For God's sake, Plath who is really Sadie McLure, why didn't you just do it?

Too precious to kill, are you, little rich girl?

Then what the hell are you doing in BZRK?

Don't you know it's a war, Plath? Don't you know this is a battle for the human soul?

Why didn't you kill, Plath?

ALSO BY

MICHAEL GRANT

BZRK

BZRK APOCALYPSE

(available October 2014)

OTHER EGMONT USA BOOKS YOU MAY ENJOY

Ashes

by Ilsa J. Bick

Quarantine 1: The Loners; Quarantine 2: The Saints;
Quarantine 3: The Burnouts

by Lex Thomas

Burn Out

by Kristi Helvig

MICHAEL GRANT

BZRK RELOADED

EGMONT
USA
NEW YORK

EGMONT
We bring stories to life

First published in the United Kingdom by Egmont UK Limited, 2013
This paperback edition published by Egmont USA, 2014

443 Park Avenue South, Suite 806
New York, NY 10016

1 3 5 7 9 8 6 4 2

www.egmontusa.com

THE LIBRARY OF CONGRESS HAS CATALOGED THE
HARDCOVER EDITION AS FOLLOWS

Library of Congress Cataloging-in-Publication Data

Grant, Michael, 1954-
BZRK 2 / Michael Grant.
p. cm.
Summary: A continuation of the events exposed in BZRK.
ISBN 978-1-60684-394-9 (hardback)—ISBN 978-1-60684-395-6 (electronic book) [1. Utopias—Fiction. 2. Nanotechnology—Fiction. 3. Conjoined twins—Fiction. 4. Twins—Fiction. 5. Science fiction.] I. Title. II. Title: BZRK two.
PZ7.G7671Bzt 2013
[Fic]—dc23
2012025064

Paperback ISBN 978-1-60684-504-2

Printed in the United States of America

For Katherine; Jake, and Julia

Being deeply loved by someone
gives you strength.

Loving someone deeply
gives you courage.

Lao Tzu

Kiss the crazy.

@Horse_ebooks

BZRK
RELOADED

[ARTIFACT]

To: Lear

From: Nijinsky

Wilkes is alive and back with us.

Ophelia is alive despite the loss of both legs below the knee.

Keats and Plath are both well and performed magnificently.

Vincent is suffering from a deep depression following the loss of one biot. The second biot was badly injured but is recovering. Vincent is being cared for, outcome very uncertain.

We failed in our main objective.

We await instructions.

[ARTIFACT]

To: Nijinsky

From: Lear

During Vincent's incapacity you are in charge of NYC cell, Nijinsky. You're the wrong person for the job. Become the right person.

[ARTIFACT]

Central Intelligence Agency—Office of Technology Threat assessment

Transcript of interview with Professor Edwin H. Grossman, February 28, 2012

(Page 7 of 9)

Q: In your opinion then, this is a serious threat but not an urgent one?

Grossman: I don't know your definition of urgent. Look, the gray goo scenario is not science fiction, not any longer. Nanotech is advancing by leaps and bounds. There is some very important research going on at MIT, and at UC Irvine, as well as in my own department at Texas.

Q: But anyone researching nanotech is aware of the danger.

Grossman: Fermi was aware of the danger of nuclear fission. Watson and Crick were aware of the danger of DNA. Alfred Nobel was aware of the danger of dynamite when he invented it. No doubt the first caveman to swing a club was aware—

Q: I take your point, Doctor, but you aren't seriously comparing nanotechnology to nuclear weapons.

Grossman: Actually, yes, I am. You see, in either case, we are talking about enormous, catastrophic power in the hands of human beings.

Q: Only a madman—

Grossman: Only a madman? (Laughs.) Has there been a shortage of madmen in human history?

AFTERMATH

Vincent felt the laugh building inside him. It was like a buildup of steam in a covered pot. Like a volcano whose time to erupt has come at last.

He was being torn apart.

His arms were handcuffed to two parked diesel locomotives, and they were huffing and puffing, and smoke was coming up out of their undercarriages, and the locomotives were so hot that the steel side panels were melting.

He stood there between the tracks.

The chains were long. The engines would be able to build up speed.

"Hah-hah-hah-hah-hah!"

He laughed, because it would be funny when his arms were ripped from his body, when the flesh tore and the bones popped out of their sockets like pulling the wings off a barbecued chicken and . . .

"Come on, man, lie down, lie down, lie down."

Choo choo. Choo chooooooo!

"You're going to be okay, Vincent."

Who was Vincent? His name was not Vincent. His name was . . . What was his name?

A dragon, one of those Chinese dragons, loomed over him, a giant face, and there was smoke coming out of its nostrils and it was the same as the smoke from the trains that were starting to move now, starting to pick up speed, now.

"Uh. Uh-uh-uh! Uh! Uhhhh! UUHHH!"

The chains clanked as the trains pulled away.

"Take this pill. Take the pill, Vincent."

Vincent thrashed, had to free his ar , they would rip his arms off, his arms would be dragged off behind the trains!

"Uhhh-uhhh-UUUHHHH!"

"Goddamn it, take the pill!"

The dragon was ripping his mouth open; he was going to split Vincent's head open so that brains came gushing out of his mouth, vomiting his own brains and . . .

The Chinese dragon was a nurse now, no, a dragon, no, no, no.

"Nooooo!"

A vise closed around his head. He smelled a masculine perfume. Vincent felt muscles like pythons around his head and something was in his mouth, and the dragon/nurse held his jaw shut even as he tried to scream and beg for help.

"Keats. Help me! Get water."

From the sky came a bottle.

Fiji water. Oh, yes, that was the one with a square bottle, sure he would drink some water, yes, dragon, I'll drink some water like a good boy.

"Get his mouth open."

But the trains!

Vincent swallowed.

A voice he heard very, very clearly but through his head not his ears said, "They'll kill you, they'll have no choice, they'll kill you, kill you, the mad king will send the mad emperor. Kill. You."

But then his arms were ripped from their sockets—Snap! Pop!—by the trains and he laughed and laughed.

And he felt sick.

He wanted to throw up.

"Like my brother," a voice said.

The dragon, who was really just a man who smelled like perfume, had an arm around Vincent's head. The man was crying. So Vincent felt like crying, too.

The other one, Vincent thought maybe he was a devil, he wasn't sure, he might have devil skin, and he had devil blue eyes.

"I don't have arms anymore, Jin," Vincent whispered.

"Jesus," the possible devil with blue eyes said.

Jin—Nijinsky, the dragon, the nurse—didn't say anything.

The drug came for Vincent. It called him to unconsciousness. As he tumbled, armless, down the long, long black well, Vincent had a moment of clarity.

So, he thought, *this is madness.*

She stood in the doorway, ready to help if Nijinksy and Keats had trouble getting Vincent into restraints.

Ready to help. Her heart was beating as if it was made out of lead. That beat, that unnatural beat squeezed the air out of her lungs; it clamped her throat.

Sadie McLure—Plath—had been just a little bit in love with Vincent. He had that effect on people. Not love love, not even attraction in the usual sense of the word—that feeling was reserved for Keats, who was working silently, quickly, to tie Vincent down. Keats looked as shell-shocked as Plath felt.

So, not love love and not attraction for Vincent, but some weird amalgam of protectiveness and trust. Strange to feel that way about someone as cold-blooded as Vincent, someone so utterly in control. Well, formerly in control.

Her fists clenched so tight that her neglected fingernails cut new and too-short lifelines into her palms. She had taken too many hits, too many losses: her mother, her father, and brother. What was left to her now?

They said what didn't kill you made you stronger. No, it left you with holes blown through your soul. It left you like Vincent.

Plath had been recruited by Vincent. She had trusted Vincent, trusted him even with her life. And at the same time there had always been the feeling that she should take care of him, not out of reciprocity, not because it was owed, but just because there was something in that impassive face, in those dark eyes that spoke to her and said, Yes, I need.

Plath knew she was not alone in this. The others, all of them, felt it.

But that Vincent, the cool, calm, relentless one whom you nevertheless wanted to shelter, that Vincent was not here any longer.

Madness.

Insanity.

It had been an abstraction, but now she saw it. Now she felt it, and brave Plath was no longer quite so brave.

She turned away, unable to watch any longer.

Ophelia would have laughed at the idea that what didn't kill you made you stronger. Her legs were gone, one at the knee, one six inches higher. She was not stronger.

But worse, like Vincent she had lost her biots. Had Ophelia been capable of rational thought she might have contemplated the comparison between legs, actual, physical legs, and the biots, which were not, after all, exactly original equipment for any human.

Her legs had burned like candles, melted like wax, down to the bone. They'd amputated the barbecued stumps in the OR there at

Bellevue Hospital. But her biots were dead long before that, incinerated in the terrible disaster at the United Nations. By the time doctors had taken what was left of her legs, what was left of her mind wasn't much.

Ophelia was guarded by FBI agents who labeled her a terrorist suspect. There was one just outside the door to her hospital room, and one at each end of the hallway, and one at the nurse's station. So, had Ophelia been sane, she probably would have been surprised to see a man standing at the foot of her bed who was obviously not a doctor despite his white coat. Underneath the white coat was a faded, lilac velour blazer. His usual jaunty top hat had been set aside somewhere, but he still had Danny Trejo's face.

Caligula—he had no other known name—came close to her, stood beside her. Ophelia gazed up at him and in a moment of clarity, a brief gap between the painkillers and the mental anguish, seemed almost to recognize him.

"You?"

"Yes, Ophelia."

"Did? Are, uh . . . Did?" she asked. It was not a coherent question, but Caligula answered as though it was, as though she could understand, even though her eyes had rolled up into her head and a manic grin had distorted her lips.

"Wilkes got out. The others are alive." And then he said, "You did good, Ophelia. You were brave."

He put a palm on her forehead, a gesture that was tender but not, because he used the pressure to hold her head still as with a single swift motion he buried the dagger to the hilt in her temple.

From his pocket he withdrew a small cylinder ending in a pointed valve. He pulled the knife out and pushed the valve into the hole. He opened the valve and let his own special mixture of white phosphorous flow into her brain.

An autopsy might just conceivably produce evidence of nanotechnology, and it was part of Caligula's brief to stop that from happening. That, and a mad Ophelia might eventually, in some disjointed rant, have given up a deadly secret or two.

The only survivor of the UN massacre in custody was now no longer available for questioning.

By the time Caligula left the room Ophelia's eye sockets were dripping liquid fire.

ONE

"Oh, I needed that."

The president of the United States, Helen Falkenhym Morales, was feeling gratified. She and her husband had just sat in bed and watched Jon Stewart take apart the Senate majority leader, a Morales foe. And for once the president had gone off-diet and actually eaten most of a butterscotch sundae.

An enemy ridiculed, and a gooey sundae: a good end to an otherwise lousy day.

Monte Morales leaned across the bed and wiped a bit of whipped cream from her chin, popped it in his mouth, and smiled.

She liked that smile; it was a very particular smile, and if it were not for the fact that her life was lived according to a rigid schedule, well . . . He was still sexy after all these years.

Her husband, Monte Morales, the first gentleman, or as most people referred to him, MoMo, was ten years younger than she and kept himself in good shape for a man of forty-five. It was one of the things the American people liked about him. They liked his good looks; they liked his obvious devotion to his wife; they liked the stories about his genial weekly poker games with some of the other spouses of important Washington players.

They didn't approve of his smoking cigars in the White House, but the American people were willing to forgive so long as he kept on being the charming, easygoing counterbalance to his wife's razor-edged personality.

MoMo was the living proof that the president couldn't be all bad—even her enemies admitted that.

"What's bothering you, babe?" MoMo asked.

She turned and frowned at him. It had sounded perilously close to criticism. "What do you mean? It's time for bed, that's all."

He sat up, swung his legs off the side of the bed, and said, "Not now, I mean generally. You've been a little weird."

"Weird?" The word was absurd applied to Helen Falkenhym Morales. Difficult, cold, critical: those were the words applied to her most frequently. No one thought she was weird.

MoMo shrugged his broad shoulders. "I mean . . . off. Just, sometimes. Little stuff. You were talking during the program."

"So?"

"So you never do, that's all."

"Really? You think ten minutes before we go to sleep is time to start questioning me?" She pulled on a robe and glanced at her pad. Nothing there that needed immediate attention. There was a coup under way in Tajikistan. That could wait.

And there was a briefing book from Patrick Rios, the new director of the ETA—the Emerging Technologies Agency. Rios, late of the FBI and a real go-getter type, was pushing hard to go after McLure Industries. What Rios didn't seem to understand was that Grey McLure and his son had been murdered in what had been—until the UN terrorist attack—the biggest headline event of the year. Go after McLure?

Well . . . why not, now that she thought of it. Rios was very smart, very capable. He reminded the president of herself, somehow. When she pictured Rios, she always seemed to see herself as a young, aggressive prosecutor.

She trusted him.

She needed to give him a free hand.

He was very like her, a good guy, reliable.

In fact, the two memories—of Rios and of herself at that age—were wired together. The president's brain could not think of Rios without thinking of herself.

"Babe, that's not what I'm saying," MoMo said. He stood to wrap his arms around her, but she moved away, heading toward the bathroom and a hot shower, her end-of-day relaxation ritual. He followed. "It's just I'm wondering if you're okay."

"Listen, MoMo, I'm tired. And until thirty seconds ago I was feeling like I had put a pleasant full period on this lousy day. So if you have something to say, let's get to it."

She slid back the glass door on the shower and turned the water on. It would take thirty seconds for the water to heat up.

"Okay," he said, suddenly very serious. "It's a bunch of little things. You've developed a nervous tic in your eye."

"It's the pollen—it's been terrible."

"You call me MoMo. You never used to. I don't mind it from other people, but that's not what you call me."

She hesitated. "Okay."

"You ate raw tomatoes."

"What?"

"You ate raw tomatoes. You hate them. You dropped the f-bomb in the Cabinet meeting. You never do that. The last couple days I see you staring in the mirror, and it's like you just go blank. The other day you snapped at the photographer. When do you ever do that?"

"I don't know if you've noticed, but I've been under some pressure lately," she said, her voice dripping sarcasm.

"You've been under pressure since I've known you, Helen, you don't snap at people who work for you, not people who can't defend themselves. It's just . . ." He shrugged helplessly. "I just wonder if maybe we should take a few days up at Camp David."

"I can't do that," she said icily. "I'm not the first lady, I'm the goddamned president. I have actual work to do."

The insult was like a knife in his ribs. He gulped, shocked by it. "See, that's not the kind of thing you say," he said finally.

She blinked.

"Sorry, Mo—, sorry, sweetheart. I'm . . ." She forced a helpless smile. "Yeah, maybe I need some time off."

"Maybe more than that. That twitch, all this little stuff, more than I can remember right now . . . maybe you should call the White House physician. Just have him check. You know . . . could be . . . I don't know."

The president nodded solemnly. "Okay. Now I'm taking a shower. Want to join me?"

"You know I'm a bath man," he said, his tone half reproach, half forgiveness.

She put her arms around him. "But I'm lonely in that big shower all alone."

When they were under the spray she considered her options.

MoMo wouldn't let it drop. He was nothing if not persistent. He loved her and he would keep pushing. And pushing.

Something was wrong with her—that was the hell of it. She had felt it. She knew it was true. Something wrong.

But she had a year until the election. This was no time to look weak. This was no time for doctors to be finding a tumor or a stroke or even just too much stress.

But what could she do? How could she stop MoMo from loving her right out of the White House?

Later she would recall that question.

Later she would ask herself how she had decided on the terrible answer.

But at this moment all she saw was that it would have to be a single swift blow. No second chances.

She pressed close to her husband. She kissed him. She ran her fingers through his wet hair, held both sides of his head tight, and with every muscle in her body smashed the back of his head against the tile wall.

MoMo sagged to the floor. Blood came with surprising force, more than she would have imagined.

She left the water running, stepped from the shower, crossed to the bathtub, and began filling it with hot water.

It took a couple of minutes before there was enough water in the tub.

MoMo groaned in the shower. Nonsense sounds, not words, but still she had to hurry.

She slid back the shower door, knelt down, put her hands under his arms, and dragged him the five feet to the tub. That much was easy: he was wet and soapy, and the floor was tile.

The harder part was pushing him up over the side of the tub. For the scenario to work it would have to seem as if he'd slipped and smashed his head against the side of the tub. It would be a long night of making sure that bloodstains were in only the exactly right places. The president would be scrubbing.

She manhandled MoMo into the rising water in the tub. Now he was moaning and moving feebly, like a sleepwalker, like a drunk, uncoordinated.

He splashed into the tub.

His eyes fluttered open as she ground the bloody wound against the back of the tub.

"Mwuh?" he managed to say.

Mustn't leave handprints. Had to do this right. She pressed her palms against his chest and leaned her weight on him until his head was completely submerged.

His dark eyes blinked, seemed to gain awareness for just a moment, and his arms came up out of the water to push back . . .

Too late. His lungs filled.

He vomited into the water.

And then she no longer had to hold him down. MoMo wasn't going anywhere.

It would be a tragedy. The nation would mourn. She would get a ten-point sympathy bounce in the polls.

Her secrets would be safe.

A sob heaved up from inside her. She loved him. She loved him with all her heart.

And she had just murdered him.

In an office in a building on the 1800 block of Pennsylvania Avenue, a very short distance from the White House, Bug Man tore the gloves from his hands.

He was shaking.

He felt sick. He climbed out of the chair, made it five steps on the way to the very nice executive bathroom before falling to his knees, gasping as if he'd been running a marathon.

He had been.

Down in the meat, down in the nano, he had been racing his exploding-head-logo nanobots, laying wire like some demented lineman from elements of the president's ego, her self-image, to images of MoMo.

Bug Man had long since cauterized a number of areas storing what might be called ethics or morality. In fact, they weren't that, they were memories of books, sermons, lectures, and—much more powerful—the images of victimization from her childhood in San Antonio that formed the basis of her core decency.

Like most politicians, and all presidents, she had a strong ego. She'd always had well-developed instincts for survival, what some would describe as ruthlessness. But it had been balanced by pity, kindness, fellow feeling, love.

Bug Man had needed a less moral, more ruthless person. He had needed her simplified—the better to manipulate, the better to convince her to give Rios and his brand-new government agency free rein to quash any unhelpful investigations, to oppose any international action.

So Bug Man had made her that. He had needed her to be suggestible to paranoia; he had needed to be able to plug that heightened aggressiveness and ruthlessness into pictures of any and all whose actions might threaten the Armstrong Fancy Gifts Corporation.

Yes.

Well.

Brains are subtle things. Some miswiring had created the twitches and tells that had alerted MoMo to changes in his wife. The president's heightened aggression combined with weakened restraint had led now to murder.

But for the last desperate minutes Bug Man had not been trying to get Helen Falkenhym Morales to kill her husband MoMo. He'd been trying to stop her.

Once he'd seen where she was going he'd tried—way too little, way too late—to make her see MoMo as an extension of herself.

The only result was that later, too damned late, she would feel remorse. Guilt. Which would only create its own problems.

Bug Man was on his knees, blood pounding in his face, stomach churning with fear, waiting for the call.

When his phone did ring it still startled him.

He wondered how long he could go without answering. He wondered if he could keep from vomiting again. Or crying.

"Yeah," he whispered into his phone.

"Oh, Anthony." The voice was not the ranting fury of the Armstrong Twins. It was Burnofsky. "Anthony, Anthony: what have you done?"

"Jesus Christ!" Bug Man wailed. "I didn't know the crazy bitch would—"

Burnofsky laughed his parchment-dry laugh. "Watch what you say. Washington is full of big ears."

"What am I . . . What do . . ." He couldn't even frame the question. His breathing was short and harsh. "The Twins . . ."

"Past their bedtime, fortunately. The only one watching the video feed was me."

It was a sign of how frightened Bug Man was that he welcomed this news. He despised Burnofsky, but he was terrified of Charles and especially Benjamin Armstrong.

"But there will be no hiding this, of course," Burnofsky went on.

Bug Man cursed, but there was no anger left in him. All was cold knife-steel fear now. The Twins—Charles and Benjamin Armstrong, those freaks—were not patient with underlings who screwed up.

The things they could do to him . . . An earlier error had been punished with a beating delivered by AmericaStrong thugs against Bug Man's legs and buttocks. He still couldn't sit in a chair without a handful of Advil. Now he had endangered everything.

"I'm a twitcher; I'm a fighter, not a goddamned spinner," Bug Man pleaded with the phone. "I took down Vincent himself. I took down Kerouac before him. I'm the best. I'm important. They can't kill me! This is—"

"Mmmm," Burnofsky said, amused, gloating, already seeing in his opium-addled brain the price the Twins might demand. "You're screwed, Anthony, my young friend. There's only one person on this green Earth who can save you. Do you know who that is, Anthony?"

Bug Man was trembling. Even now, no anger. Anger would come later, along with self-justification, but right now, with his face inches from the floor and his whole body feeling sick, Bug Man could only moan.

"Who, Anthony? Who can save you now, you arrogant little Limey shit? Say the word."

"You," Bug Man whispered.

Silence stretched as Burnofsky absorbed his rival's defeat. Then the older man said, "Go limp. Power down. Go to your hotel, screw your girlfriend, but do nothing else until I tell you."

The phone went dead. Bug Man rolled onto his side and cried.

TWO

Keats, whose real name was Noah, had not intended to go to Plath's room, but there he was. He knocked.

"Yes," she said. Not "Come in," just "Yes." Knowing it was him.

He stood framed by the doorway.

"You look like hell," she said.

"So do you."

And then they simply went for each other. They clutched and tore at each other, bruised each other's lips.

Noah's fingers dug into a handful of Sadie's dark hair, and Sadie's hands fumbled to push his shirt over his head, and his tongue was in her mouth, and her breasts were pressed almost violently against his hard chest.

They were alive when they should be dead, and sane when they could be mad.

So afraid. So lonely.

Vincent's lunatic howl was fresh in Keats's mind, still echoed in his ears, and the sight of Nijinsky breaking down in tears, and the awful memory of his big brother, of Alex, shrieking like an animal, chained to a cot in a hellish mental ward screaming, “Berserk! Berserk! BERSERK!”

Keats had imagined that their first time making love would be a study in tenderness. But this was not tender. They could hardly keep from hurting each other. They needed something that was not horror. They needed something that was not drenched in despair.

They needed not to hear Vincent howling like a dog.

Noah gasped and pulled back suddenly. He pushed Plath’s greedy hands down against the pillow.

Her eyes were confused, wary. “Don’t stop,” she said and her voice was not pleading, it was a snapped order. She expected to be obeyed. She could do that voice when motivated.

“You’re leaking,” Keats said.

“What?”

“It’s not bad, not yet.”

She understood him, then sat up, put a hand to her head. As if she could feel it. “Damn it.”

“Yeah,” he agreed.

Keats looked at her. She closed her eyes, absorbing the frustration, then snapped her gaze up at him, blazing.

But as he looked at her face he also saw deep inside her. Not in some metaphorical way. He had eyes inside her, all the way down inside her brain.

Down in the meat.

Plath had an aneurysm, which had been serviced first by her father's biots—before he had been murdered—and were now served by Keats's own biots. Two tiny, nightmarish creatures, neither as large as a dust mite, neither visible to the unaided eye. Each had six legs, a tail that could deliver a venomous sting or drip acid. A spear for puncturing the metal shells of nanobots.

There was a rack of pins only a few molecules thick slung on the biot's back. A spinneret at the rear oozed with webbing wire.

Biots were built of several different DNA strands: scorpion, spider, cobra, jellyfish, and human. The DNA of a specific human, in this case one Noah Cotton: Keats.

That DNA connection tied the biot to its creator, like a finger was tied to a brain, like a sort of detached limb, a body part controlled by his own mind. Move left. Move right. Jump. Strike. Run away.

Live.

Die.

The human DNA was most evident in the face of the biot. In addition to blank, soulless insect eyes, each biot also had structures that looked like human eyes, almost. Human until you looked closely and saw that these were as blank and soulless as the spider eyes.

The intimate connection had a very major downside. A biot wasn't just a limb, it was an extension of the mind of its controller/creator. Lose a biot and you would lose your mind.

That was why Vincent howled. Bug Man had beaten him in battle and killed one of Vincent's biots.

Noah kissed Plath, a kiss that was full of regret, and she accepted it passively.

Down deep inside her brain where a scalpel could never reach, Keats's biots, K1 and K2, stood atop the Teflon fiber barrier that had been built so painstakingly around the aneurysm. It was a bulging artery, a thin spot, a swelling, like an overinflated balloon where the blood might break out at any moment and tear apart the drum-tight membrane to flood and destroy the brain tissue around it.

Pop.

A blown aneurysm could lead to anything from strokes to localized brain death to all-over, whole-body death.

The membrane was leaking. From Keats's position it was a floor not a wall—gravity meant very little at the nano level. A floor that was gushing tiny red Frisbees, like a jet of licked cough drops. These were the red blood cells, platelets. They shot up in a jet from a tiny tear in the artery wall and floated off into the cerebral-spinal fluid, where blood was normally not allowed.

Within that garden hose of platelets were things of a paler color that looked like animated sponges, wads of mucousy goo—the white blood cells, the pale soldiers, the defenders of the body.

Keats saw this through two sets of biot eyes. The biots saw each other as well. And all the while, up in the macro, he was looking at

Plath as she stood, and he gazed with intense regret on the curve of her breasts, and the narrowness of her waist, and saw—at least in his imagination—many other details as well.

It was painful, wanting her this badly.

Keats's two biots scampered to the stash of titanium fibers. The fibers looked a little like strands of razor wire, each only about half the length of the biot itself. The jagged edges allowed them to be woven together. But care had to be exercised to avoid cutting into the artery wall and making things far worse.

"Can't you do two things at once?" She leaned into him and he did not pull away. Her open mouth met his and her tongue found his and he was breathing her breath, and his heart was pounding, pounding crazy crazy crazy.

His body, his bruised, battered, painfully taut body, did not really give half a damn about doing the responsible thing but wanted very much, very excruciatingly much, to just do, and it was almost beyond his power to restrain himself and if she kept that up then things were going to move forward to the next step, a step he wanted to take more than he had ever wanted anything else in his sixteen years of life.

His words were a rasp and a groan. "Not those two things. No. Not at once."

He held her back, his hands on her arms, and really why the hell were his arms taking sides with his brain when his body so clearly, clearly, clearly had other ideas in mind?

"I don't want to be paying attention with half my mind," he managed to say.

Plath liked that. She didn't want that to be his answer, but she liked it anyway. Yes, he wanted it to be important. He wanted it to stay with him forever. Keats was always . . . She stopped herself in midthought. She didn't know what he was always, did she? She barely knew him. They had met just weeks ago. Not a single second of that time had been anything like normal. It had been lunacy from the start.

We take the names of madmen, because madness is our fate.

Terribly melodramatic, that. Ophelia had denied that it was hopeless. Ophelia, who lay now, presumably in FBI custody, with her legs burned off.

And Vincent was the proof. Vincent, their pillar of strength. The best of BZRK, if there was a best.

How long until this beautiful, sweet boy with the sometimes difficult to understand English accent would be raving like his brother, Kerouac?

How long until he was howling like Vincent?

How long until she was alongside them?

He wasn't the only one who wanted this, he wasn't by any means the only one. She wanted him, all of him, not later, now. But that meant all of his attention, too, she supposed.

She was arguing with herself now, and either way she was losing. Plath was not good at losing.

Down deep inside her brain, Keats lifted the first of the fibers and slid one end into the weave. The platelets were pouring out, a fire hose of flat red discs. His biot bent the fiber against the current, pushing the flow aside, and shoved the loose end down, held it down while his second biot came running up with a second fiber. The platelets battered the biot's head, a Nerf machine gun.

"How bad is it?" Plath asked.

"Not bad," he reassured her. "Just an hour's work."

Plath smiled crookedly, and they both felt the moment slip away.

"You realize we may never get the opportunity again?" Plath asked him.

"Horribly aware, yes," he said.

She laid a palm softly against his cheek. He closed his eyes. He couldn't help it. He had to close his eyes because he could not look into her eyes or notice the tremor in her lips or the pulse in her throat or any of a hundred things that would destroy his ability to focus on saving her.

She kept her hand there. "I'm afraid," she said.

"Me, too."

"I told you before: I'm not the kind of girl who falls in love."

He shrugged. "I'm the kind of boy who does."

"It will make it so much worse," she whispered. "Aren't you afraid of that pain?"

"Yes," he said.

"Then let's not. We can make love without being in love, Keats. We can be . . . We can be fighters together. Side by side. We can be friends. We can do, whatever, we don't have to be in love."

He said nothing, half his focus already gone, trudging dutifully with his titanium fibers as platelets swirled around him.

"You don't need me here," she said, frustration turning her voice cold. Actually angry at him for focusing on saving her life, angry at him, she supposed, for being able to resist. Or just angry at life in general.

"I'm going to take a shower," she said.

"Yeah," he said flatly.

It took Keats closer to two hours to squeeze off the flow of blood. Then another twenty minutes to carefully check his work.

He fell asleep fully clothed, and though he would have loved to dream of her, exhaustion shut him down.

"Difficult news," Burnofsky said.

Burnofsky brought that news to the Twins right away, middle of the night. There could be no concealing it. The best he could hope for was to save Bug Man's life and leave his own plans intact. That above all: his own plans.

To that end he'd hoped to convince the Twins to take a victory lap, to take a tour of foreign facilities or even a vacation aboard their floating house of horrors, the *Doll Ship*.

Bug Man had forced his hand and disrupted Burnofsky's timetable. In a few hours, by morning at latest, the news of the first gentleman's death would be out. It would be seen as a tragic accident by the general public—but the Twins would know better.

If he was going to keep things running, he, Burnofsky, would have to get the Twins under control. Not easy. Never easy and harder now. Charles still saw reason. But Benjamin . . .

Burnofsky took the elevator up to the Tulip. The Tulip was the pinnacle, floors sixty-three through sixty-seven, of the Armstrong Building, headquarters of the Armstrong Fancy Gifts Corporation. It was the pink polymer, one-way transparent, nanocomposite-walled home and office of the Armstrong Twins.

AFGC still made fancy gifts at factories in China, Malaysia, and Turkey. They still owned and operated the ubiquitous gift stores seen in every American airport and in European and Japanese train stations. But gifts had long since ceased to be their main focus.

Weapons technology, surveillance, and communications technology, and above all, nanotechnology, now occupied the denizens of the Tulip and most of the sixty-two floors below. The gift stores were run out of an office park in Naperville, Illinois. In the Tulip they had bigger fish to fry.

Burnofsky had called ahead to Jindal so he could get the Twins up and alert. Jindal met him outside the private elevator, down on sixty-two.

"What is it?" Jindal asked, suppressing a yawn but intensely concerned despite his sleepiness.

"Why don't I just tell the story once?" Burnofsky said and pushed past Jindal to the elevator. It was a short ride.

"What in hell?" Benjamin asked the moment Burnofsky appeared.

The Armstrong Twins wore a robe, dark red silk, specially tailored for them, of course: Nordstrom and Bloomingdale's did not carry clothing in their size or shape.

Their legs, all three of them, were bare. Their feet—only the two useful ones—were in shearling-lined slippers, the third, deformed and three-quarter-size, was bare.

"Difficult news," Burnofsky said.

"Well, spit it out, it's the middle of the night!" Charles snapped.

Burnofsky tapped his pad for a few seconds, and the touch screen embedded in the twins' massive desk lit up.

It was the video from Bug Man's feed. Like all nanobot video, it failed to achieve the high standards of Hollywood; it was grainy, jerky gray scale one moment and awash in unnatural computer-enhanced colors the next. This video was worse still because it was the result of tapping directly into the president's optic nerve, pulling up the raw feed, so to speak, of rods and cones, uninterpreted by the visual cortex.

There was no sound, just a series of jerky images—a window, a wall, Monte Morales, a rumpled bed, the floor, Monte Morales again, a shower knob, a shoulder, an eye, a stream of water and then . . .

"Jesus!" It was Jindal. "Did she . . . Is that . . ."

It was fascinating to watch the reactions of the Twins. Charles's eye stared hard—at the screen, at Burnofsky, at the screen. His mouth was a straight line, set, twitching in growing fury.

Benjamin seemed almost distracted. He looked left and right. His mouth—well, it was hard, really, to judge his face fairly; it had been bashed and battered by the bottom of a glass bottle. There was a tooth missing altogether and another one chipped. Benjamin's eye was a clenched purple fist with the pupil barely showing. He looked like someone who had been on the losing end of a bar fight.

Within the raw liver that was Benjamin's eye socket, the cruel eye seemed far less interested than it should.

The third eye, the one between the usual two, seemed to agree with Charles that this was important. It focused its soulless stare on the video.

The file ended.

"It will be covered up," Charles said. He tugged at the collar of his bathrobe and, as well as he could, tugged the belt tighter. "Bug Man must be replaced at once. And punished. Punished most severely. It's that woman he has with him. She distracts him. Take her from him, get rid of her. Kill her in front of him! Bug Man will refocus. A beating for him, yes, a severe lesson, yes, that's it, a beating! And kill his woman."

"I disagree," Burnofsky said as blandly as he could.

Oh, Bug Man would owe him. He wished he had video of Charles planning Bug Man's humiliation and Jessica's murder. Anthony Elder, that snotty little black British prodigy who called himself Bug Man, would kiss Burnofsky's ass for this.

Burnofsky would own Bug Man.

"I don't care about Bug Man," Benjamin snarled. "It wasn't Bug Man. It was her. Her!"

Burnofsky at first assumed he was talking about Bug Man's girl, Jessica. But no . . . of course not.

"I want her hurt." Benjamin touched his damaged mouth. Then he clenched his fist. "Damaged in some permanent way, something she can never overcome, something that will make her remaining life a horror. Not death, no, we still need her to get at her father's secrets, but pain, such pain and despair, yes."

Not poor, dumb, absurdly beautiful Jessica. Oh, no. Benjamin was thinking of Sadie McLure.

Burnofsky suppressed a sneer. Benjamin was losing his mind. The experience with Sadie McLure had unhinged him. He'd always been the more volatile of the twins, but now? He was still "wired"—that was part of the problem. Burnofsky had volunteered to go in and pull those pins and wires, remove them before they became a settled feature of Benjamin's brain, undo, insofar as anyone could, the damage done by Sadie McLure's biots. But Benjamin couldn't tolerate the idea of someone else inside his brain.

Irony, that.

And Charles? Well, just what the hell did you do if you were a conjoined twin and the other half of you went mad?

"She was inside my brain, sticking pins in my brain, making me an animal!" Benjamin bellowed.

"Brother . . ." But Charles's voice wheezed out. Benjamin had taken control of their lungs.

"Something with acid," Benjamin said, his voice suddenly silky. "Acid. Or something taken off. Cut something off her. Cut off her nose or her hands." He chopped at the air with his hand. It was more than just a gesture of emphasis, he was using his hand as an imaginary meat cleaver.

Charles waited for an opening to speak. They each had a mouth of their own and a throat, but the lungs were shared property, and it could be difficult for one to make himself heard if the other was bellowing.

"Brother," Charles began. "Let's focus on this crisis. The next thing we need to consider is—"

"Next? Next? Next she suffers and I see it happen. I revel in it. I see it happen and I laugh at her. I stand over her and look down at her as she cries and begs and as the hope dies in her eyes. That's next."

He was shaking his fist now, a comic-book villain. But crying from his eye at the same time, a furious, frustrated, hurt child.

The "her" in question was a sixteen-year-old girl, Sadie McLure, although now it seemed she used the nom de guerre Plath. So melodramatic, the BZRKers—such romantics.

Sixteen. The same age as Burnofsky's own daughter, Carla.

Former daughter? No, death didn't make you former, it just made you dead.

Charles and Benjamin had been much more calm when they'd ordered Carla's death. They had been regretful. Charles had actually touched Burnofsky, put a ham-size hand on Burnofsky's back as he ordered the death of his only child.

Solicitous.

Considerate.

She has betrayed us, Karl. She's sold us out. You know how she would end up if we left her alone to leave us and join BZRK. Madness. Would you want that for your little girl?

Burnofsky drew a shaky breath. They might at least offer him a drink; of course, the Twins were a bit distracted. Benjamin was still ranting, and Charles was growing increasingly impatient with it.

"I was raped by her!" Benjamin bellowed. "Violated!"

Plath had managed to infiltrate Benjamin's brain with her biots. Burnofsky knew she was new at the business of nano warfare, but she had improvised, the clever, clever girl. Given the time frame she could have had only minimal training in the sophisticated business of subtly rewiring a human brain. And she'd been in a hurry and under pressure, so she had simply stabbed pins and run wire almost randomly.

She had made scrambled eggs of Benjamin's brain.

That was some of her father's intelligence in evidence. She was smarter than the brother who had died. He wondered if they had killed the wrong McLure child. Stone was a stolid, dutiful type, his sister on the other hand . . .

The result of Sadie's wiring had been severe mental disruption. Benjamin had screeched and babbled and generally made a fool of himself, straining the physical barrier that connected his own head to Charles's—very painful—and caused the unfortunate incident of the glass bottle, the results of which were still so obvious on Benjamin's face.

The membrane, the flesh, whatever the word was for the living intersection between Charles and Benjamin, had been strained and torn. The central eye, that eerie, third eyeball that sometimes joined with Charles and other times with Benjamin, and at still other times seemed to decide its own focus, was red-rimmed, the lower lid crusted with blood that still seeped from a deep bruise.

At the end Plath had let Benjamin live when she might well have killed him. Burnofsky wondered whether at this moment Charles thought that was a good thing or not. How many times must one or the other of the Twins have pondered the question of what happened if one of them died?

Their heads were melded. Some areas of their brains were directly connected. They shared a neck, albeit a neck with two sets of vocal cords. They had two hearts—one apiece—and had a sort of two-lobed stomach that fed out through a single alimentary tract.

Each had an arm. Each had a leg. And there was the third leg as well, a leg that dragged like so much dead weight. As a consequence they moved with extreme difficulty and usually chose to get around in a motorized cart or wheeled office chair customized to fit their double width.

Charles tried again. "We have important matters to discuss, Benjamin. We are on the cusp of completing Phase Three of our plan, brother, don't you grasp that? Don't you see how far we have come? But we must deal with this crisis. Bug Man's incompetence may upset everything!"

"It wasn't you," Benjamin snapped. "It wasn't you. It was me. It was me she humiliated."

"Look, we'll deal with the girl when we get an opportunity," Charles soothed. "Of course you feel violated. Of course you're angry. But—"

It was part of the strangeness of dealing with the Twins that when they spoke to each other they could not look at each other. They had never made direct eye contact in their lives.

"You think I'm being irrational," Benjamin said, sounding rational for the first time in several minutes. "But you don't understand. This cannot be tolerated. If we can be humiliated this way, then we will lose credibility with our own people. Do you think our twitchers aren't talking about it?" He stabbed a finger in Burnofsky's direction. "Do you think Karl isn't smirking?"

In fact, Karl Burnofsky was smirking, but he hid it well. His sagging, whiskered face and rheumy blue eyes did not appear to reflect any pleasure.

It occurred to him that this was his opportunity to speak. He said, "Perhaps a vacation. Some time off. We have come a long way. You're both tired. Deservedly so, the weariness of a long battle."

Charles shot a sharp, suspicious look at Burnofsky. "Are you out of your mind? This thing with Bug Man and the president, for God's sake, target number one, the purpose for which we lost so many good people. The woman has to give Rios the go-ahead."

"She did," Burnofsky said. "The initial go-ahead, anyway. I can show you the video. She finished cleaning up the blood and went to her pad, pulled up the ETA mission, and approved it. Rios has long since started planning counterattacks on BZRK. The president has scheduled a meeting with him to discuss raiding McLure, blocking their accounts, arresting individuals on suspicion of terrorism. I am confident she will give him free rein; Bug Man has succeeded in that. And gentlemen, wasn't that our goal?" Burnofsky puffed out his cheeks in a sort of world-weary gesture. "Bug Man screwed up, but—and it's a very big but—he did accomplish the goal. We own the president, and we control ETA, the agency that will deal with any nanotechnology information."

"Damn, Karl, you might have told us," Charles chided, but he was too happy to be genuinely angry.

"This thing with Monte Morales, it's a blip," Burnofsky said. "It's a bump in the road. And you're . . . tired." He tried to send a meaningful look to Charles without it being intercepted by Benjamin, but of course that was a physical impossibility.

What he wanted to say was, Look, your twin is losing it. If he goes, you go. Get him out of here. Get him some rest.

"I can handle Bug Man," Burnofsky said. "Jindal will be here running the daily operation. I can go to Washington and supervise the wiring of the president personally. If I do have to take it over, I can do it without relying on signal repeaters. Meanwhile, Rios is moving immediately against BZRK in DC and New York. BZRK will be effectively taken out, in this country at least. We've been probed by Anonymous, but we're confident they've been shut out. We have substantial control of the FBI, we have some assets in the Secret Service. Our overseas targets are being well managed. So. . . honestly? Now's a good time for a break."

Charles looked hard at Burnofsky, reading his thoughts. Charles knew his brother's stability was tenuous at best.

"You'll go to Washington yourself?" Charles asked, seeming oddly deflated. "You'll take charge?"

"I will go. I will oversee the wiring. I'll touch base with Rios. And I'll deal with Bug Man."

Benjamin frowned. Then his eye brightened, and the third eye seemed to join in sympathy. "The *Doll Ship*."

"It's in the Pacific. Somewhere near Japan, heading toward Hong Kong to pick up a very nice haul of Korean refugees, and one moderately good twitcher," Jindal reported. He had deemed it a safe moment to speak up. Jindal was a true believer, a Nexus Humanus cultist, wired and, in the favorite Nexus Humanus phrase, "Sustainably happy."

A sucker, in Burnofsky's view. A fool. A middle manager with delusions of importance.

The mention of the *Doll Ship* soothed some of the anxiety from Benjamin's face. Charles, too, softened a bit.

"The *Doll Ship*," Benjamin said, and his bruised mouth smiled.

Sick bastards, both of you, Burnofsky thought. Sick, sad, screwed-up freaks. It would be good to get them out of the way for a few days.

He had work to do.

THREE

"Rrrraaaaarrrrrgh!"

Vincent bellowed like a beast.

Like a lion at feeding time.

Plath put her hands over her ears.

"Rrrraaaaarrrrrgh!"

The sound was muffled, but the doors and walls of the safe house were flimsy and sound carried, especially at night.

Plath was due to start receiving her inheritance: at the very least, she decided, she could pay for a better safe house.

She took her shower. It was an awful little bathroom; no one ever cleaned up, and the mildew was eating the tile grout.

She could imagine it at the nano level. That was the start of the madness, the thing that softened you up and prepared you to lose it entirely. Like Vincent. Like Ophelia, probably, poor girl, wherever she was. Like Keats's brother, Kerouac. It began with that terrible parallel view. Down there. Down where human eyes were only supposed to squint through a microscope's lens, not walk among the alien flora and fauna.

Mildew. The bacteria on her own hands. The colored footballs of pollen. The mites. The soap and pounding hot water slicking it away, but not all, never all. The beasties were with us always.

I don't want to end up like Vincent.

Keats's biots were inside her head. So was one of her own. He was repairing her aneurysm, and she had one biot on board, as the jaunty semi-nautical phrase went, and another in a petri dish soaking up nutrients.

She could have gone off to find Keats's biots, down there, down in the meat. Her biot—P2 as it happened—was resting comfortably on the back side of her left eyeball. Occasionally she would move her biot as a dutiful lymphocyte came oozing along to clean up whatever this alien monstrosity was.

Had she wanted to, she could have had her own biot help Keats. But a biot face . . . Well, it was bad enough to know precisely, exactly, what vermin crawled the surface of Keats's skin. She didn't need to see the bizarro-world distortion that was his biot's face.

She liked his face quite a lot. The too-blue eyes had at first seemed almost feminine, but a gentle face did not signal weakness, at least not in Keats.

As for his mouth, well, she had always liked that, the quirky little dip in the middle made him look wryly amused. How would he look when he was where Vincent was now?

Not madness. Not that. Death is better.

A lousy, filthy, depressing, badly lit bathroom. But a good water heater at least.

She closed her eyes and aimed them up into the spray. Take that, my demodex. Hah, I bet a few of you lost your grips and are now sliding down my cheeks. Hah! How will you like it if you go swirling down the drain?

Soap, soap, soap, everywhere. Shampoo and soap and Purell. No one showers like a twitcher, she thought, and realized that was an aphorism that very few people would understand.

A voice made her jump.

"Showering off the shame?"

Wilkes. She was using the toilet.

Definitely: when she got her inheritance, it would be time to generously agree to pay for a higher-class rental somewhere. Anywhere. Just because they were crazy didn't mean they had to live like animals.

"Oh, that's a loooong silence," Wilkes said. "You didn't do it, did you?"

"Not your business, Wilkes," Plath snapped.

Wilkes had an odd laugh. Heh-heh-heh. "That's confirmation. I can't believe after all the looks and the Bella Swan lip biting—and poor Keats awkwardly adjusting his jeans any time he sees you bend over—that nothing happened. Jeez, Plath, what are you holding out for?"

Suddenly, the shower curtain was pulled back and there stood

Wilkes in a faded *High School Musical* T-shirt. Her spiky hair was less spiky, her strange tattoos almost green in the light of the cheap fluorescent bulb.

"You have a nice body," Wilkes said. "He's going to like that. You know, if you ever actually . . . Turn around, let's see the butt."

"Wilkes, I say this with affection: drop dead." Plath pulled the shower curtain closed again and heard Wilkes's laugh. Heh-heh-heh.

"If you don't want him can I borrow him?"

Plath was about to yell a heated "No!" But that would just egg Wilkes on. And anyway, it's not as if Plath had the right to say no. And not as if Keats would ever say yes to Wilkes.

"Don't stay in there too long," Wilkes said on her way out. "Scrub all you want: you can't get them all."

Something you HAVE to see. That was the message Farid sent, using all-caps for HAVE, not his usual style, that.

Farid Berbera was not a member of BZRK. Farid Berbera was a member—if you could even use that inaccurate term—of an older organization. Anonymous had been around since Farid was a kid. He was no longer a kid, although at seventeen he wasn't quite a grown-up, either. Not in the eyes of his father, the acting Lebanese ambassador to the United States. Not in the eyes of his mother, the public relations assistant at that same Washington, DC, embassy.

And truthfully, not in is own eyes, either.

Farid Berbera, tall, thin, amazing black hair, unfortunate nose, and eyes like Sal Mineo—he'd had to look that up, Mineo was way before his time—was scared.

Farid had once hacked the computers of the Food and drug Administration because the FDA was stalling a pot-based therapeutic drug. That was not why he was scared.

"Have to see?" ChickenSteak had written back. "If this is some dumb LOLcat . . ."

Farid had hacked the computers of the American Cancer Society because they had supported the FDA decision. Also not terribly scary.

He had hacked the computers of an online dating company that was selling confidential customer data, and the Randall–Georgia Institute for being anti-gay, and he'd hacked the system at Safeway's corporate headquarters because . . . well, he forgot why, exactly.

Safeway had not frightened him.

But today, for the third time in as many days, he had hacked the Armstrong Fancy Gifts Corporation. AFGC, best known for operating gift shops in airports. Also, however, known to be much more involved with weapons technology than with collectible figurines.

He was intruding on AFGC because other hackers had made their way into the systems of the cult Nexus Humanus, and there had found a surprising number of connections—personnel and finances—between Nexus Humanus and AFGC.

Why would a weird cult be so closely involved with a maker of snow globes slash missile guidance systems?

Farid had expected AFGC's system security to be tight. It was beyond tight. It was paranoid. It was not a surprise that no one had made it through before. Even drawing on the skills of half a dozen of the best hackers in the world, Farid had not made it past the bland public face of AFGC. Until he began looking at subsidiaries of AFGC.

AmericaStrong, a division of AFGC, was a security company run by ex-CIA, ex-Special Forces types. It should have been the best-protected element in the system, and they were good, but they had grown a new problem: a link to a U.S. government agency, the Emerging Technologies Agency, ETA.

And ETA? Well, they tried to safeguard their system, but U.S. government networks had been Anonymous's doormats for a generation now.

So it went like this: ETA to AmericaStrong, AmericaStrong to AFGC, and pow, kiss my ass, and he was in.

And now Farid almost wished he wasn't.

He typed into the dialog box open on the left third of his screen.

LeVnteen34: You guys seeing this?

Of course they were seeing it. He knew they were seeing it. But did they know what it meant?

86TheChickenSteak: That's the SecState.

They were seeing video. Remarkably bad video, distorted, gray scale with sudden flares of unnatural color. But that was indeed the secretary of state.

JoeyBo316: That's the Oval.

86TheChickenSteak: Oval?

LeVnteen34: The Oval Office.

There was a pause at that before Chicken typed,

86TheChickenSteak: Thefuckwhat?

The video ended in static and jerky images. Farid opened a second video file. Papers on a desk. Some kind of briefing book, but the resolution was way too weak to make out individual words.

A third video was from the point of view of someone standing at a podium speaking to a room full of people. The fourth seemed to be nothing but a blank wall.

JoeyBo316: Like someone's wearing a camera.

Farid disagreed but didn't want to embarrass Joey. The aspect ratio was all wrong for any kind of camera. But he didn't want to prejudice their opinions, better to let them see what they saw, and react.

It was the fifth video, more desk, only this time something happened.

JoeyBo316: Replay.

Farid replayed. He did it more than once. There was no getting around it: they were watching someone put on glasses. Not from outside, but from inside.

From inside the person putting on glasses.

86TheChickenSteak: Jesustitty. We're looking out someone's eyeballs.

It wasn't until they had dredged through many, many more videos—walls, desks, something that was probably a pillow, lots and lots of images so jumbled and low-res they were indecipherable—that they reached one of the most recent videos, the one Farid had saved for the end.

It showed the recognizable face of Monte Morales, the first gentleman.

Recognizable at least until two hands, a woman's hands, pushed that face under the water.

FOUR

They did not have Vincent in restraints. The sedatives they'd obtained were working for now, and Nijinsky couldn't bear having Vincent tied up.

Nijinsky stood looking down at Vincent as Vincent stared at the butcher-wrapped sandwich on the paper plate beside the snack pack of corn chips.

"You have to eat something," Nijinsky said.

Vincent sat in a plastic chair. It was one of those molded things with spindly chrome legs. The chair was beside a bed in a narrow room that held little else unless you counted cockroaches.

Not a place to rescue your sanity, Nijinsky thought.

"Come on, Vincent, have a couple bites. The alternative is a feeding tube, and no one wants that."

Vincent stuck out one finger. He slid it into the gash formed by cutting the sandwich in half. He stuck his finger into that gap and seemed to be feeling the edges of the ham and cheese and lettuce and tomato. It was almost obscene.

“Here, let me unwrap—” Nijinsky leaned forward to pull back the paper.

The growl from Vincent was like something that might come from a leopard defending its kill.

Nijinsky backed up.

For a moment regret found a way to show itself in Vincent’s eyes. He had serious eyes, Vincent, deeply shadowed by a thoughtful brow. He wasn’t a large guy—Nijinsky was taller—but Vincent always seemed older than his twentysomething years, more serious, more impressive. Vincent was a young man who tried hard to blend into the background but never would.

Nijinsky—his real name was Shane Hwang—was a completely different creature. He was Chinese American, elegant, manicured, model handsome—in fact, actually a successful model.

Vincent lost focus, blinked, looked back at the sandwich.

“Don’t go too far away,” Nijinsky said softly. “We need you. We are in trouble, Vincent. We need you. I sure as hell need you. Lear knows it, they all know it. You’re you. I’m not. And, so, listen, just try to eat.”

He didn’t say, but thought: *And I don’t want to be you, Vincent.*

He let himself out of the room and winced at the sound of the key as he locked the door behind him.

The others were waiting in the shabby, depressing common room that Nijinsky hated. They all looked up at him. Plath. Keats. Wilkes. All that was left for now of the New York cell of BZRK.

Forty-eight hours had passed since the disaster at the UN. Just two days since Vincent lost his mind and Ophelia lost her legs and BZRK lost, period.

Wilkes had gotten out with a concussion, one ear still ringing, and some superficial burns. She was an odd girl and wore her oddness defiantly. Her right eye bore a tattoo of dark flames pointed sharply down to reach the top of her cheek. A gauze bandage covered a vicious burn on one arm. With a red Sharpie she had written FUCK YEAH, IT HURTS on the bandage.

On her other arm was a tattoo of a QR code. If you scanned it, you went to a web page where a similarly defiant message waited.

Somewhere much more private was a second QR code. If you made it that far, you might learn more about Wilkes. About a high school where the football team had been accused of rape. Where the alleged victim had walked through the halls of that school one night tossing Molotov cocktails.

Wilkes. The name was taken from a Stephen King novel.

As for Plath and Keats, Nijinsky kept telling them they had behaved brilliantly, especially given their inexperience. But the question hung in the air, unspoken, unspeakable: Why hadn't Plath killed the Armstrong Twins when she had the chance?

For God's sake, Plath who is really Sadie McLure, why didn't you just do it?

Too precious to kill, are you, little rich girl?

Then what the hell are you doing in BZRK?

Don't you know it's a war, Plath? Don't you know this is a battle for the human soul?

Why didn't you kill, Plath?

And did Plath have the answer? She was asking herself that same question. What was she, Gandhi? Who did she think she was? Jesus? Saint Sadie of Plath?

"Vincent's not coming out of it," Nijinsky said. "Who's got the bottle?"

There was a bottle of vodka next to the sink in the grim little kitchenette. It was frosted. They kept it in the freezer, usually. Keats was closest to the sink. He leaned back in his chair, grabbed the bottle by its neck, and snagged a glass of sketchy cleanliness and swept them over onto the coffee table.

Nijinsky took the bottle, poured himself about three fingers' worth. He drank most of it in a gulp followed by a gasp, then a second gulp, and put the glass down with too much force.

Hair of the dog, as the saying went. A little drink in the a.m. to take the edge off the hangover you'd earned in the p.m.

You're the wrong person for the job. Become the right person.

"My brother hasn't got over it," Keats said. "My brother's still chained to a cot at The Brick."

"Kerouac lost three biots," Wilkes said. "And he was already half nuts."

"Screw you," Keats snapped. "My brother was as tough as any man alive."

"He was," Nijinsky agreed, and shot a dirty look at Wilkes, who retreated, sulking. "Kerouac was . . . is . . . the real thing." He poured another drink, shorter this time, held it up and said, "To Kerouac, who is a fucking god and still ended up screaming in the dark." He tossed the drink back.

There was violence in the hearts of those in the room. Nijinsky bitter and furious and insecure. Keats damaged, resentful, and wary. Wilkes already a headcase who had now killed and seen killing and watched Ophelia's legs burn like steak fat on a grill and was itching for a fight.

Plath saw it all. And she heard the unspoken accusations: Why didn't you kill the Twins?

"Jin," she said. Just that. And Nijinsky at the sound of his affectionate nickname sucked in a sobbing breath. He looked down at the glass and carefully set it down far from himself.

"I love him," Nijinsky said.

Plath couldn't help her automatic glance at Keats.

"Stupid of me, caring about Vincent," Nijinsky said. "Loving him. And no, I don't mean like that. I mean, if I'd had a brother . . ." He looked at Keats, who did have a brother, and there were tears in Nijinsky's eyes. "I mean if I'd had a brother, if I knew what that was like, that would be Vincent. I'd give my useless life for him. And I was too late."

In a flash Plath saw what she had missed. She wasn't the only person in the room haunted by What if? and Why didn't I?

"Maybe we could rescue Ophelia from the FBI . . ." Wilkes started to say. "She could . . . No one's a better spinner than Ophelia." She was pleading for a life and knowing better, knowing that decision would have already been made.

"You're talking about a deep wire," Nijinsky said, not meeting anyone's eye.

"Yeah, deep wire. The deepest. Take some time and get all the way down in Vincent's brain." Wilkes sat up. "Ophelia could—"

"Damn it, Wilkes." Nijinsky was pleading with her. Plath could see that he was on the ragged edge. He couldn't think about Ophelia. "Ophelia was the best."

His use of past tense did not escape anyone's notice.

Wilkes's face twisted. It was like someone had kicked her in the stomach. She jumped from her seat and walked on stiff legs to the sink. She turned on the faucet and drank straight from the tap. When she straightened up her head banged the cupboard door.

"Son of a bitch!" she screamed. She banged the side of her fist against the cupboard door. And then harder. Then both fists and on and on until it seemed she would beat her hands bloody.

Keats moved smoothly behind her, imprisoned her arms, and waited as she cursed him and struggled madly to get away.

"Was it us?" Wilkes demanded. "Was it us? Was it Caligula? Did Lear order Ophelia killed? Jesus Christ!"

After a while Wilkes said, "Okay, blue eyes, you can let me go."

He did. She smashed the cupboard one last time and headed for the door. Nijinsky's arm shot out, he grabbed her wrist, and pulled her to him. She struggled for a minute but finally collapsed, sat on his lap, and let him put his arms around her.

He spoke past her spiky hair, his voice quiet, calm. "I don't know if you've seen the news in the last hour," he said.

Heads shook in the negative.

"The president's husband is dead. Supposedly he slipped in the bathtub," Nijinsky said. "I think that's most likely bullshit."

"Why would anyone want him dead?" Plath asked.

Wilkes was listening for the answer. For Keats it all meant very little: the American's first gentleman was not on his radar.

"I doubt anyone wanted MoMo dead," Nijinsky said. "I think the other side screwed up. I think they're having a very bad wire."

Plath was the first to grasp what he was saying. "You think she did it? The president?"

"It has occurred to Lear," Nijinsky said, pushing Wilkes off and standing up stiffly, "that controlling the puppeteer is almost as good as controlling the puppet."

"We're going after Bug Man?" Wilkes said. Her incredulous expression hardened into a feral look, which in turn brought out an almost canine laugh.

"If you can't wire the target, wire the twitcher," Nijinsky said.

"When do we go?"

"This is mostly on the Washington cell," Nijinsky said. "But Lear wants us to be ready. In case they call for help."

"So we just sit on our butts?" Wilkes demanded.

"No, we go. We go. As soon as Vincent can go with us," Nijinsky said, and doubted the words even as he spoke them.

The group broke up. Plath stayed behind just a moment to talk to Nijinsky. "Do you still want me to go to the reading of the will?"

"You have no choice. It's dangerous. But you have no choice. Caligula will have your back. You think the lawyer will co-operate?"

"I know what my dad's will said. But who knows? Who the hell knows anything in this world?"

FIVE

A rebel group: misfits, borderline personalities, freaks, and definitely geeks. Who signs up to fight when the choices are death or madness?

No one joins a group calling itself BZRK expecting a country club. But among the far-flung cells of BZRK some were more conventional than others, and none was more stable, more normal seeming, than BZRK Washington.

Their safe house was on Capitol Hill, the somewhat dubious residential neighborhood near the Capitol Building where the U.S. Congress convened.

Fifth Street, Southeast, just off Independence Avenue. It was a narrow, two-story row house painted a muddy maroon color, with dirty windows in cream-colored frames.

But unlike their New York counterparts, BZRK Washington enjoyed a very pleasant interior environment. They had a gourmet kitchen. They had brand-new faux deco bathrooms. The plumbing worked. The heating worked. In summer even the air-conditioning worked.

There were five bedrooms in all, each rather small, but all pleasantly if blandly furnished. The living room had become the common meeting room where the six members could lounge on comfortable couches or decamp to the formal dining room.

There was a crystal chandelier in that dining room.

The kitchen was small but very nicely appointed, with a six-burner restaurant-quality gas stove top, a double oven, and a massive Sub-Zero refrigerator that dwarfed the rest of the room.

The kitchen was the domain of Yousef, who called himself Andronikos after the mad Byzantine emperor. He was . . . But it really doesn't matter what Andronikos was, because as he stood stirring the couscous he had three minutes left to live.

Four other members of the Washington cell of BZRK were also present. They were sipping teas and sodas—no booze or wine or beer: house rules—while waiting for the food.

They had put in a long day narrowing down the possible locations of a certain Bug Man.

Bug Man, they knew, would want to work within range of the White House and not be forced to rely on AFGC's often-unreliable signal repeaters. That meant a half-mile radius for his base of action. Probably. No one knew for sure.

But there would also be a separate abode of some sort. Living twenty-four hours a day in an office attracts attention from building management. So, two possible locations: an office near the White House and a hotel.

They were running facial-recognition software on CCTV footage, but no one had a good picture of Bug Man. All they knew was that he was a male black teen. That would lead nowhere.

But from Lear had come a solid lead. It seemed the Armstrong Fancy Gifts Corporation had a long-standing corporate discount rate with Hyatt Hotels. If they had Bug Man living at a Hyatt, that narrowed it down to seven likely hotels.

To find an office location they had gone back through occupancy permits and subtracted tenants who had been in place for more than a year. They searched the "for lease" ads for offices within the target area. They focused on those that had the greatest degree of privacy, with no shared facilities.

The list was not that long. They had fairly quickly come up with nineteen possible locations. They expected to have the exact location within three days. And with the CCTV facial-recognition software focusing on Hyatts, they expected to have the hotel pinned within a day or two.

Which was amazing work and really almost as amazing as the fact that AmericaStrong—a division of Armstrong Fancy Gifts Corporation—and the ETA had already narrowed the BZRK cell's location down to one address.

Just one.

Around the corner from the house on Fifth Street SE, what looked exactly like a Washington, DC, police SWAT team had assembled. This excited only mild interest from passersby—it was hardly the first time they'd seen a SWAT team. Even the passing patrol cops shrugged it off.

"What's that?" This from the kid—everyone called him the kid. Not The Kid, like it was some kind of cool nickname, just the kid. So he had taken it as his nom de guerre, his alias. Except he called himself Billy the Kid, because why not? Maybe Billy the Kid wasn't clinically crazy, but he was crazy. Not insane: but crazy.

Billy's real name was André. His mother had been Guatemalan. His father had been African American. The result of this interesting DNA mash-up was a boy of only medium height, with dark skin, a flat nose, and lush, long, almost girlish—in fact, no almost about it—straight black hair. The combination worked perfectly to make him feel excluded from both the African American and the Hispanic communities of Washington, DC.

André had interested, observant eyes. Nothing scary, there, just a birdlike quickness. His two front teeth stuck out a bit, which gave him a sweet childlike look and were the only physical feature he shared in common with the real Billy the Kid.

No one called him Billy the Kid. He had not found a way to mention that he shared buck teeth with the famous gunman.

Andronikos didn't call him Billy, either. Andronikos hated people looking over his shoulder as he cooked. Which is the last data point about Andronikos, other than the fact that as the front door was beaten in with a battering ram, and the back door was kicked in, and black-suited "SWAT cops" came rushing into the room yelling, "Police, down, down, down!" Andronikos reached for a butcher's cleaver and was shot in the chest, head, neck, again in the chest, and again in the head.

The hole in his neck sprayed like a fire hose.

Billy the Kid didn't so much drop to the floor as find himself knocked to the ground. Andronikos's hand dragged the couscous pot down with him, although he was dead before he hit the floor.

The couscous—little pearls of wheat, along with boiling hot water—sloshed onto Billy as he fell and Billy screamed because the heat was instantaneous and the "cop" waited until Billy was on the floor trying desperately to crab walk backward away from the couscous and the blood and the now blood-red couscous and BAM! BAM!

The cop was shooting again.

At him? At him? At a thirteen-year-old kid?

A bullet grazed his side.

From the other room, continuous gunfire. Like a jackhammer. A wall of noise. Screams. Shouting and BAMBAMBAMBAM!

The cop stepped in the red couscous and slipped. He fell to one knee.

Billy grabbed the pot. It was a heavy iron pot, but the weight was nothing to him because adrenaline and fear and the crying need for survival make the heaviest pot weightless.

He swung that pot and hit the cop's helmet.

The cop slipped a little more.

The hand that held the gun, that hand, he had landed on that elbow and that made it hard to shoot and his body armor made him awkward and he slipped again; suddenly it was all Call of Duty to Billy. He slammed the pot down with all his strength on the gun hand.

The gun fell from the cop's nerveless grip.

BAMBAMBAMBAM!

They were still shooting in the other room. And screaming. Someone actually yelled, "What the fuck?" Except that the f-bomb ended abruptly in gunfire.

Not real cops, Billy realized through the blood-mad rage that was falling over him, and he grabbed the gun and had to use both hands to get a grip on it and pointed it at the visor of the stunned man and the "cop" knew he was done for and he raised his visor so that Billy saw his face and it was a middle-aged man, a little pudgy, with a silly mustache and he was starting to say something when Billy pulled the trigger and a big hole peppered with powder burns appeared in the upper lip of the cop, taking out one side of his mustache.

Billy was up and running for the back door but bullets were flying like crazy there, so he pivoted, saw the massacre in the main room, and somehow lost all conscious thought.

The original, historical Billy the Kid was a good shot. His namesake was better. Billy could aim and he could shoot. His skills had been honed in hundreds of hours of first-person shooter games: Call of Duty, XCom, Rage, Battlefield. So he knew to be quick but not rushed. He knew that accurate was better than fast. He knew not to aim for the bodies covered in Kevlar, but to aim for the face. The visors would provide only limited protection.

He did not waste ammunition.

BAM! and the gun kicked in his hand and a cop fell and BAM! and another visor shattered and the cop dropped to his knees and his gloved hand pawed the air and Billy ignored him because he was nothing but a computer graphic and a kill and he was done and there should be a ka-ching! a point on the screen.

There was no screen. Part of him understood that because no game had yet managed to create the smell of blood, lots and lots of blood, which had a sort of salty, briny smell and an unctuousness about it, not to mention the smell of bowels loosening and bladders emptying and, of course, gunpowder smoke.

The cops, well, they couldn't call for backup because of course they were not cops at all but AFGC thugs masquerading as ETA agents, and there weren't all that many of those to call on. Not yet.

Ten of them had burst through the doors.

Five were still alive. But one of those had been wounded by "friendly fire," and was pumping his life out through a hole in his thigh.

BZRK Washington was dead. All dead. It was down to Billy and four fake cops who all aimed their weapons at him.

He dived around the corner.

Two of the cops chased him. It was a mistake on their part because damn, this is part of every first-person shooter game ever, as they rushed he popped out and BAM! and a split second later, BAM! and that was two plexi visors with neat little holes and blood gushing out beneath.

With that Billy turned finally and ran. Out the back door.

He climbed, scrabbled, rolled over the wooden fence into the backyard of whoever the hell lived back there. The back door was locked but not so locked that a nine-millimeter round through the door handle and a hard kick wouldn't open it.

Through a strange, unoccupied home with a startled kitty on the back of the couch. Out onto Sixth Street.

He stood there, panting. They weren't pursuing him. No one was after him. He was covered in blood. There were no sirens. People figured it was the cops, so what are you going to do, call the cops and tell them cops are shooting up a house?

He couldn't go anywhere covered in blood. So he jogged on nervous energy to Independence Avenue, which, if you follow it far enough, will take you all the way down to the Capitol and beyond to the Mall and the Washington Monument and all of that. Except Billy didn't go that way. He turned left and trotted back to Fifth Street SE and saw the very official-looking SWAT van and trotted on to the house, and came in through the shattered front door and saw one of the fake cops weeping and shot him in the spine where he had no body armor and another turned and opened fire, very undisciplined, and shot the wall and the clock and Billy put one right in his throat.

One more came rushing down the stairs yelling, "Aaaarrrgh!" to keep his courage up and Billy couldn't see his visor so he shot him in the knee and finished him off when the cop tumbled down the landing.

That last one was a shock. He had thought he only had two left. What was the count? Was there anyone else?

Billy climbed the stairs. The grazing bullet wound in his side was burning like fire.

He found the last AmericaStrong fake cop behind one of the beds in a bedroom. The man had removed his helmet. He had lost his gun in the madness. Defenseless.

The man was young. He had very, very pale skin. He had very, very large brown eyes. He stared at Billy the Kid. He was shaking.

"Don't," the man said.

"You started it," Billy said.

"I'm sorry about . . . about . . ." the man said, and waved in the direction of downstairs.

Billy thought he seemed okay. "You smell," Billy said.

"I pooped." The man laughed. It was a short, sharp sound.

Billy's sights were leveled at the man's face.

"Who did this?" Billy asked.

The man shrugged, but he couldn't hold it together well enough to lie. "I'm just, look, I used to work for AmericaStrong, now I'm ETA."

"ETA? Estimated Time of Arrival?"

"Emerging Technologies Agency," the man said weakly, as though he didn't expect to be believed. Or that he would be alive another thirty seconds. "My name is Joey. Joey Lamb. I . . . I didn't . . . I don't . . . Don't shoot me, kid."

"Billy. Billy the Kid."

"Okay."

"Look, it's game over, right? I won. So just, I don't know, run away."

Joey Lamb stood shakily. He had pooped all right.

"Okay, now, just leave," Billy said. "And don't call anyone. And don't come back."

Joey ran. Billy heard him clatter through the house. He heard the front door slam back on its hinges.

Billy went downstairs. He went through the pockets of his friends, harvesting credit cards and driver's licenses. He piled the laptops and the cell phones together and placed them all in a plastic trash bag.

Then he found some clean clothing, laid it out in the blessedly blood-free bathroom, and took a shower. It took a long time for the water to run clean.

Burnofsky stood up, heard his bones creak and his knees snap. Old age was coming on fast. But it wouldn't be old age that killed him.

He walked from his office out into the main lab floor. It occupied three entire floors of the Armstrong Building. It was a huge space, very white with pink accents, designed to be functional but also pleasant and innocuous. Like everything the Armstrong Fancy Gifts Corporation did in secret, it was designed to look as if it could not possibly conceal anything dark or sinister.

The lights were bright but soft. The walls bore huge plasma screens showing pastoral scenes, like slow-changing murals, a mountain stream would slowly give way to a strand of unpopulated beach, which in turn might, after an hour or so, switch to a field of flowers waving in the breeze.

The murals followed the time of day. As the sun would set outside, so the sun would set over mountain and beach and field. When full night fell the screens would light up with time-lapse pictures of crazily zooming car lights crossing the Golden Gate Bridge, or shots of the aurora borealis, or moonlight on a river.

It was really quite a lovely place to work while designing the end of the human race as it had heretofore been.

Structural integrity required the floors to have some strength, so gazing up Burnofsky looked through a loose-woven web of white tiled catwalks with pink railings and the occasional green contrast. This allowed some of the larger pieces of equipment to rise through the floors, but also created smaller, more intimate spaces.

"Dr. Burnofsky." It was Mamadou Attah. Dr. Mamadou Attah,

formerly of the Ivory Coast, later of Oxford and MIT, briefly a resident of Grand Rapids Michigan's Applegate Psychiatric Hospital, and now one of Burnofsky's hardest-working—and giddily happy—subordinates.

"Yes, Dr. Attah?"

"We did it, we sure got that extruder calibrated!"

"Good," he said.

She flashed him a huge grin. She was short and broad and, despite being brilliant, had a distinct tendency to go around giggling under her breath. She had been wired and indoctrinated, of course, all as a means of dealing with what had been crippling depression.

No more depression in her future. No more mental hospitals. Although she sometimes irritated nonwired staff to the point of rage, she was an excellent scientist and utterly devoted.

She stood waiting like an expectant dog, evidently not entirely satisfied by his wan, "Good." So he added a, "Fantastic work, Doctor. You're the best."

She grinned, made a pistol finger, and said, "No, sir, Dr. B., you're the best!"

He walked across the spotless white tile floor past white-coated scientists and pink-coated staff, a shambling, reedy, runny-eyed, corduroy-clad wreck of a human being. The door to his private lab was protected by a keypad and fingerprint ID. He punched in the number sequence and pressed his thumb against the touchscreen.

Inside was a very different space. Here the equipment was whatever putty or gray color it had been when first acquired. There were no plasma screens showing bucolic loveliness. The ceiling seemed particularly low. A Costco-size box of Little Debbie Devil Cremes spilled across his desk.

He pulled the bottle of bourbon from his desk, poured a tumblerful, and gulped it.

Back in the fabulous main lab the work of AFGC's nanotech division went on feverishly. The piece of equipment that Dr. Attah had been so proud of fixing was part of the SRN production line.

Self-replicating nanobot. SRN. But he along with everyone else involved in the project had taken to calling them "hydras," after the mythological beast that just kept sprouting new heads any time you chopped one off: in effect, a self-replicating monster.

The first large-scale field test of the hydras was scheduled to occur in just a few weeks.

Twelve hundred hydras would be released in a high-crime neighborhood in the Bronx. The test would be whether the hydras would propagate, locate hosts, and avoid detection. If they performed as expected, the neighborhood would experience a sudden drop in crime rate as thousands of residents were crudely rewired for diminished aggression.

A smaller test, just two hundred hydras bearing special radioactive tracking signatures, were to be released on the subway. They would be able to follow the spread. And these nanobots had a particular function: to do something the first generation of nanobots couldn't even begin to pull off: the implantation of an image. Actually creating a memory.

And yet, despite those specialized abilities, the hydras were poor relations to regular nanobots. They were crude, rough, and slow. The self-replicating process meant using whatever materials could be found at hand: one form or another of living tissue.

The regular nanobots were made of sophisticated alloys, ceramics, and textiles. They were the Ferraris of the nanotech world. These new tiny monsters were scarecrows by contrast.

Each hydra was serviced by dozens of much smaller micromachines, nicknamed MiniMites. These were very simple, very, very small devices whose sole purpose was to strip-mine living things for their useful minerals. They were tiny refineries, eating flesh and defecating iron, zinc, copper, calcium, magnesium, chromium, and the rest.

In the event that anything went wrong with the tests, the mayor of New York City, the governor of New York, and, if it came to that, the president of the United States should be under sufficient control to head off an effective investigation, let alone countermeasures.

Of course the whole thing had to be carefully managed. A fair amount of a human body could be consumed and turned into raw material without harming the host—most people had more than enough fat, extra bone, dead skin, resident bacteria, the contents of stomachs and intestines, and whatever brain cells were being liquefied. But uncontrolled, well, the process could be harmful. Even fatal.

To say nothing of what would happen if the MiniMites began to adapt and to chew away at buildings and bridges and so on.

But there were fail-safes and cutoffs and so on for all of that.

Foolproof stuff. And the hydras were being designed to reproduce only so many generations before dying off, and to consume only so much living tissue. The goal, after all, was to rewire the human race, not to obliterate it.

That was the plan.

That was not, however, Burnofsky's plan.

Burnofsky carried his drink to his workstation. There he had a monitor attached to a scanning electron microscope. He pressed a remote control in his pocket and the surveillance camera on the wall switched seamlessly to file video. He doubted the Twins would understand what he was doing, but there was no point taking chances: they would see only what he wanted them to see.

On the monitor Burnofsky saw nanobots. They were rather different from the ones being so carefully created in the main lab. Burnofsky smiled to see them. Busy little creatures. Hydras busy doing what SRNs did: self-replicating.

But there were a number of differences between these and the hydras beyond his lab door. Some of those differences were visible, most not.

Funny, Burnofsky thought, gazing with pride at his creations, that people talk about the gray goo scenario, and in truth the hydras in the main lab were basically gray.

But these were not.

These nanobots were blue. The exact blue of his daughter's eyes.

[ARTIFACT]

For Immediate Release

Public Affairs Office/University of Texas, Austin

The entire University of Texas family is saddened by the loss of Professor Edwin H. Grossman. Dr. Grossman apparently leapt to his death from the top of the University of Texas tower. In recent months Dr. Grossman had been under great strain. Students reported that his usual lectures on nanotechnology had taken on a paranoid character, with Dr. Grossman falsely claiming that nanotechnology was already being deployed in a bid by unnamed forces to effectively reprogram the human race.

Dr. Grossman, one of the world's leading researchers on microscopic machines, wrote a book in 2011 warning that self-replicating nano devices could run out of control with dire consequences. The book was published without the support of the University or his department.

In 2012 Dr. Grossman claimed to have been consulted by the CIA on the so-called gray goo scenario, the fanciful notion that self-reproducing nano machines could run amok and obliterate all carbon-based life-forms in a matter of days.

A student, Ling Ju Chow, who claimed to have seen two men throw

Dr. Grossman from the twenty-eighth-floor observation deck of the UT Tower, recanted when questioned by campus police and was later fatally injured in a car-on-pedestrian accident off campus.

The University mourns both of these tragic deaths.

[ARTIFACT]

Drug Enforcement Agency

New York City

Surveillance Report—China Bone

Item: Subject 49630, code name "Rocker Girl." Subject observed arriving 10:27 p.m. Electronic monitoring via her phone indicates she ordered injectable heroin. Audio monitoring produced only some singing and incoherent conversation with China Bone staff identified (tentative) as Cheng Lee.

Item: Subject 67709, unknown subject. Desc: Male, Asian, 35–40 years, 5'8". Arrived by limo. Attempting to trace origin.

Item: Subject 42001, code name "Burn Out." Arrived 12:02 a.m. Electronic monitoring via planted microphone 45-114. Subject ordered bourbon and opium pipe. Following ingestion suspect began to speak. Previous surveillance shows this is a common pattern for the subject. Transcript follows:

(inaudible) just (inaudible) deliver and then. And then, hah. Watch the bugs grow. (inaudible) baby, sorry. Sorry sorry sorry. Your bitch mother. Yeah. Oh Jesus I'm sorry sorry. But we all die. We all die, baby. (inaudible) We all surely do die and if it isn't the easy way it's the hard way and the twins would have made it hard. Bugs in your brain. Has to (inaudible) I never should have. Didn't know they'd (inaudible.) You went easy though. You went so easy, baby. Hah. Thanks to your dad. Hah. My gift baby the easy death instead of the hard. My gift . . . easy . . . (inaudible.) But (inaudible) pay up. They will pay up. My little blues will end it all end it end it. Tens to hundreds to (inaudible) millions to billions eat it all up, eat it all up eat it all up down to the rock. All . . .

End transcript.

SIX

The law firm sent a limo for Plath, but not to the BZRK safe house. The limo picked Plath and Keats up at the address she'd given them: outside the Andaz Hotel on Fifth Avenue.

Plath had not been staying at the Andaz, and a cursory investigation would reveal that fact, but it was at least plausible that she might have been there. The McLure Company maintained a suite year-round for visiting dignitaries.

Plausible.

"Why didn't you tell me you had the use of a posh suite at a hotel?" Keats muttered as the town car inched its way uptown. "Why are we staying at that miserable shit hole when we could be frolicking on clean sheets?"

"Frolicking? I seem to recall offering to frolic with you. I was going to frolic your brains out." She was determined to keep the mood light. Wave upon wave of sadness and fear had crashed on her since that terrible day when her father and brother had been murdered. More would come.

Too much.

She couldn't break. Maybe the day would come when she broke, but not yet. So she smiled and so did Keats. It felt like the first genuine smile for either in quite a while.

"Sorry, had to save your life first," Keats said. "Duty before booty."

"You shouldn't always be the good boy, Keats," she teased. "Don't you know that messed-up girls like me prefer bad boys?"

"You are toying with me."

"I used to break my toys," she said.

"Is that a warning?"

"I wouldn't break you. I might bruise you a little . . ."

"Okay, that's quite enough."

"Might bend you. There could be some chafing . . ."

Keats grinned, unable to manage a stern expression. "Now you're going past toying to torturing."

"Yes, I am."

"It's cruel."

"Mmm. I'm trying not to be the goody goody."

"No one thinks you're the goody goody," he said.

"You sure?" she asked, her tone rueful. "Jin needs me, even Lear needs me, if there really is a Lear, but I failed them, didn't I?"

Keats glanced at the driver. He didn't seem to be listening, and they were talking in whispers. Keats leaned closer. "Listen to me, Plath—"

"It's Sadie on this trip," she interrupted. "The lawyer and the others know me by my real name. So just for this trip, let's not play crazy little BZRK games. Let's act like real, normal people."

"Sadie," he said, trying it out. Liking it. Feeling flattered by the right to use it. "Do you want to know my real name?"

"Keats will do. I like it, actually. It suits you. You could totally be a poet."

Veer away from tragedy, back onto safe ground.

We take the names of madmen because madness is our fate. But Keats, the real one, the poet, hadn't really been mad, just depressed and addicted.

Plath, on the other hand: head in a gas oven while her children played in the next room.

Veer away from that, too.

"I know nothing about poetry," Keats said.

Plath said nothing for a while, watching the street go by, wondering whether Caligula had them in view. Wondering whether AFGC also had them in view. The reading of a will is not a very private matter, private in terms of the actual reading, perhaps, but not in terms of who knows it's happening.

"This could be dangerous," she said.

"Maybe," he agreed. "Do you know how to do this? I mean, this whole reading of the will. There's a lot of money involved, right?"

She nodded. "Money. And power."

"And you're okay with all that, not nervous?"

"I'm nervous," she admitted. "But I know what to say. I know what I want, and I know how my dad set things up. But that doesn't mean they'll go along with it. In fact, I'd be surprised if they did."

"So I guess we're talking hundreds, even thousands of dollars, eh?" he asked, deadpan.

"Something like that," she said.

And for a while she didn't think of Keats but of her father. Grey McLure always said he was a three-star scientist with five-star luck. But that wasn't true. He'd been unlucky enough to lose his wife, and die alongside his son. Not lucky, but smart, and far-seeing. He had laid in contingencies she had thought ridiculous and irrelevant when he told her of them.

"Don't forget," he had told her. "*Alice in Wonderland*. The You Bullshit Bank. Your mother's birthday."

"Whatever," she had replied, attention focused on thumbing a text message to some friend. The memory, like so many memories of him, came with a twinge of regret that she had not, somehow, cherished him more, him and Stone, both.

Three more blocks passed in starts and stops and her nerves were getting to her now. Small talk and banter, don't think about it, any of it, just let it happen.

"You are a great kisser," she said suddenly through her knuckles, choosing not to meet his gaze.

"Am I?"

"Don't fish for compliments. A poet would never do that."

"You're worried," he said. "You're being nice to me because you think we're about to be killed."

"A little bit, yes," she admitted. "But also, you're just a really good kisser. And you know what I like, Keats?"

"What?"

"Your chest. I like your chest. It's very hard."

"Okay, really, that's quite enough," he scolded. "We're in a limo, possibly going into danger, and you're playing the tease."

"I like your chest," she repeated. "Can I ask you a question?"

"Unh?" he said, not feeling quite in control of this conversation.

"Are your nipples sensitive?"

"I sort of hate you right now," he said, shaking his head and trying unsuccessfully not to grin.

Teasing was safe. Maybe it was foreplay leading to love, but it didn't have to be. Keep it all superficial. Make it about bodies and pleasure. The world had it all backward: it wasn't sex that was dangerous, it was love. She'd lost people she loved. It was love that brought unendurable pain.

"Death or madness, right?" She said with what she hoped was a brave, devil-may-care attitude. "There's no reason not to have whatever fun we can. You're insane for a long time and dead forever."

"We're here," the driver called back.

The car pulled to a stop beside a food stand. The driver hopped out and came around to open the passenger door. Keats had already started to open the door and now felt foolish.

The law firm's building was on a corner. There was a revolving door and flanking it regular glass doors. Security—McLure men—waited. They wore dark suits and had Bluetooth earpieces. They wore sunglasses even though it was cloudy. They screamed "security."

The AmericaStrong thugs were less obvious. They had been nicknamed TFD—Tourists from Denver—for favoring chinos and down parkas, for dressing out of a Land's End catalog. The McLure men wanted to look like security; the AmericaStrong people did not.

Four McLure security.

Six TFDs.

And all alone, a man in a long, faded black duster over even more faded lilac and leaf-green velvet. A jaunty top hat that matched his blazer.

Plath watched with eyes that had now seen violence and knew it when it threatened. She gritted her teeth, not so much afraid now as angry. There was a fine line between those two, fear and rage.

"Sadie, get back in the car," Keats said.

But she didn't. She watched, one hand on the car door, watched with eyes that now saw so much more than they ever had before. Was that what violence and fear did? Did they give you new eyes?

It all happened without any obvious action. Somehow, in some way that seemed to take place at the subliminal level, the McLure security spotted the TFDs as threats.

And somehow, those same McLure men recognized the man in the faded velvet, not as an individual, they didn't know him, no, but they knew what he was.

And so did the TFDs.

His name, at least the name he used, was Caligula.

Plath knew he would have been the one to kill Ophelia. He would also be the one to kill her, if she ever threatened BZRK. She had seen him in action and could entertain no fantasies about surviving if he came for her.

Invisible lines connected McLure men and Caligula. Invisible, intangible calculations were made. Some scent in the air, maybe, some inaudible whisper in the ears.

The TFDs walked on by.

And Plath—Sadie McLure—walked with Keats past the McLure men, all of them smiling, a tense, alert welcome, and accepted the door held open for her.

"You okay?" Plath asked Keats.

"Just relieved not to have wet myself," he said. "That won't be the end of it. They'll be waiting when we come back out."

But Plath doubted that.

Keats's hand closed around hers. She could picture what was happening at the nano level: skin like fallen leaves, fingerprints like the plowed furrows of some arid farm, sweat beads popped by the contact, mingling.

It was an absurd romantic illusion to imagine that they could avoid death so long as they held on to each other. But Plath, carrying the name of a poet, had a right to a small measure of illusion.

Dr. Anya Violet, who had been dragged unwilling into violence, into lunacy and horror, sat forgotten in her room, in her narrow, filthy room, and against all odds and logic thought of Vincent.

Oh, she knew it was all part of the same insanity. She knew that Vincent had been inside her head, that he had wired her. She was a scientist, a trained observer. She knew.

Once she had found Vincent desirable. That had been honest. That had been real. She remembered meeting him for . . . at least she believed she remembered. She searched for the memory, ran the pictures back in her head, testing them for tampering. It was hard to tell. Hard to be sure; in fact, impossible to be sure. But she believed that first meeting at least, and that first visceral impression, had been real.

She had found him interesting. And sad. Sadness was not a terrible thing to her. She was Russian by birth, from Samara, located in the middle of nowhere. She was not an American raised on the idea that happiness was the natural human condition. She tired quickly of smiling people. Have a nice day. Hey, honey, smile.

She had seen wariness in Vincent, lessons learned, pain endured, limitations accepted. He was perhaps ten years younger than she, but that was only chronology.

Where it didn't matter, Vincent was young. The other places, where it mattered, he was old, old, old, and sad.

He had touched her that first time. Yes, of course he had targeted her. She was a scientist at McLure, a biot researcher and designer, and Vincent had even then been laying out a back door to McLure, anticipating the day.

So he had touched her that first time, and yes his invisibly small biots had raced up her shivering shoulder and across the neck and into her through nose or ear or eye.

Into her brain, there to probe and discover and spy and wire her. To prepare her for a continuing relationship that he needed and she wanted.

Yes, she had wanted. Yes, that surely was an honest memory. Yes, that first liquid feeling had been real, that first parting of her lips, that first animal response to him, that at least had been completely real.

And now she loved him.

Real love? Or wired love? In the end did it matter?

They had made love. Not once, more than once. Had it been enhanced by busy biots laying wire and transponders in her brain? He had claimed not. He claimed he wired her only minimally, only to obtain her . . . professional . . . services. He wired the scientist in her, not the woman.

So he had said.

Did it matter? Did it change the fact that her heart had been a desperate animal in her chest? Did it change the way he'd made her breath catch in her throat? Did it change the fact that she had gasped and made strangling, inarticulate cries into a pillow, and he had taken the pillow away because he wanted to hear her, needed to hear her pleasure, needed to experience secondhand at least what pleasure could be?

Maybe some of it, most of it, all of it, was false.

He had told her that it was not. Vincent had sworn that he only made her more suggestible to co-operating on the building of new biots, that he would never . . . That that sort of thing was not BZRK, not what they fought for.

Did it matter?

Anya sat in her one chair remembering, and while remembering thus was unable to work on the formula she'd begun to complete on the sketch pad, covered like a college chalkboard with obscure symbols.

There was a knock at the door.

Her eyes flew open. She waited a few seconds for the unsteadiness in her voice to calm. "Yes?"

There was the sound of a lock. The door swung inward, practically halving the room. Nijinsky stepped in.

Anya didn't like him. He was beautiful and perfect and not

interesting to her. And she knew that his relationship with Vincent was deeper than her own. She was jealous of him. It annoyed her somehow that he had chosen a Russian nom de guerre. The Chinese American model didn't have a Russian soul, he was not a Nijinsky.

"Dr. Violet," he said politely. He glanced at the sketch pad, quickly at her, then resumed his usual mask of indifference. "I wanted to talk to you about . . . well, whether you've had any strange feelings lately." Nijinsky raised his eyebrows and made a slight, wry smile.

"Why don't you tell me what you mean," Anya said curtly.

"Okay. I mean that Vincent still has a biot inside you."

She nodded. The idea was not a surprise to her. "So, a little Vincent still crawling around in my hippocampus or wherever. A little biot controlled by a madman." She had to laugh. "Wasn't there a song? The lunatic is in my head?"

Nijinsky's brown, almond eyes went cold.

She noticed and shook her head derisively. "Ah, I see, we aren't supposed to say that kind of thing about Vincent, are we?"

"He cares about you," Nijinsky said. "He saved your life."

"Right after he endangered it," she snapped. "I'm not sure that counts as a net plus."

Nijinsky said nothing.

"Where are the others? His other biots? You used a singular in describing the one he had in me."

Nijinsky nodded. "One is dead. One is in a dish, rebuilding, healing. The other one I'm carrying. It's right here." He tapped his forehead lightly.

"And so you and I both get to keep a little piece of him." Anya was tired of sparring. "No. I haven't noticed anything. If anyone is wiring me I'm not noticing it, and if a . . . mentally unbalanced . . . twitcher were doing it, it would be clumsy enough for me to notice. So, I very much doubt that Vincent is even aware of the biot inside me. If he is, it's as a series of hallucinatory images that probably mean little or nothing to him."

Nijinsky nodded. "I haven't seen any activity at all from his biot."

He sat down on the edge of the bed, his knee almost touching hers. In a straight man she would have suspected a flirtation.

"What's on the pad?" he asked bluntly.

"I'm not stupid," she said. "I know you have surveillance in here. I know you've already seen and investigated."

He shook his head. Then he hung his head down and shook it again. "No, actually. We don't have the manpower for that, I'm afraid. I mean, yes, we have a camera in here, but aside from making sure you haven't hanged yourself or tried to dig a hole through the wall . . ."

"It's what I was working on before you and your charming crew decided to destroy my life," she said, but the bitterness was false and sounded it. Vincent was not something she could regret.

"Biot?" he asked.

"Biot version four," she said. "Fourth generation. What you use now is version three. Or threes with various upgrades."

"Okay," he said cautiously. "Do you want to tell me?"

"It's faster. It can jump. It has an improved rack for add-on weaponry. The legs are stronger."

"Yes?" he asked, not nearly as cool as he wanted to sound.

"And it has a rather interesting penetrating proboscis, hollow of course, with a bladder. Mosquito-derived."

"So it can suck blood?" He was puzzled.

"It goes the other way. The bladder can be filled with any number of interesting agents—chemical, bacteriological, viral—and injected. No more carrying sacks of germs with you if you want to plant something deadly."

"We don't do that," Nijinsky said.

"Ah. Of course. I forgot: you're the good guys," she mocked. "Not for you, planting a bit of flesh-eating bacteria in some enemy's brain."

"There are limits," he said.

"Just like you don't wire people."

He raised his head and looked at her. "Dr. Violet, we will endeavor to remove any alterations made in your brain."

She swallowed in a suddenly dry throat.

"We do things out of extreme necessity," he went on, sounding sanctimonious even to himself. "Vincent wired you, as little as he could, just enough to—"

"I'm in love with him," she said, and now her voice was no longer tight and controlled. "And your solution is to take that away from me? And then what?"

He looked quickly away, as if eye contact had become painful.

Neither spoke. His knee no longer touched hers. She wondered if his biots were now making the slow, laborious climb up the length of her thigh on their way to her brain. No, not likely: he could have simply planted them on her face, no need for subterfuge.

"What else?" he asked.

"The visuals are better. It will make wiring easier and more accurate. The downside? You feel pain when it feels pain. And God himself only knows what effect it has if you lose one."

Nijinsky controlled his breathing, not wanting to signal his excitement. "Can you make them?" he asked.

"Version four? Of course I can make them, they've been successfully tested," she said. "Get me to the lab and I can grow one in a few hours."

Nijinsky nodded. Not an easy proposition. The McLure labs had been the scene of a bloody battle. A massacre. But Lear had been busy, and a backup existed.

"What if it wasn't your lab?" Nijinsky asked. "What if it was a place with all the same equipment, the same samples or most of them, essentially the same data files, even better computers, and so on?"

That surprised her. "You have another lab in New York?"

"Not in New York," he said, and offered no further explanation.

She ran down a list of equipment. To each item Nijinsky said, "Yes."

"Well, aren't you clever little conspirators?" she asked sarcastically. "Yes, if everything is as you say, yes, I can do it. But why should I?"

"What do you want?" he asked.

"So many things," she said with a hard laugh.

Silence again, as the truth seeped into her consciousness. The truth was a pain in her heart. "What do I want? Don't. Don't take him from me. Don't send your bugs into me, and don't cut the wires, and don't find his last biot and take it from me." Tears had already rolled down her cheeks. "It's all I have of him."

SEVEN

A short elevator ride for two billion dollars.

"Sadie. It's good to see you," Stern said. He shook her hand firmly. Her hand was not empty. His eyes barely flickered as he palmed the note.

"Same, Mr. Stern," she said. "This is my friend, Keats." She stumbled over the word friend. They weren't exactly friends, were they? They barely knew each other.

"My friend," she repeated, as if needing to emphasize it.

Stern was head of McLure security. He'd sat by her bed when she was recovering from injuries following the assassination of her father and brother, and as far as Plath felt she could trust anyone, she trusted him. He gave Keats the same dubious, sizing-up look her father would have.

The lawyer, Don Jellicoe, was an older man, tall, spare, with a hovering grin and an open collar. He rose to shake her hand as well.

The office was a corner, with windows that looked out on the

Empire State Building and, beyond it, at the Tulip—Armstrong corporate headquarters.

She had been there, seen it from the inside. She had watched her wiring take effect on Benjamin Armstrong. She almost flinched, thinking they could see her now.

She stared, probably too long, then looked with exaggerated and unconvincing calm around the room and turned her back on the Tulip and the memories.

A younger lawyer sat discreetly in a corner. The remaining person in the room was Hannah Thrum. Thrum was middle-aged but looked younger, expensively but conservatively dressed. She had a full face and somewhat droopy eyes that seemed at odds with the well-coiffed businesswoman look.

Thrum was the interim chairman of the board of McLure Holdings, the parent corporation of McLure Labs.

"Can I get anyone some coffee? Water? Tea? We have it all," Jellicoe offered, very genial. Keats asked for coffee, Thrum ordered a sparkling water, and the younger lawyer raced off to get both.

"So," Jellicoe said. "We have copies for you, Sadie, and for you, Hannah." He handed iPads to each and tapped his own to bring up the document. "We have the small matter of two billion dollars." He grinned. "Give or take a dime."

That drew only tense stares. Jellicoe sighed, a little deflated.

"As you can see, it's quite a long document. But I wondered if we could dispense with a literal reading of every single word and you would allow me to summarize?"

Keats surprised everyone by speaking up. "Of course Pl— Sadie would get a full copy?"

"Yes, of course," Jellicoe said, and seemed amused.

"Go ahead, Don," Thrum said. Like this was her meeting.

"Well, the long and short of it is that Sadie is the sole surviving heir. She inherits the bulk of the estate. There are some bequests for some of Grey McLure's friends, relations, employees, and charities. All told those bequests are quite substantial, amounting to something on the order of two hundred million dollars in McLure stock and cash."

Keats whistled, then apologized.

"It's worth whistling at," Jellicoe allowed. "So is what's left to Sadie." He looked at Sadie, raised his Saruman eyebrows, and said, "You inherit the rest of your father and brother's shares of McLure. Added to those you already own, you hold fifty-five percent of the company. At today's prices, as I said, that's just a hair under two billion dollars. Of course the share price has dropped quite a bit since your father and brother died so tragically. But if the company is well managed, the stock value will bounce back."

"And you won't need to worry about that: managing the company is the responsibility of the board," Thrum said with what she hoped was absolute finality.

"The company belongs to its stockholders," Plath said levelly. She had not come here to be bullied.

"Yes, of course," Thrum said. "And your shares will be voted by your executor." She turned to Jellicoe, whose expression was unreadable.

"Here it comes," Keats said under his breath.

"Executor?" Plath asked, already knowing the answer. It would be interesting to see how Thrum responded.

Jellicoe sighed. "It is usual practice to assign an adult executor in the case of a minor, a wise, trusted older friend or lawyer."

Keats made a wry face.

"But in this case," Jellicoe went on, "Grey McLure specifically declined to do so. In fact, he directed me to take such measures as would ensure that his daughter not only inherited his company, but, in the event of her brother's death, should run it."

"That's absurd," Thrum snapped. "That can't be legal."

"Ah, but it is," Jellicoe said. "Grey emancipated his daughter. And with some effort—many, many billable hours, I'm pleased to admit—I was able to enact his wishes." He dropped the grin. "I think Grey, who was my good friend for twenty years, expected to die, you see. I heard it in his voice. I saw it in his actions. He expected to die."

Plath felt a lead weight pressing down on her heart. Of course her father had expected to be killed. Of course. He had guessed what was coming.

As she could guess at the terror that was coming for her. Will it be death? Or madness?

She closed her eyes, not realizing she'd done so. Silence fell around her as she remembered her father, and that day. Images of the jet screaming down out of the sky . . . Not what she wanted to remember about her father and brother. Not the images she wanted to hold on to for the rest of her life.

"Maybe he was mentally compromised," Thrum suggested. "Not competent."

Plath opened her eyes, and her lips curled into a snarl.

Jellicoe cut in quickly. "He anticipated that line of . . . reasoning. Attached to the document are affidavits from three board-certified psychiatrists who each examined Grey within a month of his signing of the will."

Thrum at last exhibited frustration. She threw up one hand. Just one. And said nothing.

Plath noticed Stern smiling, not at her but at some memory. He, too, had been with McLure for a long time, and Grey was a man who made friends for life.

"I don't want to run the company," Plath said. "In fact, Ms. Thrum, my father always said you were the smartest person on the board, and that if you hadn't been a woman you'd have been put in charge of your own family's company."

Thrum looked surprised, genuinely, this time. And she acknowledged that last point with a curt nod.

"So," Plath said, "I guess I'm appointing you as president. I'll ask Mr. Jellicoe to work out the financial terms: fair but not extravagant."

Plath had thought this next part out well in advance.

"But I have certain things I do want," Plath continued. "I want fifty million dollars—cash—in offshore banks. That's mine to do with as I see fit."

Jellicoe and Thrum both nodded warily.

"I want Mr. Stern to be my contact with you, Ms. Thrum. He was loyal and stayed by me when my family was murdered. Loyalty is important. Isn't it?"

Thrum, thrown off guard by the question, reddened and stammered, "Yes, I'm sure it is."

"Mr. Stern gets paid twice what's he's making now, and although he informs you of all relevant security issues, he works for me."

That brought a frown to Thrum's face, but only a frown.

Ah, Plath thought, hiding her emotion, keeping her eyes steady, her mouth straight. *Ah, you didn't see that coming, did you?*

Plath stood up. Keats did so as well, a few seconds later.

"Ms. Thrum, Mr. Jellicoe, Mr. Stern. The day may come when I want to take a more active role in the company. I may want to choose additional board members. But right now what I want is for the three of you to treat me with respect, to do what I ask you to—and I don't intend to ask much—and to take care of my father's company. Each of you in turn, I'm going to ask that you remain loyal to my father, and to me. Mr. Stern?"

"I'm a McLure man," he said. "Your man."

"Mr. Jellicoe?"

"I'm your lawyer," he said, and smiled.

"Ms. Thrum?"

"I'm in."

"Okay, then," Plath said. "My father was a smart and good man, who chose his allies well. I'm not as smart. I'm also not as good. For example, I'm not as forgiving as he was; I hold grudges. I can be a bitch." She softened that with a slight smile. "And I'm the bitch who owns the company."

That at last brought an honest smile from Thrum, who actually threw her head back and laughed.

In the elevator on the way down Keats said, "That was absolutely amazing. I mean . . . you just bossed those people around. You're no older than I am and you were like a captain of industry. A bloody capitalist."

Plath nodded. She was distracted and sad and worried. "I could have fired all three of them. They didn't know what crazy thing I might pull. They were all three relieved."

"Yeah, but just to stand up there with that total-domination voice, like that." He sighed. "Hot."

Plath said nothing. She just stared at Keats.

"What?"

"It was too easy," she said. "At least one of them is a traitor."

"You don't know that," he said, but he was nervous, eyes flicking back to her, to the floor indicator, then back to her.

Plath shook her head. "If they try to kill us on the way out, then they're innocent. If not then it's a setup. It's Thrum," she said. "She's the traitor. Jellicoe could easily have lost the will and substituted another. Stern had plenty of opportunity to kill me off when I was recovering. So it's Thrum: she's working for the Twins."

"I'm pulling out of aneurysm work," Keats said, buying in. "I can at least keep one eye out for nanobots."

"If they're AFGC, they'll know I'll be checked at the nano level. This is old school: they're going to track my money, see where I spend it." She bit her lip. "I'm not important as a foot soldier for BZRK. I'm only important for what I can reveal. They want my father's technology, and they want BZRK."

She wondered how Keats would react. Boys didn't always like clever girls, and if he said something stupid now, well, at least then love would be off the table. She would never love a dull boy.

Keats's absurdly blue eyes narrowed. "If they think you don't know . . . That's an opportunity for us, then."

So, not stupid. Not that she'd really had any doubt.

Damn.

The elevator reached the lobby. The McLure security men were waiting. Caligula was nowhere in sight. The limo steamed at curbside.

No TFDs.

The limo driver had changed.

"What happened to the driver?" Plath asked the back of Caligula's head as they pulled away.

"He had some vacation time coming."

"What happened to the TFDs?"

Caligula shrugged. "One tried to put a tracking device on the car. It was an amateurish job. I resented it."

She saw his eyes in the mirror, as deep as desert ravines, creased with sunbaked lines.

"It's all a setup," she said. "The TFDs looking tough when I got here? That was a show. If they really wanted to kill me there are buildings all around, windows with perfect sight lines for a sniper."

Caligula's eyes wrinkled in merriment. "They gave you exactly what you wanted, didn't they?"

"Yep," she said. "They lined up and rolled over like well-behaved puppies."

Caligula laughed, delighted. "I'll pass that description along to Lear."

"Lear needs to contact me. Directly."

Caligula said nothing.

"You tell him or her. Or them. Or whatever, that I'm going to keep financing BZRK, just as my father did. But not unless I know who I'm dealing with."

He did not answer. He neither nodded nor shook his head. It was getting on Plath's nerves, which were already frayed.

"Ophelia," she said.

Caligula nodded slightly, as though he was expecting it. "She's gone."

"Was it . . . was it easy for her?"

Caligula pulled the car over to the side of the street. He turned around and looked at her. She did not flinch. "It's never easy. It's death. And death is terrible and profound."

"And when it's me or Keats you have to kill?" Plath demanded, shamed by the quiver in her voice.

"Then that, too, will be terrible and profound," Caligula said.

Pia Valquist was forty-one years old. Her hair had always been blonde. First because her DNA had dictated that color, and now because her hairdresser made it so. Her tired eyes had luggage—dark bags. Her feet were a source of constant pain made worse by the snow that seemed to laugh at boasts of waterproofing for boots.

A long time ago she had been tall and moderately pretty, with the kind of body you expect from a five-foot-eleven-inch Swedish girl.

She was still tall.

And she was a spy. A very cold spy as she tramped from the rented Saab she had reluctantly left parked at the gate. It was a long driveway, but no one had answered the call box, and well, she'd be damned if she was going to stop now. It was very dark, but then this time of the year, this far north, it was dark almost all day. The sun was nominally visible for a few hours on either side of noon, but today's sun had been a distant, helpless light filtered through mist. It was long gone now.

People know that all the great powers have intelligence services, the Americans, the Russians, the Chinese, and of course the famous MI6 of James Bond fame.

People do not expect that a small country, a small peaceable country like Sweden that had last fought a war in the nineteenth century, would have spies. They didn't have many. The Militära underrättelse- och säkerhetstjänsten—the MUST—did not have a giant complex like the CIA. They didn't have their own array of satellites. They didn't blow people up with missiles fired from drones.

The KSI—Kontoret för Särskild Inhämtning—MUST's most secretive branch, had even fewer people, a relative handful. The advantage of small size and a lack of current war, or likelihood of war, meant that the KSI could tolerate individual strangeness to a degree that one of the tight-jawed, do-or-die, save-the-world spy agencies could not. It could, for example, allow Pia Valquist time to obsess over the Natal Incident.

Three years earlier a very strange thing had occurred in the northern Brazilian city of Natal. A ship's boat had come ashore there in the wake of a devastating hurricane. The ship's boat belonged to a converted, repurposed amphibious assault ship purchased through shell corporations from the U.S. Navy. It was an older ship, Vietnam

War–era. Originally, when it had been a U.S. Navy ship, it had been the USS *Tiburon*.

The boat that had come ashore showed signs of having been at sea for a long time. Weeks, perhaps. And it showed signs of having been occupied for that time, because there were three sets of footprints crossing the sand away from the boat toward town.

That same day local police found a mad, filthy, bearded man wandering the streets of Natal and picked him up for questioning. He told them a wild, disconnected story of having been kidnapped from a yacht sailing from South Africa. Then there was some nonsense having to do with a two-headed man and hideous experiments and brainwashing. The police dismissed him as mentally unbalanced.

That night the man hanged himself in his cell. With a belt that was not his.

The second and third sets of tracks were never identified. One matched the suicide victim, another appeared to belong to a grown woman, and a third could have been those of a teenage boy or girl.

The only reason that Pia Valquist knew anything about the matter was that she'd been visiting a Brazilian friend who happened to be the regional police lieutenant. He also happened to be absurdly handsome and wonderfully romantic and quite infatuated with Pia.

The fling had gone nowhere in the end—how could it? But it had left Pia with the kinds of memories that still brought a smile to her face years later.

And a mystery.

For two days she had assisted her friend's investigation into the boat and the suicide and the unexplained footprints. The mystery had gotten its hook into her.

When she had returned to Sweden, she'd taken another look at maritime incidents in that time frame. She'd come across reports of a body washed up in Madeira. And an unconfirmed report by a freighter captain who claimed to have seen a ship foundering in the storm. The ship matched the description of the USS *Tiburon*.

The best official guess was that the ship was involved in drug running or human smuggling. But Pia had observed the questioning of the "madman." She thought that explanation was nonsense.

The incident was officially forgotten. But not by Pia Valquist, because she wasn't someone who gave up a good mystery. She was, in the words of her boss, unique, by which he meant difficult, by which he further meant that she was a pushy obsessive who just would not let something go.

Valquist knew better than to go chasing every highly fragrant bit of nonsense that crossed her desk, but she had sensed something very wrong going on. For one thing: people who smuggled immigrants or drugs did not own amphibious assault ships. They moved people and drugs around in tramp steamers and rickety fishing boats.

Valquist had searched every record she could find. From the ship's decommissioning in Norfolk, Virginia, to its purchase by a cutout corporation, to a brief appearance off the coast of Tisno, Croatia, and Tunis, and the Ivory Coast, to an equally brief appearance off the coast of Capetown, South Africa.

Capetown, South Africa, where two people had been reported missing in the time frame, and where a yacht had been found floating empty, thirty miles out, with no sign of crew or passengers.

One of those missing people looked exactly like the Natal suicide. Had in fact been that unfortunate man.

Of the seven disappeared, the average age was seventeen. And in precisely zero cases was there an explanation.

Here is what Valquist knew about smugglers: they didn't go around kidnapping Croatians or Tunisians or Ivorians or South Africans.

And then she had begun to look at mysterious disappearances in port cities even further back in time. Two in Ireland. Three near Southampton, UK.

It went on.

And no, there was no way to prove that the mystery ship had been in each of those locations. But, critically, it could have been. Given normal sailing times it could have been in each place where the disappearances occurred.

Now, Valquist was convinced that she had at last tracked one set of those footprints in the sand all the way from far-off Brazil to relatively nearby Finland.

The house was rather grand, very un-Finnish. It had the look of a fort. It was large, made of a pale stone, one corner a tower, a sort of stunted mockery of a medieval castle. The windows were narrow, as if the person who had built it was anticipating a siege, with crossbows and lances.

The front door was well-maintained oak, thick enough to discourage a battering arm.

To the left was a detached garage. To the right was what might have been a small guest cottage but spoke rather of guardhouse. This suspicion was confirmed when a man emerged carrying a rifle. He had been interrupted in his lunch: there was soup in his beard, already beginning to solidify as it froze.

"Stop," he ordered.

She stopped. Automatically she turned gloved palms out: no weapon, nothing to hide, no threat.

"What do you want?"

"To show you my identification," she said. She held her fingers up, pincers, ready to reach into an inner pocket and pull out her ID.

"Go ahead," he said. His accent was not Finnish or Norwegian or Swedish. Israeli, she thought. Well, poor man, he was a long way and many degrees Celsius from Tel Aviv.

She pulled out her official MUST identity card and handed it to him.

His eyes widened.

"I'm here to see your boss," she said.

"Do you have an appointment?"

"Do you think it's likely that I have an appointment?"

"This isn't Sweden," he observed.

"No. And I have no official standing here," she admitted.

He was a small man, a good six inches shorter than her and certainly younger and more fit. And he had a gun. She waited.

He pulled out a cell phone and made a call. "There's someone here. She's Swedish." He considered his next words. "Swedish intelligence."

There was quite a long wait then, during which Valquist and the Israeli looked at each other.

Finally, he said, "Yes, ma'am."

Sixty seconds later Valquist stood dripping melting snow and offering her chilly hand to an old woman with a hard-looking face. The woman did not speak. Instead, she stood aside as though ushering Pia forward to the more important person in the room.

"You're here about the *Doll Ship*," said a dark-haired girl with only one arm.

Pia Valquist had never heard or imagined the words, "*Doll Ship*." But she looked the strange young woman in the eye and said, "Yes. I am."

EIGHT

"You have fifty million dollars," Keats said.

They were walking down lower Broadway, having been dropped off by Caligula at a discreet distance from the safe house. If anyone was following them, Caligula would spot the tail. And he would, as he would have said, resent it.

"Actually, I have two billion dollars."

"I can't think about numbers that big. No one should have two billion dollars."

"You're not going to be that way, are you?" she asked wearily. How strange was it that this familiar city, these familiar sidewalks seemed so alien? When had she last walked down a city street? She wore a hat and had the collar of her jacket turned up. She might still be recognized, but she doubted it: New Yorkers don't look people in the eye.

"What the hell are you doing in this stupid game, in this stupid war?" Keats asked. "You could go anywhere."

"And take my biots with me?"

"Yes, take your biots, yes."

"And what about when they die of old age, or whatever it is that kills biots?"

She could see that this was not a new thought for Keats. "We don't know how long they live. Maybe by then there will be some sort of answer. You could always spend a billion figuring it out."

"When you say 'billion' there's an edge to it," she pointed out.

He didn't answer. In fact, he didn't look at her.

Plath sighed.

"It's ridiculous," Keats said at last. "You and me. What would I be? Your butler? It's *Downton Abbey* and you're the duchess or whatever, and I'm the footman."

"Keats, don't do this, okay?"

"It's why you could talk to them that way. With that whole I-get-what-I-want tone of voice. It's the voice your class are born with."

She stopped, and after a couple of steps, he stopped, too. "Listen, Keats, I don't want to do this. I don't want to have to defend myself from you. I have more than enough to deal with."

"Yeah, well, saving your pennies so you can afford to take a girl to the movies isn't one of them."

He looked genuinely angry, and that fact made Plath genuinely angry. "Hey: I'm not responsible for you being poor. Or working class. Or whatever you call it."

"I didn't say you were," he muttered. "We should keep walking. Caligula is certainly watching this. From somewhere."

"I don't care what he's watching," she snapped. "He killed Ophelia."

They walked for a block in silence. Then he said, "We could just go, Sadie. If you don't mind being with a footman, we could just go. Just go. Get on a plane to . . . to . . . Africa."

She didn't answer at first. They dodged around street vendors selling cheap copies of designer bags, and vendors selling cheap copies of designer watches, and tourists buying same.

"Costa Rica," Plath said at last. "The Pacific Coast. I could learn to surf."

It was his turn to fall silent now, brooding.

"Or Africa," she said. "What is it?"

"What?"

"Your name."

"Noah."

"No? Why not, do you think it really matters?" she snapped.

"Not 'no.' Noah. Like the old Hebrew with the big boat full of animals."

"Oh. Noah," she said. "That's a strange name for a footman."

He sighed.

"The thing is . . ." he began, then cut himself off.

"The thing is what?" she demanded.

"The thing is, sometimes I get myself through something with a story. You know, a fantasy."

"Yes?"

"A fantasy. Imagination."

"Yes, I know what a fantasy is," she said, irritated again. "What's yours?"

He made a bitter laugh. "I haven't worked out the details, but somehow you and I end up together. And not in a mental ward, but like, together. Like I say: I haven't worked out the details. There's a house. Nothing grand. You know. Just a place."

"You've moved straight to marriage? You've only known me a couple of weeks."

"Fantasies don't have to make any sense," he snapped. "That's what makes them fantasies. They aren't meant to be logical, they're meant to keep you from losing your mind or panicking or wanting to kill yourself." He noticed the way she was looking at him and said, "No, for God's sake, I'm not bloody suicidal. And I'm not proposing, either. Forget I said anything."

They were walking slower now. Both had decided they wanted to extend this time, not cut it short.

"I have a fantasy, too," she said. "It's that this is all an elaborate dream and I wake up and I'm only seeing through one pair of eyes and I'm not noticing that it's time to move away from that lymphocyte."

A bike messenger barely missed running them down. They were both city kids, London and New York, so neither missed a step.

"So, all a dream, eh?" Keats asked.

"A dream. Yeah. Everything goes back to normal."

"And I'm not there."

She stopped. He stopped.

"Oh my God: you are there." She made no effort to hide the surprise in her voice. It was true and it startled her: even when she imagined everything going back, no Vincent, no Caligula, no biots or Armstrong Twins, no terrible plane crash killing her father and brother, Keats was still there.

"I assume I'm your footman."

"You're the guy who saves up his pennies to take me to a movie," she said, shaking her head as the truth of it came home to her. "I buy the popcorn. Large, of course, because I'm rich."

They moved close together. He put his arms around her waist and drew her closer still.

"In this vision I'm ridiculously attractive? Incredibly sexy?" he said.

"Not at all," she said, deadpan. "You look just like you do now."

He laughed a bit crookedly at that, and she found herself needing to touch his face. "We're in this together."

"But not in love," he pressed.

She hesitated. She couldn't say it, didn't want to even think it, knew it was nonsense.

"Together," she said at last.

She glanced at a clock scrolling by on a neon marquee. She had an hour. It would be tight, but Stern would wait.

Hide in plain sight. Keep the lie simple. And say the one thing sure to dissuade any male from asking follow-up questions.

"I need tampons," Plath told Nijinsky. "There's a Duane Reade down the block. I'll be back in half an hour. Do you need anything?"

He frowned. Suspicious? No, just thinking. "ChapStick," he said. "Plain, not cherry or whatever."

Stern, in obedience to the note she had slipped him, was waiting in the shaving-supplies aisle, seeming to take his time choosing a razor. Stern did not look at her, nor she at him. They were back to back, him looking at razors, her looking at shampoo.

"Sadie," he said.

"Mr. Stern."

"You're in trouble of some sort."

"I'm in trouble of every sort. Listen. My father and brother were murdered by Charles and Benjamin Armstrong. Is that idea a surprise to you?"

Three seconds of silence. "No," he said at last.

"My father trusted you."

His voice was husky when he said, "I was honored by his trust."

She leaned back just enough to make the slightest contact, stretching her fingers back to touch his sleeve.

"Mr. Stern, have you heard of something called BZRK?"

He was silent for what felt like a long time. Then he said, "I thought it might be that, when I saw the man with the, well, the fanciful hat." He sighed. "I know some of it, not everything. Your father didn't want McLure security getting involved with . . . with those people."

"I don't want you involved with them either," she said, surprising herself with the force of her conviction. "I want you to work for me. Just for me."

"Whatever you need," he said.

Here it came. How much to ask? How much to trust?

"I want an escape route. For me and . . . and for the boy I was with earlier."

"Yes."

She hesitated. "The man in the hat. He's on our side, but be careful of him."

Stern said nothing.

"My father financed these people. I'm going to do the same. But Thrum is a traitor, she's working for the Armstrongs. She's going to trace my spending."

"If that's true, then yes, she certainly will."

"So, I want to give Ms. Thrum something to watch, Mr. Stern. I want her and the Armstrongs to be unsure which side I'm on. I made it clear that I trusted you, so they'll be watching you. I want you to start looking for a person who calls him- . . . or her- . . . self, Lear.

For all I know it's not a real person, or may be several people, but he, she, or it, is running BZRK. Spend some money on that search. Let Thrum see that you're looking."

She heard a soft, satisfied chuckle. "You're capable of deviousness, Sadie. Your brother . . . I loved him because he was the boss's son. But there's more of your father in you."

She fell silent at that and covered the silence by bending down to select a bottle of conditioner and appearing to read the ingredients label. Memories of her brother, Stone, had come rushing back. How had he been at the end? How had he felt knowing that the plane he was on would crash?

He had been brave, she was sure of that. She pushed away a sob and sucked in a sharp breath.

"In my father's study, on the shelf, there's a copy of *Alice in Wonderland*. In the spine, there's a key. It goes to a safe deposit box at UBS, the bank, in Manhattan. My father said I'd remember it by thinking of You Bullshit Bank. You B.S. The box number is 0726, my mother's birthday. They'll ask you a verification question. It won't matter what the question is, the answer you give is 'pepperoni pizza.' In the box are bonds worth two hundred million dollars. Let Ms. Thrum watch the fifty she knows about. We'll use the two hundred she doesn't to keep BZRK going and to find me an escape route."

"Aren't you worried I'll take the money and run?"

Her answer was bleak, not glib. "I have to trust you. I don't want to, honestly, because I'm scared. I'm in a trap. But I have to, I have to trust someone. So it's you."

"And the boy," he said.

"We'll see about that," she said. "Don't follow me and don't try to protect me. I know you'll want to, but don't. Caligula . . . the man in the fanciful hat? He'll . . . he will resent it. Find me an escape route." She started to walk away, hesitated, then over her shoulder added, "Something near the beach, in Africa."

Billy the Kid had spent the night after the massacre at the foster home where he had not been in the three weeks since joining BZRK. He could think of nowhere else to go, and he felt hollowed-out and stretched very, very thin.

The man in the foster home, Daddy Tom as he liked to be called, let him in without a word and said nothing as Billy trudged wearily to the bedroom he shared with a boy named Marshall.

Daddy Tom smirked as Billy came in, but to Billy's relief he didn't insist on seeing what was in the bag. In the morning an only-slightly-rested Billy walked out onto cold streets beneath threatening clouds.

He needed to think, and he needed to figure things out. Everyone from BZRK Washington was dead. They hadn't really liked him anyway, and the feeling was mutual. The Washington BZRKers kept telling him they'd let him play the game, but they never did. He heard about biots, he knew what they were, they'd let him see some very weird video. But they had not given him a biot.

It was in online gaming forums that he had first heard from someone calling himself Lear. Billy had posted some impressive numbers, and he'd let it be known that he was a foster kid, unconnected, sick of where he was, looking for . . . well, looking.

Joining the Washington BZRK group had set off an uproar, with some of the others demanding to know what the hell was going on if they were down to recruiting children.

Well, they were all dead, weren't they? And he was the one walking around with their credit cards and their phones and their pads. So much for being a child.

The others had died like newbies. They had barely gotten off a shot, like this was the first time they'd ever really played an FPS game. They'd been surprised and they had panicked.

Newbies.

And he was the child?

Suddenly he saw that house again in memory, the common room with the twisted tangle of bodies on the floor and blood all over the walls and the stink of urine and feces.

He threw up thinking about it and looked up to realize he was throwing up within sight of the White House. How weird was that? It made him feel . . . well, something made him feel . . . strange, sick, like he wanted to be even sicker. But no, he wasn't having any of that.

He stopped and sat on a park bench and searched the phones for

Lear. Lear was the big boss, right? Well, didn't Lear owe him now? Who had killed all those phony cops? Not the so-called adults. Billy. Billy the Kid.

BANG! Hole. Smoke. Blood.

That was new, that's what still made him feel wrong: real blood. And real death, which was so much dirtier than the gaming version.

A car went past, horn blaring, and he realized he'd stepped into traffic, like he had lost consciousness or whatever, like his brain had stopped functioning.

He reached the far curb, shaking. His lungs felt congested. The wound in his side burned with fresh pain. He had put some Neosporin and Band-Aids on it and managed to sleep with a couple of Advil. But now, walking, walking, the scab that had formed was chafing. He looked under his jacket and saw blood staining his shirt.

There were tears in Billy's eyes, and he couldn't explain why. The pain was bad but not that bad.

The rain started then and he ran to shelter in an office building's doorway. There were some people there smoking cigarettes. He ignored them, and they ignored him. He continued thumbing through the calls made and received on the phones but found nothing that looked like it might be either to or from Lear. Then he started on messages. Also nothing.

That first phone had used 1111 as its password, which was just plain dumb, but breaking security on the second phone was more time-consuming. Any time he guessed wrong he was shut out for a while. It was going to take all day. Then, he knew the answer: 2975, because on the alphanumeric keypad 2975 spelled out BZRK.

"Smart," he muttered sarcastically.

Of course no one was going to have "Lear" in their address book, that would be too much to hope for. And unless they were complete idiots they'd delete calls to or from Lear. But they could be slightly less stupid and yet still forget to delete the number from their trash.

The rain stopped and he headed off again. There was always the fear that some well-meaning adult would begin to wonder what a kid was doing standing with the smokers in the shelter of the building.

The second phone also yielded nothing.

He had plenty of cash, so he bought a couple hot dogs and a Pepsi and wolfed it all down in a steamy, overheated diner. It was well past lunchtime, though you couldn't tell from the gray-on-gray sky outside.

And then, on the third phone, he had something. It was in the trash, as he'd expected. A number. He Googled the area code, curious because it had a strange number that began with a plus sign. The prefix was a country code, and the country in question was Japan.

Time to make a decision. If he was still part of BZRK—and where else did he have to turn to—then he had to contact Lear. So he composed a text.

DC got burned bad. But they didn't get me. Billy the Kid.

He hit Send.

Then he added, *This is not my phone.*

He hit Send again. And waited. Nothing.

He wanted to cry then because he had halfway convinced himself that Lear—if this was really Lear's number—would instantly respond and come to his rescue. But nothing, and the diner was shutting down, the cook had begun to clean the grill.

So Billy went back out onto the darkening street, heading toward the big green space on his map app.

Rock Creek Park, as the name implies, runs along Rock Creek at the western edge of the city. He figured he could find a place to hide out overnight, think things through. And indeed he came upon a stone bridge that crossed the creek.

Trolls lived under bridges, at least in games. And when he slid down the muddy embankment a troll is what he found. A man, large, maybe a crazy street person, maybe not.

"Hey. You," the man said. "This is my place. Get lost."

The man came closer. His rough, pendulous features brightened with avarice as he saw the not-very-large boy. The rain was back, and Billy was tired.

The man made a suggestion for just how Billy could pay for the right to stay dry.

So Billy stuck a nine-millimeter pistol in his face and said, "Go away." It was getting to be a habit.

The phone chimed.

The man laughed, thinking the gun was a toy.

"Get over here and—"

The explosion lit up the bridge overhead. The bullet, aimed past the man's face, but not much past it, hit the water in the rain-swollen creek.

"Jesus!" the man yelped.

"I already shot a bunch of people yesterday," Billy said. "So I can shoot you."

Billy was alone when he read the text message.

Stay hidden. Help coming. Lear.

A few hundred miles north, in New York, Burnofsky watched the data flow on his screen.

Four Hydras had each made a copy of themselves.

Eight Hydras had each made a copy of themselves.

Sixteen Hydras had each made a copy of themselves.

Thirty-two . . .

Sixty-four . . .

One hundred and twenty-eight . . .

Each round took seven minutes. So in a little over half an hour, the four hydras had become more than a hundred.

256. 512. 1024. 2048. 4096. 8192. 16,384.

That was the number after a dozen cycles, requiring eighty-four minutes.

32,768. 65,536. 131,072. 262,144. 524,288. 1,048,576.

It had taken eighteen cycles, two hours and six minutes, for four hydras to become more than a million. And of course that meant at least twenty million MiniMites.

He had used a live mouse as building material. Burnofsky pulled up video of the mouse, at first indifferent, then agitated, then desperate as tail and legs and ears were chewed away by the hydras and their MiniMites.

When he sped the video up he could watch the whole sequence as the mouse's back erupted, as it died, as it grew gruesomely smaller and smaller and nothing but a few bones and shreds of flesh and then all gone, all of it completely gone, replaced by a seething mass of blue-tinged nanobots. They looked, he thought, like uncooked egg white, or the stuff that ran from a punctured eyeball.

Goo, he supposed, for lack of a better word.

The world would die in agony and panic. And of course Burnofsky would die as well, but last, he hoped. Last and best and floating on an opium cloud.

But not just yet.

NINE

Farid had never met anyone from Anonymous in the real world. The fact that he'd even been asked for a meeting was extraordinary, and it made him paranoid as hell.

Since the intrusion into the AFGC system he'd been jumpy. His family was supposedly immune to prosecution thanks to diplomatic immunity, but that immunity would be a pretty thin defense if the American security people came after him. They might not be able to snatch him off a street themselves—Americans were very devoted to the illusion of law—but the city was full of American allies with no such scruples. The Saudis, maybe, or the Israelis.

Now this request for a face-to-face from d0wnb1anki3. Blankie's name carried some weight. Even so Farid had been sweating bullets sitting in the Starbucks on Connecticut Avenue. He was trying not to be too obvious in looking for the "black woman carrying a backpack decorated with a picture of Bob Marley."

He waited until the appointed time. He waited until ten minutes after the appointed time. Jumpy from too much caffeine and too little sleep, he got up to grab a cigarette outside.

And there she was, just as described. An African American woman carrying a Bob Marley backpack. She was hurrying across the street, looking very much like a person late for an appointment.

Farid sucked hard on his cigarette, assuming he'd have to put it out in a few seconds. But in fact the woman walked right up to him, gave him a dubious look, made a V of her fingers, then a give-me gesture. Farid shook out a Marlboro for her.

He lit her cigarette with his Marilyn Monroe lighter, and she said, "Let's walk."

She did not give her name, and he didn't ask. She led the way, south toward Dupont Circle. The sidewalk was busy—it always was—but they were walking slow, and Washingtonians—the most self-important people on Earth—were all rushing past them. Anyone following them at this slow pace would have been instantly obvious, so Farid looked around and convinced himself that things were cool.

"This is some very dangerous stuff," the woman said.

"No shit."

They walked on for a block past boutiques, crossing the street through the eternally impatient traffic.

"You need to wipe it all," the woman said.

"What are you talking about?"

"Wipe it. Burn it. Bury it in a deep hole and then forget you ever saw it."

Farid thought about that. He frowned. "Wait. What? We're supposed to cover this up?"

The woman made a cynical face. "It's Washington, kid. Cover-ups are what this city's built on."

Farid stopped. After a few steps, so did the woman.

"Yeah, but we aren't about cover-ups. We're about exposing the truth. I mean, this is profound stuff. This is craziness."

"You think this is the only time the president has murdered someone? She sends drones out every day to kill people; you're a Muslim, you should know that. Look, this whole thing needs to go away." She waved her cigarette, trailing smoke. "And you need to tell me who else is aware of this intrusion."

Farid was shaking his head and wishing he had a second cigarette going. "No, no, no. There's more going on here. I'm all up in the AFGC system now. Those guys are deep into some serious nanotech."

He saw a flicker on her face at that.

"They're building nano robots. Ever heard of the gray goo?"

"Sounds like the name of a band."

He stared hard at her. What she'd said sounded like a joke, but her eyes weren't on the same page as her tone. He didn't know her. She was someone supposedly sent from people up the food chain in Anonymous, but how did he know that for sure?

Now she was telling him to walk away? Destroy data? Give up names?

"I don't think I want to talk to you anymore," Farid said.

"What's the matter? Getting paranoid? Walk another block with me. Let's get this straightened out."

"What's a block from here?" Farid demanded.

"Okay, just stay where you are," she said in a very different voice. A cop voice: ordering and controlling.

Suddenly Farid was aware of two men moving swiftly up the street behind him. A black sedan roared up and hit its brakes.

His next move was purely instinctive. He was standing just outside a bookstore and coffee shop. He ran for the door. The woman cursed and leapt after him, but he caught a break, a shopper emerging through the narrow door let him in and unintentionally blocked the woman's path.

It was just a few seconds, but it was enough.

He glanced around frantically, looking for a way out, a weapon, a savior, something. The coffee shop was full of the usual latte-sipping, laptop-tapping crowd.

"Listen to me! Everyone! My name is Farid Berbera. I'm a Lebanese citizen with diplomatic immunity. That woman is trying to kill me."

He pointed a finger at the woman with two men at her back, all now clearly revealed as security types.

"Armstrong Fancy Gifts Corporation is creating nano robots. They have video from inside the president's eyes as she murdered her husband!"

He didn't expect to be believed; he barely believed it himself. But he expected to be heard, and Tweeted and texted.

"They're trying to stop us from finding out," Farid yelled. He held his hands up in the air, the universal language of helplessness.

The black woman no longer carrying the Bob Marley backpack hesitated, nonplussed, and then Farid saw the reason for her hesitation: a Washington DC cop was picking up a coffee to go and holding a small bag of some sort of pastry.

"Officer! Officer! You have to help me, I have diplomatic immunity!" He fumbled in his pocket and out came the passport, the blessed diplomatic passport with that lovely word, *Diplomatic*, in big, gold-embossed letters. The policeman would have seen passports like that many times before.

"People are watching!" Farid warned. "People are watching! Farid Berbera, Lebanese Embassy." People were watching, but they were not on his side. So he said the thing he would never before have imagined saying. "I'm part of Anonymous. They're trying to stop me before I can tell what I know."

The woman and her two agents moved then, grim-faced, but the policeman was setting down his coffee and pastry and said, "Hold up, just a second there. This is my beat. I'm calling this in."

"You are not calling it in," the woman snapped.

"What are you, FBI? Let me see your shield," the policeman said, and a voice in the crowd said, "Hell yeah."

Phone cameras were coming out.

"This man is a dangerous criminal," the woman said. "We are federal officers. Put down those cameras and—"

"Show us your badge," a second voice yelled.

The policeman was definitely on guard now, torn between his instinctive need to control the rowdiness and an unfamiliar sensation of having people actually take his side.

"Just show some ID, ma'am. If you're feds, we'll work it out." He was preparing to call it in but a bit perplexed at what code would apply. Was this a 10-31? Or more of a 10-34?

"We're with the ETA," the woman said. She flipped her ID open.

The policeman frowned. "Sorry, I'm not up on all the—"

"Emerging Technology Agency."

The policeman blinked. Stared. Laughed. "You gotta be pulling my leg."

"They're trying to stop me from telling what I know. AFGC. Nanotech. Video of Falkenhym killing her husband. Gray goo scenario." Farid was just repeating it over and over, frantically, in a loop, as the cop confronted the feds, and the store denizens blasted the entire scene out over the Internet. "Farid Berbera. Anonymous. Lebanese diplomat."

"Lady," the cop said, "in this city I got to put up with FBI, Secret Service, DEA, but I have surely never heard of an ETA, and you aren't arresting—"

BANG!

It wasn't until the explosion that Farid even noticed the gun in the woman's hand.

The police officer was wearing a Kevlar vest. It did not protect his face. Or stop the bullet from punching a hole out the back of his neck, spraying bits of spine and blood all over the coffee counter.

"Kill them all," the woman said. "No witnesses."

Three guns began firing.

Somehow, he would never be able to explain how, Farid ended up on his elbows behind the counter, crawling and whimpering as BANG BANG BANG BANGBANGBANG! The glass display case full of croissants and pre-made sandwiches shattered. People screamed. People yelled nonsense like, "Hey, what are you doing?" Tables were overturned. Smoke filled the air.

"Stop it, stop it!"

Steam was venting from the espresso machine through a bullet hole.

The woman, still with a cigarette in her mouth, was around the counter now and BANG! shot the cringing barista and BANG! fired at Farid and missed as he jumped up and ran, screaming into the stacks, grabbing at handfuls of books and slinging them over his shoulder.

BANG! and the bullet hit a thick political text and blew it apart in midair, making confetti of the pages.

The shots and screams from the café were dying down, and now there were sirens too late, way too late, as Farid tripped, fell against a table loaded with books, slipped to the floor, and saw himself staring up at the muzzle of a gun.

He said, "No!"

BANG!

His head jerked. Stabbing pain in his mouth.

Smoke drifted.

She was looking right at him, the muzzle no more than two feet away. Ash fell from her cigarette. He could see the way her finger tightened on the trigger. All slow motion now.

Snap.

Instantly the ETA agent reached for a new magazine, but Farid was up and scrambling, leaping, sobbing, tasting the blood that filled his mouth, not knowing what had happened just knowing: run. RUN!

The store had a second entrance, out on Nineteenth Street. He was on the street before he knew it, nearly ran into a passing taxi, raced north up the street and the taxi, amazingly, miraculously, thought he needed a ride, thought he was chasing it.

The cab driver stopped.

Farid ripped open the door and collapsed into the seat. "Go! Just go!"

The driver looked skeptical until he heard the gunshot from behind. The driver had not survived the waves of war in Sudan just to die here in Washington, DC.

He floored it.

The cab sped away. It was then that Farid realized the bullet had gone in his mouth and out through his cheek. It had taken the top off a molar in the process, but he was alive.

Jessica gazed longingly out of the window at the city, Washington, DC, as she sat astride Bug Man and rubbed his narrow back with long, steady strokes.

The sun had gone down and painted the Washington Monument orange. Then the rain came, and the landscape disappeared in gloom. It was depressing. Surely over there, somewhere, was a club, a night spot. Something.

It was right there, across the river. All that history. And probably shopping as well. Restaurants. Boutiques. And the White House and all that.

It was a curiously squat city, more like Brooklyn, where both Jessica and Bug Man—she knew him as Anthony—lived, than like Manhattan. It didn't look to be such an important place.

"Can't we go out tonight?" she asked. To ask the question she leaned down, flattening herself against him, and tickled the back of his neck with her lips.

"We can't go out," he muttered. "I've told you that about nine times."

She pouted. He failed to notice.

"Couldn't we at least go downstairs to one of the restaurants?"

No answer.

She had known Anthony for much longer than she had loved him. At first he'd been nothing to her, just a boy two years her junior, not especially handsome, definitely not tough or rich or exciting.

But over a very short time she had come to first notice him, and then to like him, and then to want and need him almost desperately. She would do anything for him.

And yet he still wasn't objectively attractive in any way.

It puzzled her sometimes. She puzzled herself sometimes. She still remembered what she had found attractive in other boys and men. She still found hard muscles—which Anthony lacked—and long muscular legs—which he also lacked—and a quick wit—ditto—to be the things that turned her on.

Yet Anthony—too short, too weak, too sullen—had a devastating effect on her. She worshipped him. What he asked for he got, and if he failed to ask, she gave it anyway.

Well, Jessica thought, *life is a mystery, isn't it?*

"It's boring here," Jessica said, resuming the massage. He was always tense. But more so since yesterday. He was so tight, it was almost as if he worked out and had muscle tone.

"It's a boring place," he agreed.

"At least you get to go out," she said.

"I go to work."

"How long is this so-called temporary assignment? We had more fun in New York," she said. She knew the answer, but he hadn't told her to shut up, yet. When he did she would, of course, shut up. But he hadn't said it yet, so she asked.

"Don't know," he said into the mattress.

"I can't just stay in a hotel room forever," she protested.

He reached back blindly, fumbling with one hand until he touched her thigh. "Hey, you've got me, right?"

"Mmm. Yes, I do."

"Okay, then shut up."

And she did.

But as she pressed her lips together she remembered a dream. She almost told him about it, but he had told her to shut up.

In the dream she had been somehow buried up to her neck. Just her head stuck up above the ground. She couldn't move. She had wanted to put her hands to her head, had wanted to press her palms against the side of her head and squeeze, really hard. She didn't know why.

Jessica had been very angry in the dream. That's mostly what she remembered. That she was very, very angry, because she didn't want to be buried in the ground and someone had done that to her.

Sometimes she could almost see who it was. But she couldn't turn her head far enough to make him out. She rolled her eyes back and forth but she couldn't see him because he kept scuttling out of sight.

Even now, recalling the dream, she was angry. It rose up in her, that anger, like boiling oil rushing through her veins.

But Anthony didn't like her to be angry. So she wasn't. And the boiling oil turned slow and sluggish as it cooled. It became thick, like jelly.

Jessica breathed for the first time since the memory of the dream had come to her. Her hands were kneading the back of his neck. From where she sat it looked almost as if she was choking him.

Bug Man opened his eyes and stared at the sheet beneath his face. He hadn't meant to do that, to tell her to shut up. It made her seem like a robot. Like a machine. Any other girl would have argued, but no other girl had quite as much "wire" in her brain as Jessica.

She was in many ways his greatest accomplishment, second only to taking down Vincent and Kerouac. She was so beautiful, a tall, elegant African beauty with amazing eyes and a perfect body, and a mouth that, oh, God, and even now it hurt him to think about how much he had wanted her. She was so beautiful, she could silence a whole noisy restaurant just by walking in the front door. And she was his, all his, 100 percent his.

She was amazing. When she was on his arm, she made him a king. Men looked at him with baffled respect. Women looked at him wondering just what it was about him that could command a girl like Jessica.

But Jessica didn't really have much to say. When they watched movies together, she would wait until he had expressed an opinion and then parrot him. He could see she hadn't really liked *Tron:Legacy* until, as the credits rolled, he'd said he loved it. And then, so had she.

When a minute later he said that the truth was it kind of sucked, she agreed.

And agreed again when he changed his mind and praised it.

That could have gone on for hours.

It was creepy. It was boring. She would say what he wanted her to say. She would do what he wanted her to do. She was, he realized sadly, like a game you've already mastered completely. She was Portal 2 in a Portal 3 world.

He eased her off him, stood up, and went to the window. "It's a boring town, anyway," he said. "I don't think there's much to do."

She was about to agree with him, and the prospect made him cringe. "On the other hand, maybe we could sneak out for a little bit, right? Maybe just to my place where I work. Whatever."

She agreed with him. It seemed sincere.

Go limp, Burnofsky had told him. Do nothing for now. So he would do nothing. But he could still watch, right?

[ARTIFACT]

Preliminary investigation of suicides and psychotic breaks.

Notes of Dr. Nigel Blankenthorpe, Chief Medical Officer, *Doll Ship*.

I have sufficient data to confirm what I have suspected: the suicide rate among wired subjects is almost six times higher on average than would be predicted by standard models. The rate of sudden psychotic break is almost as high.

There were seventeen suicides between January 1 and June 1. Given the ages, backgrounds, and mental histories of the population, no more than three suicides should have occurred.

In that same period five individuals out of the combined populations of Benjaminia and Charlestown attacked staff or fellow townsfolk with sufficient violence that injuries resulted. One death occurred.

The question that had to be answered is whether these rates are a result of the unique conditions aboard the *Doll Ship*—separation from family, a constrained environment, etc. Or whether these suicides and psychotic breaks are some sort of reaction to the wiring process itself.

At my request Dr. Aliyah Suleiman at AFGC New York sent me additional data that confirm that what I am seeing here on the *Doll Ship* is part of a pattern associated with wiring.

I have thus far performed three autopsies—two of suicides, one of a patient who became so violent staff had to resort to deadly force—and my preliminary observations suggest that in these cases the brains began a sort of counterwiring. Dense clusters of new brain cells that grew almost like cancers, or as if in mimicry of the wires, formed in the hippocampus, in the nucleus accumbens, even in the frontal cortex.

The sample size is too small to reach conclusions. But my hypothesis is that some brains grow fresh tissue spurred by the wire. In the cases observed, this new growth can predispose toward depression and thus suicide, or incoherent rage.

Fortunately this appears in only a minority of cases. Though when it is extended to the entire human race I would expect to see tens of millions, perhaps hundreds of millions, of suicides and violent psychotic outbursts.

Recommend that AFGC begin a much wider investigation of this phenomenon.

Tables and charts attached.

TEN

Word had gone throughout Benjaminia that the Great Souls were coming.

The Great Souls!

People with fixed, jawbreaking smiles and wide, glittering eyes and way too much energy wouldn't stop talking about it.

Everyone was busy cleaning up the town. In this case it meant using buckets of a gentle acid wash to scrub the curving nickel alloy walls with long-handled brushes. The walls were already clean—cleanliness was part of sustainable happiness—so this was more an act of devotion than of simple housekeeping.

More immediately noticeable was the touch-up painting on the great pillar that rose through the center of the sphere, as well as similar work on the entrance to the tunnel that connected Benjaminia with Charlestown. The most adept artists touched up the painted sky with its wondrous image of the Great Souls reaching out a hand to God on their left and Darwin on their right.

It all would have gone much easier but for the storm that raged outside, producing waves so steep they sent the weak of stomach racing to thoughtfully placed buckets.

Fortunately Minako McGrath did not get seasick.

The nickel steel sphere that defined Benjaminia was forty meters—131 feet—in diameter. The great pillar rose up through the middle. A flat, level platform of plywood—also in need of some grass-green touch-up paint—flattened the bottom of the sphere, providing a level surface, a sort of lowest floor.

Fourteen-year-old Minako had never been a math whiz, but she cared to an insane degree about numbers. Forty meters in diameter was not a good number.

The floor of the sphere, that wooden platform, was also an even, easily divisible number: twenty-four meters diameter.

Minako was not happy. Not "sustainably happy," in that obnoxious Nexus Humanus phrase, nor any other kind of happy. She was sad to the point of desperation. It had been just ten days since she had been hauled, kicking and punching, aboard this nightmare ship.

Ten, also, was not a good number. It was not prime, nor was it divisible by either three or seven. There were good numbers and bad numbers, and the numbers in Benjaminia all seemed to be bad.

Six days earlier Minako had been walking along the beach at Toguchi. Toguchi wasn't much of a place, a small town even by Okinawan standards. You couldn't even brag about the beach. There were no resort hotels or boardwalk, just vibrant green bushes and low-slung, wind-chastened trees edging right up against the narrow strand.

Minako had been thinking, and of course counting her steps—the number to hit was 701, a prime—and pausing occasionally to look out to sea and wish the clouds weren't so thick and low and the sun could be seen setting. Her OCD—obsessive compulsive disorder—was often worse in the fall and early winter when the days grew shorter. It was almost as if sunlight banished her compulsions, or at least lessened their demands, so that she could lie out on this same beach without quite as many numbers careening around inside her head. But now, with the sea turned gray to match the sky, her carefree season was over.

A boat had come ashore, a Zodiac. There were three men in it, all dressed in rain slickers. Two were white, one Asian. Minako saw herself as Asian, though her father was an American marine and her mother Japanese.

The men saw her, stared at her a bit actually, so that it made her uncomfortable, But then two of them—one of the Caucasians and the Asian—had gone off across the beach into town.

Three was a good number. One, two, three, five, seven, eleven, and thirteen: the first seven prime numbers. The one man left behind, that was okay. The two who left were okay as well.

Which just went to prove that numbers aren't everything.

This late in both the season and the day there wouldn't be much going on in Toguchi town for the two men to do—they might find a bowl of noodles and some tea, but there was no nightlife. They were a long way from the lights of Naha.

Minako wondered why she assumed they were hungry. They looked like men who wanted something. And what else could it be?

She continued walking along the beach, coming closer to the boat and the man guarding it. He was smoking a cigarette and avoiding looking at her. He seemed jumpy. Was he a smuggler? A drug smuggler? If so, she should run.

But running away seemed like a strange overreaction. There was no crime in Toguchi. Someone being picked up by the local police for public drunkenness was a crime wave by Toguchi standards. Minako knew: her mother was the only police officer in the area.

Minako curved her path away from the shore and away from the boat. It would mean a possibly very difficult count adjustment. Her routine required her to walk from the southern path along the beach, down to near the high-water line where the driftwood scattered. The steps from the tree line down to the high-water line didn't have to be counted. But once she turned and started walking north she needed it to be exactly 701 steps. Then, if she had done it properly, she could turn back toward the town and be able to aim for the path home. Curving or avoiding made it harder to calibrate. She could end up having to take some ridiculous mincing steps to get the count just right. That would work, yes, but it would be unsatisfying.

Out at sea was a ship. The light was poor and it was hard to make it out, but it looked strange, like a sort of white peapod with four white domes half-protruding above decks. Four troubling domes.

Had it been three it would have been better.

That's where the men had come from, that ship. Had to be. In which case they were not likely to be drug smugglers. Still, Minako considered for a moment phoning her mother. It was not Minako's job to be an informer—as she had repeatedly had to reassure the older brothers and sisters of her friends when she saw them smoking pot.

Still . . .

She compromised and sent a text. *A Zodiac has landed at the beach with 3 men.*

That made her feel better: duty done.

Three hundred and eighty-two . . .

Three hundred and eighty-three . . .

Minako was a pretty girl, with long hair the color of darkest honey and unnaturally large light brown eyes. The flaw that bothered her most was that her mouth sometimes looked a little crooked, and her chin could be pointed when seen in profile. That, and she had a sprinkling of freckles across her upper cheeks.

Of course, at her school, she was quite a freak. She was not the only Japanese American—after all, there had been thousands of U.S. marines on Okinawa since World War II—but unlike many she looked as white as she did Japanese. Her father had been an Irish

American, and no, her mother had not been a prostitute or some party girl. Minako's parents had been married legally. They had been madly in love.

But Captain McGrath, USMC, had been sent to Afghanistan when Minako was just three years old, and he had been killed in an ambush.

Minako had his picture beside her bed. But she did not really remember anything about him. Just the picture.

She had reached step number six hundred and forty-five when she saw the two men returning. Each carried two heavily weighted plastic shopping bags from the grocery store. The bags bulged with rice wine, French Cognac, and cigarettes.

Six hundred and forty-six . . .

Six hundred and forty-seven . . .

Almost there. But now, if she turned to shore, she would walk directly into the two men. It would look deliberate.

Minako felt a stab of panic. She really needed a good count. It had been a bad day. And if she didn't get her number the Unspecified Bad Thing would happen.

They had come back too quickly.

Six hundred and fifty-two . . .

Six hundred and fifty-three . . .

Just forty-eight more steps.

"Hey, girly," the Asian man said. He was speaking accented

English. Minako spoke English fairly well, her mother had insisted, and of course her school taught the language as well.

"She'll do," the Caucasian man said. He spoke with a Russian accent.

The two men moved apart. Their arms spread out a little—awkward with the heavy shopping bags.

Minako's first reaction was confusion. What were they doing? She was so close to finishing her steps.

Six hundred and sixty-one . . .

Forty more steps and she would have her 701.

"What's your name, honey?"

In Japanese she said, "I don't understand," and made a shy little shrug of apology.

They were only twenty yards away now, and she was still thirty-five steps away, and suddenly they swept toward her. No choice, she had to break and run, she took one more step—number 678—and broke stride, started to run, and hit the sand, facedown.

The one from the boat had come up behind her and shoved her. There was sand in her mouth. She cried out, but her voice was masked by the sound of the waves.

She tried to roll over but there was a heavy weight on her back.

"Stop fighting," a man's voice said, far too near her ear. "No one is going to hurt you. You're going to the happiest place on Earth." There was something sardonic about that last phrase.

Minako opened her mouth to scream again, but a rag was in her mouth and a roll of duct tape made a tearing sound as it went around her head once, twice, tangling in her hair.

A second set of hands had her legs.

"We could have ourselves a time before we take her in," suggested the Asian one.

She screamed into her gag.

"No one bothers one of the villagers." The voice of the one from the Zodiac. The one who had shoved her down. The one now sitting astride her back as his mate wound the tape around her ankles. His cigarette ash fell on her cheek. "Don't be a stupid boy, KimKim."

"Zoob, I'm just saying . . ." the one they'd called KimKim said.

They wound the tape efficiently around her wrists. The one named Zoob searched her pockets, found the cell phone, switched it off, and stuck it in his jacket pocket.

The Russian laughed. "You're just saying? Listen, stupid boy: we grab a villager, that's what they want, yes? Good. So if the mate finds out that we also picked up cigarettes and Cognac on the way, well, we can make him happy, da? 'Here, Dragoslav, have a bottle, have two packs.' No problem, right? But you don't mess with the villagers."

Zoob hauled Minako up off the sand as if she weighed nothing. He casually tossed her over one shoulder and walked to the Zodiac. He set her in the bottom where water sloshed several inches deep.

"Get this straight, KimKim, before you dig your own grave. This isn't the merchant marine," Zoob said as they gunned the outboard engine. "This is the *Doll Ship*. There are rules that you can break . . . and maybe you get some extra punishment duty. But. But there are other rules that if you break, you find yourself trying to swim ashore from twenty miles out with six feet of chain around your ankles."

The young one thought that over. Then said, "Nah."

But nevertheless, Minako had made it to the ship unharmed.

What they had done instead was ignore her outraged protests and pleas. For six days she had been in this place, and all they had done was show her videos from some group called Nexus Humanus. And she'd been given reading materials, also from Nexus Humanus. Mostly she'd been told about her benefactors—Charles and Benjamin Armstrong, the Great Souls.

And she had been assigned a "lodge" in Benjaminia.

The steel sphere that was Benjaminia had nine levels. Each level was a steel catwalk that went all the way around the sphere. Level 5 was the largest. The circumference of the sphere was 125 meters at that point.

But Minako was not assigned to level 5—a prime number. She was given a lodge on level 4. Four was not a good number for her. Worse yet, her lodge was one of fourteen lodges on her level. Each lodge was a slightly wedge-shaped space—wider at the outer edge where it met the nickel sphere and narrower where it opened onto the connecting catwalk.

There was a raised metal IKEA bunk bolted down. Beneath that bunk, a desk and chair. There was the sort of tiny bathroom you might find on a boat—a toilet, a sink you could barely fit your hands into, and a shower that used the entire bathroom as a stall.

The bathroom was the only place where there was any privacy. The rest of the lodge was open metal grille below and above. Minako could look up and see the soles of the shoes of the man who lived up there. When she looked down, she saw the girl who lived beneath her on level 3.

She was not allowed to talk to either. Talking was done only out on the connecting catwalk or down on the assembly floor. And there was no point.

Every conversation:

"I've been kidnapped. I want to go home. I want my mother!"

"You've been liberated, freed! Wait until you see. Wait until you understand!"

"I don't want to be here. What is this awful place?"

"We call it the *Doll Ship*. We're like the beloved toys of the Great Souls. It's so happy here!"

The words would change, but never the conclusion, never the message, never the smiling acceptance.

They loved her. She was going to be so happy.

The top of the sphere was the big painting, the one that showed God the Father and Charles Darwin. Between those two was a disturbing creature that could only be meant as some sort of metaphor. It showed a completely—embarrassingly—nude man with what amounted to two heads. The two heads were seemingly joined together, allowing for a third eye.

Minako figured the third eye was meant to evoke wisdom and knowledge. The possibility that this painting—and that third eye—was anything other than a metaphor did not occur to her. It simply never occurred to her that the sky painting was of a real person.

There were seventy-six people in Benjaminia, but there were lodges for more. The residents of the sphere—the town—ranged in age from ten or eleven, on up to middle age. And all of them she had encountered—all of them—were happy.

Very happy.

Consistently, sustainably, happy. It was a madhouse. A floating insane asylum. A lunatic cult hidden inside a liquefied natural gas ship.

At the announcement that the Great Souls would be coming for a visit, the residents were more than happy. Word had come over the public address system and everyone had come rushing from their lodges and raced down the spiral staircases to the assembly floor to hug and cry tears of joy. It reminded Minako in some way of a nightmare version of *The Wizard of Oz*. No Munchkins or witches, but a terrible falseness and suppressed hysteria in everything.

They said she would understand soon. Someone they called

Toblerone—like the chocolate bar—had taken sick, so they were without an adjustor until he recovered. But don't worry, Minako, they said, Toblerone will be back, or someone just like him, and your happiness will be assured.

You will be as happy as any of us.

Have you watched the third video? Wasn't it the best ever?

Have you read the pamphlet titled "Youth and Happiness: They Really Do Go Together"? Didn't you find it amazing?

But Minako overheard two of the proctors—those in charge of the village of Benjaminia—talking in hushed voices. Toblerone had died. Meningitis, they said. And now, in the wake of a suicide by someone called Joe Carpenter, there was no "twitcher" on board, no adjustor.

That left her, Minako, the only unadjusted person aboard, aside from much of the crew.

All of this was mysterious to Minako, who spent her days worrying about her mother and her little brother. And sketching on the paper they supplied her. And pretending to read the boring Nexus Humanus pamphlets.

And counting.

And crying.

And plotting escape.

Helen Falkenhym Morales lay in her bed alone. So strange. She had spent nights without MoMo while on overseas trips. Rare, but it happened. But in the three years she had slept in this room in the private portion of the White House, she had never been alone.

Now, alone.

Her staff was walking on eggshells with her. They were keeping things from her, trying to give her time to come to grips with the tragic death of her husband.

Morales saw the moment in memory, saw her own hands as they grabbed MoMo's head and SLAM!

It had made a sound like a cracking walnut. That was how hard his head hit the tile.

Crack.

She'd been lucky the tile didn't break.

As it was, everyone had bought her story of finding MoMo dead in the bathtub when she got up in the night to relieve herself.

Now she had a cover for any strange behavior. People would say, Oh, she's coping with the grief.

But what she was coping with was the question: What in God's name had happened to her? How could she have done that terrible deed? She was not a murderer.

Her heart was broken. She had killed him. She had bashed in the head of the only man she had ever loved.

Something . . . a gear had slipped. Like when she was little and riding her bicycle and suddenly the chain would fall off the sprockets and the pedals were no longer connected and the bike would wobble as she tried to regain control.

That's how she felt.

She was scared. The pain in her heart was so terrible it had to be physical, it couldn't just be her emotion squeezing her like that, like an iron fist that wanted to stop the beating.

Reality did not leave the president alone to grieve. She wasn't the only one who seemed to have slipped a gear, the entire country had gone nuts: the bizarre death of Grey McLure and the indescribable horror at the stadium; the UN massacre; a terrible mass murder in a house on Capitol Hill; and now early reports were coming in that some of Rios's ETA people had lost it and shot up a bookstore, supposedly in a gun battle with a terrorist.

The thing on Capitol Hill was at least a local matter. So far. The rest was all on her plate. She was getting hourly updates on the investigation into the UN terror attack, each report amounting to the same thing: we don't know. Now she was getting word that there was a full-scale turf war going on over the bookstore massacre, with FBI and Washington police fighting over witnesses.

She had picked a very bad time to lose her mind.

There was Cognac in the nightstand, very high-end Cognac, a gift from the French president. She'd already had one snifter. Now she had a second one. She downed it in a gulp.

No one would blame her for having a drink.

Except of course that she didn't drink. Never had liked the stuff.

[ARTIFACT]

The White House

Office of the Press Secretary

For Immediate release

Summary: White House releases details of memorial service for First Gentleman Monte Morales.

WASHINGTON, DC, Today: The White House office of protocol announced today that the funeral for First Gentleman Monte Morales will take place on Saturday. It will be a strictly private event. Mr. Morales, a U.S. Air Force veteran with service in the Iraq Theater of Operations, will be interred at Arlington National Cemetery.

Following the funeral service and interment, a public memorial service will be held at the National Cathedral.

In addition to the POTUS, foreign dignitaries will include British Prime Minister Bowen and Mrs. Victoria Poplak-Bowen; Hanna Ellstrom, First Lady of Canada; Claude Dehaye, First Gentleman of France, and Mexico's First Lady, Sofia Soto.

The full list of dignitaries is appended.

[ARTIFACT]

Notes for book proposal: *Billionaire Freak Show*

by Jan DeVoor

Lengthy prelim interview with Carmela Fazenda. Claims she was a maid working at the Armstrong household NYC yrs, 1982 to 2008. Cuban native hired by Arthur Armstrong. Worked as general downstairs maid later assigned to work specifically for C and B. Later, subsequent to AA's death, worked for C & B.

Much talk of Arthur's fanatic anti-communism. Fazenda sympathized as a Cuban expat. Liked C & B much pity etc. C was the cool calculating one. B maybe smarter but volatile.

Says twins raised in near-total isolation. Attempts to intro them to staff children generally disastrous. An attic space was eventually set up as a sort of artificial environment. Mannequins dressed and posed in artificial environments. Twins would pretend they were real. (Note: mannequins believed purchased from Bloomingdale's. May have searchable records.)

The attic space was called the doll house.

Relations betw AA and C & B were good. AA fascinated by his grandchildren. Believed them a sign from god.

Fazenda says things changed when AA became ill. Twins panicked. What would become of them etc. Spent more time in attic mannequin menagerie. AA orders them out of attic to focus on business.

AA disease degenerative ups and downs and C & B start to use the time to learn more. Take to business.

Fazenda believes C & B may have assisted AA suicide. Fazenda witnesses conversation between C & B. "This dies with us, brother. As dead as him."

Fazenda retired, replaced by woman Ling (last name? first name?). Warned not to speak to press. But now terminal herself she is talking.

Second interview sched for Monday.

Update: Fazenda dead after fall on subway tracks.

ELEVEN

"The attic," Benjamin said. "I was thinking of the attic."

"I often remember it," Charles admitted, but he didn't like talking about their childhood.

The Twins traveled by private jet. There was no other practical way. Their jet had a specially built seat, and handrails bolted to the overhead so they could hold themselves upright for the trip back and forth to the specially built bathroom.

They stayed aboard the plane during refueling in Novosibirsk, Russia. They did not get off until the plane had landed and taxied into a secure hangar at Hong Kong International.

The Twins had traveled with three bodyguards, a personal assistant named Samuel, and an old Vietnamese woman named Ling. Ling was a piece of work—ancient, wrinkled, short but squat and amazingly strong. There would never be a need to wire Ling to ensure her loyalty—the Twins owned her body and soul after they had bribed the communist authorities in Hanoi to release Ling's son from prison.

At the airport Charles and Benjamin transferred to a helicopter.

It, too, was specially equipped. It belonged to the *Doll Ship* and had been flown to shore to accommodate them. The only problem with the helicopter was that it was too small to take all three of the bodyguards. There was room for only the Twins, Ling and a single AmericaStrong operative whom everyone called Altoona after his hometown.

The helicopter whined its way to full power and tilted out through the doors of the hangar. The weather had turned nasty, with low clouds and gusting winds. Rain and worse wind was ahead. Already the flight conditions were less than optimum for a landing on a pitching ship. But they hadn't come all this way to be denied now.

"Our friends were mannequins," Benjamin said bitterly, spitting the words.

"Listen, brother, you must fight these memories. She wired you, that McLure girl. You know that. You know that these memories are given too much prominence because she wired you."

Benjamin stared dully ahead. "My best friend was Poppy. Do you remember her, brother? I imagined going out to the movies with her. With a mannequin. With a thing. A thing made of plaster over a metal frame, topped with a yellow wig."

The helicopter lifted off with a lurch that upset the stomach they shared. The city stabbed up at them with a hundred bright skyscrapers. Then the busy harbor. And finally they were out over gray water.

"I wanted to look under her dress," Benjamin said. "A mannequin."

"For God's sake, let it go. We aren't those children anymore, Benjamin." The words were painful. The memories were painful. Worse than painful, shameful. Humiliating.

"Aren't we those children, Charles? And yet we are en route to the *Doll Ship*, and what is the *Doll Ship* but the doll house with anatomically correct mannequins?"

"The whole world will change, Benjamin. We are going to change the whole world. Do you understand that? I know you do. All of that, all the . . . all the past, will be a prologue and everything will be—"

"We will still be what we are, though, won't we?"

"If the world changes, how can we be the same?" Charles asked. "It's going to be better, Benjamin. It will be better. And soon. For now, there's the *Doll Ship*."

The *Doll Ship* had passed from the Philippine Sea into the South China Sea. Minako, in the nickel steel bubble of Benjaminia, knew nothing of it. All that could be noticed inside that eerie pressure cooker was that the swell of the ocean now had a shorter interval—smaller, faster waves, and sometimes the whole place would sink into a trough before taking a hard slap that would have people reaching for handrails.

"They are on their way!" the public address system blared. "The Great Souls are in the air and on their way!"

English was the language of the *Doll Ship*. But Minako heard cries of pleasure and excitement in half a dozen languages. The girl downstairs—her name was Fatima—spoke Spanish and despite being aboard the *Doll Ship* for six months had not acquired much English.

What she did know were mostly slogans from the endless Nexus Humanus books and pamphlets and videos.

She was happy. "Sustainably happy," although Minako doubted she understood the words.

Minako was not happy. She had wondered if she should climb up to the highest level and leap off the railing. The fall would be something close to a hundred feet, more than enough to kill her.

How long a fall? Two seconds? Three?

If only she could be sure it was not four seconds . . .

The loneliness choked her sometimes. Choked the air from her lungs. Her mother. Her friends. Her bedroom. Her things. All of it gone. All of everything that had ever seemed normal had been traded for this floating madhouse, these bright-eyed lunatics.

Fatima had seen her crying and come to stand outside Minako's quarters, speaking from the catwalk outside. "No be sadness, Minako. Be happy. Be joy!" She pronounced that last word "yoy."

"I don't feel joy," Minako had said. "Why would I? I've been kidnapped. My mother cries every night, I am sure. I can see her in my mind, I can see her crying for her daughter. I can see her eyes all red."

"No, no, Minako. The world entire will be happy. *Tú mamá* she is happy you. Happy you."

"Don't you miss your parents?" Minako had asked.

And a bleak, hollow look had come into Fatima's dark eyes. "No?" She had said it as a question. Then, more confidently, "No. They are come, the Great Souls."

"Who are these Great Souls?" Minako had asked.

"You have not look at photos?"

Minako shook her head. "No."

"Yes. Toblerone, this is why. His sicking."

"What is so special about these people?" Minako asked.

Fatima smiled mysteriously. "Very beauty. Most beauty men." Then she said, "I have photo in my lodge."

And if only the timing had worked out a bit better Minako might have had a chance to see what Fatima could show her. But before that could happen, the announcement came.

"Everyone assemble in the commons, wearing your cleanest clothing and happiest face!"

Fatima had yelped and run off, forgetting entirely her offer to Minako.

Minako had only one change of clothing, the *Doll Ship* was not known for its style. Women wore black slacks and powder-blue blouses. Men wore khakis and white shirts. Young girls wore a sort of school uniform: pleated skirt and white blouse. There were no young boys, a fact that only at that very moment dawned on Minako.

None of the clothing fit very well, but the laundry kept things very clean and very well pressed. Even the knee socks were ironed, Minako knew, because it was her job to work in the laundry.

A strange laundry it was in a belowdecks space between Benjaminia and Charlestown, with workers from both towns, all happy, happy to be doing laundry, sorting, loading into the big industrial washing machines, using the padded steam-iron machines to press trousers, all of it so very, very happy.

Except when a young man named Xander had evidently climbed inside one of the big industrial dryers. It must have happened at night when the laundry was quiet. He had set the cycle, pushed the Start button, and used a wad of tape to pull the door shut behind himself, triggering the dryer to start.

Minako had not found him, but she had been in the area when the first scream announced the grisly results. Proctors had come running and pulled the bloody, burned body from the dryer. Minako had seen it slip from their grip and hit the floor.

Suicide by dryer. So. Not everyone was happy, happy, happy you.

Ever since she had reached puberty and the obsessive compulsive disorder had worsened, Minako had suspected she was crazy. But it was impossible that these people could be genuinely happy, deprived of their families, taken from their homes, kept in an awful steel ball and made to do drudge work all day. Xander was the proof, wasn't he?

Either they were mad or Minako was, and for the first time in Minako's life she had begun to suspect that here, at least, she was the least crazy person around.

She changed clothing, acutely aware, as she often was, of a sense of being watched, even when she changed clothes. Even when she used the toilet or showered. There were no secrets aboard the *Doll Ship*. No need for secrets when everyone was so happy they sometimes locked themselves in a dryer.

She joined the rush of people down to the commons, the flat space at the bottom of the dome; there was no alternative, and she hoped, somehow, that these Great Souls would be rational. In any event she would get to see the men responsible for this place, the gods of this monstrous sphere. Maybe they would see that they had made a terrible mistake taking her and that she—she somehow being different than all these other people—should be returned to her home.

The word *home* made her throat tighten.

The Twins for their part could now see the ship through the Plexiglas canopy. It couldn't be mistaken for any other ship, there were few such LNG carriers: four huge spheres that looked like they'd been dropped into an oversize canoe. Two of the spheres actually carried liquified natural gas. This was the brilliant coup that allowed this *Doll Ship*—the second vessel to carry that title—to travel the world unsuspected and unmolested.

This *Doll Ship* could travel from one LNG port to the next, take on LNG in Bontang, Indonesia, and carry it to Punta Guayanilla, Puerto Rico, or to Kochi, India. And no one ever asked why they were here or there. No one from customs ever asked to look inside the tanks. Why would they? The various sensors all showed the expected readings.

What, you want to stick your head into a vat of supercooled, highly volatile gas?

No, you don't.

You really don't, Mr. Customs Inspector.

"We're going to crash," Benjamin muttered. "Charles and Benjamin Armstrong dead trying to reach their dolls."

"Why don't you shut up?" Charles snapped. The helicopter was pitching and vibrating as the rotor hit pockets of vacuum where the blades chewed at nothing.

The helicopter landing pad was aft, behind the superstructure where the crew lived. The crew were not all wired, in fact most were not. It wasn't necessary. They didn't need to believe, not yet, they needed only to be paid. Well paid and threatened.

Charles considered calling it off: they couldn't very well be killed in a fiery crash when they were so close to making major strides in their work. Ah, that would be painful irony, wouldn't it? To have control, or something very like control, over the heads of the world's most powerful nations, and then to die because a landing skid caught and pitched them into the sea?

Then those skids hit the deck with a frightening impact.

"Ah!" Charles cried out.

But now the whine of the rotors died, and crewmen in bright yellow slickers rushed out to attach cables even as the clouds dumped the rain.

Two crewmen appeared with umbrellas. They opened the helicopter door. There was a gust of cold, wet air, and suddenly the noise of the turbines and the thwap-thwap of the rotors were replaced by the rush of the wind and the thrum of the ship's engines.

With Ling's help, they climbed awkwardly down the steps, dragging the almost useless third leg, swinging side to side in their awkward way.

A crewman blanched and looked away.

"Get that man out of our sight!" Benjamin yelled.

The crewman looked relieved when the captain tapped him on the shoulder and jerked his head to indicate that the indiscreet lad should find somewhere else to be.

An umbrella shielded the twins' heads, but cold rain drove against their legs.

"Thank you for having us, Captain Gepfner," Charles said cordially.

"We are honored." The captain was a gray-bearded man with haunted eyes and the red nose of an alcoholic. He managed a bow of sorts. His first officer was indifferent, a gray-eyed American named Osman who stared past the Twins.

The Twins sank gratefully into the golf cart. Captain Gepfner personally fastened the clear plastic tarp that kept the rain at bay. Ling was with them. The AmericaStrong security man, Altoona, was not—seasickness had driven him to the railing to throw up.

Charles wondered whether the ship would be able to make contact with their assistant back on shore. It was vital to keep in touch with New York and their many other offices and facilities around the world. Jindal was a tool of limited use, and Burnofsky . . . Well, how could you ever totally trust a degenerate genius?

But though it was important to stay in touch, it was not as important as simply being able to touch. That was what Charles craved most. Benjamin was different: he enjoyed the sense of power. But for Charles the vital importance of the *Doll Ship* was that it allowed him to touch another human being. To be touched in return.

Hand on hand. Finger on skin. He was suddenly almost nauseous with desire for human touch.

He had rarely touched another human being. And only on the *Doll Ship* could he touch without seeing that look of terror and revulsion in her eyes.

Her eyes. In his innermost thoughts it was always a her, a woman, who would recoil in horror. Many had.

Benjamin became enraged when that happened, when they looked that way at him, when they swallowed hard and drew back. Sometimes they fainted.

Sometimes they cried.

Screamed.

Vomited.

The Morgenstein twins, what beauties they had been, those two, and yet they really hadn't known how to behave. The vomiting, that had been the worst of it.

That's what had pushed Benjamin over the edge. It had been Benjamin's idea to have those two pitying, puking little rich girls kidnapped and taken to the first *Doll Ship*.

Twins. They should have been nicer. They should have had at least some sympathy.

Well, they hadn't been twins like him and Benjamin, had they? No, they were the sort of twins people thought were cute. Leering boys fantasized about them. Rich young men in expensive clothing courted them.

But Benjamin had taught the Morgenstein twins a lesson. Charles had tried to stop him, but there was no denying the justice in Benjamin's plan.

Was there?

So pretty? So cute? Having fun being a pretty, rich twin, are you, Sylvie and Sophie? Well, welcome to our world, girls. It's amazing what a motivated surgeon can do.

"You're thinking of them, aren't you?" Benjamin asked suddenly.

It would be silly to deny it. Charles said nothing.

"Remember how they cried when they woke up?" Benjamin asked.

Charles remembered. "None of that will be necessary now, Benjamin," Charles said. "That was all left behind when the first *Doll Ship* went down. There will be women here who want us. Who will be honored—"

"That McLure girl," Benjamin interrupted. "She heard our cries. It would be only justice if we heard hers."

"None of that," Charles repeated sharply. "These are our people aboard this ship. We must treat them well. You know that. They are one with us."

The golf cart was driven by one of the ship's crew. It wasn't a long ride, but out here on a cold, pitching deck there was no chance that the Twins could manage the walk without falling.

They passed along the starboard side of the ship heading aft. They traveled to the second sphere. From the outside it was nothing but a giant white-painted beach ball, but Charles and Benjamin knew what was inside.

A set of metal steps ascended from the deck up to the catwalk that went along the tops of the domes. Pipes ran alongside, connecting the tanks for loading and unloading, for drawing away the boiled-off LNG that powered the ship's engines.

A motorized chair lift ascended alongside the stairs. It was a specialized piece of equipment, a sort of cagelike metal bench that climbed—a bit like the first rise of a roller coaster, with an audible whir and clank.

It stayed level as they rose and afforded them a view of the wide, white-topped sea. Unfortunately the tarp cover wasn't very effective at keeping out the rain, and they were fairly drenched by the time they reached the top.

Up there, at the top, two ship's officers waited, wearing slickers, inured to the cold and wet, rolling easily with the swell.

"Mr. Armstrong, and Mr. Armstrong," the second mate, Dragoslav said. He offered both his hands to shake, and each took one, awkwardly.

Human touch.

The top of the dome was a cunningly concealed hatch raised by motors from within. A gust of warm air, smelling of human bodies and the singed smell of metal, rose as the lid came off.

Through the hatch then appeared a sort of elevator, though it was open and really little more than a bare-bones balcony. The Twins hobbled aboard it. Ling guided them but then stepped back: their grand arrival must be by themselves alone. It swayed a little under their feet, and when the ship hit a trough, Benjamin yelped out a curse.

The platform began to descend, running down the central pillar, down into Benjaminia.

They would appear to those below to be descending from the painted sky.

Charles could not see his brother's face, but he sensed he was at last relaxing. The chafed skin that connected their faces was drawn tight by Benjamin's growing grin.

The whole of it came into view as they slowly, majestically, descended from the sky. The platforms that ran around the inside of the sphere were bedecked with handmade and thus authentic banners welcoming the Great Ones.

WELCOME TO BENJAMINIA!

YOU ARE HOME!

THANKS YOU, CHARLES AND BENJAMIN!

The English on that last one was a bit off, maybe, but it was a very international assortment of people. You could hear it in the odd inflections as voices rose up from below them, singing. Singing the official song of Benjaminia.

It was a perkier, more upbeat version of the old Beatles song, "Julia."

All of what I say is magical.
But I say it for I love you . . .
Ben-ja-min.

There were people on each level waving Nexus Humanus flags and yelling their lungs out. It brought a tear to Charles's eye. Men, women, young women, all looking at the Twins with acceptance. And more than acceptance: wonder, joy. Like teenagers gazing at rock stars.

Now Charles's own smile broke out. "Hah," he said. Then again, a chuckle. "Hah."

He was looking at other people, face-to-face, albeit from a distance. Seeing them and being seen in return. Not cowed employees, not the hired AmericaStrong thugs whose tolerance and impassivity was bought with dollars and pounds and euros. Not the disdain of the twitchers, or the seething, barely concealed contempt of Burnofsky.

Here was true acceptance. Here was adoration.

Here was love.

They descended, and at last the platform was nearing the commons floor, where the bulk of Benjaminia's happy residents waited, arms upraised, waving.

Charles searched each face, winked at some he recognized, raised a hand slightly to old friends. Or at least people who thought of themselves as old friends, though none of the villagers on this second *Doll Ship* had been here longer than two years, and in that time the Twins had been able to visit on only three occasions.

Then . . . a new face. A girl. Tall, but obviously young. Pretty. A beauty, even, maybe, though the freckles across her nose made him think of . . .

And then her eyes widened.

Her mouth formed an O, and the girl with Sadie McLure's freckles screamed.

TWELVE

"We're going," Nijinsky announced as soon as Plath walked in and tossed him his ChapStick. "Pack up."

"What do you mean we're—" Plath demanded.

"We're out of here, Washington cell was wiped out yesterday. Killed. Lear just told me, or maybe he just found out, in any case . . . There's a single survivor." His face was the color of cigarette ashes. "Grab whatever gear you have. You two are on a plane. I'm going to drive down with Wilkes and Anya."

Keats walked into the room, and Plath handed him a Snickers bar she'd picked up at the drugstore. He took it, made a dubious face, and stuck it in his jacket pocket. "What about Vincent?" he asked Nijinsky. "You're not leaving him . . ." A terrible thought occurred to him. "Tell me Caligula is not coming for Vincent."

Nijinsky wiped his mouth with his hand, a nervous gesture. He was a wreck; that was plain to see. "No. Lear has left that decision up to me."

"Up to you?" Plath asked, not meaning to sound incredulous.

“Up to me, that’s right, up to me,” Nijinsky snapped. “I’m taking Vincent with us. We’re going to grow some new-generation biots and try a deep wire on Vincent. If that works . . .”

“If it works he lives . . . and if it doesn’t?”

“Do me a favor,” Nijinsky interrupted. “Don’t lecture me. And don’t give me your outrage, I have no time for your outrage. Pack. Now. This place could be hit next.”

Keats said, “If this deep-wire thing works on Vincent, it could work on Al . . . on Kerouac. My brother.”

“Let’s not get ahead of ourselves,” Nijinsky said. “Let’s just get out of here alive.”

“He means don’t start hoping,” Wilkes said sourly. “We’re BZRK. We don’t do hope. You know who had hope?”

Nijinsky gritted his teeth. Wilkes came right up to him, her face up next to his neck. “Ophelia. She had hope.”

“I didn’t order that, goddamnit, Wilkes!”

“Nah, but you would, right? Because you’ll do whatever it takes to impress Lear. Right?”

But Plath had a different take. She wondered why Lear would have let Nijinksy decide Vincent’s fate, but not Ophelia’s. Was Nijinsky lying?

Pia Valquist finished her report, logged it, and saved it into the system. It would be automatically encrypted.

It would also be forgotten. The story was horrific. Ghastly. It would have been unbelievable but for the missing arm and the terrible scars.

What the Armstrongs had done to that girl . . .

Sophie Morgenstein confirmed that the *Doll Ship* had indeed sunk in the South Atlantic, and that her sister had died. She herself had almost bled to death.

Valquist used a mapping app to lay out what she had gathered from Morgenstein's account of her fellow passengers. Thus far Valquist had correlated five coastline kidnappings or disappearances. Sincheng, Taiwan. Funakoshi Bay, Japan. Pismo Beach, California. Ensenada, Mexico. Port-au-Prince, Haiti.

But of course in reality there were probably far more. Sophie Morgenstein estimated the captive population of the *Doll Ship* as over a hundred, not counting crew, guards, and the despicable medical personnel who used drugs and even lobotomization to create a docile population.

Her recitation had left Pia shaken. She was not unaware of human cruelty and depravity, but this was monstrous. Even now her hands trembled with suppressed fury.

Pia entered the data into the map and calculated the cruise times between her five known points. Yes, a ship moving at, say, fourteen knots, could do it quite handily.

Then she noticed something. The number of unexplained coastal disappearances did not appear to decline following the sinking of the *Doll Ship*.

Valquist frowned and then rubbed the frown away with her fingertips. She took the short walk to the coffee room, made a cup of Nespresso, and came back to her data.

Two women missing from Freeport, Texas. A girl missing near Cameron Parrish, Louisiana. Panama City, Florida. Punta Guayanilla, Puerto Rico, a teenager. Pampa Melchorita, Peru. Alaska. Vladivostok. Northern Japan, quite recently.

Okinawa just a little over a week ago, a Japanese American girl.

Fighting down a growing excitement, Valquist began plotting the places out on Google Earth. Yes, sailing times worked if you assumed a slightly greater speed of fifteen knots.

She paused, looking at the satellite imagery of Point Lookout. Something just north of there: a series of white dots.

She zoomed in closer. Tanks of some kind.

She checked the location of the tanks: Dominion Cove, it was called. A liquified natural gas port.

She immediately Googled all the more recent kidnapping reports that fit the profile. She had eleven in all. Of those, six were within close range of a liquified natural gas facility.

A chill went up her spine.

That was not coincidence.

There was a second *Doll Ship*.

She rechecked her data, took a deep breath, and burst into the office of her supervisor, Georg Gronholm.

"I need Naval Intelligence."

Georg shrugged. "I can introduce you to—"

"Not ours. I need NATO. I have a friend with the Royal Navy."

"So? Call this friend."

Valquist shook her head. "It's not the sort of thing for a phone call. He happens to be in Hong Kong. I need to fly there. Immediately. On the next flight. Now."

The New York home of BZRK was abandoned. None of them believed they'd ever return.

No one had the slightest affection for the place, with its peeling paint, filth, and stink of grease from the deli downstairs. But it was what they had. A place. A spot.

Without it they were just three teenagers—including one certified nut—a gay male model, a crazy person, and a Russian scientist. Somehow within the safe house it was possible to believe they were significant. Out alone? Plath and Keats in a cab on the way to the airport? The others in a rented van?

Ridiculous, that's what they were.

The cab drove past the Tulip. Keats looked up at it and whatever tiny flame of hope he'd held on to flickered like a tired candle flame in a breeze.

Airport scanning machines could see guns. They could not see biots.

Plath and Keats wore theirs in their heads. In specific, Plath had two biots—P1 and P2. Keats had one biot in his own head—K1—and K2 in Plath's brain, working—whenever he had a spare moment and could focus on it—on strengthening the aneurysm wall.

The flight from New York's La Guardia Airport to Ronald Reagan Washington National Airport took only an hour. The problem was that Sadie McLure was a recognizable person. If she were spotted there would be media, there would be people sneaking video of her and uploading it to the Web.

But she was not, despite all the incredible media focus on the terrible crash of her father's jet and her own near miss and the hundreds of casualties, as well known or recognizable as a major movie star. A little effort at camouflage, a minimal change of hair color and perhaps a baseball cap, should do the trick.

Did, in fact, do the trick. For most people.

Plath and Keats sat in row 14, just behind the wing. The plane was three and three: three seats on the starboard, three seats to port.

Keats took the aisle seat, and Plath took the window seat (they had an empty seat between them), where she could pretend to be asleep and pull the brim of her baseball cap down over her eyes and go unnoticed.

It worked.

Until she had to go to the bathroom. And even then the cap and the dark glasses would have worked had not a particular passenger also been on his way to Washington, to deal, as it happened, with the flip side of the same problem.

When Karl Burnofsky looked up he saw, and slowly recognized, none other than Sadie McLure.

Plath went into the bathroom, peed, washed her hands in the tiny sink, and squeezed out of the door. A passenger, an older man with a ragged, Keith Richards face, was very impatiently waiting to get in. He pushed past her, practically knocking her aside.

He reached across her as if desperate to grab a paper towel, and as he did his hand brushed against her neck.

Plath returned to her row. She slid past Keats and sank into her seat and stared out of the window at hard glittering lights below and the trailing edge of the wing. It looked cold out there in the night.

She had a book to read, but she wasn't reading it now. Keats had a book as well, but he just gazed moodily down the aisle. They knew better than to talk about anything of importance. Nijinsky had warned them.

Keats summarized his life. Brother in a mental institution. Parents indifferent, glad to have him gone, no matter how thin the excuse. In love with a girl who had two billion dollars and had told him flatly that she did not love him back. And two biots. One in Plath's head, trudging back and forth, building the wall of titanium. The other in his own eye, sitting there, watching red blood cells surge beneath its feet.

Death or madness.

He stole a glance at Plath. He wanted her, but more than that he wanted her to want him. He wanted her to need him.

And why? Because he was so reliable? Because he really could save her? No. He wasn't fool enough to believe that. She had more resources than he did. She was probably smarter. She was certainly too beautiful for the likes of him.

And yet . . .

And yet.

Seven rows back Burnofsky smiled slyly to himself. What were the chances? And what an interesting problem. He had Sadie McLure, the daughter of his old friend and nemesis, within his reach. Had her dead to rights.

The Twins would forgive Burnofsky anything if he could deliver The McLure, dead or alive. Yes, the plan had been to use Thrum to use McLure to get to BZRK. But that plan had been laid in place before Sadie McLure had invaded Benjamin's brain.

Charles would be upset if Burnofsky altered course suddenly to go after Sadie. But Benjamin? Oh, Benjamin would love nothing more than to have Sadie McLure in his power.

The question then was: What was best for Burnofsky?

Obviously Sadie was being sent to Washington because Lear knew his Washington cell had been obliterated. The New Yorkers were being brought in to take over. Their mission was obvious: take back the president.

Burnofsky smiled at the thought that he was playing chess with the mysterious Lear. Burnofsky moved a pawn, Lear moved a rook, Burnofsky moved a bishop. And Burnofsky's king was half mad.

Well, he thought, *most kings are at least half mad.*

When they landed, Sadie would go one way and he would go another. She and the boy with her would in all likelihood go far out of range. He could lose them. He had some limited ability to track nanobots, but it was sketchy and imprecise.

Follow her? Yes, that would be the right move. Do his best to stay with her. He had placed twelve nanobots on her neck during their brief encounter at the restroom, but it was a crude, inert transfer. He was not at a twitcher station, and nanobots were not biots; they could not simply be controlled with thoughts. What he had done was to use what they called a "packet." A packet was about the size of a single grain of table salt. Twelve nanobots packed tightly together and covered with an adhesive. He kept two of these with him at all times. One under his left pinkie fingernail, one under the right. It was one of these packets that he had "accidentally" wiped onto Sadie's neck as he passed her.

But if he lost her now he might never be able to activate the nanobots.

Burnofsky played it forward in his mind. He would be met at the airport by a limo. The driver would be an AmericaStrong thug with instructions to drive him to the Crystal City Hyatt to meet Bug Man. The driver would follow Burnofsky's orders, but would he be able to track whatever limo or cab or bus Sadie McLure took? BZRKers tended not to be fools: they would take steps to throw off any pursuit.

The jet touched down and taxied to the gate.

The passengers clicked off seat belts and stood en masse. Burnofsky stood.

There had been no time for Burnofsky even to get a drink on the short hop from New York to DC. And he badly needed a pipe. He had the address of a place in Washington . . . No one claimed it was as nice as the China Bone, one of the world's great opium dens, but it was apparently the very best place to find a pipe, or indeed whatever you wanted, in Washington. The rumor was that two congressmen, the secretary of education, and the White House doctor were regulars.

The plane's door opened. Keats hauled his bag down from the overhead locker. Plath hauled her own down as well. They did their best to act as if they didn't know each other, Sadie and the boy, but no close observer—and Karl Burnofsky was quite a close observer—would miss the tiny clues. The way they refused to make eye contact. The way he moved reflexively to help her when her bag slipped but stopped himself. The indefinable energy field that vibrated between them.

Oh, they more than know each other, Burnofsky thought. *There's some powerful something going on there.*

The plane emptied and Burnofsky followed docilely behind them. Would they have a car waiting? He didn't see one.

Now it was either off to the cab stand or the bus or . . .

No, they were heading toward the car rentals. No way. That wasn't going to happen, was it? They were too young to rent . . . Unless of course they had fake IDs.

Damn it. That would make things awkward.

A husky black man in dark livery carried a sign that read BELVEDERE. That was Burnofsky's fake name for this trip.

"Give me your card and wait here," Burnofsky told the man.

Burnofsky followed Sadie and the boy. Watched them stop to stare in some bewilderment at signs indicating that car rental could be reached on foot or by a shuttle. Saw them head off pulling their bags behind them to reach the place on foot, no longer even really trying not to know each other, though still not touching.

The boy reached up to rub his eyes. But it wasn't rubbing, it was a very special touch, and Burnofsky should have seen that. He really should have seen what was coming next. But he believed he was the predator, not the prey.

Suddenly they turned.

Burnofsky was caught off guard. His eyes were not sufficiently bland, not appropriately disinterested. Gazes met. His first instinct was to bluff it out, keep walking.

"Hey, there," Sadie McLure said to him.

"I . . ." he managed to say before the boy, the blue-eyed naif, stepped in fast, confident, and suddenly the boy's hand was on Burnofsky's throat, and Burnofsky was suddenly terribly aware of how old he was, how feeble, and the boy, not cold-blooded but angry, pushed his thumb right into Burnofsky's eye.

"You know what just happened old man," the boy hissed.

People were passing by on either side, hauling their luggage, sleepy, weary, resigned, impatient, completely uninterested. And it wasn't like Burnofsky was being mugged. What could he do? Cry for help? To whom, the police?

The AmericaStrong driver was far behind, out of sight, probably grabbing himself a doughnut.

"I don't know what the hell you're talking about," Burnofsky bluffed.

The girl wasn't having it. "Yeah, and yet you're not screaming your head off for the cops, are you?"

"Let me ask you this," Burnofsky said, switching tactics. "How do you get your biots back?"

"By taking you with us," the boy said, but Burnofsky could see the concern on his face. The kid was new to this war. He hadn't thought it through. He'd just done the brave/stupid thing and not considered that his biot was now a hostage.

"Not so easy to do, is it?" Burnofsky laughed his rasping laugh. "Throw me over your shoulder here in the airport? Carry me to the rental car?"

"Or just keep you trapped long enough that I can do some interesting wiring. Or blind you," the boy said.

It was Burnofsky's turn to flinch. It wouldn't be easy, even with acid and claw, to cut the optic nerve, but it wouldn't be impossible, either. And if the boy knew some anatomy there were easier ways. An artery that could be punctured, for example.

He would have to take his chances. He would have to break and run. He was carrying his own special hydras and a portable twitcher control; he couldn't have them pawing through his things.

One problems with that: he was old and slow.

"No!" Burnofsky cried suddenly. "I won't let you steal my money!"

He shrugged, and winked at the boy, then he bolted for the door.

The McLure girl and her friend easily kept pace, but now that Burnofsky was yelling, people were paying attention. A middle-aged woman made a vague gesture, as if she was going to get in the middle of it, but thought better of it and instead yelled, "Someone needs to help this man!"

A businessman looked on skeptically.

Burnofsky made it out the door with the two kids right behind him. Traffic whizzed by, buses, cabs, limos, and the noise level rose, which made it harder for Burnofsky's hoarse voice to carry. There was a police car parked a hundred yards away, looking in the wrong direction.

A shuttle bus was bearing down.

Limos glided by.

"Grab a taxi!" the boy shouted to Sadie McLure.

"They're trying to rob me!" Burnofsky cried, but few heard and none seemed to care.

The boy pressed close behind him and pushed his knee into the back of Burnofsky's knee. Burnofsky lost his balance, the bag swung forward, forcing him to step into traffic and the boy wrapped an arm around him, hauled him back, and to the inquiring, anxious face of a passerby said, "My uncle's recovering from a stroke. Hardly knows where he is."

"Get the police!" Burnofsky yelled.

"Now, uncle, you know that's nonsense."

Burnofsky was beginning to get really afraid. Then he had an inspiration: maybe no one would rush to rescue an old man. But there was another way. "Sadie McLure! Sadie McLure! It's the girl from the Stadium Massacre! It's Sadie McLure!"

Yelling a celebrity's name had more effect than yelling "Help," but it drew only eyeballs, not offers of assistance.

Then Burnofsky saw the burn line. It was right through his field of vision. He knew what it would look like to the boy's biot. Down there, down in the nano, the biot had laid a trail of acid. Only a few cells in width and at most a millimeter long, but it was there, a blur, like someone scratching a diamond on a windowpane.

If the goal was to scare him, it had succeeded. Irrationally, perhaps, but he could not work without sight. It could finish him. In any event, no one was helping him anyway.

Burnofsky stopped yelling. He stopped struggling.

"Stop it, stop it," he said.

"I was going to see whether I could burn 'BZRK' into your eyeball," the boy said.

A limo came tearing up in reverse, fishtailing as it rushed madly against traffic and screeched to a stop.

Keats didn't need an invitation. He yanked open the door and threw Burnofsky in. He slid in beside him. Plath was at the wheel.

"You stole this car?" Keats asked breathlessly.

"Borrowed," Plath said, and hit the gas pedal. "The driver was wrangling some luggage and talking to his passenger. In two minutes the cops will have the plate number, so we need to get somewhere fast and switch cars."

Keats pulled out his phone and opened the map app. "You're coming up to Interstate 385. Go east. East! It takes you into the city."

They merged into fast-moving traffic.

"What do you two young fools plan to do with me?" Burnofsky asked.

"Search you for a start," Keats said. He thrust his hands into Burnofsky's pockets and came up with a wallet and a phone.

"Power the phone off," Plath advised.

"No," Keats countered, "he may get interesting calls. We just need to turn off his GPS."

Keats next flipped open the wallet. A driver's license in the name of Richard Belvedere. The picture matched the man seated beside him. There was an American Express card in the Belvedere name, too, but two other credit cards were in a different name: Karl Burnofsky.

To Plath he said, "What do you like, Belvedere or Burnofsky?"

He saw Plath's eyes in the rearview mirror. She said, "My father knew a guy named Burnofsky. The name stuck with me because I always picture someone burning."

"I'm going to text Nijinsky."

"Ah, Nijinsky is in charge in New York, is he?" Burnofsky asked. He laughed. "So: poor Vincent. No longer with us, eh? Bug Man will be absurdly pleased."

Keats sent the text.

He hauled Burnofsky's suitcase onto his lap and unzipped it. Inside were shirts, underwear, more toiletries and medications than might be expected, an iPad, and a very old-school Xbox. There was also a tin of Altoids that felt too heavy.

"That's probably a nanobot controller," Keats said, poking at the wires and game console. "What's this?" He held up the red-and-white tin.

"I like to have fresh breath," Burnofsky said tightly.

Something rolled inside the tin. Keats opened it and saw two Duracell batteries. He closed the tin again.

Plath turned off the highway and plunged into the city of monuments.

Keats's phone lit up with a message.

Hold him. Awaiting instructions from Lear. Jin.

Keats absorbed that, wondering what it meant that Nijinsky had to ask for guidance from Lear.

"Let me guess," Burnofsky said. "The male model kicked it upstairs to Lear." Burnofsky coughed, swallowed, and shot a wry look at the boy. "Yeah, kid, I know the name. I'll admit, we don't know who it belongs to. But yeah, we know about Lear. So melodramatic, don't you think? The whole noms-de-guerre thing? Taking the names of madmen. Not very British, really, is it? More of a Hollywood thing."

"Am I meant to be impressed that you know I'm English?" Keats said. "I'll say this: you have the whole stiff-upper-lip thing down. Very cool under pressure and all that. Let's see how you feel when you get desperate for your next drink or your next fix."

Burnofsky's eyes glittered in the dark. He had swallowed reflexively at the mention of a drink. His coated tongue licked dry lips.

"I've known a few junkies, seen a few in my old neighborhood, and God only knows how many drunks," Keats said. "I know the look."

Suddenly Burnofsky grabbed for the door handle. The boy let him: Sadie had locked it from the driver's seat.

A police car, siren screaming, tore past.

Plath said, "We need to switch cars. Google 'how to hot-wire a car.'"

"You're serious?" Keats demanded. But he Googled it. "I've got a YouTube."

Plath pulled over suddenly and killed the lights. They watched the YouTube. But first they sat through an ad for a new Avengers movie.

"Looks good," Keats said.

"Boy movie," Plath said. "But save your pennies. I'll get the tools from the trunk."

"Trunk?" Keats asked.

"The boot," Burnofsky explained helpfully.

"We'll need an older car," Keats said. He scanned down the street. They were in a residential neighborhood. Through the gap between two houses he could see a slice of the Capitol Building, a bright ivory dome.

Plath returned with the tools. "No wire cutter but there was a Swiss Army knife. How about that old Toyota over there?"

It was not as easy as it had been on the YouTube video. But neither was it terribly hard. Ten minutes later, they were in the Toyota, and Burnofsky's wrists were bound in electrical tape.

The phone chimed. Keats read the message. It was not from Nijinsky.

Pick up "Billy" at 18th and Q NW. Then to Stone Church. Beneath altar.

Keats gave Plath the address. "We're picking someone up. Then, there's a church."

"I wonder who this Billy is." Plath said. "The survivor?"

"I'm going to guess another sociopathic gamer who will soon be turned into a raving schizophrenic ex-gamer," Burnofsky snarked. "Like Vincent."

They found the corner. It was a quiet space with three apartment buildings and a couple of well-lit embassies across the road. There was no one waiting but a mixed-race kid carrying a torn black plastic garbage bag.

"Kind of young to be a homeless person," Plath observed. She rolled down her window. "Kid. What's your name?"

The boy was wary. He looked up and down the street. "Who you looking for?"

"Our friend sent us to pick someone up. The friend's name is Lear."

That was good enough for the boy. "I'm Billy. Billy the Kid."

"Of course you are," Burnofsky said dryly.

The boy started to get into the backseat, realized it was crowded, and took the front seat instead.

"I'm Plath. That's Keats. This is someone from the other side. A prisoner."

Billy turned to look, and Plath took the opportunity to check out the boy in the hard greenish glow of a streetlight. He was a cute kid, she decided. And by kid she meant he was, what, three years younger than her?

She decided immediately not to do that. Not to treat him like a child.

"What's in the bag?" Plath asked.

"Laptops and phones. And guns."

"Laptops and phones and guns, oh my!" Burnofsky parodied.

"I grabbed it all after we got shot up," Billy said.

"Shot up?" Keats asked, as Plath turned a hard left.

"They pretended to be cops and came in. Bang bang bang."

Plath saw Keats's eyes in the mirror. She asked the question on both their minds. "How did you get out alive? And have time to grab laptops?"

Billy shrugged. "Everyone was dead by then. Except the one guy I let go."

"You let one go?" Plath could not help but be intrigued.

"It was over by then," the kid explained. "He surrendered. Plus he pooped himself, so it didn't seem cool to shoot him."

"Jesus," Burnofsky said, disgusted, but at the boy, not at the disgraced man.

"There's the place," Plath said, leaning down to see out of the windshield. "We'll get out. Then I'll go ditch the car and come back. Do you have a gun on you now, Billy?"

"Yeah." He drew it out from under his sweatshirt. It looked absurdly large.

"If Mr. Burnofsky here tries to run away will you shoot him?"

"If you want me to," Billy said.

There as an awkward and overly long pause. Finally Keats said, "Yes, that's what we would like. If he runs or cries out, shoot him."

"The good guys and their child soldiers," Burnofsky said.

Not far away Helen Falkenhym Morales was writing the eulogy for her husband.

She had speechwriters, but it seemed wrong to ask one of them to write a eulogy for her husband. The whole country would be watching and weeping when she read this speech.

And so far she had written the words,

I loved him. I don't know why he had to die.

She was using a laptop, a highly secure laptop, of course— no one hacks the president's laptop. So she could write here, in the privacy of her office—not the Oval, that was the official office—she could write the truth or at least what she knew of the truth.

I don't know . . .

Something happened . . .

Bad things happen . . .

Sometimes . . .

It was like bad haiku.

She swallowed Cognac. How had she ever disliked the stuff? Why did she like it so much now?

There was a bill in Congress to . . . something important. Very important.

Wasn't it?

And one of the justices of the Supreme Court had been caught on tape making calls to a porn site. And that would blow up in the press.

The Iranians were . . .

The Euro . . .

Terrorism . . .

Rios . . .

I didn't mean to hurt him.

I loved him.

I still do. I miss him. But something . . .

Backspace—erase.

There were six nanobots tapped into her optic nerve. Left eye. Getting actual visuals was hit or miss, but with multiple nanobots tapping simultaneously, sometimes you could get a pretty good picture.

Bug Man could see what she was writing.

He was in his twitcher chair, in the office space, and Jessica was standing beside him. He was showing her. She had never seen it before, never even guessed at what Bug Man did at his "job."

"See, I'm down there inside her head," he explained.

"What are you doing there?"

Why was he telling her this? If the Twins found out, they'd kill her. They'd flat out kill her. Or maybe not: maybe they'd make him do it.

Or maybe they'd make him rewire her even more.

Once when he was maybe six, seven, he'd heard his mother talking to her sister, his aunt, about some dude named Mills, an American. His mother and aunt had been drinking gin and tonics, not drunk but not sober, either. There had been a lot of laughing and he'd ignored it all, in the next room, playing a game. But when the laughing stopped and the conversation grew quiet, he'd put down the game and crept closer to eavesdrop.

When his mother talked about this man, this Mills person, her voice grew heavy with emotion. It seemed like every three words there was a sigh. She had cried, and Bug Man's aunt had comforted her and said things like, "You had him for a while, be grateful for that."

"He loved me," his mother had said.

"He loved you more than he loved life itself," his aunt confirmed.

That cliché phrase had stuck with Bug Man, with Anthony Elder. More than life itself. That's how Jessica felt about him. She loved him more than life itself. Of course that DeShawn, whoever he was, he hadn't been made to love. No one had wired him to feel that way. Somehow it had just happened.

What would be left if he were to start tearing out the wire he had laid in Jessica's brain? What would she see when she looked at him? What did she see now?

He looked at Jessica speculatively, watching her watch the monitor. Watching her understanding what he was and who he was. How powerful he was. How important he was.

Why was he showing her?

Why was he even here? Burnofsky had told him to go limp, to do nothing, but how could he do that? What if Morales pulled some other crazy bullshit? What if she went nuts and killed someone else?

"She's saying she loved him." Jessica said softly, reverently. "She must be sad. Strange, kind of, huh? I mean, the president being sad and all. Because she's so powerful."

Bug Man wiggled one of the probes just a little, hoping for a better resolution.

I hurt him and I hurt myself in the process, and I don't even know why. Is that normal? Do you all understand how that happens?

Backspace—erase.

I was so determined. I knew at that moment what I had to do.

Backspace—erase.

Bug Man felt weakness in his arms. His breathing was shallow.

"I'm in trouble, Jessica," Bug Man Anthony Elder said.

"You're the best, Anthony," Jessica said. It was automatic. He knew the connections that made her say it. He had laid that wire.

"They'll kill me if this goes wrong," he said. "They'll fucking kill me."

She laid a hand on his shoulder. She leaned down to nuzzle his neck. "I can make you not so tense," she said.

Jessica was beautiful, as beautiful as when he had first seen her, and he wanted her so badly it hurt, wanted her so badly he'd pay any price. . . .

I loved Monte the first time I saw him

And his head made a sound like a walnut

Backspace—erase.

"Did she kill MoMo?" Jessica asked, and suddenly it was a little girl's voice. A voice full of wonder and sweet, innocent worry.

And even as she worried she was caressing his face and neck, doing what he had programmed her to do, and something like panic rose in Bug Man's chest, making his heart beat too fast and then too slow and he felt sick.

Oh, God, how did it come to this?

That's what the president typed. And Bug Man read it and thought, *Yes, yes: How?*

THIRTEEN

The Stone Church was evidently abandoned, though perhaps not so long ago. It was the sort of building that might have been considered historical, perhaps, but was small and ugly and too patched up to quite make one think of George Washington in attendance. It seemed squeezed and oppressed between a coin-op laundry and a halfway house.

Needless to say, it was not one of Washington's tonier neighborhoods. Local residents had decorated the stone exterior with graffiti, none of it terribly original, none of it rising to the level of street art.

Keats used the tire iron from the car to pry plywood from the side door. It was a noisy job. Billy slid through the opening and pushed from the inside. Once in, Plath and Keats used the lights from their phones to find a switch. Amazingly, the switch lit up a pair of clamp lights hanging from scaffolding.

As their eyes adjusted they saw a space that was more impressive from the inside than it had been from the outside. The only window was a small, peaked, stained glass set beside the door. It was protected by Plexiglas so it had not been broken, but it had been largely obscured by graffiti. Its much, much larger cousins were in a shallow dome in the ceiling. It was impossible to see the scenes clearly, but Plath counted ten panels. The moon shone through one and revealed a scene of a man in a red robe raising a knife in a threatening manner. The Ten Commandments, maybe, with "Thou shalt not kill" the only one now illuminated.

A dozen long wooden pews had been pushed aside for the scaffolding. The purpose of the scaffolding must have been to begin some restoration project, but there were cobwebs and maybe spiderwebs as well and dust everywhere, so it had been abandoned some time ago.

There was an altar, a two-step platform topped by a large rectangle decorated with lacquered tile. A wooden podium or lectern was tipped onto its side. Above the altar on the wall was a cross in rough wood, probably a fairly realistic reproduction of the original. Someone had gone to a great of trouble to climb up there and set beer cans at the ends and at the top. Two were green Rolling Rock cans and one was a dented Colt 45 Malt Liquor can.

Billy had hauled his bag inside and set it down on the altar. He searched behind it.

"We need Burnofsky tied up," Plath said. She glanced around. There was plastic rope, neon orange. She and Keats sat Burnofsky on a folding chair and tied him to the scaffolding. The placement of the metal pipes of the scaffolding dictated an odd, asymmetrical arrangement that left one of the man's arms stretched out and the other raised over his head. If he pulled hard enough he might just be able to pull the whole rickety structure down on himself, but they were too shaken and weary to think of any better arrangement.

"This is hardly necessary, I'm an old man," Burnofsky said, not really putting much conviction behind it.

"Tape his mouth shut?" Keats wondered aloud.

Plath shook her head. "No. Maybe he wants to spill his guts."

Keats grinned at her. "Seriously? Americans really say things like that? Spill his guts? That sounds very *Law & Order*."

"That's probably where I heard it," Plath admitted.

"You two make a cute couple," Burnofsky said dryly.

"Beneath the altar," Keats said, recalling the text from Lear. He joined Billy and the two of them tipped the altar over.

"There are stairs," Keats said. "No light switch, though. I'm not keen to walk down there with nothing but the light from an iPhone."

"Wait for Jin," Plath suggested. "I'm going to see what the old man put on me." She sounded tougher than she felt. She had come to more or less accept that nano-scale images of her own eyes or brain were simply a part of her consciousness, but traveling out over her own skin still held terrors for her. She would have liked to take a good long shower first at least. You never knew what microscopic monstrosities you might encounter.

"I can do it," Keats offered, stepping back from the altar.

Plath shook her head. “Bad enough I’ve got you in my brain. I don’t need you crawling over my epidermis.”

“Then I’ll update Lear and Jin,” Keats said.

Plath motored her two nanobots around her own eye. From the massive Golden Gate Bridge cable–size nerve onto the eyeball itself.

The back side of the eye was very different than the front. If the front was a sort of eerie frozen lake with an awful black pit in the center surrounded by stretched chewing gum muscles, the back was an alien landscape of seemingly impossible constructions formed by nerves and muscles and surface veins like tree roots.

Or perhaps the veins were more like pythons. She could see the shape of the blood cells that surged and slowed, surged and slowed with each heartbeat. The platelets were a sort of slurry in the larger veins, then branched off into smaller veins, and capillaries where they piled up, single file like impatient children pushing in line.

It was impossible at this scale to see blood as liquid. They were objects, each cell tiny but distinguishable. Wet red stones being forced through a pale sausage casing.

Then there were the muscles, giant bundles of rubber bands that fused into eyeball and jerked incessantly, though at the nano level she didn’t so much feel the motion as see it when the slanting rubber bands would thicken in contraction, stretch out in release, endlessly adjusting as though somewhere there must be an absolutely perfect angle for the eye and the muscles were determined to find it.

Plath's biots came around into the light on the lower edge. Bottom eyelids move less and could be more easily climbed than the swift-rushing upper eyelid. The edge of the lid was a shoreline of tall bluffs topped by scaly, curving palm trees. Eyelashes.

The lower lid jerked and the line of palm trees shot toward her. The lid and lashes rushed with startling speed, slid over her and blotted out the feeble light. She jumped both of her biots simultaneously and caught the wet membrane above.

This movement she felt, the impact, as the eyelid suddenly reversed direction and swept her back and away. Now clinging upside down to the lid, the eyeball itself swept by above/beneath her.

She steeled herself for the next part as she climbed—upside down, but in the nano up and down mattered very little—to emerge in the line of eyelashes. There, face-to-face with her, a demodex.

In the m-sub—micro-subjective—the demodex was almost as large as she was. Its face was a crude spider's mouth and two utterly blank Hello Kitty! button eyes. God only knew what it saw—surely not much. The demodex was calmly munching a dead skin cell that looked rather like a fallen leaf after a rain.

The demodex did not respond to her presence—nothing in a demodex's evolution had prepared it for this—it just kept eating.

The shortest way forward was to clamber straight over the mite. With a shudder Plath sent her biots scampering across, through the scaly trees, and out onto broken ground.

In and out of desert ravines, past scattered balls of pollen in half a dozen different colors and shapes. The pollen grains looked oddly like an assortment of footballs and soccer balls left carelessly on a playing field.

Onto the cheek. Here the skin was smooth—no more ravines. Those would come no doubt with age—but for now her skin was a carpet of leaves, dead cells drifted onto a living substrata. As she watched a handful of dead cells broke loose and fluttered away.

The biots could not see distances well. So Plath knew that the massive, Everest-size mountain off in the distance was her nose, but she wouldn't easily have recognized it as such.

"Ahh, what the hell?" she cried. A long, low, dark berm was directly ahead. The rough blanket of skin cells suddenly rose, looking like some kind of burial mound, like some dark tumor.

"Freckle," she said, relieved to realize what it was.

"I like your freckles," Burnofsky said up in the world. "I'm sure your English friend admires them as well."

She skirted the freckle and saw more of them across the landscape ahead.

As she neared her lip the fine hairs appeared, much smaller than eyelashes, less like scaly palm trees and more like widely scattered stalks of wheat. It was impossible to avoid the sensation that she was racing across a fantasy landscape, something out of a science-fiction movie. And while that was happening she was accepting a can of soda from Billy, who had been sent to the 7-Eleven down the block to bring in supplies.

Her biots saw the soda can—an unimaginably large object, a *Hindenburg* rendered in lurid red—arise from the horizon and seemingly crash into the landscape ahead.

The Coke went down her throat.

"There's a slight scratch where he brushed against you, I think," Keats said, up in the world. He was looking closely at her neck. "You're sweating. Don't move."

She turned her biots and saw the wall of water racing toward her. It was a glistening ball, more like a water balloon rolling down a hill than a drop of water, solid rather than liquid.

She cut sideways sharply but just then a pillar came stabbing down out of the sky.

In the macro she saw Keats's finger. He touched the drop of sweat. He was very close to her, which may have been why she was sweating, or maybe it was that she hadn't taken off her coat and it was humid in the church.

At the nano level something the size of the world's largest sequoia intersected the sweat drop, bursting its illusion of solidity. His fingerprint was turned toward her, a desiccated farmland of weirdly plowed furrows. It stabbed into the yielding flesh of her cheek, which bent the very fabric of the "ground" beneath her feet.

She saw his face. Both versions. One with concerned blue eyes, a vertical worry line between his eyebrows, a mouth pursed in concentration.

And the other version, a sky-filling enormity, a falling moon with distant smears of features, a towering volcano with twin calderas, two lakes so vast you could sail them, an elongated red spot to rival the one on Jupiter: his mouth.

"Thanks," she said.

"No problem," said the red spot. The wind from his mouth bent the reeds and ruffled the pollen grains.

Plath noticed Billy standing to one side, staring. "You know about this?" she asked him.

"The game? Biots and all? Sure I know."

"The children's war," Burnofsky said. "The game. Always the game."

In both the nano and the macro Plath saw Keats's eyes widen. The huge sky-wide face turned away. "Shut it, old man. You work for the Armstrongs? Then this is your fault. Your doing. So if you want to smirk, you know what, maybe I can get past my usual reluctance to smack a helpless old man."

Burnofsky's pale eyes rolled, but he fell silent.

Plath continued all the while racing down the length of her cheek. "Put a finger near the scrape you said you saw."

Keats did. His finger touched her throat. It was further to the right than she'd expected, she must have come too close to her own lips. Now she corrected her course, barreling toward the finger pillar.

She was away from the downy hairs now, upside down beneath her jaw in deep shadow cast by the harsh bare bulbs. Her neck was at right angles, but the curve was gentle and almost unnoticeable to her weightless biots. The tiny talons in her twelve legs easily gripped the dusty . . .

And there it was.

It lay on the surface of her skin. It was a gooey ball, almost like a wad of gum, or spit, a roughly spherical wad that adhered to her skin.

She slowed to approach it cautiously. One biot to the right, one to the left, two visuals added to her own true eyes, each a picture formed in her visual cortex. The pictures didn't so much overlap as coexist, separate but simultaneous, a large-screen macro and two picture-in-picture smaller visual fields.

"I see it," she said. "You can pull your finger away."

"What does it look like?" Keats asked.

"Wow," she said. "It's . . . Okay, it looks about twenty feet in diameter m-sub."

"About as big as a grain of table salt," Burnofsky said.

"It's . . . It's nanobots. Like, a lot. Maybe ten or so. They're all intertwined and covered in goo."

"Yeah. Goo," Burnofsky said, and laughed.

"Back away," Keats said urgently.

Plath shook her head. The movement twisted the ground beneath her. "They aren't moving. Burnofsky doesn't have a controller. They're just stuck there."

It took them a few seconds to realize what had happened, and then Keats grinned at Plath. "You mean we just captured a dozen nanobots? I've got to believe that will be useful."

Nijinsky drove from New York down to DC. Down the Jersey Turnpike. Night traffic, cars zooming past the rented van, his eyes bleary, attention fading, eyes peeled for a Starbucks because he needed a serious jolt of caffeine.

A triple cappuccino. Yeah. That would get him most of the way. He was fantasizing about it. Imagining the foam, the bitterness underneath it . . .

There was a loud bang. Not the first, but still startling. The madman shackled in the backseat kicked at the seat and growled.

Strange, Nijinsky thought mordantly. He would have pegged Vincent as a quiet sort of crazy. Not a kicker. Not a growler.

Anya Violet was beside Vincent, occasionally laying a soothing hand on his arm, saying little.

Wilkes rode shotgun. She seemed nervous.

"I don't like going through Maryland," she muttered.

"It's not a very big state," Nijinsky said.

"Big enough," Wilkes said. "This is where I come from. Where I had my . . . you know."

"Ah," Nijinsky said. "I forgot it was in Maryland."

"What was in Maryland?" Anya asked.

Nijinsky shot a look at her in the rearview mirror. "Not your concern, Doctor."

"Arson and attempted murder," Wilkes said with relish. "Arson. True. Attempted murder? Not true. I had a sort of disagreement with the football team at my school."

"Disagreement?" Anya asked. She was bored, ready for a story.

"They thought they could rape me and I couldn't do anything because I was just the freaky chick and who would believe me? They were right that no one would believe me. But they overlooked the fact that I could set the bleachers in their gym on fire. And also their locker room." She smiled a dangerous smile. "Yeah, that was our disagreement."

Anya asked from the dark backseat, "Did you get them?" There was a hard edge to her voice.

"I wasn't out to kill anyone. Like I said: the attempted murder charge on me is crap. Arson, sure. Molotov cocktails. You know . . . Hey, you would, right? Weren't they a Russian invention? Then you probably know: you get wine bottles and fill them with gasoline and stuff a rag in."

No one said anything. So Wilkes added, "The trick is you have to break the bottle after you light the rag. That was the hard part, actually. It's easy to get them burning, but it's not like in the movies where stuff just blows up. They'll just burn like a candle unless you throw them and smash them."

"Yeah," Nijinsky said, because he couldn't think of what else to say. He was fully awake now. That was good.

"I kind of had to side-arm them up against the metal bleacher support poles. Easier in the locker room because they had barbells. Those broke the hell out of the bottles."

"Good for you," Anya said, garbling the *r* sound with her Russian accent. "Take back what is yours: pride."

Nijinsky glanced up in the rearview mirror and saw her smiling. Was he the only sane one in the van?

"Anyway, I'm not popular in Glen Burnie, Maryland," Wilkes said.

Which was the point when Nijinsky's phone lit up with the text from Keats and Plath. "Read this to me," he told Wilkes, and handed her the phone. Then added, "Please."

"'Have taken AFGC guy possible name Burnofsky. Instructions?'"

Wilkes read him the text and burst out again with her weird, heh-heh-heh laugh. "Go Keats. Capturing some bad guys. I'd do Keats in a heartbeat. What about you, Jin? You hot for our English friend?"

Nijinsky veered toward an exit that suddenly presented itself. They parked at the far, dark end of a Hardee's parking lot. Nijinsky sent a text to Lear.

"Can't make that decision yourself, Jin?" Wilkes asked.

He sent a text back to Keats. *Hold him. Awaiting instructions.*

He decided against answering Wilkes's barbed remark because he was asking himself the same thing. Would Vincent have handled that himself? Was this an example of Nijinsky being the wrong person?

He glanced at the navigation system as Vincent once more yanked on his chains and said something like, "Hurrrr!" Forty minutes to go, and that was if there was no traffic.

He was in a van with a crazy girl, a raving lunatic, and a woman who probably wanted to kill him. In the parking lot of a Hardee's. In the middle of God knew where in the dark. Waiting for instructions from a man or woman or for all he knew computer program to tell him to live or die, kill or be killed.

People were pulling into the drive-thru, getting burgers and fries and shakes. Normal people with normal lives. A family, two fathers and their two girls, sat in a Subaru wagon, pointing at the neon menu, and Nijinsky thought for a moment that in another universe that could be him.

How in hell had he ended up here, doing this, with these people? He had wanted a little adventure, a sense of doing something mysterious and important. He wasn't even a gamer; he had come to BZRK because of a chance meeting with Grey McLure at some stupid society party where Nijinsky had been invited as eye candy.

Somehow he had fallen into conversation with McLure, and before he knew it he was telling McLure his life story.

"You're too smart to just walk around looking good in a tux," McLure had said.

"Maybe, sir, but that's my skill set." At the time he'd halfway thought McLure was hitting on him. He wouldn't be the first straight guy to consider a little experimentation.

But no, that wasn't it. McLure had found something genuinely interesting in Shane Hwang, underwear model and party tux-wearer. Finally he'd asked McLure straight out why he was paying attention to him.

McLure tilted his head, looked at him, and said, "You have no family, you have no connections, really, you have no direction. You strike me as a gentle person, but not weak, very intelligent but unfocused."

Nijinsky had frowned. "Is this a job interview?"

"I know someone who may need a young man like you, Mr. Hwang. This person needs a sort of, well, I don't quite know the word for it. He needs someone to be a right hand to a young man who is very talented and in a leadership position but is not good at handling people."

"Like a personal assistant?" The idea had disappointed him.

"No. Like a brother in arms. Like a balance. Yin to his yang."

"It doesn't sound like—"

"Your life would be in danger. Your sanity would be at risk. You would see things, and do things . . . unimaginable to you now."

McLure had smiled. "You would have purpose. You would be doing very, very important work . . ."

Nijinsky saw that the Subaru family had finally gotten their order straight. He sighed.

The yin to his yang, or was it the other way around, he could never remember, was chained in the seat behind him. Kerouac was mad. Renfield was dead. Ophelia was dead. And unasked for, Nijinsky was in charge. He had never wanted it, not for so much as a millisecond. He'd been a good second in command to Vincent.

But he had never—

An app opened on his phone, unbidden.

Suddenly he was looking at a night-vision shot of the common room in the New York safe house, taken from one of the security cameras.

Men in Kevlar vests and helmets were in the room, swinging their weapons left, right, looking for opponents.

"They're hitting the New York safe house," Nijinsky said, then regretted it because Wilkes was all over him in a flash, wanting to see.

"Goddamn!" Wilkes said, twisting his hand so she could see the phone better. "They missed us by what, three hours?"

"They're going macro on us. They hit DC. Now they're hitting us in New York."

Her chin was on his bicep as she looked in fascination at the gray-scale video. The cameras switched from room to room in steady rotation. There were armed men in every room now.

"You've got to do it, Jin," Wilkes said.

Nijinsky said nothing. The phone trembled in his hand.

"Jin, you have to do it. If you won't do it I will."

"What are you two talking about?" Anya asked.

"Blowing up the New York place." Wilkes tried to sound casual, but Nijinsky could tell that even she, even hard little Wilkes was shaken by the idea.

He punched in a twelve-character code to get access to the Kill button. It was a green button.

Cheerful.

"I have to check with Lear," Nijinsky said.

"There's no time for that, Jin," Wilkes snapped, her voice as ragged as his own. "It can take hours for Lear to respond. You know there's instructions for all this. Everyone's biots are outta there, we're outta there, you know what we're supposed to do."

"I don't think—"

"It's what they did at the UN, what they did to their own people to hide evidence, and they burned Ophelia's legs off!"

"So we do what they do?" he demanded, wanting somehow to blame her.

"There are fingerprints, hair samples, personal stuff, clues. Evidence. Whatever the hell. Jin. Jin!"

"I'm the wrong person for this," Nijinsky said quietly.

"Give it to me," Wilkes said. "If you don't do it you're putting all of us and our families at—" She stopped. Because Nijinsky's thumb had pressed down on the button.

The video feed went blank.

They sat there, silent, until Nijinsky said, "Anya, would you mind driving for a while?"

FOURTEEN

The instant Nijinsky, Anya, Wilkes, and a heavily drugged Vincent arrived at the church, Nijinsky held up his phone for Keats and Plath to read a text. It was from Lear.

Karl Burnofsky: inventor of the nanobot. Murdered daughter on orders of Twins. Hold at all cost. Kill before you allow escape.

Keats read it twice just to be sure.

Burnofsky saw all this. He sighed. "I assume that's about me. Am I a dead man?"

No one answered.

"Anya, would you help Vincent to a room?" Nijinsky asked.

There was something wrong with Nijinsky, it was obvious to anyone, something that was not just about a long drive on the turnpikes and freeways. He looked old. He looked as if he could be his own father. His voice was a whisper. He was carrying a paper bag from the liquor store where he had stopped off en route.

Keats took the bag from an unprotesting Nijinsky and set it on one of the pews. He drew out a bottle of vodka. He crumpled the bag noisily, making sure to draw Burnofsky's attention to the bottle.

Burnofsky licked his lips, and for a few seconds an expression of terrible desire ruled his face.

Keats saw and understood. He'd been right about Burnofsky. An addict.

"So there he is in the flesh," Burnofsky said, deliberately looking away from Keats and the bottle. "The great Vincent. Look what you fools have done to him."

"We didn't start this," Plath snapped.

"Of course you started it, your half of it," Burnofsky said. "We started our part, but no one made you take the other side. Did they? Your father was a friend of mine, you know." He glanced at the bottle. "We used to drink together, Grey and I. He worked for me at one point. Did you know that? Used to enjoy a drink together."

Plath, despite herself, was drawn to listen. She was hungry for anything that made her father real again.

"What a brilliant man, your dad. And a good father, too. Better than I was to my daughter."

"You have a daughter?" Plath asked, keeping her voice neutral. Information was power, and there was nothing to be gained by telling Burnofsky what they knew.

"Had," Burnofsky said. "Had. Had a daughter. Had. Just like you had a father and a brother. And of course your mother, oh, God, I'd have traded my soul for her." He smiled wistfully. "Beautiful woman. Nothing like you," he added cruelly.

Plath showed him nothing.

Wilkes lifted a loose brick off the scaffold, stepped close, and calmly smashed it into Burnofsky's mouth.

Blood erupted from his lips and gums.

She put the brick, smeared red, back in place just as it had been, as if it was an heirloom resting on the mantel.

"Beat a helpless old man?" Burnofsky cried as he spit blood. "It's like that is it? Fucking little bitch!"

Wilkes made a "Who, me?" face.

Plath waited for Nijinsky to call Wilkes out, to order her to stop. Nothing. So she said, "Maybe not, huh, Wilkes?"

"She's the nice one," Wilkes said, helpfully pointing to Plath. "I'm the other one."

Billy the Kid watched it all from beneath lowered brows.

"So who the hell are you?" Wilkes asked Billy, not unfriendly, just sounding like Wilkes.

"Billy."

She stuck out her hand to shake his. "Having fun so far?"

"Burnofsky here's got a nanobot controller in his bag," Keats said. "We were just going to get it out. He placed a sort of pod of nanobots on Plath's neck. Hard to count, but maybe a dozen."

Keats picked up the vodka bottle, twisted the lid off, and carried it to Burnofsky. He dragged an empty plastic paint bucket over and set the bottle on the can, just a few feet from the older man.

"What are you doing?" Nijinsky asked dully.

"He's a drunk or a junkie or maybe both," Keats said.

"Fuck all of you, you deserve what's coming," Burnofsky said, and spit blood at Plath.

"Oh, but we'll be best of friends once we're absorbed into the hive mind and spouting Nexus Humanus nonsense, won't we?" This from Wilkes. Plath was surprised to see her take the lead. Nijinsky barely seemed to be in the room. "You'll forgive us then, right? I think I'll smack you again."

"Yes, what you have now is so much better, isn't it?" Burnofsky snarled. "So much better. A hundred thousand years of violence, starvation, torture, betrayal, brutality, rape, and murder. So much to be admired in *Homo sapiens*, eh? Not an inch of this planet that hasn't been drenched in blood." As he spoke blood bubbled on his lips. "Yes, what a lovely world it is that brings you young thugs together to beat up an old man tied to a ladder. Yes, that's worth fighting for, right?"

"It works for me," Wilkes said.

"We're fighting for the right to go on being human," Nijinsky said quietly. "We're fighting for freedom." He frowned, as if he was hearing this for the first time and not sure if he found it convincing.

Burnofsky barked a laugh and a piece of tooth went flying. "Of course you are. Freedom. The freedom to do what, exactly? Don't worry, Mr. Hwang, you'll still be able to pleasure strangers in bathroom stalls after the great change."

Nijinsky went paler still. Plath carefully avoided making eye contact with him.

"Shane Hwang," Burnofsky said grandly. "Nijinsky. Of course we know who you are, you're on posters all over Manhattan, although you do look different with clothing on. Your father disowned you after he found you bent over his kitchen counter . . . entertaining . . . the cable installer. Oh, we know all about you, Nijinsky. We could have taken you out at any time, but why bother, eh?"

Wilkes sighed theatrically and picked up the brick.

"Go ahead! Beat me! Show me your moral superiority; show me what you're fighting for."

Wilkes hesitated.

Nijinsky, his voice straining to remain calm, said, "He doesn't know who you are, Wilkes. Or Keats. Doesn't know Billy, I'm guessing. He's bluffing. Pretending to know more than he does."

"I know what they are," Burnofsky shot back. "The losers. The damaged. The victims. Life's little rejects, all except Sadie McLure of course, no, she's the rich daughter of privilege out for revenge." He shook his head. "Every war in history was fought by the cannon fodder. All for the benefit of someone who stayed safe and above it all. They get you into the fight with high-flown rhetoric, and then they blood you, don't they? They make sure you've seen a friend's blood and drawn blood from an enemy. You're pushed into their fight but now you've lost people, so now it's personal. Now it's too late to get out because you've done things . . . unimaginable things."

Nijinsky jerked almost violently.

Burnofsky didn't seem to notice. He was on a roll. "You've been hurt, so now, by God, it's your fight. Yours. Oldest game in history: idealists and patriots turned into vengeful killers. Somewhere, Lear is laughing."

As if on cue a terrible moan came from Vincent, whom Anya had drawn away into a far corner of the church. It was a moan that rose higher and higher before suddenly falling off a cliff and tumbling down in manic laughter.

"Your friend's meds are wearing off," Burnofsky said.

Keats picked up the vodka bottle and held it close to Burnofsky's ruined mouth. As if he was going to pour. A ragged need transformed Burnofsky's face.

"I believe your meds are wearing off as well," Keats said, and set the bottle back down again.

Minako McGrath had screamed.

She had not fainted, but as she screamed something had hit her in the back of her head, and that buckled her knees.

No one had warned her, no one had told her that the fanciful, mythological painting on the ceiling of the dome was of a real person. People.

It had simply been too much. She was not so delicate as all that, she had seen many people with deformities and she had never felt anything but compassion for them. And maybe, no certainly, she would come to feel that same compassion for these unfortunates. Except that these were no helpless beggars. These were the Great Souls, the ringmasters of this floating asylum, the bastards who had kidnapped her.

She lay in her quarters. There was a bruise on the back of her head. Someone had brought her here, someone had smeared antibiotic ointment on the back of her head, matting her hair.

She sat up. The headache was an explosion in her skull.

There was singing, loud and not very good.

One mind.
Two great guides.
No more war.
No more hate.
It's never too late.

Minako did not recognize the tune. She stood up and fought down a wave of nausea that almost did make her faint.

She went to the door. It was locked. She could see out into the sphere, but the door was locked. The railings were crowded with singing, banner-waving people. Through the gaps she could see that the floor of the sphere was crowded with ecstatically happy celebrants. It was all like some weird melding of rock concert, celebrity red carpet, and political rally.

The monsters were still in the elevator cage, which had come to rest just a few feet above the crowd. People reached out to touch them, tried to push their fingers through the wire. Like teenage fans with a pop star.

The song went on and on, and Minako had the distinct impression that it had been going on this way for quite some time. The sphere throbbed with it.

Finally the recorded music played a rousing finale, and the singing devolved into yells and cries and shouts of "Charles! Benjamin!" and "Benjaminia welcomes you!"

We love you!

Sustainable happiness!

Charles waved his arm expansively, soaking it all up. Benjamin was less obviously pleased. His face had endured some damage and his expression was more a scowl than a smile.

It mattered not to the admiring fanatics.

Benjamin! Our wonderful Benjamin!

Our prince!

Our guide!

Minako felt a very different sense of sickness, not nausea but terror. A chant was building, all the voices together, an inexorable rhythm.

Ben-ja-min!

Ben-ja-min!

Charles was pointing to his brother, a ringleader, cheering on the cheerers. He was deliberately drawing attention to his twin. And it seemed to be working, a little at least. The scowling Benjamin waved his arm before letting it drop to his side.

But then his eye drilled straight into Minako. He could see her. She recoiled from that terrible stare.

Only then did Benjamin smile.

Minako fell back, out of sight, and sat on her bed. This was all a nightmare. A nightmare. It couldn't be real.

She was shaking. The sheer malevolence in that single eye.

They were going to hurt her.

The chant had changed now.

We are everyone!

We are everyone!

We'll be everywhere!

We'll be everywhere!

Three men appeared at the door to Minako's quarters. They were crewmen, not inhabitants of Benjaminia. One was the young Asian from the beach, KimKim, the one who had wanted to abuse her. But he was not leering now; he was standing very stiff and proper. The second man was older and she had never seen him before. She knew the third one was an officer; he had epaulettes on his shirt.

"You're coming with us," the officer said brusquely. He had an accent she couldn't place.

She shook her head. "I don't want to go anywhere."

Minako backed into her room, as if that would stop them.

The officer said, "If you fight it will be worse."

Until that instant she had not been sure she would fight. She had no weapons. She wasn't going to win. Nor would she even manage to hurt them. But she would fight.

The two sailors stepped into the room and Minako threw the useless pamphlets at them. They reached for her and she kicked and scratched and none of it had any effect but to make her ever more enraged, enraged by her own impotence and weakness.

The younger one soon had her around the waist and threw her onto the ground. Once again a roll of duct tape was produced and wound quickly around her ankles and wrists.

"You're all crazy! You're all crazy!" Minako cried at the top of her lungs. "This is a madhouse!"

They tried to tape her mouth, but the older one dropped the tape and it rolled out of the door and bounced over the short lip of the catwalk to fall out of view.

"Idiot," the officer said. "Just grab her."

The two sailors hefted her up onto their shoulders. She kicked and squirmed and smashed her head against the young one's temple. She contracted her stomach muscles and made them both stumble as they carried her out onto the catwalk.

For a terrible moment she thought they meant to throw her over the side. Maybe that would be better. At least then it would be over quickly.

Did they mean to hand her over to the chanting mob? They had caught sight of her, the others standing on the catwalks, and soon a new chant began.

Join us! Join us!

They weren't angry words, but the chant grew ever more intense. From encouraging to angry to hateful.

Join us!

It was a curse.

Join us!

It was a threat.

They hustled her down the stairs and through the now-enraged crowd. People spit on her. Someone punched her, then others. Her shirt was ripped. Someone pounded her calf repeatedly.

"You're all crazy! You're all crazy!" she screamed.

Someone in the crowd punched her in the mouth and various voices yelled, "Shut her up, shut her up, join us, join us!"

The officer and the two sailors were now having a hard time getting through the mob. KimKim slipped and Minako fell hard to the floor, crashing on her neck. A kick caught her shoulder. Feet were stomping all around her.

KimKim bent over her, shielding her with his body. He was scared, she could see it.

"You're all crazy!" Minako screamed, on automatic now, as caught up in the madness of the moment as the fanatics around her.

"My friends!" a huge voice bellowed.

"It's Mr. Charles!" some cried out. "The Great Souls!"

The amplified voice repeated, "My friends! My friends! Calm yourselves! Calm yourselves!"

The kicks and punches lessened and the legs receded around Minako. But she did not stop screaming, "You're all crazy!"

The sailors manhandled her up off the floor and half carried, half dragged her to the elevator lift. She saw the legs, the two and the one, and suddenly she was deposited at their feet, at the feet of Charles and Benjamin Armstrong.

Charles's voice boomed again as the lift began to rise. "My friends, do not hate this girl. She is simply unenlightened, as are too many in this sad world. But never fear! Our time is coming. The future belongs to us!"

Cheers rose like a tide all around her, and yet still she screamed, "You're all crazy!"

Benjamin's foot moved. The toe of his shoe was against her side. He pressed his weight down and ground the skin of her waist against the metal.

Minako heard Charles say, "We don't have a twitcher aboard, brother."

"So much the better," Benjamin said. "The old ways, then. The old ways."

"Where the hell is Burnofsky?" Bug Man asked Jessica. Back in the hotel room in Crystal City. Back to just the two of them, claustrophobic, the walls closing in again.

Go limp.

The president was doing whatever she was doing. Writing her crazy eulogy.

Bug Man was doing nothing.

Jessica was watching *Evil Dead 2* on the TV. That kind of thing had never been her taste back in the old days. That kind of thing was Bug Man's taste.

"I don't know who Burnofsky is, baby," Jessica said. "Do you want to have sex?"

"For God's sake no!" Bug Man said, exasperated. "Jesus Christ, why would you think that? That's not the answer to everything. That's not—"

He was arguing with himself.

He was arguing with what he had done to her.

She turned her still-amazing eyes, those incredible hazel eyes that looked so alien in her African face, on him, all liquid willingness to please, and he wanted to punch her. Honest to God, he wanted to punch her in the face and see whether she responded with a bland, programmed response.

He could. He could punch her and she would ask him if he was tense, if he needed something to relax him, a massage perhaps, or a blow job.

Where the hell was Burnofsky? Bug Man had checked the flight and the traffic. There was no way it could take Burnofsky this long to get from National Airport to Crystal City. He could walk it in less time.

Go limp.

It was ridiculous! He had his nanobots all up in the brain of the single most powerful person on Earth, and he was sitting here doing nothing nothing nothing, waiting for some old burn-out junkie to show up. Go to the office and watch passively, as he had earlier, or sit here and cycle through the movies and TV shows.

This was not the game.

The game was going on without him.

Anthony Elder had a sudden, unbidden memory of himself in London. Of his life changing when he found a mate from school who had a high-speed Internet connection.

Anthony had practically moved into Mike's home. They had played Batman Begins and Call of Duty 2, mostly. But the friendship began to wane when it became obvious that Anthony's skills far exceeded Mike's. Mike was not a talented gamer, and Anthony—who had adopted the online name Bug Man—was not just a good player, he was one of the best.

Tensions had come to blows and Anthony had come out on the losing end. It finished his friendship with Mike and forced him offline.

He might as well have been a junkie: he needed the game that badly. He sought out other kids at his school to replace Mike, but Anthony was not very good at making friends. He was arrogant and unwilling to hide it. He didn't do particularly well in his classes, but no one believed it was from lack of ability.

Anthony just didn't care.

He thought of the time between falling out with Mike and before the blessed day when his mother could finally manage a fast Internet connection as a sort of time of emptiness, of longing. Without the game—some game, any game—Bug Man was just Anthony.

He had Burnofsky's number. He dialed it. It rang through to voice mail.

No game was anywhere near as good as twitching. He was a twitcher. He needed it. He needed to be down in the meat.

He glared at Jessica, just sitting there, looking beautiful, gazing out of the window at the lights of the city, sighing occasionally, bored but obedient.

It struck him then what he had done. "I hacked my own game," he said. Jessica was like any game where you knew all the shortcuts, where you had all the hacks. The game lost any value.

He had a portable twitching controller.

He had nanobots of course.

"Come here, Jessica. I just need to poke you in the eye."

FIFTEEN

African beaches. Or was it Costa Rica they had talked about? Africa, yeah, that was it.

She would get Keats and they would drive away. Stern would meet them. Then, somehow, African beaches. Bodyguards. And a message would be sent to the Armstrong Twins: We are out of this war of yours.

We are civilians now.

Leave us alone.

Nijinksy shone a flashlight down the dark hole beneath the altar. "It was a bootlegger's hideout," Nijinsky said, cutting off her fantasy. He led Plath and Anya down a surprisingly well-built set of concrete steps. After some searching they found a wall switch, and Nijinsky flicked the light on.

It couldn't quite be called a cave, it was more just an underground pit dug out of the clay soil. Dirt walls, dirt roof held up by a lattice-work of recently added four-by-four and two-by-four beams.

The floor was covered by interlocking steel mats. A big rock protruded, and the steel flooring went around it. The entire space was large enough that it had to extend beneath several adjacent lots.

There were dusty, dried-out casks, the big ones you might see at a traditional winery, against one wall. Farther on the lighting improved dramatically, and the metal flooring had been covered by a thick blue plastic tarp.

It was in this section, an area that smelled less of mold and must, more of fresh-dug dirt, that the lab equipment was set up.

"A lab in this hole in the ground?" This from Anya, who stepped gingerly onto the tarp and went from one hulking piece of equipment to the next, marking them off a mental checklist, powering each one up, checking read-out panels.

Keats was upstairs with Wilkes and Billy, checking locks on the back door and the small window, barricading with the pews and assorted scrap lumber. All the way down in the sub-basement Plath could hear the dull impact of a hammer driving nails to strengthen defenses.

Burnofsky's words were still buzzing in her brain.

It was true, wasn't it? She had been suckered. She'd been tricked into this. She was a rich girl on a revenge high, but led into it by the eternally unseen Lear. Who else had sent Vincent to recruit her?

Who was Lear, exactly? And who the hell did he, she, or it think he, she, or it was to do this to her?

You've been hurt so now, by God, it's your fight. Yours. Oldest game in history: idealists and patriots turned into vengeful killers. Somewhere, Lear is laughing.

"Very well done," Anya said, giving her verdict on the underground lab.

Nijinsky nodded. "Good. Then we may as well get started. Assuming you're ready, Dr. Violet."

Anya Violet turned soulful eyes on Plath. "Is she ready?"

Plath blinked and brought herself out of her dark reverie. "Ready for what?"

Nijinsky stood with his back to the lab. He faced her in what was almost certainly a calculatedly frank and honest way. She could have sworn he was striking a pose, and he knew how to do that. But it wasn't working.

"There's some new technology," Nijinsky said.

Anya snorted.

"We have something very special we need you to do."

"What's with the royal we, Jin?" she demanded.

"The what?"

"We. Who is we? You and Dr. Violet?"

"We," he said, sounding a little exasperated. "We. BZRK."

She stared at him, searching his eyes. They were anything but inscrutable, that old cliché. Nijinsky did not hide his feelings well. He knew he was asking something he had no right to ask; he knew he was leading her into danger.

"What is it you have planned for me?" she asked.

"There's a new version of the biot. Version four. It has a number of improvements," Nijinsky said, almost as if he was trying to sell her a new car.

She stared at him. "What?"

"We think . . . I think . . . No, we think . . ."

"Oh, man," Plath said.

"With the version four we think you can pull off a deep wire. On Vincent. That maybe you can bring him back."

Nijinsky and Anya watched her, very different expressions on their faces, waiting. Nijinsky waiting to offer up some compelling argument, but his attention elsewhere all the while, like he was watching a movie in his head. Anya with a sadness that went deep.

"You want me to take on another biot?" Plath asked dully. "Each new biot . . . I mean, what happens when . . ." She felt a chasm opening up beneath her. They were going to make her just like Vincent. Each new biot was a risk. Each new biot was another opportunity to draw the "insane" card from the deck.

"We . . . I . . . think you have the skills, Plath. The empathy. If she were . . . we'd have asked Ophelia," Nijinsky said, obviously aware of the lameness of his plea.

"Yeah, but she's dead."

Nijinsky nodded. "Yes. She's dead."

"Killed by us."

"The FBI had her," Nijinsky argued.

"Yes, the FBI. Our FBI. The guys who chase bank robbers and terrorists, except now, suddenly they're the enemy."

"Listen to me," Nijinsky said, stepping toward her. "I want you to listen to me, Plath—"

"My fucking name is Sadie!" she screamed.

There was a long, ringing silence. Anya Violet was looking at Nijinsky, watching to see how he responded.

"Listen to me, Plath," Nijinsky said with barely contained panic. "I heard what Burnofsky had to say. And some of it's true. Yeah, you're trapped. Yeah, it sucks. But we are still the good guys. It wasn't us who killed your father. We loved your dad. This is your dad's fight. Your dad helped to create this, this, this . . . BZRK."

Plath found she was having a hard time breathing.

Nijinsky pressed his advantage. "Your dad bankrolled us. Your dad saw where it was going, saw what was happening. And they murdered him. Your brother, too."

"My afterthought brother," Plath said bitterly. Then, "I miss them."

"Look, I'm not trying to play the saint here," Nijinsky said, hands spread in supplication. Those hands were shaking. "You want to say there're some shades of gray here? You want to say we're not always ethical or whatever, yeah. Did we k—" And suddenly he couldn't say it. A sob just choked him in midword. The next words had to be squeezed out. "We killed Ophelia, who was my friend, who I would have died for? Is that what you want to lay on me? Because I've had a long day, too."

Plath had seen Vincent stark, staring, twitchy, raving. This was almost as bad. Tears rolled down Nijinsky's cheeks. He was falling apart.

"Plath . . . Sadie . . . I don't know . . . I just know we are . . . maybe not right, but more right than them. We have to be. That's all I've got. We're more right than them." He shrugged helplessly. "We believe in freedom. And your dad believed in it."

Plath found her gaze drawn away from the desperate, sad Nijinsky to the seemingly eternally, organically sad Anya.

Anya said, "I love Vincent. Maybe you can save him. I cannot, but maybe you can."

"He wired you," Plath said, somewhere between scorn and pleading.

Anya made a helpless gesture with her hands. "And your friend, Keats, did he wire you? He is in your head."

The idea shocked Plath. No way. No.

Anya said, "Listen, I am not saying he did. I don't think he did. But you care for him. Because you like his face. Because you think he is attractive or funny or smart . . . What is the difference?" She shook her head impatiently. "What is the difference?"

"The difference is what this war is about," Nijinsky said. He was reluctant, but he couldn't stop himself; he couldn't let it go by that there was some equivalency between genuine, real, honest emotions and the man-made results of nanobot or biot rewiring. "It's about free will."

Plath made a sound of disbelief. "Maybe we should get off this philosophy because it's going in circles. Just tell me why we are in such a hurry with Vincent."

"Because we are talking about taking on Bug Man inside his own brain. If we take him down and do it without the rest of Armstrong finding out . . . Their most trusted soldier would be ours. And we could wire . . . unwire . . . the president."

"You don't think that you, me, Keats, Wilkes—the four of us together—could take on Bug Man?" Plath asked.

"Put us on a number line," Nijinsky said. "One to ten, in terms of skills as a twitcher. I'll start with myself. I'm a three. Wilkes is no better, she's brave, but she's still a three. You, Plath? You're an unknown. You haven't really been tested. Keats has talent, and he may be as good as Bug Man some day. But Bug Man has the experience. You're not getting the math right: Bug Man is the best. He's a ten out of ten. If we all four go against him, all he has to do is make one kill against each of us." He held up a single, manicured finger. "One kill and we're done. That's our weakness. All four of us at once? We'd be giving Bug Man a chance to wipe out our whole cell in a single fight."

"Even if I can somehow help Vincent," Plath said, "what makes you think Vincent can beat Bug Man this time around?"

"He will also have the new biot. Faster, stronger, better armed," Anya said. "We're going to grow one for him."

"Also, we have no choice," Nijinsky said. "It's Vincent or we lose."

Charles Armstrong had fought with Benjamin before.

Age twelve. Living in their grandfather's gloomy mansion. Up in the doll house.

The mannequins all wore clothing of recent vintage, the current styles. All had eyes and mouths—the more abstract mannequins with mere suggestions of faces were not for Charles and Benjamin. No, their mannequins were people with personalities and opinions. And hair.

Ludamilla, one of their grandfather's maids, dressed the mannequins. The outfits came from buyers at Bloomingdale's and Macy's. The mannequins themselves came from mannequin supply companies.

On the occasion of their twelfth birthday they were presented with a particularly attractive mannequin pair, both females, one with a wig of long, stiff, honey-colored hair. The other, identical except for the wig, which was pert, dark, and short. The boys named these new creatures Jessie and Betty.

Jessie and Betty were made part of the schoolroom tableau, along with the teacher, Mrs. Munson, and the four students in desks, Tina, Tony, Terrell, and Ty.

Jessie and Betty were to be the school nurse and the new music teacher.

Betty, the dark-haired one, was the music teacher. She had a saxophone draped over one shoulder. Her eyes were blue and never looked at you, always looked, by virtue of some artist's design or simple error, away.

Benjamin was the first to suggest that the two new mannequins might be made into the equivalent of Charles and Benjamin.

"We would just need a saw," he'd said. "A saw, some glue, some clamps."

This had not started the fight. The fight had started because Charles had felt they should have identical hair, but Benjamin had liked the fact that they had this small difference.

They had been sawing awkwardly away at the tough plastic when the fight turned ugly. Charles had threatened his brother with the saw, waving it around furiously as they conducted their argument in the reflection of a tilted, oval-framed mirror on a floor stand.

Benjamin had started screaming, "Use the saw, use it, use it to saw us apart! Saw us apart!"

Then Benjamin had yanked a hinged arm from Jessie and started beating Charles with it.

Not their first fight or their last.

But the two of them had always found a way to manage. They loved each other. What was the alternative? They were stuck together.

"We will not mutilate this girl just because she reminds you of Sadie McLure," Charles said.

"Look at her," Benjamin sneered. "She thinks she's beautiful. Does she think I'm beautiful?" He glared at Minako. She was handcuffed wrist and ankle to the gurney. He tried to force his face down close to hers but Charles resisted. They came close to toppling over. KimKim, who had been lent to them as servant, steadied them with a timely grab for Charles's arm. He let go as quickly as he could. Ling, who had been across the room, glared poisonously at KimKim.

"Brother, we cannot make ourselves beautiful by making others hideous," Charles pleaded. "You know that this is not the way. We are here with our people. They love us."

"They have no choice!" Benjamin raged.

"Just as people have no choice but to fear us," Charles argued.

"I'm sick of it. I'm sick of it all. Enough. All my life . . . I want . . ."

"What do you want, Ben?" Charles could feel his own heart and lungs clenching, tightening from his brother's emotion.

"To no longer be this," Benjamin cried out. "To be a man and not a freak. To smile at a girl and not have her run screaming. It's pathetic, isn't it? I should accept my life. Pathetic."

"We aren't accepting it," Charles snapped. "And please stop, we're hyperventilating, I can barely breathe! We are accepting nothing. We are changing the world! We are remaking the human race! We've begun on this ship, my God, did you hear the cheers and the cries? It was love, brother. It was love for us."

Benjamin said nothing, just stared at the terrified girl with the sprinkling of freckles. At long last, in a dreamy voice, Benjamin said, "I've thought of having Burnofsky wire me."

"What?"

"But it wouldn't work, would it. Do you know, Charles? Because when you wire a brain, you can only connect those things that are already there. What is there in my brain, in my memory, that could be tapped for happiness? For joy? When that evil girl, that spawn of Grey McLure, was in my brain, what was she wiring together? Old hates and new. Old pain and new pain. Emptiness, brother, you know it's true, emptiness. That's what she made me face. That's what I couldn't pretend away. Wherever she stuck a pin she hit sadness and rage and pain. And nowhere happiness."

"There were good times," Charles said weakly.

Benjamin made a small laugh. "Do you know what memory she tapped into? Certainly not what she had hoped, but there it was, the memory of that day, that morning, when Sylvie and Sophie Morgenstein awoke."

Charles bit his lip and closed his eyes, remembering now as well.

"How they screamed," Benjamin said. "Not because they saw us, but because we had made them into us. Pretty twins sewn together. They saw the horror of the rest of their lives stretching out before them. They saw the horror of being us."

"They were in pain," Charles said. "They were startled."

"I was never so happy again as at that moment," Benjamin said.

Charles remained silent. How could he argue? The memory was clear to him as well. The feeling of . . . what? Revenge? Yes, revenge. Not just on the Morgenstein twins, but on everyone who had ever sneered or mocked or shrieked.

Revenge.

The word must have filtered into Benjamin's brain because now he took it up. "Revenge on all of them. On our father and mother. On life. On God."

Then Charles swallowed in a dry throat. "Those tactics are no longer necessary. We have the technology now. This girl, we don't want her to scream, we want her to sing, like all the others on this ship. Besides, it won't be the same. She's not a twin."

"She's not a twin," Benjamin conceded. Then his eye brightened. "There's no twitcher. But the equipment is aboard. There are nanobots."

"We've never . . ." Charles began, but he was intrigued.

"We've seen it done many times," Benjamin said. He stroked the side of Minako's head and she tried to pull away, as though his very touch was foul and poisoned. "She cannot go unpunished. I won't allow it. Not after what the McLure girl did to me. No, that is the last time I will be humiliated and made a fool of."

Charles was troubled, but this was better than the alternative. And it fit within the beliefs they now had, the enlightened understanding that had come hand in hand with the power to rewire minds. Terrorize and inflict pain, yes, but only if necessary. This act, conquering the girl down in the nano, would empower Benjamin, hopefully without feeding the growing madness in him.

"Then, let's go, my brother and friend," Charles said. "Let's go . . . what is it the twitchers say?"

"Down in the meat," Benjamin whispered. "Down in the meat."

Pia Valquist had understated the nature of her contact in the Royal Navy. Understated both in terms of his position—rear admiral—and relationship. They had been friends. Close friends.

There was something very nineteenth century about Admiral Edward Domville. He was not particularly fit or trim, he was beefy, long-armed, short-legged and his face was the cheery red you might expect of a man who had spent years climbing masts and running out cannon. Of course he'd done neither; he had mostly served in submarines.

Pia had not been attracted to him because of his looks, but rather for his intelligence and completely unaffected sense of humor. His family stretched back to the Norman Conquest, with many an admiral or general or member of Parliament in that long lineage. Possibly even a marquess (or was it a baron?), if she recalled correctly.

They met in the lobby lounge at the Intercontinental Hotel. Most of Hong Kong was within a stone's throw of water, but the Intercontinental was very nearly in the bay.

"Pia, my God, you've let yourself go completely," he said, grinning around a missing tooth.

"Eddie, I can't believe they still let you wear that uniform."

They did a cheek kiss that went on a bit longer than it might if they'd really been only casual acquaintances.

"Let me! Hell, they've given me extra decorations. The sheer weight of them is wearying. How have you been, Pia?"

They looked at each other like old friends, in fact were old friends. The admiral was beginning to show his age in the jowls and the bulbousness of his nose. On the other hand, the extra decorations he'd alluded to were not for merely standing around and looking distinguished.

They took a table that looked out through prismed windows onto a stunning view of Hong Kong harbor and across the water to the wall of skyscrapers that was a sort of mirror of the similar wall of skyscrapers just behind the hotel.

"Tea is coming," the admiral said. "Neither milk nor sugar, as I recall. But what can one expect of a Swede?"

"I have something rather bizarre, Eddie. You're going to have a hard time believing what I have to tell you."

"Am I?" His eyes narrowed and he got that conspiratorial bad-boy look that she liked.

"Have you ever heard of the Armstrong Fancy Gifts Corporation?"

"I believe they deal in gift shops. Also weapons systems," he said dryly.

"And you know about the Armstrong Twins?"

"In a general sort of way," he admitted. The tea came, and they spent several minutes performing the small rituals of pouring, parceling out sandwiches, tasting, complimenting.

"They are a tragic case," Eddie said. "Or perhaps I should say tragic cases, plural."

"Do you recall an old American surplus amphibious assault ship that foundered off the coast of Brazil a couple of years ago?"

"Oh hoh," he said. A tiny sandwich hovered in his hand, forgotten.

"Eddie, it was a floating house of horrors. The Armstrong Twins were kidnapping people, often very young people, and using drugs and lobotomization and quite frankly Nazi techniques to . . ." She fell silent when she realized from his expression that none of this was news to him.

Eddie sat back in his chair, and the cheery face was less cheery by several degrees. "I have heard rumors."

"The hell," Pia said hotly. "You knew?"

Eddie shrugged. "There isn't a great deal that goes unknown on the high seas. If the Royal Navy doesn't know it, the Americans do. In this case, we both had suspicions."

"Eddie, don't dance around on this, please. I've met and interviewed one of the survivors."

That surprised him. "Have you?"

"She's in Finland. And let me tell you that her story would give you nightmares. She lives in fear, surrounded by former Mossad and dogs and electrified fences."

Eddie looked grim. "By the time we knew anything about it, it had sunk. There was nothing actionable."

"Actionable?" She chewed on the word. "You've spent too much time with Americans."

He laughed at that. "Oh, no question. I'd far rather be spending my free time with lovely and ageless Swedes."

"Eddie, there's another."

"Another man? I'm shocked."

"Another *Doll Ship.* That's what she called it: the *Doll Ship.* It's a human doll house for the Armstrong Twins. And there's a second. A replacement for the one that sank. They are still at it."

Eddie's face darkened. His eyes went from interested to predatory. "Is there indeed? Do you have proof?"

"I have evidence. Circumstantial evidence. I need you to supply proof." Pia sat forward and spilled a little tea in the process. "Eddie, they kidnapped a young Japanese American girl from Okinawa just a week ago. A fourteen-year-old child. The *Doll Ship* is near."

She let that hang in the air. The wheels were turning in her friend's head.

"The *Albion* has completed maneuvers with the Five Power Defense Arrangement and is steaming toward Hong Kong for a bit of a show. . . ."

The admiral made a tiger shark smile that must have come down through generations of prize-seeking Royal Navy captains and a few privateers as well. His eyes were dreamy. He said, "I was just this very minute thinking that the *Albion* could do with a sudden, surprise inspection by a senior officer. Do the Americans know anything about this?"

She shook her head. "I came straight to you."

"Better and better," he said. "Do you have a description of this *Doll Ship* of yours?"

Pia nodded. "I believe it is a liquified natural gas carrier."

The admiral opened his briefcase, an ancient leather object with far too many buckles. He pulled out a pad and began tapping away. "Yes," he muttered.

"Yes what?"

He held up a finger to silence her. Tapped some more. Swiped. Frowned. "Interesting. As luck would have it, there's an LNG carrier on a course that would have brought it past Okinawa at roughly the right time."

Pia's heart leapt. "Where's it heading?"

"Practically to our table."

He went back to his pad. "But there is no way to have *Albion* intercept this ship. . . . It's the SS *Gemini*, that's the registered name."

Their eyes met. "*Gemini*," Pia said. "The twins."

"We don't want some sort of fight with a dangerous LNG carrier inside Hong Kong harbor. They are floating bombs, really, if mishandled."

"But you said your ship can't intercept them."

"No, but the *Albion*'s helicopters certainly can. I'll fly out as soon as I've taken care of a few things here." Then, innocently, "I don't suppose you'd want to come with?"

"It would take more than one aging admiral to stop me," she said.

SIXTEEN

It was too intimate.

Plath was inside Vincent's brain. She was touching his memories. She was seeing things he would never have shown her. Things no one would ever voluntarily show another person.

Plath lay back on a dusty IKEA Poäng chair. She wore sweater and jeans. No shoes, but two pairs of socks so her feet wouldn't get cold. It was chilly down in the sub-basement.

She lay back, eyes closed but not asleep. Sometimes she would gasp or suck air like a person surfacing after a deep dive. Sometimes her fists would clench on the paint-spattered blond-wood arms of the chair, only to be released by conscious effort.

She was aware that Nijinsky, leaning against the side of the biot hatchery, did not want her to narrate. He didn't want the details of what was in his friend's head.

The new biot—the very first of the four series—was accompanied by one of her older biots. The difference in main visuals—what she saw through her biots' eyes—was noticeable, though still grainy and distorted.

The bigger difference was the input from sticking pins into the brain matter beneath her feet.

Normally a biot either wiring or pinning a brain could bring up a sort of sketch of the reaction it was causing. Stick a pin in a particular neuron bundle associated with a particular memory and you'd get an idea of what you were pinning, but only an idea, a hint. You got a sort of scratchy, jumpy snatch of video or more likely nothing more detailed than a vague feeling.

You didn't get the equivalent of HD quality.

This input was HD and 3D, too.

Plath had done some wiring before. She'd done some practice work, and she had been inside the twisted brains of the Armstrong Twins.

This . . . Oh, boy, this was different.

"I can't see this . . ." she said. "I can't be looking at this."

"You need to know enough to help," Nijinsky said, his voice flat.

"I don't need to . . . I'm not even sure if what I'm seeing is real or memories of imagination, of things that never really happened."

Nijinsky didn't answer.

"I'm not a voyeur," Plath said.

Oh, but she was. Unwilling, maybe, but she was a voyeur all right, a Peeping Tom, a creep looking through the curtains, a pervert with a buttonhole camera.

Stab a pin. Vincent is hearing a blues song. *I worked five long years for one woman, and she had the nerve to kick me out.*

Stab a pin. A beach. He's a small child and has to pee. "Just go in the water, Michael," a voice tells him. But it's too cold.

Vincent's real name is Michael. Plath had not known that. But it seems right.

Stab a pin. "Don't you like that?"

"Like?" Vincent answers. "It doesn't hurt."

There's a girl laughing. She's four years old, just like little Michael. He doesn't understand the sound she's making. He feels shame.

And now a scene that makes Plath extremely uncomfortable. Nothing wrong just nothing a stranger should see. She moves on.

Look out, the Christmas tree is falling over!

A long wind-swept beach. It's not at all like the South African beach she's been seeing in her own mind's eye. This is black seaweed and twisted driftwood on white sand under a dark sky.

A cigarette. Vincent says, "I don't see the point."

"Tripped on a root, fell down, cut the hell out of my knee," Vincent says.

"Sine, cosine, tangent," he says.

"I don't need it," he says. "I see it in other people, and it makes me curious. I wonder what it would be like. But I don't think I need it."

Plath said, "Jin."

"Yes."

"He can't feel pleasure, can he?"

The three-second delay in his answer was the answer. "He has anhedonia. He doesn't experience pleasure. Not in the usual sense."

Plath tried to remember if she had ever seen Vincent smile. Even now he was Vincent to her, not Michael. Vincent he had to remain.

"I'm not some kind of psychiatrist, here," she said plaintively. Nijinsky had moved out of her view. Anya Violet was there. Was that jealousy in her eyes? "I don't know what any of this means. All I know how to do is scramble someone's brain, I don't know what to do to help him."

Nijinsky didn't answer. She waited . . . and nothing. Because he had nothing. Because this was desperation time, and no one really knew how to help Vincent.

The best they had come up with was finding a way to excise the memory of the fatal battle. Somewhere among billions and billions of cells in Vincent's brain there were memories of the dead biot. Memories of defeat.

If you take a brain and flatten it out, it makes a surface about the size of two pages of a newspaper. That was then crumpled up and shoved into a fluid-filled sac, which is in turn squeezed into the cranium. In the m-sub even a square inch is a large area. She was doing the equivalent of walking around on a football field in which someone had buried a single Easter egg.

She was poking that field blindly with a stick, hoping to find the egg.

Nijinsky's phone rang. "Yeah."

A plant he had once grown from an avocado pit. Dead on return from a family vacation. Sadness. He could feel that.

Getting a flu shot as an adult. He likes the prick of pain.

"Okay," Nijinsky said and clicked off. "Wilkes says Vincent is reacting, his eyes and mouth are moving. Like . . . Never mind, keep going."

Plath had not wanted to be in the same room as Vincent. Somehow that would have made it worse.

In a gloomy classroom, the desk all the way to the left, a spitball hits the side of his head.

Bong hit, lungs hurting, coughs and can't stop. Someone laughs. He feels strange.

Anya Violet wearing nothing but red panties walking toward him on bare feet. He's intensely aroused. It's almost painful.

"That's recent," she whispered, embarrassed to be seeing this. But yes, now she's a voyeur, because she wonders, fleetingly, if this is how Keats sees her, how he feels when he looks at her.

They could find out. Somewhere far from here. The beach, the mythical, not-real beach. And what would that be, she asks herself, a date? A really long date? She who refused to consider falling in love was now seeing herself in hiding with Keats? For the rest of their lives?

Her biots, which had been traversing millimeters between probes, now barely moved. Would more recent memories be in closer proximity?

She placed a marker exactly on the spot she had stuck. Now she began probing in a circle around the spot.

A boat? A ferry. A ferry moving through dense fog. "Michael Ford. Don't turn around."

Plath froze.

Vincent, resting elbows on a chilly steel railing. His skin was clammy from the fog, his hair felt limp. There was a girl wearing a biking outfit seated to the right, far enough away not to overhear anything. The girl had cast one or two impassive-but-interested looks at Vincent.

He had looked at her when she bent over to retie her shoe. Desire. He could feel desire. He wanted while nevertheless knowing he would gain no real enjoyment.

He could want.

But he was here for a purpose and the bike girl with the long legs was not the point.

He felt someone approaching. He guessed this was it.

A whispered voice. "Michael Ford." Not a question, a statement. "Don't turn around." An order. Obedience was assumed.

Curiosity. Vincent felt curiosity, too. His other emotions were intact. Only this one thing was missing: joy. He could fear, he could care, he could loathe.

Could he love?

Plath opened her eyes, and Anya was staring at her. Her dark eyes were wet with need.

Vincent listened, tried to analyze the voice he was hearing. Male or female? It was subtly masked by electronics.

Vincent's mind searching for clues. Was the figure in the fog tall or short? Fat or thin? White, black, Asian . . .

"Who are you?" Vincent asks.

"Lear," the unidentifiable voice says.

"The mad king betrayed by his chidren."

"'As flies to wanton boys, are we to the gods; / They kill us for their sport.'" It was obviously a quote from something. Plath didn't recognize it.

"You're fighting them?" Vincent asks.

"Who, the gods?"

"The Twins. Nexus and the Armstrongs," Vincent said. "The whole mess."

"What is it you really want to know, Michael? This once you ask a question. After that, you take orders. One question."

Vincent waits. He knows the question, but he isn't sure it's what he should ask. He's not sure Lear won't hear the question and simply walk away.

He doesn't want Lear to walk away. He realizes it. He wants this. Vincent wants this . . . purpose.

"Are you good or evil?" Vincent asks.

"We, Michael. All of us. We," Lear corrects him. "We, Michael, are good and evil. But we are less evil than them."

Vincent hears this and—

"Goddamn it!" Plath cried. The memory ends there. She pushes the pin slightly deeper and finds only an unrelated memory of a funeral for a neighbor's cat with a very young Vincent solemn in attendance.

"What?" Nijinsky asks.

She can't tell him. Lear's identity is sacred, defended by Caligula. She can't even admit she came close.

Vincent had gone looking for it. Vincent had wanted in. He had chosen this path. Did that make him better than Plath? Or had he always been a bit too close to crazy?

"That's enough," Plath said. "I'm pulling out."

She sent her biots toward the exit, toward the long walk through Vincent's brain to the optic nerve.

"No. There's no time for that, Plath. Stay in there," Nijinsky orders. "Biots in place. Take a break. Have a sandwich. Play some music. Whatever. Then get back to it."

Farid learned a number of useful facts after being shot in the mouth.

Fact One: Even with lidocaine being injected into your cheek, sewing up a bullet hole hurts.

Fact Two: Even with novocaine, grinding a shattered molar down to a stump for a temporary crown hurts.

Fact Three: His father was nominally in charge of the embassy, but when the attaché for cultural exchanges—in reality the Washington station chief for Lebanese intelligence—gave him an order relating to security, it was obeyed.

By the time Farid got back, exhausted and rattled, to his bedroom at the embassy, his laptop was gone. They'd taken his phone while he was still at the hospital.

The TV news was all about the bookstore massacre wherein—according to reports—an unidentified suspect falsely claiming to be a federal agent went on a shooting spree, severely injuring a Washington, DC, police officer, and killing three others.

"You are going home," his father informed Farid.

"Father, you don't understand what . . ." Farid has started to say. But how was he going to explain any of it? Confess to being a hacker? He would never get access to another computer.

"I understand that you were almost killed by some madwoman! This country is crazy. You are going home!" His father had hugged him so hard it hurt. Then he had drawn back almost as if to slap Farid. Then he had burst into tears.

Fact Four: he was going home.

Fact Five: he would not be the person deciding the fate of the American president, others would. They would know he was off the grid, and they would know he was being sent home. If there was one thing he was sure of, it was that what he had learned would not simply disappear.

"I feel funny, Anthony."

"Do you?" He had goggles on that covered his eyes and half his forehead. His hands were in thick gloves. A tangle of wires ran from a strap around the back of his head down to what looked like an old Xbox. More wires ran from the gloves to the box.

"I feel . . ." She bit her lip.

"Tell me what you feel, baby."

He had six of his nanobots in her brain. The wire was everywhere in the hippocampus and in the nucleus accumbens. It had become overgrown, like a cable laid through a jungle. The wire was still bright where it showed, but much of it was completely obscured. Lymphocytes had swarmed as they usually did, but they had failed to either absorb or rip open the wire and now only a few sniffed around the alien intrusion.

A much bigger problem was the brain cells themselves. They came in various shapes and sizes, none as large as a nanobot's sensor array, but some like stretched octopi, others like cross sections of kitchen sponge, or lichen. All, of course, had been artificially colored by the software, creating weird tableaus of broccoli green, and a sort of pulsating maroon, and a vivid blue unlike anything in nature. The corpses of lymphocytes were painted pearly white by the software, like cow skulls in the desert in an old cowboy movie.

Like vines the cells grew over the wire and encrusted the pins that stuck up like so many arrows shot into pulpy soil. It was like discovering the ruins of a long-abandoned factory deep in a jungle.

The nanobots had to move hand over hand, so to speak, pincer claw over pincer claw, perhaps, in the environment of gently circulating cerebral-spinal fluid. Losing your grip could mean floating away. It was a bit like an astronaut working in zero G.

Two claws to grip, two claws to rip.

Six nanobots. Six sets of visuals, front and back, twelve screens in his goggles. Bug Man controlled it all, all at the same time. It was nowhere near as cool as battle, but it was enough for now, because he was doing something new. He was unwiring a brain.

The pincers yanked at pins, some of which slid out easily, others of which could not be budged unless he used two or three nanobots at once.

The pins came out, though, one way or the other. And as they came free, trailing a few scattered cells, the nanobots shoved them into their back-mounted quivers.

The wire was simply ripped up, like pulling up a half-buried garden hose. Rip and tear, rip and tear, and oh, that definitely brought the white cells pulsing and oozing. But what to do with the wire? It was spooled out from within the nanobot when it was laid, but there was no procedure for retrieving it.

So Bug Man set two of his nanobots to the job of collecting the used wire, spooling it, stacking it in a central location, a deep fold where the cerebral–spinal fluid current wouldn't carry it off.

"I feel," Jessica said. "Do . . ."

"What? What do you want to ask me?"

"Do you want sex?" It was a plaintive voice. A confused voice.

"No, babe. Not now. Maybe later," Bug Man said.

"Those goggles scare me. You look like a monster."

He hesitated then. The nanobots all froze in place. What if she utterly rejected him? What if she was disgusted by him? What if she said, "Oh my God, I can't believe I've been with you. You!"

You toad.

You nobody.

He sucked in a deep breath. It wouldn't be like that. Probably. But anyway, it didn't matter anymore, because he was doing it, and whatever happened happened. This was the game, for now.

"Can we go out now? I want to go out," Jessica said.

"What if I don't want to go out?" Bug Man asked as he ripped up a long strand of wire that pulled a few cells loose as it came up.

Jessica hesitated. The hesitation went on for quite a while.

"What if I say no, we can't go out, Jessica?" He was pulling an encrusted wire, like a robin pulling an earthworm from the dirt.

"I want to go out," she said.

Bug Man pulled off the goggles and set them aside. He took off the gloves.

He stood up and said, "Okay then. Yeah, let's go out."

SEVENTEEN

Here is what Plath knew about Vincent after what felt like a lifetime sticking pins in his brain: that he was anhedonic; that he once stuck a pencil into a boy's arm when the boy called him a wuss and shoved him from his place in the elementary school lunch line; that he didn't understand why people liked animals; that he experienced drunkenness in an extraordinarily self-aware way; that he had been slapped by his mother for failing to appreciate the cake she made for his eleventh birthday and then had watched helpless and lost as she broke down crying.

Plath knew about the mild allergy to cashews and mangoes.

She knew that the combination to his locker in tenth grade was 11-41-23.

She knew that he once became furious watching a film in school about atrocities in the Congo and vowed to kill the bastards responsible. He was suspended for three days for inappropriate language.

Once she had touched the spot where he first experienced the nano world. But the memory did not lead her anywhere.

"I'm tired," she said. She had eyeshades on. She had her feet up. She had a soda with a bendy straw within reach at her side.

"We're all tired," Wilkes snapped. Wilkes had taken over for Nijinsky. He had gone with Anya to observe Vincent, the actual physical Vincent, upstairs in the church. "Ophelia's dead tired."

That hadn't made any sense, but it caused Plath to fall silent.

After a while Plath began to confuse Vincent's memories with her own. Was it Vincent or her who had ridden the pony? Was it her or was it Vincent who had gotten poison ivy? Was it Vincent or her who had recruited Nijinsky?

First bloody nose.

First bath as a baby.

First time he had slid his hand up a girl's leg.

First time tumbling out of his crib.

First time eating popcorn.

Then, suddenly, she was seeing herself through Vincent's eyes. He had found her attractive. In the macro she blushed. He had first met her when she was in a bathtub.

She saw Kerouac, Keats's brother, as he was in Vincent's memory. He wasn't much like Keats. He was more athletic, not larger but muscular, tough. His eyes did not have Keats's tenderness. She would never have wanted to run away with Kerouac.

She had never pictured Kerouac smiling, somehow, laughing, but Kerouac had enjoyed life. He was telling Vincent a story about teaching his little brother to play goalkeeper. And laughing. And Vincent had wondered what it was like to take vicarious pleasure from another person.

Suddenly Plath saw images that could only be digital. There were stunted game creatures with swords.

And then, a thrilling ride through a bizarre alien landscape.

Digging into a sort of Lego-like world.

Passing through magical doors.

Games. Games, a dizzying array of them. Game controllers, touch screens, racing and leaping and . . . not joy, not for Michael Ford who would later be called Vincent. But a suspension of the strangeness that was always with him. And a rush. Very much a rush.

There were people—just names on a leaderboard, but with humans behind them—and Vincent knew them, knew their strengths and weaknesses, and they knew him.

He was somewhere rather than nowhere.

And he was someone. MikeF31415.

"Wilkes," Plath said. "Google MikeF31415."

"Why?"

Plath didn't answer, but she heard the distant sound of fingers on a touchscreen.

"There's a lot of hits," Wilkes said. "Game sites."

"I've seen that handle before." This from Billy the Kid, who had crept downstairs after being ignored by the others. He was looking over Wilkes's shoulder. He sounded respectful. "Whoa. Whoa." Pause, then, and in a deeper register, "Whoa, this dude is good. I mean, way good. Respect."

Games and more games. This tiny corner of Vincent's brain was a library of games. And with them came feeling. Not pleasure, but not numbness, either. Michael Ford AKA Vincent had found something he cared about.

And then, there it was: Bug Man's nanobots.

They were racing toward Vincent's biots, their center wheels down for speed. The exploding head logo that marked all of Bug Man's nanobots was seen in flashes.

The sight sent chills through Plath. She froze in place, pushing the probe ever so gently to the left, to the right, back, center again.

She saw the ripped off legs of Vincent's biot spinning away in the cerebrospinal fluid.

Worse, far worse, she felt Vincent's fear.

"Unh!" she said.

"What?" Wilkes. Bored, but hearing the change in her voice.

"Get Jin," Plath said. "Get him now."

The twitcher station on the *Doll Ship* was as complete and up-to-date as the ones back at the Armstrong Building, and better than the one Bug Man had in Washington.

In addition, there was a portable model to be used as backup. The controls for the portable unit were less sophisticated, and the visual feedback in particular was less efficient.

Charles would get one, Benjamin the other. Charles knew Benjamin would end up with the better equipment—that was the problem in dealing with an irrational, emotional person: they could simply dig in their heels and outlast you.

Making a virtue of necessity, Charles said, "Take the more comfortable equipment, Benjamin."

Benjamin did not demur.

They did not need Minako to be present in the room with them. In fact, Charles would have preferred she not be, but here again Benjamin had his way.

So Minako had been immobilized in a metal chair with handcuffs.

"Don't hurt me," she said in her charmingly accented English.

"We are not sadists," Charles said, sounding wounded. "This is not some horror movie. We are going to help you."

"Just let me go. Please. Please, I want to go back home."

Charles was fitting the equipment to his head. It took two hands, which meant he and Benjamin had to cooperate, though Ling was there to help, and they'd been given the services of the crewman named KimKim.

"Fasten it around the back, KimKim, if you would, please," Charles said. "Yes, it can go tighter."

It was extremely uncomfortable, the two of them wearing the helmets—neither could go all the way on, obviously, so contacts were imperfect. The lighter portable model fit better, offsetting some of the advantage Benjamin had.

And why am I thinking in terms of advantage? Charles wondered. This isn't a competition.

Of course they must look grotesque to both KimKim and the girl. As always, Ling remained silent.

"We are not going to hurt you, Minako; we are helping you," Charles said. "You have lived your entire life alone, whether you recognized it or not . . . Yes, now get the first syringe, KimKim. We need to link to the nanobots. This is exciting, isn't it?"

"Yes," Benjamin said curtly.

"I'm sorry," Minako cried. "Whatever I did, I'm sorry, please let me go."

Charles's bifocal vision—his depth perception—dropped out. This was a common experience. The center eye, the shared eye, could link either to him or to Benjamin. It was always obvious to whom the third eye was linked at any moment, because when it was active it provided depth of field otherwise lacking.

KimKim lifted the syringe from its stainless steel cradle. "I don't know how to give anyone a shot," he said nervously. Then added, "Sir." Then amended, "Sirs."

"It's not really a needle," Charles explained. "There's no sharp tip, you see. You just need to place it very close to Minako's eye and squeeze the plunger very carefully."

"You cannot do this," said Minako. "Please. Please, please."

"Young lady, there is nothing to be afraid of," Charles said, working on his best friendly voice.

"Who's to stop us?" Benjamin snapped.

"You should understand that we are doing this to make you happy, Minako. Think of it . . . think of it as if there was a disease in your brain and we are going to cure you. When we are done you will feel happier. You'll find that you—"

"I see!" Benjamin cried. "I can see through their eyes! I'm seeing through the nanobot eyes! Hah!"

KimKim carefully placed the tip of the needle—it might not be sharp, but it certainly looked like a needle—as close as he could to Minako's eyelid. She squeezed her eyes shut and yelled, "Someone help me! Help!"

KimKim pulled back. "If you don't sit still I'm going to poke you!"

"I can see through all their sensors, oh, oh!" Benjamin said. "I see all the other, all my . . . all the nanobots, we're all jumbled together, oh!"

KimKim used two fingers to pry Minako's eyelid open and quickly pushed the plunger.

"Ah!" Benjamin cried. "Like a roller coaster."

"Now me, now me, the second syringe!" Charles ordered. "In the other eye!"

KimKim raced for the second syringe and now Minako was sobbing on the edge of hysteria. She started babbling numbers. "One, two, three, five, seven, eleven, thirteen, seventeen."

"What is she doing?" Charles demanded, distractedly.

"Prime numbers, you dolt," Benjamin snarled.

"Nineteen, twenty-three, twenty-nine, thirty-one."

Charles tried to ignore his brother's condescension—Benjamin had always been better at math—and focused instead on the virtual control panel that appeared in the screen the helmet projected—lopsidedly—onto his eye. His fingers twitched in the gloves. The interface was a virtual touchscreen. He searched for the button labeled, Register.

He pushed it by barely moving his index finger. A second prompt opened up. Did he want to register nanobot package six? Yes, he did.

And then, "Ah!"

It was startling, though he'd seen it many times on video. All at once he was looking through six sets of sensors. It was hard to make sense of what he was seeing. A tangle of mechanical legs and sensor arrays and immobile wheels. The nanobots were not neatly stacked but rather tangled in a ball.

KimKim hit the plunger and the nanobots all exploded down a steel pipe and landed in a spare splash of liquid in Minako's eye.

"Thirty-seven, forty-one, forty-three, forty-seven!"

The visuals were too much, too overwhelming, too many eyes

looking in too many directions. What was it Bug Man did when he had too many nanobots to control individually? Platooning. And there was the prompt in the form of a question: Platoon?

Charles said, "Yes," then realized this was not a voice-activated control. He drew a finger around the six nanobot avatars and touched the Platoon? prompt.

The nanobots moved automatically into a formation, two lines of three.

Sudden darkness.

Charles awkwardly shifted the helmet to see out into the world. He looked at Minako. KimKim had let go of her eyelid. She was squeezing her eyes tight shut again, still rattling off prime numbers. He felt a moment of pity for her fear.

But pity was weak tea compared to the fascination of feeling himself actually down—physically in—a place he'd only seen second-hand. He pulled the eyepiece back into alignment.

There was no sense of touch. He poked a leg at the eye surface beneath him. All six of his nanobots did the same. No sensation. But the visuals were amazingly convincing. He was there, actually there!

He had much to learn, and Charles knew he would never be Bug Man or Burnofsky. But oh, Lord, it was amazing.

Then with a flick of a finger he sent his six nanobots racing. The center wheels dropped into place, the legs spread out like a canoe's outriggers.

And zoom!

Zoom!

The speed was breathtaking. Charles had never even walked quickly, let alone run, let alone this wild motorcycle speed.

"Ling," Charles said. "Call to the galley and order us some coffee and sandwiches. We'll be here for some time."

Can a damaged mind be cured?

Can a damaged mind be cured by subtraction?

Can the thing, the one thing, that sent you over the edge merely be removed from your brain?

Is it like writing a book, where the author can simply highlight a scene and hit the Delete button and change the course of the story?

Is it all just a data file? Is that all the human mind is: a sort of computer made of meat? Highlight folder: Delete. Empty trash. All gone.

All better now.

Shane Hwang, who called himself Nijinsky, considered these philosophical questions and badly, badly wanted not to make a decision.

"There's cutting," he said to Plath, who was still in her easy chair but not looking at all easy. "And there's burning with acid."

"Jesus," Plath said. "I . . ." She stood up. She paced away, looking strangely tall beneath the low dirt ceiling, turned, and came back. "I think it's as close as he ever came to some kind of . . . not joy, that's not the right word. Gaming, I mean, it's as close as he came to feeling like he belonged."

Nijinsky noticed that Keats stood awkwardly, wanting to make some physical contact with Plath, not doing it for fear of . . . something.

"He's upstairs growling like a dog," Wilkes said in a grating voice. "We have to try something, right?"

"We might be cutting his soul out," Plath said, twisting her fingers together.

Wilkes made a rude sound. But she didn't argue, she couldn't. Instead she pushed a thumbnail into the flesh of her arm. Hard.

Speaking of crazy people, Nijinsky thought mordantly.

Like any of them were normal. Keats and Plath might have come in normal, but they wouldn't stay that way. Wilkes had always been a little nuts. And maybe he himself had been normal, or something like it, once upon a time.

What did you think this was? Nijinsky asked himself. Did you think this was a romance novel? It's war.

What did you think you would become when you got into this? Did you think you were a hero? You pushed the green button, Shane. You didn't see the results, but you know what happened. You know that those men were killed.

They were there to kill us, all of us. Kill or be killed.

"What would Vincent want?" Keats asked, speaking for the first time.

"To be making the decision himself, not leaving it up to all of us," Nijinsky snapped, drawn out of his circular contemplation. Interrupted in the act of chasing his own tail.

"And what would his second choice be?" Keats asked, looking Nijinsky in the eye, very steady.

Nijinsky resented it. "What would your brother want?" he shot back. "If we were talking about operating on—"

"He'd want me to make the call," Keats said. "If he couldn't do it himself, he'd want me to do it. I don't know Vincent very well, but my guess is he'd want you to decide, Jin. He'd want you to try and rescue him from where he is."

"Like I failed to do when it mattered," Nijinsky said. "When Bug Man had him. Rescue him now like I didn't do then."

There was a long silence.

"Yeah," Keats said finally. Because someone needed to.

The strange thing was, Nijinsky was relieved at the answer. He had needed his guilt recognized.

Wasn't that what they were fighting for? The right to feel every jolt of pain life had to give? The right to suffer? To not be sustainably happy?

"I'm not the right person to lead this," Nijinsky said to three blank faces. "Unfortunately none of you are, either. So, I'm it." He nodded and felt his chin quiver and decided it didn't really matter if they saw that. "Send your model four out to take on a load of sulfuric,"

Nijinsky said to Plath. To Wilkes, he said, "Go make sure Dr. Violet is with Vincent. Have her prepare the acid for Plath. Then stay there with him, report to me."

Wilkes ran off immediately, leaving Plath and Keats with Nijinsky.

After a while Nijinsky realized the awkwardness was all about him. He excused himself.

But he went only as far as the stairs, waited there out of sight, listening. Because that's what the right person would do. Because the right person would want to know what Plath and Keats said to each other.

He overheard.

"Don't do this," Keats said.

"I have to try to—"

"Like hell you do."

Plath felt like the basement was out of air. She clenched a fist until the nails cut into her palm and thought, *Jesus, just like Wilkes.* She said, "I thought you were saying it was the right thing to do!"

"For Vincent, yes," he said. "For you . . . You have to get out of this, Sadie. I see it in your eyes, you want out."

"I want us both out," she said in a near whisper.

She had turned away. He didn't want to talk to her neck. He took her shoulders and turned her around. It was not roughly done, but it was more definite than Keats had been before. He wasn't asking her to face him, he was demanding.

"Together?" he asked.

"Yes, together," she said, shaking off his grip but facing him nonetheless.

"But you said—"

"Don't fucking tell me what I said!" Her head jerked forward with the force of it, making him back up. "I was making sense. I was being mature. I was trying not to hurt you or hurt me."

"And now, what? Now you don't care?"

"Listen to me, Noah," and all at once it wasn't Keats, it was Noah. She repeated the name, defiant. "Listen to me, Noah. If this works, if we save Vincent, we may be able to save your brother. And someday we may be able to save each other."

"Don't do this for me or for my brother," he pleaded. "Don't. You can get out. You can escape. This doesn't have to be your life."

She took his face in her hands.

He closed his eyes.

It was not a kiss as prelude to desire. It was a kiss that sealed fates.

EIGHTEEN

The new version-four biot—biot 4.0—moved more slowly with its internal bladder filled with acid. It was also carrying a separate bladder full of acid, just a sort of plastic trash bag really. It moved slowly back along the tortuous path it had followed earlier. Across the frozen lake of the eye with its below-the-surface rivers of swollen capillaries.

Follow the long curve, down beneath the eyelid, a long walk it was, it felt like a mile. Around and around until the muscles, like bridge cables, merged into the slickery ice surface now more pink than white.

The muscles twitched. Vincent's eyes, well, he didn't sleep much, which all by itself made him twitchy. More so when he was strapped down. They had cut down on his meds to let him react more normally. At the moment, to react normally meant to laugh softly, madly, to himself, to occasionally bark like a seal, and other times simply to roll his eyes up as far as they would go. It felt to Sadie like he was trying to turn his eyes all the way around and look back at his brain. Which given what he knew made a certain amount of sense.

Plath's biot could not make out human speech very well, less well when she was down in the meat. She heard what she knew to be a voice, a soft, soothing voice, Anya no doubt, but it was like hearing a truck rumble by on the street outside.

A routine move (God, how had she come to think of this as routine?) down the optic nerve. The nerve cells were jittery, firing gigabytes of optical data beneath her biot feet. She hesitated, looked down with her biot eyes, and saw the cell beneath one foot begin to divide. It was surprisingly sudden in the final phase, looking like invisible hands were ripping soft bread dough in half. She almost laughed at how much it looked like something she'd seen in high school biology.

Her own nerves were stretched to breaking point. It had been one thing to feel brave alone with Keats. He brought out the tough girl in her, made her feel strong, like she had when she was with her brother. In fact, now it seemed as if the two were similar, though she'd never made the connection before. Noah and Stone McLure. She had, of course, loved her brother. And though she had tried to resist it, she loved Noah—she was pretty sure of that—though in a very different way.

The optic nerve was a long cable but so thick at this point that she could barely see the curve. The only light came from two illuminating pods that cast the faintest of greenish light—enough to allow her compound insect eyes to see motion, but barely enough to let her humanlike eyes interpret artificially enhanced color.

The optic nerve goes deep into the brain. The brain tissue presses in close all around, but not so close that a biot couldn't crawl along beneath a weird, sparking sky of brain cells that warped in long, sensuous waves.

Suddenly she saw something she had not seen on previous trips. Her first impression was of maggots.

It looked like a corpse, roadkill, but completely covered in maggots the size of kittens. They seethed over it—white, gelatinous things with neither head nor eyes nor any other recognizable feature.

Lymphocytes. The defenders of Vincent's body and blood. White blood cells.

It was his biot. His dead biot. The lymphocytes were consuming it, eating it, slowly wedging legs away from body, slowly absorbing its crushed and extruded insides.

"What can you see?" Keats asked, as Sadie drew in her breath.

"His biot," she said.

"What?" Wilkes asked. She had checked on Vincent, tightened his restraints, then come back, unable to be in the room with him.

"His . . . It's his biot. The reapers have it."

That was the term of art in BZRK: reapers. The slow-moving but deadly lymphocytes—they came in different shapes, colors, and sizes—were reminders that bodies have their own defenses. They were here cleaning up the mess, disposing of one of millions of invaders. Mindless. Relentless.

"Why the hell would his dead biot be in here?" Plath demanded.

"I brought it to him after we retrieved it from the president. I carried it out. It seemed the right thing to do," Nijinsky said. "You give the dead child back to his parent."

The lymphocytes had dislodged one of the legs. Its pointed claw stuck up in the air, waving slowly back and forth like some desperate flag of surrender as the cells ate at it like it was a drumstick.

She raced back to the safety of her previous path, sick to her stomach. Her real stomach. Her biot had no stomach.

Don't fear the reapers,—a song went through her head.

Through the eyes of her old series-three biot Plath saw the approach of her new, sleeker, more capable biot, making its way laboriously, hauling the sac of acid like some foul egg nestled between its hind legs. She felt the twin shudder of recognition as her two biots saw each other and saw the eyes that were so like her own and yet so different.

There is no explaining a biot face. There is no way to paint a fair picture of that awful melding of soulless insect with eyes that look like smeared, crushed-grape versions of human eyes, which somehow convey the image of the face from which they are derived.

The biot 4.0, the new kid, drew up alongside where the older biot was keeping station at the exact location, the very spot they meant to destroy.

The end of a long needle protruded from the brain beneath their feet. The needle was shoved almost all the way down. The biot had one claw gripping it. It looked like a murder scene.

The acid sack, the festering off-white egg filled with a burning yolk, was dragged into position. Plath had been instructed to poke a small hole in it. To let the acid ooze out, and to flow the acid down the needle, down into the sparking brain cells, burning as it went.

"I'm there," she reported.

"Okay," Nijinsky said. He had a phone line open to Dr. Violet, upstairs with Vincent. "Dr. Violet. We're about to do it. Observe carefully."

A small tinny voice came through the iPhone's speaker. "What do you expect? To see him suddenly well? To leap up and cry, 'Huzzah?' It won't be so easy."

Nijinsky didn't answer, just pressed his lips tightly, took a deep breath, and said, "Do it, Plath."

She maneuvered the sac directly against the pin. With one clawed hand she tore a small—it seemed only an inch or so, m-sub—hole. At first the liquid would not come. She used a second leg to press gently on the sac. A droplet formed. It would be invisibly small to anything but a very good microscope up in the world.

The droplet hung, golden in the artificially colored world of her biots' vision.

Then it dropped.

The destruction was immediate. Between her front legs, just below her sleek insect head, the brain cells burst open like a stop-motion depiction of fruit rotting.

The cells popped. There was no sound, but they popped. Burst, spilled the goo inside, as the acid attacked in detail. She could see mitochondria squirming as though they were tiny insects.

Fumes rose from the melting flesh. She had no ability to smell, and her hearing was not attuned to the hissing sound. She could only see it.

"It just burned a few cells," she reported.

"Push the pin to one side, see if you can open a tunnel," Nijinsky advised.

She did, pushing the pin as far as she could, leaning her tiny weight into it. The flesh resisted as though fearing what was to come. A small hole was opened. The problem seemed to be that the acid's droplets were too large to fit into the narrow tunnel. Her second droplet melted just a few cells, which now congealed, like cooling lava.

"It isn't working. I can't get it to work."

"Use a second pin. Widen the hole."

"I'm making a mess." She looked at him, pleading, weak, wanting to get out, turn it off, walk away.

"Plath," Nijinsky said.

She pulled out a second pin and slid it down precisely beside the first. Now she was hit with a second wave of memories. Not all of it was games.

Vincent, spanked by his father for cursing.

Vincent, a baby, so tiny those little hands reaching for his mother's breast, vision all skewed with lurid flares and colors that looked like something from damaged film stock.

"There's other stuff, other memories. His mother—"

"Do it, Plath, damn it, we are out of time," Nijinsky said in a terse, angry voice that was his version of yelling.

With her biots working together she wedged the pins apart, and yes, now she had a hole opened into the depths of his brain. With a third limb she reached to widen the tear in the sac.

"Aaahhh!" She swore and jumped halfway out of her chair. "It broke, it broke, it broke!"

The sac had simply disappeared like a balloon that's been popped. Acid flowed everywhere. Droplets splashed and burned in the cerebral spinal fluid, like the flowering of anti-aircraft fire in some old World War II movie. Some of it sank into the brain, burning, exploding cells, obliterating all it touched.

And some of it splashed onto her biot body, eating with insane intensity at her middle leg's shoulder joint, causing that leg to flail wildly as if it had caught fire.

The new biot could feel pain.

"AaaaaAAAHHH!" she cried.

"Goddamn it, get her out of there!" Keats yelled.

Some, maybe even most of the liquid flowed into the hole. Plath gritted her teeth and kept the pins apart even as she watched one of her claws melt and curl up like a burning scrap of paper.

"Jesus, it's everywhere!"

"Are you hurt?" Nijinsky demanded.

"Yes, I'm hurt!"

The acid had splashed across both biots, she now saw. A tiny droplet was burning neatly through the carapace of the series three.

From the hole in Vincent's brain rose a boiling mix of acid and melted flesh. It burned the brain cells and blew apart capillaries and frothed heavily like some awful parody of an undersea volcano.

"Dr. Violet?" Nijinsky asked tersely.

"Nothing," she answered promptly.

"It hurts like hell," Plath yelled.

"It's just in your head," Nijinsky said.

"Of course it's in her head," Keats snapped. "Pain always is. Get her out of there!" When Nijinsky didn't react immediately, Keats yelled, "Sadie! Get out of there."

"It's starting to melt the pins," Plath reported, "and I am out of there, have to back away, Jesus!"

"Stay close enough to see," Nijinsky ordered.

"Fuck you, Jin," Keats snapped. "Sadie: get out."

Plath motored both biots backward. She turned them to look one at the other, seeing through both sets of eyes at once. A leg fell, burned away, from her older biot.

The pain was intense but not worsening. Not like life-threatening pain. But pain, definitely pain.

She had pulled back a few meters m-sub.

The hole in Vincent's brain was bubbling still, but like a dying fire. Whether the acid had maintained strength down to the target zone she couldn't guess. But it had devastated an area that seemed at that scale as large as a small backyard.

The first lymphocytes were oozing along, heading toward damage. The earliest to reach the damaged area were burned by the acid and burst open like water balloons filled with oatmeal.

"I can't reach the pins to pull them out," Plath said. "The acid is eating at them, but they're still there."

"Okay, okay," Nijinsky said at last. "Withdraw."

Faint dawn was illuminating the stained-glass panels in the shallow dome atop the Stone Church one at a time. Anya had seen enough now to be sure that they did, indeed, illustrate the Ten Commandments.

Thou shalt not.

Thou shalt not lie, steal, covet, commit adultery, kill. The numbers were off a bit: Anya had learned her commandments in the Russian Orthodox church her grandfather attended. She had never been a believer, but she loved the old man, a disillusioned communist who nevertheless had remained a devout believer.

How has that worked out for you, Jehovah, the commandments and all?

Anya Violet touched Vincent's face. He had become very still. His eyes were focused, no longer darting around. Focused with terrible intensity. But not on her. She felt invisible.

He was looking at something. Seeing something.

Nijinsky emerged from the hole beneath the altar. He crouched beside Anya. "Dr. Violet. What are you seeing?"

"I'm not a psychiatrist."

"What are you seeing?" Nijinsky pressed.

"He's . . . he's not moving. Not moving at all. He's breathing. But his eyes, they are not moving. Not at all. His hands aren't moving, his arms are just hanging."

Nijinsky looked at Vincent. Vincent showed no sign of awareness. He was utterly still. Then, slowly, like a toppling redwood tree, he fell backward on the pew, then slid to the floor.

Nijinsky and Anya leapt. She touched his face. Nijinsky took his pulse.

"He's alive," Nijinsky said. "He's alive."

"He's catatonic. What have you done to him?"

Nijinsky slid a hand under Vincent's head and raised him up. Vincent's eyes never moved. No change of focus.

Nijinksy slapped his face, not hard.

Anya drew back, but she did not object. Instead she said, "Harder."

Nijinsky delivered a stinging slap.

Nothing. Not a flinch. Not a blink.

"Again," she said, and somehow now she was in charge, delivering orders.

Nijinsky took a deep breath. This time no open-handed slap. He delivered a short but very sharp closed fist punch to the side of Vincent's head.

Nothing.

Both of them drew back, staring in horror at those blank, empty eyes.

Then Nijinsky saw something that made him gasp.

But what he saw was not in the room.

Perched at the back of his own eyeball, one of his own biots gazed passively at Vincent's still, inactive biot.

"What is it?" Anya demanded.

"Just . . ." And he didn't say what it was, because he didn't know, all he knew was that the flesh on his arms rose in goose bumps because for the first time, Vincent's biot had stirred.

Nijinsky felt a chill. He could barely breathe.

"What is it?" Anya demanded.

Vincent's biot turned eerily Vincent-like eyes on Nijinsky's own biot. Then, while the real, macro Vincent stared blankly, catatonic, seeing nothing, his biot walked uncertainly to Nijinsky's creature and extended a claw to touch.

"Anya," Nijinsky said, his tone awestruck. "He's . . . He's aware."

NINETEEN

"Aren't you a bit young to be playing with guns?" Burnofsky asked Billy.

Burnofsky looked bad. He'd spent the night tied up and staring longingly at the bottle of vodka. Jealously when he'd watched Nijinsky come and take a long pull.

Billy the Kid said nothing, because he had wanted to say, "I'm not playing," and then there had been this huge rush of memories and it was like he'd swallowed poison or something. Like he wanted to heave up his guts and he'd already done that.

"Certainly young to be a murderer," Burnofsky said.

Again, Billy was on the verge of saying something and stopped himself. What he wanted to say was, "I'm not a murderer. I just defended myself."

Except that wasn't quite true, was it? He had gotten out, after all. He had then walked around the block and come back into the bloody safe house.

He had been safe. Free and clear. And then he had gone back.

Of course he'd thought all the bad guys were dead. Right?

Right, Billy?

As if he could read Billy's mind, Burnofsky laughed. It was a bitter, angry sound.

"Maybe I'll shoot you," Billy said, irritated.

"Might as well," Burnofsky said. "If you don't, one of the others will. Or more likely they'll wire me."

Billy noticed him glance at his suitcase. And Burnofsky noticed the curiosity.

"Ever run a nanobot, kid? Ever twitched?"

Billy shook his head.

Burnofsky said nothing more, just waited, and glanced at the suitcase again, and looked at Billy from half-closed eyes. Billy reached impulsively for the suitcase. He unzipped it. There was a clean shirt, underwear, a toiletries bag, and a zippered nylon case.

Billy glanced toward the stairwell. He hauled the zippered case onto his lap, wedged his gun under his leg, and opened the case.

"Looks like an old Xbox. Kind of. The glove . . ." It was like watching Burnofsky gaze lovingly at the bottle. Billy wanted to slip the glove on.

"Go ahead. It tingles. It's much more sensitive than anything you've ever used before. You can set the tolerances, of course; at maximum, you barely need to move to twitch."

Billy stalled, trying not to look greedy for the game. "Where are the nanobots?"

“Where? Ah, well, we have two kinds, you know.”

“Uh-huh.”

“Let’s call them the grays and the blues.”

“Okay.”

“The grays, well, they’re easy to move around, obviously. In fact, the biggest worry is losing them. See the two batteries?”

Billy had of course seen them. They were nestled in an peppermints tin. Two very average-looking batteries, a single AAA and a single AA.

Billy pulled the batteries out and cupped them in his hand. He prodded them with his index finger. He frowned and then pinched the protruding nub of the positive end of the AA and pulled. A cylinder slid out. Inside the cylinder were six glass tubes, each not much thicker than a sewing needle.

“Each of those contains two dozen nanobots,” Burnofsky said. Then he said, “Of course those are the grays.”

Billy heard the subtle disparagement in his voice. He looked up. There was a challenging, teasing look in the old man’s eyes.

“What’s the big deal about the color?” Billy asked.

“It’s not about the color,” Burnofsky said in a near-whisper that forced Billy to lean in close. “It’s about capabilities. I mean, you’re a gamer, right, Billy?”

Billy the Kid had come up along a mean path strewn with bad people. He was not naïve despite being young. His instincts warned him that Burnofsky was up to something.

But he could handle Burnofsky. He slid the glove onto his hand. It seemed to come alive. It closed in around his hand, not squeezing exactly, but forming itself to fit perfectly. Like it had been made to order just for him.

He could feel thousands of tiny rubber needles pressing, tickling, itching for him to twitch just a little.

He grabbed the second battery and pinched the nub with his free hand. It was awkward now with the twitcher glove on. But he didn't want to take the glove off.

"How do I get them out?"

Burnofsky's look was unreadable. Something deep and dark was going on there. Something big. Finally he said, "You just snap the glass pipette. See the one end the way it's scored? Snap it off and just upend it on any surface. The inside of the pipette is specially coated so the nanobots can't grip. They'll slide right out. Takes about five seconds."

Billy held a single pipette up to the light. There was a suggestion of faint blueness, nothing more.

"What's better about these?" Billy asked.

"Well, Billy, those are special nanobots. Those are very special nanobots." Burnofsky's voice was a whisper again. "Why don't you empty them out in your palm?"

Billy was past hesitation. Without needing to be told, he slipped the goggles into place.

He snapped the pipette with his teeth, spit out the end, and held it so the open end was against his ungloved palm.

Two dozen nanobots slid onto his hand.

The goggles lit up with screens. Twenty-four separate visuals. It was a magnificent jumble of imagery. Mostly what he saw was nanobots—nanobots looking at nanobots—the whole tumbling melee of spidery legs and spinning central wheels and seeking metallic eyes.

And he saw, for the first time, the world of the meat. The nanobots lay, stood, staggered around in what seemed like a deep ditch. Like a ditch where leaves had fallen and collected on the ground without any trees nearby.

Crossing the ditch were smaller cuts in the "ground," the smaller lines of his palm. The ditch, wasn't that what they called a lifeline or something? Wasn't there something about your lifeline, long or short? Stupid, but it was weird being down there.

And the funny thing was that with the goggles on, it was almost impossible to think of himself as anywhere other than down there. That reality immediately took precedence over the macro world. Burnofsky was all but forgotten.

Superimposed over the various visual fields was a menu, glowing radioactive orange.

One choice was 1x1.

Another was Platoon.

Replay.

And one labeled SRN Rep.

Billy said, "One by one probably means play them individually. Okay, and Platoon . . ." He twitched a finger, the button showed a flare, and suddenly all twenty-four visual fields began to align, all looking in the same direction like a well-disciplined army on parade. There were secondary options—he could choose how many platoons of what number. There were subroutines being suggested.

"What does SRN Rep mean?" Billy asked.

"Ah," Burnofsky said dreamily, "That's the best part. It means replicate. But I doubt you're up for that."

And here's the thing: Billy knew Burnofsky was provoking him. He knew the man wanted him to push SRN Rep.

He just didn't know why. Billy the Kid, who was always being underestimated, assumed the old dude wanted to see him humiliate himself. Like he couldn't handle whatever replicate meant.

He did not guess that the old man had just decided to obliterate all life on the planet.

"Probably shouldn't . . . ," Burnofsky said, letting it hang there.

Billy pressed SRN Rep.

To escape the Crystal City Hyatt was not easy. Bug Man was not there alone. AmericaStrong security occupied the rooms on either side. AmericaStrong agents regularly rotated in and out of the lobby, keeping an unobtrusive but constant watch on who came and went. Bug

Man was a big asset to the Armstrong Fancy Gifts Corporation.

They had of course bugged his room. And he had, of course, found those bugs, disabled all but one and looped that last bug into a program that simply replayed audio from TV shows.

Jessica had dressed up and looked stunning. Bug Man . . . Well, he had done what he could. He was never going to be George Clooney, or who was that other dude all the girls liked?

"Let's go see some sights," Bug Man said. He took her hand. She looked at his hand holding hers and frowned as if she was trying to remember something.

"Things are going to be a bit strange," he said. "For a while, at least."

"Strange?" She didn't know what he meant, but she was unsettled.

Suddenly he felt doubt. He had almost convinced himself that nothing would change. She would still adore him, but maybe be just a bit less servile. A bit more honest.

Instead she was looking at him as if he presented a baffling mystery.

What am I doing with him?

"That's okay, that's okay. It's going to be okay." He was doing what he hadn't had to do since about three days into wiring Jessica: he was placating.

And his nanobots were still inside her. If things got too weird . . .

He had long since planned a way to evade the watchful eyes of the AmericaStrong watchdogs. He knew where the passage was to the room-service elevators. It went down to the kitchen and beneath that to the laundry.

Ten minutes later he was outside, holding Jessica's hand, wishing he had a warmer coat. It was a short walk to the Marriott, where they could get a cab without being spotted.

Bug Man felt wild. Like a kid skipping out on school. He felt free. Even the cold wind accentuated his sense of having escaped something. And if Jessica's hand was a little less confident in his, well, that was all right too, because he would win her over. He would make her . . . no, scratch that . . . he would convince her to love him.

And the next time when she made love to him it would be real.

Minako lay in her bunk, staring up at the wire mesh overhead, and at the shoes of the man up there.

The monster . . . It was what she had to call them, no compassion anymore, they were the monster! The monster had made her feel awful things.

One minute she had been terrified and the next she had begun laughing hysterically and the next she was crying, sobbing, tears running unchecked down the side of her face and into her ears.

The monster's faces had laughed and sneered, and the smiling one had congratulated the other one on discovering this wonderful new game.

How many squares were formed by the wire mesh floor above her? Count and multiply. One, two, three, four, five, six. She counted to fifty, noted that the fifty-first square had a little smudge of green paint; that would make it easier for her to go back if she lost count.

Fifty-two, fifty-three . . .

At some point they had reached her motor controls and had made her right leg twitch painfully.

"Look! Look at that!" Charles had exulted.

"Hah!" Benjamin had said. "Do it again!"

So Minako had sat there spasming, her leg squeezing and relaxing, squeezing and relaxing, a human puppet.

"Imagine what else we could do," Benjamin said in a voice that made Minako's flesh creep.

"Alas, we must return to the more important business of helping this girl to let go of her fear. She is in need of our help, yes?"

Benjamin didn't answer. But the wild jerking stopped, and a while later the confused memories began to play out again.

There were one hundred and seventy-eight squares in the mesh along the longer axis. Now to count the shorter axis. One, two, three . . .

She had suddenly remembered her father, as a huge, moon-size face looking down at her in her crib. There was a mobile of blue-and-gold birds beside him. She had not understood his words. She didn't yet understand any words.

She had found herself scrubbing her hands in the bathroom sink while her mother called to her to hurry up. In those days the OCD had been all about hand washing. That symptom had lessened, thankfully, but had been replaced by counting.

She saw disjointed, irrelevant visual memories—sand, a leaf, the bars on her playpen, her best friend from fourth grade, Akiye.

She heard audio memories, like a corrupted download that skipped from snatches of conversation to the sound of the wind to a barking dog to something that scraped to something else that pulsed.

A heart. Not hers, but so close. Her mother's heart, as she had heard it in her mother's womb.

They were opening her up like a book and reading her. Not that they understood, not that they saw in detail, for their comments were more general.

"That seemed sad," Benjamin would say, and his brother would say, "Mine felt angry."

They were leeches attached to her emotions, feeling what she felt in some way that was both distant and intimate, like being groped by someone wearing thick gloves.

And then—

"Gah," said Benjamin. "The little pig has wet herself."

She had felt the truth of it. She had wanted to start crying, but she had never really stopped.

"Disgusting. I can't go on, not until she's cleaned up. KimKim take her back to her lodge," Charles had said.

"I need a rest anyway," Benjamin agreed. "Ling! I'll have a cocktail. I've earned it, eh?"

KimKim had hauled Minako, shamed and defiled, back to the lodge. "Take a shower. Change clothes," he'd said harshly.

And now she lay counting the squares in the mesh and hoping against hope that when she multiplied the two sides she would get a lovely, beautiful number.

TWENTY

They danced.

Anthony Elder and Jessica . . . He had forgotten her last name. How had he forgotten her last name?

They danced in a club where two hundred dollars and a plausible fake ID did the trick. There were advantages to being the AFGC golden boy.

They danced on a parquet floor crowded with twentysomething white guys in suits, their ties loosened and sweat matting their conservatively cut hair. They danced amid women in sexy-mannish business suits who wore moderate, serious-lawyer heels and threw their hair around a lot.

The music was pretty weak, but it didn't matter. It didn't matter. They were dancing, a dude and his girl. His girl who blew away every other female in the room.

That last part, the part about walking around with a stunning beauty, he'd almost become used to that. The looks. From the guys, from the women, the looks that said, Man, you are so not in that girl's league. But now it was different. He was still not in her league, but now she was free, and every moment she spent with him . . .

"Having fun?" he yelled into her ear, straining to be heard over the music.

"Uh-huh."

"Really?"

He heard the insecurity in his own voice. He sounded needy. Then she smiled, and it was a different smile. No one else would notice, but he did. She was flushed with pleasure. Her eyes, her amazing eyes, were bright, and they watched him.

Gratitude. That's what he felt. How strange. Gratitude. Like he wanted to thank God up in heaven.

It was real. That was the thing: it was real.

The dream came back to her as she danced.

Buried up to her neck.

Napalm in her veins.

She hummed along with the music, which was really all beat and not much melody. She looked past Anthony. There was a muscular man, black, maybe twenty-five, a gym rat, biceps stretching his leather jacket. He was checking her out. Nothing new there, they all did, but this one, this man, had something different happening. His gaze was professionally observant. He wasn't just looking at her face, her breasts, her legs, although he was certainly doing that. He was watching more closely. Sober. Thoughtful.

Suspicious. That's what he was: suspicious. When he glanced at Anthony, there was shrewd suspicion there.

So Jessica watched him back. It became a mutual thing. And then he did something casual but deliberate. He twisted on his barstool and let his jacket fall open. He had a holster and a gun on his hip, not showy, professional.

He was a cop. Some kind of cop anyway.

Jessica disengaged from Anthony.

He turned when he saw her walking away. He followed her as she walked—not sure why, not sure what she was planning—to the muscular man in the leather jacket.

"Hi," Jessica said.

"Hey," Anthony said. "Get back here."

The man said, "Hello." To Jessica, not to Anthony.

"Jessica, get your ass back out there with me," Anthony snapped. "I brought you here because you begged me."

"I like the name Jessica," the man said.

"Yeah, well, she belongs to me," Anthony said, and grabbed her arm.

The napalm in her veins caught fire. Suddenly it was as if all of her was burning, burning away the soil that held her trapped. She spun and delivered a stinging backhand to Anthony's face.

The big man moved with trained speed. He stepped between

them, said, "Whoa, whoa, whoa. Let's take it easy, right?"

Anthony, though, was not prepared to take it easy. "Fuck off, she's mine."

And that's when Jessica lost it completely. What happened next she would never be able to recall in detail. All she remembered was fists and kicks and screams of rage, and all of it coming from her.

Somehow she ended up out on the street in the cold night air. The man set her down, held her out at arm's length, and said, "Okay now, relax, ma'am."

The "ma'am" was as much a giveaway as the gun. Regular people did not call teenage girls "ma'am," that was cop-speak.

"Take it easy, he's gone," the man said. "You're safe."

The rage was cooling, but the memory of that sudden explosion filled Jessica with a different warmth. She was sweating and shivering all at once. "Who are you?"

And out came the badge. "Agent DeShawn Franklin, Secret Service."

She was nonplussed. "Secret Service. Then . . . You know? About Anthony?"

"Is that your boyfriend in there?"

"He's not . . . He's my . . . I . . ."

"Take a breath. It's okay. You're safe. What is it you think I know?" He made a wry but wary grin. "Look, if you're holding drugs, that's not my thing to worry about. Secret Service, not DEA."

"You take care of the president."

"That's one of the things we do, ma'am. Jessica. You want to tell me something, I can see that."

"Anthony," she began, then glanced over her shoulder as if expecting him to be behind her. He was nowhere to be seen. "Anthony, I think he did something to me. And I think he's doing it to the president, too."

"Plath," Keats said.

"Sadie. Sadie and Noah. Let's try that."

"Sadie."

They had found a place: the stunted bell tower. The stairs leading up were narrow and rickety, and they'd had to bow their heads and press steadying hands against the wall as they climbed up. But at the top there was still a bell, an actual, old-fashioned bell maybe a foot across at the base. It had not been rung in a very long time, and spiders had taken it over as an arachnid condo.

The space around the bell was cramped but swept relatively clean by breezes blowing through the low, open windows. They could at least stand upright, and a series of tiny horizontal ventilation slats gave them a sort of film noir view of the world outside.

It was cold. They could each see the other's breath. A small slice of the brilliantly lit Capitol Dome was visible, but it looked cold, too. "You know what I wish?" Noah asked. "I wished I smoked cigarettes.

It would be lovely to stand up here and sort of contemplatively smoke a cigarette."

"Contemplatively?"

"Of course I imagine a cancerous lung must be a hell of a thing to see down in the nano."

"All things considered I'm not so worried about cancer."

"No?"

"Normal people are worried about cancer."

"And that's not us?"

She forced a short laugh, wanting to acknowledge the weak attempt at humor. "Do you think either of us ever was? Normal?"

"I was," he said.

"Tell me."

"Tell you what?"

"Tell me about normal."

"What, me? Well, Miss McLure . . ."

"Ms." she corrected.

"Really? All right then, Ms. McLure. Here's my normal. Up early. It's cold in the flat because the radiator in my room doesn't work very well, and if I want to be warm then my mum's room has to be the Sahara."

"Can't you get it fixed?"

"Well, yes, normally I'd ring for the butler—"

"Don't start," she snapped.

"Why are you so touchy about being rich?"

"Because I want to be loved for myself." She said it lightly, a toss-off, as a joke.

"I didn't think you wanted to be loved at all," he said.

"Ah. Well, there's a difference between wanting to be in love and wanting to be loved." She shivered. "I'm freezing."

"Shall we go down?"

She shot him a look from beneath lowered eyelids. "How do you not recognize a cue to offer me some warmth?"

He put his arm around her.

"Still cold," she said.

He took her in his arms. She put her arms around his waist and pressed against him, the side of her face flattened against his chest. She breathed deeply. She felt her breasts flattening against his abdomen.

He was breathing in her hair.

"So it's cold in your room," she prompted.

"Sorry?"

"You were telling me about normal."

"Was I? Sorry, I was busy thinking about football. Desperately thinking about football. Remembering all the details of a particular match . . ."

"Mmm," she said. "You like sports?"

"Yes. I find sports to be an excellent distraction."

"From?"

But she had lost interest in banter, really, and he didn't bother to answer. Instead he ran his fingers through her hair and pulled her close for a kiss.

Her heart wasn't in it. She was distracted.

"What?" he asked.

"Keats . . . Noah . . . Those beaches we were talking about. What if it was possible? I mean, what if I had a way to—"

A scream.

Keats and Plath froze. "That's not Vincent," she said.

"Billy!"

They bolted for the stairs.

Billy saw the palm of his own hand as an unworldly terrain, gently rolling hills crossed by an irrational crosshatch of ditches, some shallow enough that his nanobots could step over them easily, others deep enough to hide a nanobot from view.

He experimented by closing his hand slowly. The land curved up around his nanobots. It lifted him at the same time as it began to shut out the strong light. Fingers . . . They looked so huge! Like someone had made sausages the size of Metro trains. They were even segmented like a train, each section of finger like a car. They came together as they closed, blocking light, creating deep canyons in the sky. The surface was again covered in slashes, left, right, diagonal, in every direction. It looked like some arcane script, like writing in a language he could never hope to understand.

He opened his hand slowly. The massive scarred fingers swept back and away, like watching one of those time-lapse things of a flower opening its petals, bud becoming blossom.

Light flooded over his troops, his nanobots.

His tiny army.

But enough of palms and fingers, he wanted to see more. He wanted to see what the older BZRKers had always talked of in awed tones. He wanted to go down in the meat. He wanted to confront the beasties. He wanted battle.

He wanted game.

He glanced at Burnofsky. The man looked at him with an expression that reminded Billy of rats he had seen in the alleys behind his foster home. Knowing. Wary but not fearful. Contemptuous.

Billy sent his nanobots speeding across his palm—leaping, cavorting, even lowering the center wheel for a bit, though this proved to be not a practical idea on this terrain. He cartwheeled a couple of the nanobots in the process of learning this fact.

The nanobots raced madly, legs motoring along like blue-tinged cavalry. He picked the middle finger to climb. And it was a climb now: when they slipped the nanobots fell backward, like Jack and Jill falling back down the hill. But gravity hadn't too much meaning for nanobots. A slip, a fall, meant little, which gave him a reckless courage.

He laughed.

"Fun, eh?" Burnofsky said. "Hurry and get off your hand. Get somewhere more interesting."

Billy shot him a suspicious look. Burnofsky prodded him. "Don't be scared, little boy," he crooned. "You'll be part of history. A first. And I've got a ringside seat."

"What are you talking about?"

Burnofsky made a lopsided grin. "It doesn't matter. Game on, Billy the Kid."

The nanobots reached the end of Billy's finger.

He raised that finger toward his face.

In the up-is-down and none-of-it-matters world of the nano, the fingertip seemed to plunge down toward the face. Like a massive rocket aiming for impact, and Billy was riding that rocket.

Yee-hah.

Billy went around the circumference of his finger. He crossed from plowed farmland to an eerie moonscape, like the dried-out salt flats of Death Valley, hard-baked shale plates, not nearly as smooth down at the nano level as fingernails were up in the macro. Down here what was up there was like roof shingles.

But ahead, oh, there was the stuff, there was the world-wide wall of meat, the cheek, and above it a globe like the moon sunk into a pulpy earth. The eyeball. His eyeball.

The nanobots leapt from the crusty ground of the fingernail

onto an endless curved plain of fallen leaves, and then slowed.

"Three minutes," Burnofsky said. "It will begin now."

The nanobots deployed curved hooklike blades from the ends of their rear lègs. The front legs continued to power forward and the rear legs sank into the dried outer layer of epidermis, those fallen leaves of dead flesh, and began to plow them up.

When they had plowed a furrow—and there was no pain in harvesting dead skin cells—they stopped.

They turned.

Billy punched the virtual controls. He frowned, and Burnofsky saw that frown.

"I wish I could see what you're seeing, Billy."

The nanobots revealed then a feature that was unexpected. A jaw, toothless, but curving like the Joker's slashed mouth, opened at the bottom of the nanobot.

The ripped and torn skin cells were sucked into the unhinged jaws.

Within seconds the nanobots began defecating a pinkish paste.

What happened next was a blur Billy couldn't even see. The nanobots ' legs moved like a spider on speed. Or like a sculptor, wasn't that what they called guys who carved statues? A shape began to emerge from the pink goo.

Other things—tiny needles, busy sculpting cilia, jets of flame, on and off in an instant. A faint haze almost that was the MightyMites crawling across the nanobots like fleas on a dog, a scarcely visible blur of activity.

He was seeing programmed activity, he knew that much. He was seeing something that he was not controlling.

He looked for a Stop button. He searched the controls, punching this and that, trying to distract the nanobots, trying to make them do this or that. Or anything.

But his controls were no longer controlling. A prompt appeared, demanding a code.

"What's happening?" Billy asked.

"Watch," Burnofsky said with an almost sensuous whisper.

"The controls aren't working."

"No, they won't now unless you punch in the code. Thirty-two characters, alphanumeric," Burnofsky said. "If you just start guessing, you should be able to hit the right sequence within, oh, probably a year—"

"Give it to me!"

It was now clear to Billy what was happening. New nanobots were being built from the pink goo.

As he watched the new monsters rose. They were crude, post-apocalyptic versions of the original nanobots, less sharp-edged, rougher, simpler.

And then, they began to dig.

It was then that Billy screamed.

Minako woke from troubled sleep. She gasped as memories came flooding back.

She rolled onto her side, swung her legs off the bed, and stood up. She still smelled of urine. She had not had the strength to shower before.

Would they come for her again?

Please, no. Please. No.

The ship was pitching and rolling far worse than before. Somewhere outside, in the world beyond this terrible gleaming sphere, a major storm must be raging. She felt sick to her stomach and ran, wobbly, to the tiny bathroom. But by the time she made it there the nausea had lessened. She closed the door with barely room to sit down on the toilet.

She had to lace her fingers together to keep them from shaking, but even then they trembled, and the trembling went all the way through her.

She sat and there was the door directly before her and there was something on the door.

A piece of toilet paper, just a single square held there with a tiny piece of tape.

Someone had written on it in pen.

It said: *Be strong. You are not alone.*

"Yes, I want a goddamned cigarette."

"But, Madam President, you don't smoke."

That was from her chief of staff, Ginny Gastrell. Gastrell was painfully thin, with a sort of concave chest, knobby elbows, and hands that could almost have belonged to a man. She was often described by detractors as looking like the weak horse in the third race at Belmont.

"I did smoke, though. I gave it up. Now I want it back," Helen Falkenhym Morales said. She was in the Oval Office, staring through the bulletproof glass at the South Lawn. "I gave it up and I want it back. I want a cigarette. Surely someone in this place still smokes."

"Madam President, you—"

"I want a goddamned cigarette! I'm the goddamned president of the goddamned United States, and I want a goddamned cigarette!"

"Yes, Madam President. I think one of the Secret Service agents . . ." She let herself out.

The president went back to reading a report on her pad, an endless, dire report on the rash of bizarre terrorist or suspected terrorist incidents.

The plane crash in Jets stadium.

The bombing and shootout at the United Nations.

The murder of the sole surviving suspect from that bombing—she had been identified, finally. A good girl, of course, weren't they all, from a good Indian American home in Connecticut. Someone had gotten into her secure hospital room, incapacitated the FBI agent in the room with her, and pumped liquified white phosphorous into her brain. By the time anyone had discovered her, she had a meatless, empty skull sitting atop her shoulders.

A massacre in a house right on Capitol Hill.

Worst of all, for the moment at least, Washington, DC, police were all over the massacre in the bookstore. The FBI had tried hard to federalize it and been told in no uncertain terms to drop dead. A cop had been shot. No way the PD didn't investigate.

And what they were turning up was Rios's ETA. Evidence was mounting that the witnesses had been right: the lead shooter had ID'd herself as ETA and she was, in fact, ETA.

The president had scheduled a meeting with Rios. She liked him. She liked him a great deal, although she seemed to remember that at first she hadn't. He'd grown on her, then. Lately she had come to think he reminded her of an early political mentor, Senator Reynolds, a man of unshakable integrity.

Not that Rios looked or sounded or acted anything like the senator. Just . . . well, there was some connection there . . .

But now she and her administration were about to be jammed up over Rios's disaster of an agency.

"And that's why I need a cigarette," she snarled.

Gastrell reappeared. She held a single cigarette in her hand, and a green Bic lighter. She placed them on the desk in front of the president, every fiber of her being radiating disapproval.

"You're too much a Puritan, Ginny. Live a little. I'm going to. What do you think: How soon after the memorial service can I start dating?"

"Have you finalized your eulogy?"

"I've finalized everything. Final." She lit the cigarette and inhaled deeply. "Oh, sweet home." She looked at the chief of staff and said, "Let me have women about me that are fat / Sleek-headed women and such as sleep a-nights. Yond Gastrell has a lean and hungry look. / She thinks too much. Such women are dangerous."

It was a speech from Shakespeare. From the play *Julius Caesar.*

"Madam President," Gastrell said, choking down her anger. "I have to tell you something. You may get a question about it."

A deep inhalation. The president blew a smoke ring and laughed at it. "What now, Ginny? What now?"

"There's a video. It just showed up and it already has two hundred thousand views. It will hit ten times that within twenty-four hours."

"An especially cute kitty?"

"It's a fake, of course, but it's very well done. It appears to be video of you. No, not actually of you. Video as if someone had a camera mounted . . . actually . . . Let me show you."

The chief of staff leaned in with her own pad, turned it to landscape, and tapped the screen.

Rough, jerky, maddeningly low-quality video showed various scenes, all apparently within the White House private quarters.

"So?"

"Wait."

Suddenly the picture changed and there was Monte Morales.

There he was lying on his back, chest bare, face contorted.

And there he was talking, though there was no audio.

And there he was with hands, feminine hands, on either side of his head.

"Ah-ah-AHHH!" the president cried. She wanted to cover her mouth but instead grabbed her own blouse as if roughing herself up.

Gastrell put a hand on the president's shoulder. "I'm sorry, I should have warned you. It's despicable. Even by Internet standards it's vile."

And now Monte was being dragged.

And now he was slipping below the water in the tub, and the blood was a swirling smoke pattern around his head.

"Ah," the president said. "Ah. Oh. Oh, God."

"We can try to get it taken down, but it's already propagated everywhere. Anonymous is claiming credit. They claim . . . well, it doesn't matter."

The president's fist clenched around the cigarette. It burned into her palm and gave off the sickening barbecue smell of burning flesh.

"Are you all right, Madam President?"

"It's a fake. It's a fake."

"Obviously. But it's well done, as I said. The backgrounds look very much like the actual bathroom. The Secret Service is analyzing it, so it can be thoroughly debunked."

"Debunked," the president whispered.

"I wanted you to know."

"Debunked." She opened her hand and saw an angry oval burn in her palm, right over her lifeline.

"Get out," the president said.

"There's the briefing on the Azerbaijan situation in twenty minutes."

But the president wasn't listening. She pushed abruptly away from her desk and ran toward the private quarters.

TWENTY-ONE

KimKim, a second crewman, and a middle-aged woman from two levels up came for Minako. Minako had seen the woman around. She thought she might be Australian.

"My name is Kyla. You must be so honored," the woman gushed.

"I want out of here," Minako said. "I want to go home. You people have no right to keep me here! Let me go!"

"Oh, that's silliness, dear. Everything is fine. Everything is wonderful. This is the most wonderful place in the world."

"You're brainwashed. You're crazy!" How many times could she say that? What was the point in yelling at crazy people?

"Oh, don't be ridiculous," Kyla said. "I couldn't be happier."

"It's what they've done to you," Minako said, trying desperately to communicate, to make the woman understand. "You aren't thinking right. This place . . . those horrible men, those monsters!"

The slap came hard and fast. It was open palm and hit its intended target perfectly. Minako's cheek stung, and she was shocked into silence.

"I'm sorry, sweetie, but you simply must not insult the Great

Souls. They know best. They're geniuses, don't you see that? You're too young to understand."

"Enough, let's go," the second crewman said impatiently. "The bosses said fetch her, so let's fetch her and be done with it."

"Absolutely!" Kyla said. "And quickly, too!"

The two crewmen each grabbed an arm.

"This one wants to hurt me, is that part of your madness, too?" Minako demanded of Kyla.

"Nothing happens in Benjaminia or in Charlestown, either, unless it is the will of the Great Souls," Kyla said. "I wouldn't worry."

Back in the room. The same machine lay waiting. The monsters had not yet returned.

"You can go," KimKim informed Kyla.

"I'm sorry, but you don't dismiss me," Kyla said. "You're just crew. You aren't even enlightened. You are not sustainably happy."

"Whatever, just bug off," the second crewman said.

"No!" Minako cried. "Don't leave, they'll do terrible things to me! It's a trick!"

"It is a bit of a trick," the second crewman said with a sigh. His left fist shot out, and Kyla's head snapped back. She fell straight back onto the deck, her head bouncing from the impact.

Minako yanked free of KimKim but didn't make it far: he was quick. His hand closed around her arm like a vice. And he said, "You are not alone."

Minako froze.

Then, in Japanese so flawless it could only have come from a native speaker, he said, "My full name is Kenshin Sugita—KimKim is my nickname. I work for the Naichō, the intelligence service of Japan."

"But you tried . . ." she gasped.

"No. I knew they would never break the rules, the men are too afraid. But it made them trust me."

She looked at the second crewman, who shrugged and said, "Listen, I've only been on this floating hell for a couple of weeks. I needed work. Bad. But enough is damned well enough. My name is Silver. Formerly Gunnery Sergeant Silver. U.S. Marine Corps."

"My father is . . . my father was a marine."

"That's why I'm going to get myself killed with this crazy Nip, here," Silver said. "And you should know better than to say anyone was a marine, past tense. In or out of service, alive or dead: once a marine, always a marine."

Minako drew a shaky breath. "Semper fi?"

"Damn straight. Now, let's get the hell off this boat."

"How . . ." Minako began, faltering. Then she tried again. "How old are you?"

KimKim looked at her like she might already be crazy. "I'm twenty-nine."

"As I recall, I'm forty-seven," Silver said, puzzled.

Minako smiled her first smile since Okinawa. Twenty-nine and forty-seven. Both were prime numbers.

• • •

Keats took the rickety steps two at a time, with Plath hot on his heels. Burnofsky was still tied to the scaffold. Billy had a twitcher headset on, a glove on one hand, the other hand clawing at his face.

Billy shrieked. "They're eating me!"

"What?" Keats shot a hard look at Burnofsky, but the old man seemed to be almost dreamy, a slight smile on his bloodless lips, eyes half closed.

Nijinsky and Wilkes came running.

Keats ripped the twitcher goggles off Billy's head and settled them onto his own.

Plath said, "It just looks that way, Billy, you've never been down in the meat before."

But while she was placating, Keats was seeing.

At least two dozen nanobots were busily scraping at Billy's skin. There was something like pinkish ash lumped here and there in piles. And as he watched a stray dust mite came lumbering along, oblivious to everything, nearly blind, a harmless but grotesque consumer of sloughed skin cells.

The mite was about the size of the nanobots, a fat, swollen spider-like creature with stubby legs. The nanobots ignored the mite as they tunneled eagerly into epidermis. Then the mite blundered into one of the nanobots and in an invisibly fast motion the nanobot cut the mite into two pieces. Other nanobots rushed to help, and the mite spasmed as it died.

The nanobots ate the pieces of the mite.

Other nanobots ate Billy's skin.

They began to extrude a paste, and other biots rushed to that paste and with a blur of tiny tools and jets of flame—

"They're building more nanobots!" Keats said.

"What?" Nijinsky had come running from downstairs. He angrily snatched the goggles from Keats. He looked. He pulled the glove from Billy's hand and slipped it on. Like he was the responsible professional who would tell them all . . .

"Can't be," Nijinsky said.

"Oh, I think it can," Burnofsky said.

Nijinsky took the goggles from his head and dropped them on the floor. "Self-replication is biological, not mechanical," he said, repeating what he'd been told once, somewhere. "Those nanobots are complex machines."

"Indeed," Burnofsky said. "And I appreciate the compliment." He turned to Plath. "Of course, I was building on your father's work—"

"His work wasn't this," Plath said. "He didn't do research so he could destroy, he—"

"He did it for the same reason we all do it. For ego. To say he'd done it. To not only play God but to be God!" Burnofsky shouted. "You spoiled little brat, you aren't the pimple on her ass. If she was alive, she'd—" Suddenly he seemed unable to catch his breath.

"Who? Who are you talking about?" Keats asked. "That daughter you murdered?"

"Give me a fucking drink!" Burnofsky yelled, spittle flying.

"Tell me how to turn off those nanobots," Nijinsky shot back.

"Oh, no, I don't think so," Burnofsky said. "I don't think I'll do that. And we call them hydras. Cute, isn't it?"

"It's starting to hurt," Billy said, almost like he didn't want to interrupt. A thin trickle of blood ran down his cheek.

"Stop them," Nijinsky said. "You know what happens in this scenario. You can't want that."

"Give me a drink, pretty boy," Burnofsky said. "Hold it to my lips and pour."

Nijinsky froze, indecisive.

"Jin, give him the drink," Plath said.

Wilkes snatched the bottle, stuck the entire neck of it in Burnofsky's mouth, and upended it. Burnofsky gagged and swallowed and choked, but Wilkes kept the bottle elevated.

Finally she pulled it away. "Now talk. How do we stop it?"

Burnofsky coughed until the cough turned into a laugh. His voice was a harsh rasp. "I never said I'd tell you anything."

"You guys need to help me," Billy said urgently.

"Hah," Burnofsky said. "They need to incinerate you, kid. That's what they need to do."

"What?" Billy asked, his voice quavering. "What does that mean?"

"Nothing," Plath snapped.

"You're going to do this to a child?" Nijinsky demanded.

"A child? A child, singular?"

"I don't believe it," Keats said, shaking his head. "No matter how degenerate you are, no matter what you've done, you can't sit here and watch it happen."

Burnofsky's stare was from very far away. "Well, my little Limey friend, it won't be the first, will it? The first time, I saw it very close and very personal. She looked at me. . . . She didn't know . . . but she felt it, inside her . . . She felt death, you know, she felt it, even though she was young and what did she know about death? She looked at me and said, Daddy . . . And she never called me Daddy that way before. Not in a long time, not since she was a little girl . . ." He lost the thread for a minute, then recovered, lifted his chin up off his chest. "I'm doing it to them all, all the children. I'm doing it to the whole human race. All of life. I'm cleaning this filthy planet. All of you," Burnofsky said. "All of everything. Welcome to the end of the world."

TWENTY-TWO

"Give me that." Keats took the nanobot controller from Billy.

"We don't have the code," Nijinsky pointed out.

"I'm not trying to stop the hydras, I'm going to kill them. I'm going to switch over and use the dozen nanobots Burnofsky planted on Plath. And I'm pulling my biots from Plath and Burnofsky."

Burnofsky snorted. "Try to run biots and nanobots simultaneously? I don't think so."

"Wilkes?" Keats said as he slid on the twitcher glove. "If he argues, give him the brick again. Just don't hit his right eye, I'm walking my biot out that way."

"This isn't a fight against Bug Man," Plath pointed out. "These hydras are on automatic, right? Uncontrolled? I'm getting in on this, too."

Burnofsky said, "Don't be stupid. By now there will be too many for—"

WHACK!

Wilkes did not have to be prompted. The brick smacked

Burnofsky's head with enough force to stun him into silence.

"You two are not playing hero by yourselves," Wilkes said. "I'm in, too."

It was a strange battle muster. The forces were spread far and wide, and yet, in the macro they were all within a three-foot radius.

Plath rallied all three of her biots, two fresh from their nutrient baths and functioning normally. Keats withdrew his first biot from Plath's brain and his second from Burnofsky. He took charge of the nanobots Burnofsky had planted on Plath—these, at least, were controllable.

In Keats's brain there was an explosion of awareness. He saw through K1 and K2, his two biots. One raced across Burnofsky's eye. The other was racing to escape Plath's brain. But at the same moment all twelve visual inputs from the nanobots appeared in his goggles.

He was seeing fourteen distinct visuals, the nanobot inputs unfamiliar, crude seeming, compared to the direct mind-to-mind control of twitcher over biot.

Fourteen creatures under his control, on Plath, on Burnofsky, all needing to be moved as quickly as possible to Billy's cheek. It was somewhere between deadly serious and absurd.

The problem was: it was impossible. Keats knew that, felt his heart sinking as he realized that no one, not Bug Man, no not even Vincent, could manage this army. He platooned the nanobots, but if he was going to hunt down and kill every last hydra he would need to control his nanobots individually.

Impossible. He took a step back and must have seemed about to faint because Nijinsky caught him.

"Billy, haul that pew over here," Nijinsky said. "I'll do the transfer. First, I'll touch Plath's cheek to get the nanobots."

"Yeah," Keats said. Then, not meaning to say it out loud, "No way."

He could control the nanobots well enough to race toward the massive finger that lightly touched Plath's face. He could send them scampering along the polish-tarred fingernail. And having done that, he could march one biot down Plath's optic nerve and another from Burnofsky's eye through the fringe of eyelash trees. But not all at once.

The hydras would continue to replicate. Every passing second would mean more foes to be destroyed. And he would have to get them all, every last one. Leave even a single hydra alive to start the process all over again and Billy would be eaten alive.

Fail, let even one hydra survive, and they would have no choice but to destroy Billy themselves—kill him and burn him to ashes.

Suddenly, in one of his far-too-numerous visuals, he saw the first of Plath's biots. It was hideous, a bug, an attenuated grasshopper, a mite, a tiny monster that loomed six feet tall in the nano subjective. Its face—an insect's eyes joined by eyes that were an awful parody of Plath's own eyes. The effect was disturbing and haunting, as if the face he loved had been skinned from her and then blowtorch-melted onto a spider's face.

"Is that you?" Plath asked him up in the world, but it felt somehow as if it was coming from the biot.

"I guess so," he said.

"You're better at this than I am," she said. "I'll follow you."

"I'm coming in behind you two," Wilkes said.

Keats started to say that no one was better at this, because no one could possibly be good at this. But nevertheless he moved his two biots and dozen nanobots forward.

Like cavalry and infantry, he thought. The nanobots would be the foot soldiers, the pawns, he could lose them. The biots were more precious. They were the king on this chessboard: to lose one was to lose all.

A second Plath biot joined up, and a third, the new one. Keats wondered about its capabilities.

"I may not be able to talk later," Keats said. "I may . . . Anyway, I know you don't want to hear this, but I love you, Sadie."

Burnofsky cleared his throat.

"I still have the brick," Wilkes warned him. "So shut up and leave Katniss and Peeta alone."

Plath should have told him she loved him, too, but those would have just been words. Instead she sent her biots racing forward after his, determined that she would not let him lose this fight.

They reached a rushing, tumbling avalanche of red disks—the

blood flowing from the hole in Billy's cheek. It was a surging flood of licked red cough drops, rolling by like a rocky whitewater river. In with the red disks were spongy white blood cells. And something Keats had never seen before, a kind of thick spiderweb that threw weak and inadequate ropes over the rushing platelets.

"Clotting factor," Plath said. She was beside him on the pew. He couldn't see her with the goggles in place. He knew he could move his leg slightly and make physical contact with her, and wanted to, but he worried it might distract her.

They raced along beside the red, red avalanche of blood toward the rim of the volcano that spewed this body-temperature lava.

Keats slowed the pace of his biots and saw that Plath was following suit. The nanobots kept on at full speed.

Ahead, a single blue hydra could be seen atop the crater's rim, gobbling up passing platelets.

"Mine," he whispered to Plath.

The front of his first platoon of nanobots hit the single hydra. Six nanobots tore into the hydra and ripped it apart. Hydra legs went flying through the air.

Easy. An easy kill.

"Come on," Keats said and Plath heard him, of course, and followed him. Twelve nanobots and five biots powered over the crater rim. They were staring down into a witch's cauldron, a stew of blood cells—red and white, plus clotting factor stretched like fishing nets out from the sides of the hole. The cells spilled steadily over the side, dragging clotting nets with them.

Hydras—an uncountable mass of them—were pushing down through the blood cells, swallowing some, pushing others aside. You couldn't call it swimming, it looked much more like giant bugs digging their way into soggy gravel.

The main body of hydras was chewing through the deeper epidermal layers, tunneling sideways. They were tunneling beneath the dead outer layer, down through spongy pinkish-gray meat.

Keats faced decision time sooner than he'd hoped. Two groups of hydras heading in different directions. No more platooning. He had to pursue in both directions. Six nanobots, one biot; to Plath, he said, "Stay up there on the rim, catch anything that comes back out. When Wilkes gets here, she comes in behind me."

"I do. Care," Plath said.

But Keats didn't hear it. He let himself go and fell into the pictures in his head. The movements of his fingers would be sequential, one then another, then another, but there was no way, no way in hell to do it unless he lost himself.

Fourteen microscopic creatures to move in two radically different environments.

Don't think.

K1 and six nanobots dived after the hydras heading down into the blood.

K2 and six nanobots raced after the ones tunneling into the subcutaneous fat of Billy's face.

Keats heard nothing. He lost awareness of the room he was in. Forgot Plath. Did not feel the hard pew under his thighs. Was not thirsty or hungry. His heart did not beat, he did not breathe, not so that he noticed, anyway.

Once before, when he had been tested, all the way back in London, he had gone away like this, lost himself in the game, felt nothing, ceased to exist as a consciousness.

Within the red gravel a hydra leg. One of Keats's nanobots clawed it and reeled the hydra in. The others swarmed over the first and over the shredded hydra using both as a ladder, fighting the surge and pause, surge and pause of the red avalanche.

Seven different views of platelets and lymphocytes and clotting fibers. Seven sets of arms and legs, all swarming, all searching, catching a second hydra, ripping it apart, another and stabbing it, and another and another, catching up to a massed body of the replicated hydras, weak, shambling disjointed creatures built with only one ability: to build more of themselves.

The hydras did not fight, they were not controlled, they were as simple and mindless as mites, no one in charge; they were on automatic. They didn't fight, they didn't flee, they just gobbled up flesh and shit out carbon while the MightyMites did their sub-visible work, building more, ever more hydras.

Not Keats's concern. Just kill them.

A millimeter and a world away K2 and six nanobots squeezed through fat cells like partly deflated beach balls made of wax, all white with clinging platelets and strands of unknown fibers. The hydras had stopped tunneling and now were digging and consuming, creating a sort of cavern in the skin as they entered a new replication cycle.

They were everywhere in the cavern, top, bottom, sides, all busy and oblivious and Keats tore into them, slaughtering, dismembering. It was like work in a meatpacker's plant, assembly-line chopping and hacking, killing as fast and efficiently as he could.

The bodies of massacred hydras clogged the cavern until his nanobots were forced to dig through the debris of their bodies to find more to kill. Lymphocytes were oozing into the chamber, adding their slow-moving predation to the slaughter.

And then, a very different creature. Also blue, also a hydra, but gleaming with sharp, distinct lines, with bristling weapons. But even this, a first-generation hydra, a factory-made hydra not a cheap replicant, was uncontrolled. Mindless. Programmed.

K1 yanked out two legs and left it crippled and helpless. The lymphocytes would finish the job.

Heedless, a mad rush now, just rush, all fourteen visuals at once, and oh, God, it was good.

It was blankness. Emptiness and fulfillment. A wild beast, fourteen wild beasts, chasing and killing and chasing and killing.

• • •

Plath, not wearing the goggles, able still to see in the macro, up in the world, saw an ecstatic smile on Keats's face. She had never seen him smile like that, lips trembling, teeth bare.

She felt her gaze drawn irresistibly to Burnofsky. She expected to see him gloating at the animal revealed in Keats. But he was not gloating. His mouth worked, and he chewed his lip. His washed-out eyes were hungry.

He was jealous. He was a junkie watching another addict mainlining the ultimate drug.

Plath felt sick. Her biots waited on the crater as Wilkes's two biots came rushing by and swan dived into the blood. Clotting nets were slowing the flow now. Plath couldn't see Keats's nanobots or biots, just the tumbling platelets and, riding that red tide like driftwood, the nanobot legs, heads, and insides.

A tear rolled down Burnofsky's cheek.

Keats's blue, blue eyes had disappeared behind the bug-eyed goggles.

Wilkes was laughing to herself. Heh-heh-heh.

He'd said he loved her, and she had not answered. Now she wondered if she gave him everything he wanted, her body, even her love, would any of it matter as much to Keats as this terrible game?

"What's happening?" Billy asked her.

"Madness," Plath answered.

• • •

Pia Valquist and Admiral Edward Domville rode through the storm aboard a Royal Navy Sea King helicopter. It was not the very best way to travel through high winds and lightning. The natural background noise of the helicopter itself was deafening, but when you added shrieking winds and sudden thunder like God tearing the sky open with his bare hands, you had a great deal of noise.

And a great deal of movement as pockets of wind acted like surprise elevators, dropping the Sea King hundreds of feet, or shooting it suddenly upward, all the while buffeting it back and forth. There was something about the constant bobbing and weaving that made Pia think of a boxer in the ring, always keeping his head in motion.

Admiral Domville was less inclined to be thinking of colorful descriptions. He was busy being sick into a plastic bucket.

"Seasickness is nothing to be ashamed of!" Pia yelled at the top of her lungs.

"Nelson was frequently seasick," Domville yelled back during a brief moment of coherence.

Then, quite suddenly, they were through the storm, and the massive piles of dark gray clouds gave way to scattered clouds lit by a fading sun. The noise was still ferocious, and the motion of the helicopter was still erratic, but it was nevertheless a relief.

A crewman came back and motioned to the tiny window. Pia reluctantly disentangled herself from the jump seat and stutter-stepped over to look out; she saw the *Albion* sailing serenely below them.

She gave a thumbs-up signal.

"We can land," the crewman said. "We won't have to use the winch."

"The what?" Pia asked. It was the first anyone had mentioned a winch. "Did you say 'winch'?"

The landing was fairly smooth. The reception was Royal Navy spit and polish. Domville played his role, but as soon as was decent he drew the *Albion*'s captain aside. Introductions were brief and to the point.

"Captain, I'm going to ask for the loan of some of your marines."

"Certainly, sir," the captain said, as though nothing could be more natural than an admiral dropping out of the sky in company with a Swedish spy and demanding to abscond with a platoon of his men.

"We need to have a conversation with an LNG carrier that is rapidly approaching Hong Kong harbor." He gave the course and position of the *Doll Ship*.

"We'll have to step smartly if we're to intercept before they reach Chinese territorial waters," the captain said.

"Indeed."

"Just time for a cup of tea before you go," the captain said briskly.

Minako did not want to get her hopes up, not yet. Hope would just make her heart beat faster, and she could barely draw breath as it was.

Were they really here to rescue her?

"Only two ways off this ship," Silver said. "We take a lifeboat, or we steal that helicopter. I can fly the chopper, but it's been a good long while, and that's a pretty good storm raging out there."

"It's supposed to blow itself out," KimKim said. "If they see us take a boat they'll be on us in a heartbeat. It has to be the helicopter."

"Yep," Silver said.

Neither man looked happy about it.

With his gun hand low and out of sight, KimKim cracked the steel door and peeked out.

Minako noticed that only KimKim had a gun. Silver did not. Silver was a big man, but Minako did not believe in magic or in Jackie Chan. One man with big fists was nothing against the mad villagers of Benjaminia and Charlestown.

The prime numbers helped. But many more men with many more guns would help more.

"Down the hallway, take the stairway down two decks, out to the landing pad. We hole up in the flight tech's quarters. If the pilot's there, we convince him to help us."

Silver nodded. "You're the James Bond here, I'm just a grunt."

"Minako. Stay close." KimKim opened the door followed immediately by Silver and Minako.

One-two-three-four-five . . .

They clattered down and that's when Minako saw her mother

standing there, standing right there on the steps and she stopped and cried out and KimKim walked right through Minako's mother and so did Silver.

Like she wasn't there, no, impossible. And yet, she was.

Minako had counted the thirteenth step. And there was her mother.

She took another step, number fourteen, and her mother was gone. Like she had never been there. And of course, how could she have been?

Fifteen-sixteen-seventeen-and nothing, no mother, just the two scared but determined men glancing over their shoulders to make sure she was keeping up.

The first flight of steps counted nineteen, a prime. If the second flight was the same, that would be good.

One-two-three . . .

She counted to thirteen and—her mother, as real as anything she had ever seen, as real as real could be except that KimKim and Silver again stepped straight through her.

Minako froze.

The two men reached the bottom, noticed she wasn't with them and Silver said, "What's the matter, honey?"

"I . . ."

"Are you okay?" KimKim asked her in Japanese.

"I see my mother. I see her. Right there!" She pointed a finger at what was empty space to both men. "The thirteenth step. The same as the last time. The thirteenth step."

Shaky, she took the fourteenth step and her mother disappeared. "There's something . . . They did something to me. To my brain."

KimKim took the steps two at a time to reach her. "That may be, Minako; that's what they do. They do things inside your brain. You must ignore it. You must follow me and Sergeant Silver, and pay attention to nothing else."

Minako sobbed. "I'm not good at that. I'm not . . . not good at ignoring things."

"Yes, but you are a brave girl, and you will do it," the spy said. He had taken her hands in his, an awkward embrace that pressed the chilly metal of his gun against her wrist.

The door at the bottom of the stairs opened. A crewman looked up, took it all in and looked shocked and confused. He saw Minako. He saw the pistol in KimKim's hand. He saw Silver.

He hesitated.

"Keep your mouth shut and walk away," Silver said. "Don't volunteer for trouble."

The crewman nodded once and pushed past them up the stairs.

"Will he tell on us?" Minako asked.

"Fifty-fifty," Silver said. "Come on."

They made it down the stairs and stepped out onto the helipad. The rain was coming down, but it was vertical, no longer horizontal. The swell was still heavy and the ship wallowed fore and aft, up and down.

"Not so much of a cross sea," Silver commented. "And the wind is dying. Maybe an hour."

KimKim led the way to the pilot/mechanic room, which was directly off the helipad and tucked beneath an exterior stairway. He stepped in without knocking.

The pilot was there, bent over a workbench, twisting something metal with two sets of pliers. He was a man in his thirties, with longish black hair falling back from a receding hairline.

"What do you want?" he demanded, and narrowed his eyes suspiciously when he saw Minako. Silver closed the door behind them and threw the lock.

"What the hell is going on?" the pilot demanded.

"What's going on is that I have a gun," KimKim said, helpfully showing the pistol. "So that means I talk and you listen."

"I'm not scared."

"Then that's stupid, you should be scared."

The pilot forced a laugh and set the pliers aside. "I am happy," he said. "Deeply, sustainably happy. Fear has no place in happiness."

"He's one of them," Silver said contemptuously.

"Yes," KimKim said with a sigh.

Silver took one quick step and snapped a hard left into the pilot's face. His second blow was an uppercut that turned the pilot's legs to jelly. Silver bound the man's hands and ankles with wire.

"So it's up to you to fly us out of here," KimKim said to Silver. "Do you think—"

The door opened. A man was framed in the doorway. An officer. KimKim leapt but the man was too quick. The door slammed back in KimKim's face.

KimKim threw open the door, but it was too late. There was no one in sight.

"We have about ten seconds to figure something out," Silver said.

"Get that helicopter in the air!" KimKim yelled.

The three of them bolted for the helicopter. The cockpit was not locked, but the craft itself was tied down to the deck, lashed with padded chains.

"Cast us off!" Silver yelled, and climbed up into the pilot's seat. Minako hauled herself into the surprisingly spacious and oddly configured backseat, and sat there drenched, teeth chattering. One-two-three . . .

When she got to thirteen, her mother was standing outside in the rain. The illusion was perfect. Her mother's hair was blowing. Her police uniform was turning a darker shade of blue as the rain stained it. The only thing missing was any kind of real reaction to Minako or to her environment. It was as if her mother was a very limited computer program, like the illusion knew how to be affected by the environment, but not how to respond to it.

Fourteen.

And her mother was gone.

"You down there, back away from the helicopter." It was a voice magnified by a megaphone; even then it was half snatched away by the wind.

Minako leaned forward to look up and out. There. Two ship's officers in yellow slickers.

KimKim continued throwing off the straps. Silver was flipping switches in the cockpit. Minako pulled the harness belts tight around her but they weren't made for anyone her shape. She realized, suddenly, that the seat was built for Charles and Benjamin.

The officers were motioning. Men were rushing from aft, from behind Minako's line of sight.

KimKim aimed fast and fired. A man went down, clutching his leg. That reversed the charge of crewmen.

Minako heard an electrical sound, a sort of whine. A gust made the helicopter tremble.

KimKim was fighting the last tie-down strap, but it was jammed.

The rotor above began to move. Slow. . . slow. . . gaining a little speed . . .

How many revolutions per minute? Minako wondered. Was there a set number? Was it a good number?

Suddenly a riot of people, all rushing toward the helicopter. These were not cautious crew, these were residents of Benjaminia and Charlestown.

"No!" Minako cried.

KimKim threw back the last strap. He stood, facing the wave of bodies. He fired the pistol into the air.

No one stopped.

"Oh no, no, no," Minako pleaded.

KimKim lowered the pistol, took aim, and fired.

A red flower appeared in the exact center of a man's chest. The man fell backward.

This, finally, sent the mob into retreat. They didn't run far, but they had stopped charging. They might still escape, if only they could get the helicopter into the air.

The rotor was moving, but so slow, so slow!

"People! Our people! We are under attack!" Benjamin shouted. He saw the one KimKim had shot. Dead. One of his people. He had once spoken to the man. Or maybe it was some other man like him—it didn't matter, all of the people of Benjaminia were his.

Benjamin said, "Captain, open the spheres. Let all of the people out on deck, every one of them. We'll soon deal with these scum. Every one of them! We'll swarm them with sheer numbers."

The spheres began to split open like sliced oranges. From their spot on the bridge the Twins could see down into the nearest sphere, down into the structure of catwalks and braces. They saw faces suddenly turned skyward, suddenly seeing the sky for the first time in weeks or months or years.

"Rise up!" Benjamin cried, his voice ecstatic. "All of you, out onto the deck and destroy the traitors. Don't fear, attack!"

Out into the wind and rain and light they came, stumbling over unfamiliar territory, climbing over one another like ants. The people of Benjaminia, the people of Charlestown, hundreds of them, scraping their shins on sharp metal, banging into bulkheads, mad with excitement.

"Get them!" Benjamin cried. "Kill the men and save the girl!"

A woman tripped and fell into the gears of the sphere; she fell and screamed and was drawn slowly down and out of sight, like meat going into a sausage grinder.

But the sustainably happy did not hesitate. They had their orders. They had their targets in sight.

The dolls of the *Doll Ship* had come to vicious life.

And then one of the officers on the bridge yelled, "Captain! Captain! We have targets incoming!"

Every eye on the bridge swiveled to follow the direction in which he was pointing. Two Sea King helicopters, moving as fast as race cars and so low and close to the heaving waves that no radar could see them, flew, relentless, toward the *Doll Ship*.

Binoculars were snatched and sighted. "Royal Navy!"

"Shoot them down! You said you had missiles!" Charles whinnied in terror.

"They're too close, they'd hit us and blow the ship," Captain Gepfner said. "And those are Royal Marines."

"We're only half a mile from Chinese waters," the first officer reported.

But it was irrelevant information for the moment, because the nearest Sea King banked sharply, roared overhead like the wrath of God, seeming barely to miss the bridge, so close that Charles could see the faces of the men inside the Sea King's open door.

With startling speed the helicopter came to hover over the melee in a well-practiced maneuver. The second Sea King floated a hundred feet away. A swivel-mounted machine gun pointed its muzzle directly at the bridge.

Charles felt his heart stop. There was no way the deadly calm marine behind that gun would miss.

"Stop them!" Benjamin demanded.

"If we're taken it's prison for the lot of us," Gepfner said, ignoring Benjamin and speaking to his officers. "If they take us in Chinese waters it may be a firing squad." He glanced around sharply and saw the consensus form. "Life or death now, gentlemen. Break out the RPGs and issue them to the mob."

"No, sir," a junior officer said. "I am not firing on Royal Marines, sir."

Gepfner drew a pistol and without warning shot the officer in the chest. As the explosion echoed in the metal box of the bridge, he said, "I'm not ending my career in a Chinese prison waiting for a bullet at sunrise."

"This is a fight for all we love," Benjamin shouted into the loudspeaker. "Die if you must. Die for me!"

TWENTY-THREE

For the second time in a very few days Bug Man was shaking. He had run from the club, run straight out the door, raced down the street through crowds of young professionals who now, when they looked at him, did not see a very lucky guy with an amazingly hot girlfriend, but saw instead a scruffy-looking kid who was most likely running from cops.

He forced himself to stop running. Forced himself to walk, but he could not force himself to stop scraping his hand over his head again and again, as if he was trying to scrub something out of his hair.

Jesus, they would kill him for sure this time. They would kill him. But that was only Fact Number Two turning endlessly, endlessly around in his brain. Fact Number One was that she had betrayed him. The bitch! The skank! After all he had done for her, after all he had given her. Gifts and . . . He was sure he'd given her gifts. A necklace! That's right, he had given her a necklace once.

And he had given her himself. Had he ever hurt her? No. Had he ever raised a hand to her? No.

Without a backward glance, without a second thought, she had just dumped him. Dumped him. Him! The bitch! Had none of it been real? After all they'd done together, the minute he unwired her she turned on him? The minute!

The outrage built in him, feeding on itself, growing ornate and detailed, and was almost enough to force the thought of what would happen next from his mind.

The bitch. She was going to get him killed. He had shown her the president. He had taken her to the office. What the hell? And now she was with some kind of cop? What were the odds of that happening?

Where was Burnofsky? That was the question, where the hell was he? It was his fault. If Burnofsky had shown up none of this would have happened.

He had to call him. He wasn't supposed to, it was a security breach, but damn, what wasn't a security breach now? Jessica was with some kind of cop, and she knew. She knew!

He moved away from the drinking crowd and onto a quieter street. Bug Man ran the conversation in his head. Burnofsky, Jessica has gone rogue. She lost it and ran up to some cop or coplike person.

Burnofsky would ask how the hell that happened. And Bug Man would lie. He'd say nothing about unwiring her, and he definitely wouldn't talk about the way she'd looked at him suddenly as if he was some kind of lousy insect. Like he was nothing!

And for sure nothing about letting her see the nanobot feed from the president. Why had he done that? Because he thought she cared, that's why, because he wanted her to see that . . . Never mind, why wasn't the question.

Yeah, it was just one of those weird things, Burnofsky. Sometimes, you know, there's a failure rate with wiring, right?

If you have to kill her, Burnofsky, no problem, man, because she represents a threat. So, do what you gotta do, Burnofsky. The thing is, it wasn't my fault.

You want to know why was I out in the world? Why was I in some club? Because . . . because she had run off and I was trying to get her back, that's why.

Yes, that would all work. Maybe he wouldn't die. Maybe.

He reached for his phone. He kept it in the back pocket of his pants, but it wasn't there, nor was it in the front pockets, or the other back pocket, and he checked each again, because maybe he missed it.

She had it. That was it. The bitch had his phone! Or else it fell out in the cab when he was reaching for his wallet, damn, yes, he had accidentally pulled it out and set it on his knee while he was . . . and now what? Now what? Call from a pay phone? There were no damned pay phones!

The hotel. He had to get a cab and get back to the hotel right now and call Burnofsky. To hell with security, this was an emergency.

He hailed a cab, which drove on by. So did the next three.

Wait, it wasn't far to the office. He could walk there.

It was a five-minute walk, time that he divided between fearing for his own safety, wishing death and hellfire on Jessica, and feeling terribly alone.

Some new area of consciousness had opened up for Keats. He'd been lost, consumed by the game, and any self-awareness would have fatally distracted him. But this was different. This was an awareness as unreal as the state of the rest of his mind, a new feeling, a new type of consciousness.

He wasn't Noah Cotton looking at Noah Cotton, he was . . . someone. Some nameless observer. Some attenuated, thin-stretched, overheated mind watching his own brain from far away.

Look at him go, this new awareness thought. Look at the moves! Hah! Now that's game.

He remembered the testing he'd undergone what seemed like a long, long time ago under Dr. Pound. A chainsaw, the real thing, had been sawing toward his leg. Electrical shock. And yet he had stayed in the game, lost himself in the game.

What he was seeing himself do now was so far beyond that. This wasn't juggling two balls in the air, playing two games at once, it was a mind-altering expansion of the limits of his brain's function. It was an acid trip. It was nirvana.

He heard a phone ring. His new distant self was aware of Nijinsky getting up to find the phone and say, "It's Burnofsky's phone."

The hydra targets were fewer now. He was no longer killing in dozens, he was chasing down single individuals, crawling after them as they plunged into fat and blood, ripping through capillaries, plowing through a pustule of tight-packed football-size bacteria.

He killed his last one there, in the base of a pimple, having to shove seething bacteria aside while ripping the hydra apart.

The ringing stopped, Nijinsky did not answer. "Googling the number."

Each of the fourteen visual inputs now showed no hydras in sight. None in the blood, none in the fat.

The new awareness began to fade, slow as a sunset. His normal consciousness began to return. He began to feel his own heart. He knew the goggles were rimmed in sweat. His skin was cold but seemed to vibrate, like his body was plugged into a massager. His ears were ringing.

Nijinsky said, "The number is an office building in the city, looks like a main switchboard number—it ends in double zero. Not far from here, maybe eight, ten blocks."

"Bug Man?"

The phone rang again, same number.

"Did you get them all?" Billy asked him.

Keats was silent. He tried to answer but he couldn't. Words

wouldn't come yet, like that part of his brain–body connection was numb and needed to get circulation back.

"Did you get them all?" Billy asked again.

Keats was pulling out. Nanobots crawled back through the rush of platelets, easier coming back out with the current, though the current had slowed now as the clotting factor webs adhered and began to twine together. Nanobots and biots cut their way back through the fat cells that had sagged to fill in the tunnel. It was like digging out after a mine cave-in. He felt an edge of claustrophobia he hadn't experienced earlier in the mindlessness of battle. He was conscious of Wilkes's biots joining him.

Plath's biots waited as Keats's army emerged.

He wanted to ask her whether any hydras had come this way, but he wasn't all the way back yet, words still . . . Instead, one of his biots made a gesture, sweeping a claw around the crater.

"Three came back this way," Plath said up in the macro. "I got them. Take the goggles off, Keats. Do you hear me?"

Still Keats didn't speak, but a hand went up to his head and peeled them off.

His eyes moved slowly to focus on her. Then he looked down at his hand, where the goggles lay. She took them from him and he did not protest.

Wilkes pointed a finger at Keats, looked at Plath, and in a voice that was half awed, half laughing, said, "Your boyfriend here is a son of a bitch down in the meat. I mean, damn!" She nodded her head fast. "Oh yeah, honey, game. Game! He got them all, I maybe got a dozen; he didn't leave me any, he got them all."

"Nonsense," Burnofsky said. But his voice lacked any confidence. He was going through the motions, trying not to sound defeated.

"The replicants are easy to kill," Plath said. "They aren't controlled, they're just programmed, and they can't defend themselves. Even the factory models were helpless without a twitcher."

She looked from the stunned Keats to the feral Wilkes; from Nijinsky to Burnofsky. "Your big secret weapon can be killed, Burnofsky."

"Once they're in their millions you'll never stop them! You won't even find them until it's too late!"

Plath stood up. Her joints cracked from the tension. "Jin, what are we doing?"

"What do you mean?"

"I mean that call. From the office building. You know who it is, or at least who it probably is."

"It's probably a big building. It's getting light out. . . ."

Plath stared at him. Was he looking for an excuse to do nothing?

She looked around the gloomy church. In the far corner sat Vincent with Anya. Vincent actually seemed to return her gaze, almost as if he knew her.

She reached and touched Keats's cheek. He looked up at her, but he did not speak. He was shattered, for now at least. He had not lost any biots, but he had just played and won a game no human should have been able to play. He and Vincent, both lost for different reasons in the same war, both, she hoped, coming home again.

She looked at Nijinsky, who had not been the same since arriving in Washington. He refused to meet her gaze.

Three broken men. And Billy, who was holding the tail of his shirt to the small hole in his face.

Burnofsky's phone rang again, again the same number. Someone was desperate.

"We have to go after Bug Man," Plath said. "It's why we came here."

"Enough for now," Nijinsky said. "I'll update Lear. He'll—"

"I'm curious about something, Jin," Plath said.

"Yes?"

"Earlier, when we were going after the hydras, before Keats just . . . well, did whatever he just did. Wilkes jumped in with her biots, you didn't. Why?"

"I would have."

"You didn't."

"Are you calling me a coward? I set off a bomb, Plath. I just killed a bunch of men tonight. Are you calling me a coward? I'm not the one who didn't have the courage to take out the Armstrong Twins!"

Plath recoiled. There it was, out in the open.

Nijinsky was shrill, over-the-top outraged. Too much to be real. "The only reason this whole thing isn't over is because you didn't step up when you had the chance, Plath!"

"Oh, tensions mount," Burnofsky taunted.

To Plath's surprise, Wilkes spoke up. "Because she's a normal kid, Jin, and normal people don't like killing. How did you like it?"

Nijinsky blinked. "She can't just call me a coward," he said weakly.

"I'm not doing that," Plath said. "I'm saying why didn't you volunteer to throw your biots into it? Because I have an idea why."

Nijinsky swallowed. He was breathing heavily. He started to say something but stopped.

"I think you couldn't do anything, Jin, because it would mean revealing where your biots were," Plath said.

Wilkes was looking hard at Nijinsky. "Where were they?" she asked. When he failed to answer, she turned to Plath. "Where were they?"

"Where they still are. In me," Plath said. "Wiring me."

Keats was remembering a scene from one of the Bourne movies, Jason Bourne so far down underwater that it seemed impossible that he would ever reach the surface. That's how he felt, but instead of water it was blood and skin and he had to claw his way back to daylight.

He'd done that, actually, yeah. His biots and the nanobots were all up and out but his mind was not yet breathing fresh air. He wondered in some abstract way if he had done permanent damage to his brain.

It was confusing. It was mad. It was impossible. The human brain created only one person, one self, and yet somehow he was no longer singular but multiple. Multiple Noah Cottons had played the game and hunted the hydras.

Now he needed to fold all of that back into a single person again, reassemble himself from component bits. Multiple personalities? Was that it? No, multiple functionalities.

Then—and goddamn, there should have been some kind of cool sound effect for it—suddenly all the parts snapped back together and he said, "Ah!" really loud.

Then, "Ah-ah-ah, oh, hell, ah-ah!"

He jerked up from his seat and hugged himself with his arms, paced three steps left, sudden turn, three steps back, rubbing his head hard, making an even bigger mess of his hair.

Every eye was on him. And now he was self-conscious and feeling as if he'd been very inappropriate. He was embarrassed.

"Sorry," he said. Then, seeing that they were still staring, he added, "Kind of a rush. Hah! Kind of bloody amazing."

"Are you all right?" Wilkes asked, less mocking than usual.

"Aside from being taken apart like I was made out of Legos and then put back together? I think I'm all right." Then, sensing that he'd missed something, he said, "What?"

"We were just discussing why Nijinsky didn't want to bring

out his biots," Wilkes said with a significant look at Plath.

Keats's memory provided the last minutes of conversation. His face darkened. "You wired Plath?"

"I'm in charge while Vin—"

Keats hit him, a looping, somewhat inaccurate right that caught Nijinsky on the jaw, snapped his head back, and elicited a loud, "Ow! What the hell?"

"I think our boy here may not have all his Legos back in place just yet," Wilkes said.

"You wired one of us?" Keats yelled, ignoring Wilkes. "You wired Plath? To do what? What did you do to her?"

He was advancing with unmistakable menace on Nijinsky. Nijinsky stood his ground until Keats was almost nose to nose.

Nijinsky didn't answer. So Plath did. "He's been ensuring my loyalty. Isn't that it, Jin?"

"Nothing that wasn't already there," Nijinsky said. "I . . . strengthened your existing attachments. You would have felt it all eventually. We don't have time for eventually."

"Attachments?" Keats whispered menacingly. "To?"

Nijinsky's recovered, belligerent look said it all.

"You bastard," Keats said. "You made her care for me."

It was Burnofsky who said, "Soldiers don't fight for king and country. They fight for each other. They fight for the poor deluded, trapped bastard in the next foxhole."

Nijinsky didn't argue. He just said, "Vincent was out. Lear laid it on me to be the right man. He laid it on me."

"Vincent swore to me he would never wire me or any of us," Plath said. "He said if we ever discovered it, it would destroy our trust in him and he'd be worth nothing as a leader after that."

Nijinsky moved back a step, almost like he'd been shoved.

"And you know what, Jin? He was right."

"Yeah, well I'm what you've got for a leader," Nijinsky snapped. "I may not be the right person, but I'm it."

"Nah, I don't think so," Wilkes said. "I don't think so. I like you, Jin, but dude, I'm not taking orders from you anymore."

There followed a long silence. Finally, almost sobbing with something that seemed strangely like relief, like a massive weight had been lifted from his shoulders, Nijinsky said, "Yeah? Well, who else then?"

Wilkes jerked her thumb. "The rich bitch, here."

Plath felt the blood drain from her face. "What?"

Keats said, "She's right, Sadie. You know she's right."

"You're a better twitcher than I am," Plath pleaded.

"Yeah. But I saw the way you handled Thrum and Jellicoe. I saw how you called out Caligula. I also, by the way, saw you slip a note to Stern. You have the money; you have your own private army. More important, you're a natural. Like I am down in the meat you are up in the macro. Until Vincent gets all the way back to us, you're it."

"Yeah, what pretty boy blue eyes said," Wilkes said.

"But I'm too young for this," Plath pleaded.

"So was Alexander the Great." To everyone's surprise, this came from Anya, who had walked Vincent over to join them. Vincent was calm and quiet, but he was still not with them. "So was Joan of Arc."

"David killed Goliath and cut off his head when he was just a kid," Wilkes said. "What? Why the looks? I've read the Bible. It's mostly slaying and screwing."

Plath felt like someone was squeezing her heart inside her chest.

Nijinsky breathed in like he was taking his first breath in five minutes. "Huh," he said. And then, a smile spread across his face, showing perfect teeth, and he laughed. "Lear was right. I'm the wrong person."

"What's your vote, Burnofsky?" Wilkes asked him. "Who worries you more? Handsome Jin or Freckles McMoneybags here?"

Burnofsky said nothing.

"I'm sorry, Sadie, but you're it," Keats said.

Was there a part of Plath that was flattered? Yes. Was there a larger part that was horrified? That, too.

"Okay," Plath said. "Until Vincent is back. Only until then. And I hope that's soon."

"Yes," Nijinsky said, but not in a resentful way. He looked too relieved. He was having a hard time not jumping up and down. He was like a condemned man who just got the right telephone call from the governor.

"Okay, then, two things," Plath said. "First, Anya, are you with us? Not as a prisoner or whatever, but as one of us?"

"I'm with Vincent," she said. "Which means I am with you, too."

Plath nodded. "Billy? We can get you away from all this to somewhere safe. I can arrange that."

Billy shook his head. "No, ma'am. I'm good. I can help."

"Okay then," Plath said. "We're going to hold on to Burnofsky, and we're going to turn him. We're going to take Bug Man and do the same. And then we're going to unwire the president and stop the Twins and . . ." She stopped herself there.

Wilkes laughed her heh-heh-heh laugh. "She was going to say, 'and save the world.'"

TWENTY-FOUR

The sun was up, and Bug Man was scared.

He had tried seven times to call Burnofsky.

Then he had called Jindal. He hadn't told Jindal anything, just that he had to talk to the Twins. Jindal said they were traveling and unreachable. He insisted on knowing what was going on.

"Burnofsky never showed up," Bug Man said. No other detail, just that. That was enough. Jindal told him to hold while he tried to call Burnofsky, and then texted Burnofsky when he got no answer. Then Jindal tried to use the phone locator app. It showed Burnofsky's GPS had been turned off.

"Where are you?" Jindal asked Bug Man. He was sounding desperate, and part of Bug Man thought, *Welcome to my world.*

"I'm at the office," Bug Man said.

"Then you have to . . . I . . ." Jindal said. "Okay, keep working on the president. Just, you know, keep working."

Bug Man tried not to reveal his relief. "Are you ordering me to keep working on POTUS, because it looks like you're in charge, Jindal."

"Yes. Yes, just keep doing that."

Bug Man hung up the phone, his mind racing. Okay, so, he was doing what Jindal ordered him to do. That was his defense: Burnofsky had gone off on some epic drunk or whatever, so Bug Man had called Jindal, and at that point, it was all on Jindal.

Maybe Burnofsky was dead. That would leave the Twins even more dependent on Bug Man. That was a happy thought.

Out in the hallway he heard something. He strained to hear, then relaxed. A vacuum cleaner. Just the cleaning crew. He made sure the door lock was set.

Okay. Back to the game. That would get his mind straight.

He settled into the twitcher chair.

The vacuum cleaner was closer. Someone was slipping a key into the lock! Bug Man bolted from the chair and raced to the door just as it opened.

He pushed against the door but the damned vacuum cleaner blocked it. Behind the vacuum cleaner was a girl who looked too young to be working a cleaning crew. She had a weird tattoo under her eye. She also had headphones in and was obviously listening to loud music as she vacuumed and didn't even notice Bug Man as he blocked the door until her vacuum cleaner banged into his foot.

Then she looked up and seemed puzzled.

"Go away," Bug Man said, not quite yelling but speaking loudly enough for her to hear over her music.

The cleaning woman sighed and removed one earbud. *"Qué?"*

"Don't come in here," Bug Man said.

The cleaning woman turned off her vacuum cleaner. It was suddenly quiet. *"Tengo que limpiar aquí.* I am . . . I am must cleaning."

"No, you don't," Bug Man said. "No, um, no necessitatay. Whatever. No."

"Is my *tío*, my, in English my sister? No, no, my uncle! Is my uncle his job. He be anger me."

"I don't give a fuck about your uncle being anger you!" Bug Man yelled. He reached through the gap and tried to push her vacuum away. Her hand shot out and caught him around the wrist.

"Please no break *el aspiradora!*" Wilkes said, and was incredibly pleased with herself for dredging up the Spanish word for vacuum cleaner. Who knew ninth-grade Spanish would be useful someday?

"I'm not going to break anything," Bug Man said heatedly. "Unless you keep from closing this damn door."

"Chinga tú madre!" Wilkes snapped, and gave him the finger.

He closed the door. He locked it. And for good measure he manhandled a large potted fern over to block it.

Then he sat down at his twitcher station, breathed deep, and never even considered that three biots—two of Vincent's originals and one new fourth-generation version—were racing from his wrist up his forearm.

Nijinsky was left behind with Billy and Burnofsky.

"What do you think, kid?" Nijinsky asked him. "We don't have time to build you a biot right now, but we happen to have a whole bunch of unused nanobots. Want to see the inside of a degenerate murderer's brain?"

Billy picked up the goggles and the glove.

"The first thing you need if you're wiring someone is a plan," Nijinsky said. He poured himself a short shot from the vodka bottle.

"A plan?"

"Yeah," Nijinsky said, and threw the shot down his throat. "What is it we want to do to Mr. Burnofsky here? We want him to change his mind. We want him to change sides. We want betrayal from Mr. Burnofsky."

Billy shrugged.

"We have here a drug addict, a drunk. Hates himself, you know. Isn't that right, Burnofsky?"

"You're too weak to lead but tough enough to take on a helpless old man," Burnofsky said.

Nijinsky nodded. "Yeah, that's about right. I would never have had the strength to murder my own daughter on orders from some freaks. Yeah, that's strength, right? And then rather than own what you've done and who you are, you decide it's time to kill everyone in the world."

Nijinsky touched a finger to Burnofsky's eye. Billy gasped as through nanobot eyes he saw his first biot. Nijinsky translated into biot was not nearly as handsome.

"Ever hear of the nucleus accumbens, Billy?"

"No sir."

"Well, some people call it the pleasure center. That's a bit simplistic, but it's not far wrong."

"Yeah?"

"So, here's my idea," Nijinsky said. "We reverse things. See, now every time he thinks about what he did, he feels self-loathing. He hates himself for it. So he self-medicates and then he turns it all outward into hatred. So we change that."

Nijinsky leaned close to Burnofsky and said, "What do you think of that?"

Burnofsky said, "Complicated. You have to locate the memory. Then you have to do what? Connect it to all my better angels? Or just burn the memory out?"

"Yeah, I could do that, thanks to my spiffy new four-point-oh. But Plath nearly fried herself playing with acid down inside Vincent. So I think I'll stick to good old-fashioned wire."

"Maybe you could make me queer," Burnofsky spat.

Nijinsky shook his head. "We're not recruiting. No, I think I have a simpler approach: I think I'll find that memory, the one that tortures you so badly, and I'm going to wire it to your accumbens."

Burnofsky had nothing to say.

"So you'll remember it, you'll remember killing her. And when you do, you'll experience deep, intense pleasure."

"No." Burnofsky shook his head.

"The emotional need for drugs will diminish, you won't be self-medicating anymore. You won't need to. The rewiring will alter your entire motivational structure. That murder will become your greatest source of joy."

"No," Burnofsky said. He shook his head violently. "No. No!"

"Kind of interesting, isn't it?" Nijinsky said. "Grey McLure became involved in nanotechnology in hopes of saving his wife and later his daughter. His motivation was to save his daughter, and yours flows from the fact that you killed yours."

"You won't stop it," Burnofsky blustered. "If I don't do it the Twins will. Sooner or later they'll come to it. Right now all they want is acceptance and love. They'll come to it, though, the gray goo. Even without me they'll see the truth—that it's all foul and filthy and degenerate and deserves to be wiped clean."

"Feel free to keep ranting, Burnofsky. Billy, since we have your nanobots to do some drilling, we're going in through the nose, up into the sinuses. It's easier to reach the nucleus accumbens. It will be fun!"

"No," Burnofsky pleaded. "No, don't do this. She was my daughter! She was all I had!"

"The man who would kill us all begs for his humanity. Rich," Nijinsky said. "Follow me in, Billy."

They had let themselves into a vacant office two floors down from where Bug Man was slipping into the twitcher station. They had the keys, of course; a janitor had given up his pass key for the six hundred dollars Plath withdrew from a nearby ATM.

Vincent sat almost comatose in an office chair beneath a dusty wall-mounted sign that read SCHATTEN GMBH. There were old computers and old office supplies, and it looked as if no one had occupied the place for some time. The electricity had been turned off. What must once have been an orange, left on the windowsill, had collapsed in on itself and grown a fine coating of green mold.

Plath, Keats, Wilkes, and Anya perched on chairs and the edges of desks. The four of them tried not to stare at Vincent.

Only Plath had any idea what was happening with Vincent's biots. She had sent all three of her biots along with Vincent's aboard Wilkes's hand, and transferred from there to Bug Man's wrist. Wilkes's own biots were hanging back, waiting in the grooves of Bug Man's palm.

Plath's job was to watch Vincent's biots make their approach, then to peel off and gain access to Bug Man's eye and see what he saw. It seemed insane to her—an apt word, insane—that Vincent could still be nearly comatose in the macro but responsive in the nano. But she could almost understand it. (Which might also be insane.) A biot was not an "other." It was not outside of you, it was part of you. It was like a finger or a leg.

Still, accomplishing the mission would require Vincent to understand at some level, to know where his biots were and why. Did he understand? If not, Bug Man would destroy him once and for all. There would be no coming back from further losses.

Vincent was going into a fight he absolutely had to win, and yet he might not even know the fight was on.

"He's moving," Plath reported. Everyone glanced at Vincent. She corrected, "When I say he's moving . . ."

"Yes, his biots," Keats said. He smiled at her.

She did not return the smile. She knew how vast the brain was down there, down in the meat, and she knew that Nijinsky could easily enter her brain and lay wire without Keats's own biot having spotted him. But it was still hard to shake the suspicion that Keats had known what Nijinsky was up to and had just concealed it from her. Could she really trust even him?

The rational, reasoning part of her knew better, understood that because Nijinsky knew the location of her aneurysm he would of course easily avoid Keats's biot. Keats would never have known. And yet . . .

"Down the rabbit hole," she whispered to herself. "And all of us as mad as hatters."

TWENTY-FIVE

Vincent was running free. So good to be running free. He was two, a twin, but not identical. Half of him was familiar, the sights, the sensation, the speed, but the other half over there, no right here, was faster, stronger, and saw more clearly.

Two halves of him. The real, true him, running wild over dead skin cells, threading through widely spaced, dark spikes like branchless palm trees, bent almost parallel with the ground.

He was conscious of another creature, much like himself, but different, following behind, keeping pace. She—and he was somehow sure it was a she—was no threat. A friend? Possibly, but certainly no threat, no, he had an image of the threat; he remembered them, the other game pieces, the ones with the center wheel, the machines that zoomed along on six legs or lowered that wheel.

He remembered their dangerous claws and spikes and vulnerable visual array.

There was something else, too, a vision in his head of large, slow-moving, gloomily lit creatures arrayed in a semicircle. Noises came from them. Sometimes he almost understood those noises. And sometimes they reached toward him with long five-pointed starfish hands that never touched him, not him, the real him, the mismatched twin him that raced now toward an ascending wall of impossible height.

Up the arm. Onto the shoulder. Toward the neck, yes, he knew what all those things meant: they were geographical features of the game space. They were roads that sometimes presented obstacles but not now as he ran like a tornado across an Oklahoma wheat field.

Somewhere ahead would be the frozen white lake and the pulsing capillaries and then on to the darkness within. Down in the meat.

Down in the meat. Back to the game. The thought of it triggered feelings in him. Fear. Or was it anticipation?

Joy? Something like it, not joy, but something satisfying, something that flooded him with a dark, wild urge that balanced the fear, that turned fear into rocket fuel.

One of the gloomy dark creatures in that other reality made a noise. "Look: he's smiling."

Ropes coiled down from the lead helicopter. Before the rope ends touched the deck, the Royal Marines were descending. They came down so fast it was as if they were simply dropping from the sky.

The first of them hit the deck and was instantly overwhelmed by the mob that poured from the open spheres.

The second saw what was happening as he dropped. He fired off six quick rounds over the heads of the mob, warning shots aimed carefully toward the open sea. His bullets made tiny splashes in green-gray waves.

He slid down to rescue his buddy but was knocked to the deck by a middle-aged woman and had his hand stomped by a furious little boy.

The mob was unafraid, unimpressed, enraged, energized by some power that went even beyond the motivations of loyalty to the Great Souls: they were human beings who had been locked in a cage, had their brains crudely rewired, had been fed a diet of propaganda and carefully avoided feelings that sometimes rose up from within like a geyser, feelings of fury and loss and confusion.

And now they had targets. They had someone to attack and permission to unleash all that was buried deep inside them, all the emotion that had been papered over by sustainable happiness.

They were fearless because in that moment, caught up in the hysteria of the mob, they were insane.

A teenage boy bit into the hand that had been stomped. The marine shrieked in pain.

A flash-bang grenade went off, a noise like the crack of doom. But out in the open the flash meant little.

More ropes coiled down and with shocking speed the marines dropped to the deck. First two of them managed to link up, then a third, then a fourth to form a little square, back to back, hammering with their rifle butts at every target that presented itself, men, women, children, smashing and yelling and now the professional discipline was paying off against the untrained civilians.

The square of marines grew to eight, old school, like some desperate Custer's Last Stand, back-to-back, side by side, a formation so old it was old by the time of the ancient Romans.

"Masks on!" their sergeant roared in a voice that could nearly be heard three miles away on shore.

They took turns slipping gas masks over their faces. The Sea King veered sharply away to lessen the rotor downdraft. Then from the Sea King came rocket-propelled gas grenades, fired straight into the mob. Some of the grenades hit people, knocking them flat. Gas swirled and some choked, but the wind was too strong and the fumes were soon carried off.

But the marines had gained a precious foothold. There were a dozen men now, backs to the helicopter where Minako screamed in sheer terror.

Pia Valquist, aboard the second Sea King helicopter, said, "Let's come at them from behind!"

The admiral nodded, and the Sea King veered away just as the first rocket-propelled grenade was fired. It shot past the helicopter and exploded in the sea.

"That was close," Admiral Domville observed with no apparent concern.

The Sea King zoomed along the length of the *Doll Ship* and came to hover just over the bow. Pia saw Hong Kong harbor now unmistakably close, tight-packed skyscrapers with every known type of craft from oil tankers to pleasure boats in the foreground. The city lights were coming on as darkness fell.

The marines from the second Sea King now began sliding down to the undefended bow.

"You know how to do this?" Domville asked Pia.

Pia slid a pistol into her pocket, grabbed a line, snapped on a friction carabiner, and said, "I think it will come back to me." She swung out into the air and dropped toward the deck thinking it was a hoary old action-movie cliché but, in fact, she really was too old for this shit.

It took about three minutes before it clicked for Bug Man. He was back at the twitcher station, hooking into the president's nanobots when it occurred to him that offices are cleaned at night, not in the morning.

Even then he froze for a few seconds, not wanting to believe it. Surely not. Surely BZRK hadn't found him? How could they? And if it was BZRK, why hadn't the girl with the strange eye tattoo just pulled out a gun and shot him?

But even as he raced through the steps to understanding and accepting, he already knew: they were going to wire him.

He shoved himself out of the twitcher station, tore off the glove, and ran for the small bathroom. Where had the phony cleaning lady touched him? His wrist? How long a run from wrist to eyeball or nose or ear?

The bathroom must have been some long-ago executive's pride and joy. It wasn't large, but it had a sink, a toilet, and a very small shower. Jindal had rented this office for the bathroom—twitching jobs could go on for a long time and they couldn't very well have Bug Man running down the hall every time he needed to pee.

Bug Man turned the shower on hard and hot. He stripped off his clothes, dropping them to the floor, grabbed a washcloth and soap and began to scrub. He opened his eyes and stared up into the powerful jet. It hurt like hell and he couldn't do it for more than a few seconds.

Then he vigorously, even brutally, scrubbed his face with the washcloth and soap, rubbing like he was trying to remove his own skin.

There was a second's warning. Plath saw that the quality of the light had changed, from soft to harsh. Then a roar, like a waterfall.

She jumped from her chair, grabbed Vincent's arm, and said, "Shower! He's on to us!"

At that moment, down at the nano level, she was just crossing from horizontal (and upside down) to vertical as she rounded the long arc of Bug Man's jaw. Vincent's biots were ahead of her, barely visible.

The water hit like a dense meteor shower. In the m-sub the first drops of water were the size of swimming pools. They exploded across the skin with unimaginable force. Plath sank her biot talons into dead epidermal cells and crouched low.

The first drops had missed Vincent, but he must have seen them because he appeared frozen in place. And that was the last she saw of him because now the water was coming down like a fire hose. She could no longer make out individual droplets; it was like a tropical downpour where every drop falling was the size of a house. The violence of the assault was shattering, indescribable.

One biot managed to reach out and grab a hair, then pulled itself to that hair and held on. Her other biots kept having to grab new skin cells as others gave way like roof shingles in a hurricane.

Then the spray moved away, but her biots were still completely submerged in rivulets of water, each a rushing whitewater river.

Then the sky turned white and down from above came the washcloth, bigger than a circus tent. It was a massive, undulating wave, a fabric of rough cables woven together, with frayed ends like shrub-size bottlebrushes. It dropped across the landscape and moved swiftly down, then reversed direction, up, and suddenly one of her biots, P-1, was torn from the epidermis. It was on its back, underwater, surrounded by a forest of massive threads.

Plath bit her lip and tried to climb back up one of the terrycloth threads to reach the skin again. She climbed over and through a cluster of bacteria like tiny blue tadpoles, also trapped in the material. The bacteria made her shudder, but she'd seen them before. They swam blindly around her biot legs like she was wading through a tidal pool of guppies.

P1 fought its way atop the bottlebrush thread, but then the water came again, pounding her through the cloth, beating her between bottlebrushes and skin, unable to grasp either firmly.

Loose!

P1 was caught in flowing water, like a child carried away on a water slide, slipped from the cloth, rushed madly over skin, grabbed frantically at anything that passed. Suddenly a deep pool that swirled like a draining toilet, madly around and around.

She was in Bug Man's navel.

Then just as suddenly she was spilled out, caught by the raging torrent and carried into a dark forest of curling, leafless trees. She grabbed hold, one leg, then a second, holding two hairs where they met and rubbed together.

She chose one and held on to it for dear life.

Her other two biots had held on much higher up on Bug Man's body. But Bug Man knew how things were down in the meat, he knew the resilience of biots.

P3, the biot 4.0, now saw something terrifying. It was a football field in length, a rectangle containing three full-length steel blades each capable of leveling a forest. The razor's edges didn't seem especially sharp in the m-sub, but they had a terrifying perfection that was alien to biology. In the gaps between blades Plath saw stubs of hair.

Bug Man was going to shave everything from face to wrist.

The blades touched down, pressed against the epidermis, and hurtled toward her biots. P2 was close enough to the left edge of the razor to make a mad dash to the side, racing from hair to hair like some demented Tarzan swinging through the trees.

But P3 was flat in the razor's path.

She was watching a car crash, seeing what was coming, powerless to avoid it. She could only hold on and hope as the first of the blades flew harmlessly by overhead, a scythe that missed its wheat stalk.

But the second blade, a tenth of a second behind the first, snapped the tree P3 was holding on to, and she was jammed between blades in a Pick-Up-Sticks jumble of broken hairs, random skin cells, and soap.

She felt, with the P3's superior senses, the sudden swoop up, away, through the air.

Bug Man thrust the razor up against the showerhead where the power of the water was irresistible.

P3 was blown out of the razor.

It fell, trapped inside a water droplet. Fell like a missile toward the shower floor.

Pia and Admiral Domville had the sense to stay behind the advancing phalanx of marines that now worked its way back with swift efficiency toward the melee on the stern.

Neither had any business participating in the action, one was a Swedish intelligence agent and the other a portly, middle-aged, very senior naval officer.

Pia was tense and frankly afraid. Domville was neither. Somewhere in the back of his mind he was wondering how in God's name he could possibly explain this to his own superiors—quite possibly a committee of Parliament, God forbid—but most of his brain had been swept up in a giddy froth of testosterone and adrenaline. Several of his ancestors had swung cutlasses and fired cannons, and Domville was thrilled to be carrying an assault rifle and going into harm's way.

This was fun.

Unless of course it ended badly, and he was forced into early retirement.

The first group of marines retreated under renewed pressure and the haphazard but deadly assault of hand grenades. No order to mow down the mob had been given, but one marine was dead and another was bellowing in pain from shrapnel in his knee, and as well trained as the marines were, their mood was nevertheless ugly.

Domville's detachment came rushing up the starboard side, out of view of the mob, then attacked with a loud hurrah using rifle butts and kicks to push them back.

Finally, the mob broke. First a few ran, then more, then all but a handful were racing back to their familiar spheres.

"Keep them bottled up!" Domville shouted. "Lieutenant, I'll take three men to the bridge."

The lieutenant detailed three marines as Domville and Pia began to run up the series of steep metal stairs that led to the bridge.

As he climbed, Domville's earpiece informed him that a Chinese coastal patrol vessel was on an intercept course and the *Doll Ship* was now in Chinese waters. He had to wrap this up and present the Chinese with a fait accompli. He could claim he was in hot pursuit of an obviously illegal vessel holding international citizens as hostages. That might work.

The fact that half a dozen of those international citizens now lay dead and bleeding on the deck would, however, be a complication in that narrative.

They were racing up the last stairway to the bridge when a crewman appeared holding a rocket-propelled grenade launcher.

The first marine fired his weapon and the crewman staggered back spraying blood from his neck—but not before he squeezed the trigger.

The RPG flew a mere ten feet before hitting a crossbeam. The explosion knocked all of them back down the stairway, and had it not been for the blood landing on Pia's legs it might almost have been comic.

She crawled out from under the tangle of bodies, all still living, thankfully, though one corporal had a gushing wound in his arm.

Domville was stunned but already leading the charge back up the stairs, roaring for the others to follow him.

By God, Pia thought, the man needs a cutlass.

They burst onto the bridge. Captain Gepfner raised his pistol and was shot a dozen times before he could so much as twitch. He was dead when he hit the deck.

The other officers raised their hands and yelled, "Don't shoot! Don't shoot!"

Pia found herself panting, heart pounding, face-to-face with something . . . someone . . . unlike anything she had ever seen before. The body was too wide, the number of legs all wrong, and the head, that two-faced head . . .

"No reason to shoot," Charles Armstrong said.

"I've talked to the surviving Morgenstein twin," Pia said, panting. "There's every reason to shoot."

"We are not armed. We are in your power," Charles said, placating.

"Who is in charge on this bridge?" Domville demanded.

"I suppose I am." The second mate actually raised his hand, like a schoolboy.

"Then get this ship headed away from land, back into international waters," Domville ordered him.

"I can't sir. The helm is not responding."

"What? Nonsense. Put this ship about this instant!"

"Sir, the helm is locked out. All controls are locked out. The captain did it, sir. It's all computer-controlled. He locked it out when he realized we wouldn't be able to stop you."

Every eye looked toward the bow. Off to the left there was a very strange sight: Sleeping Beauty's Castle rising in spotlights peeked up from Disneyland Hong Kong. All around the ship was a series of small green islands like lumps of bread dough waiting to rise.

Directly ahead, what looked to be waterfront warehouses and blocks of residential skyscrapers. Ahead and to the right a veritable wall of skyscrapers, twinkling now, some limned in neon, loomed over swarms of cargo ships, tankers, cruise liners, and smaller craft cutting phosphorescing wakes in the water.

Already the small craft were scattering as the *Doll Ship* plowed on at a relentless fourteen knots.

There were now two Hong Kong Police vessels racing to intercept, but both were relatively small patrol boats. A larger Chinese ship kept its distance, but Domville saw them unlimbering a deck gun.

"All engines stop!"

"Sir, as I said, we are locked out!"

"Then we'll go to engineering. Sergeant, you'll stay here with Ms. Valquist. You two, and you, mister," he said, indicating the baffled and increasingly worried second mate, "you are with me and if you hesitate in the slightest I will have you shot."

They ran from the room.

"It looks as if we'll run straight into the harbor," Benjamin said. "I wonder what happens to the natural gas tanks when that happens."

"Do you have a way to stop this ship?" Pia demanded.

"The only one who could seems to be dead." Charles waved an arm at the dead Captain Gepfner.

"The admiral will find a way," Valquist said, projecting confidence she didn't feel.

"I devoutly hope so," Charles said.

"There will be quite an international contest to see who gets to try you two first. I hope the Chinese win. Unlike my country, or Britain, they still have a death penalty."

To her amazement, Charles laughed. "Don't be ridiculous. We're mere passengers aboard this vessel. You'll find nothing proving that we own this ship or hire its crew."

"You think your lawyers and your money will protect you? You'll be tried for a thousand different felonies. Kidnapping, torture, murder. You're monsters."

"Don't call us that," Benjamin said, twisting his mouth into a brutal snarl.

"None of the people on this ship will testify in your courts," Charles said smugly. "You'll find they are absolutely loyal. They are happy, and we are the source of their happiness. We'll produce a hundred witnesses to every one of yours."

Pia felt rather than heard an explosion down deep within the ship. Suddenly the whole ship careened sharply, turning radically to starboard.

Pia staggered, slammed into the captain's chair, saw the Twins fall over onto their back.

The small Asian woman, Ling, lurched into the remaining marine.

Pia heard a strangled sound, dismissed it, then realized too late what it was. A knife was buried to the hilt in the marine's throat.

The remaining crew bolted en masse.

Pia turned her pistol on Ling, fired, missed, and suddenly the smaller woman was on her, delivering sharp blows to Pia's midsection, head, and throat.

The blow to her throat stopped her breathing. It was like sucking air through a collapsed straw. She fired again and Ling spun and dropped.

Pia fell to her knees, dropped the gun, and tried to squeeze her throat open, digging desperate fingers into her windpipe, but now blood was filling her mouth.

Ling, shot but not dead, got up, whipped off her belt, stepped behind Pia, wrapped it around her throat and twisted.

Pia thought how unnecessary it was to strangle her when she was already choking.

That was not her last thought.

Her last thought, her very last thought, was that she hoped someone would take care of her cat back in Stockholm.

[ARTIFACT]

Council on Foreign Relations

Liquefied Natural Gas: A Potential Terrorist Target?

Natural gas is at least 90 percent methane, which is combustible. Though in its liquid state natural gas is not explosive, spilled LNG will quickly evaporate, forming a vapor cloud, which if ignited can be very dangerous. Yet the likelihood of this happening is somewhat remote: in order for a vapor cloud to combust, the gas-to-air mixture must be within the narrow window of 5 percent to 15 percent. Furthermore, the vapor is lighter than air, and in the absence of an ignition source it will simply rise and dissipate. Under windy conditions, which frequently exist on the waters where LNG tankers sail, the likelihood of such a cloud forming is further lessened.

Nevertheless, should one of these vapor clouds catch fire, the results could be catastrophic, says James Fay, professor emeritus at the Massachusetts Institute of Technology (MIT). Describing one scenario, he says that a hole in an LNG tanker could result in liquid leaking out of the storage vessel faster than it would burn off, resulting in an expanding "pool fire." A 2004 study by the Sandia National Laboratory, a division of the Department of Energy, suggests that such a fire would be hot enough to melt steel at distances of 1,200 feet, and could result in second-degree burns on exposed skin a mile away.

The most attractive terrorist targets are the boats: 1,000-foot tankers with double hulls and specially constructed storage tanks that keep the LNG cold. A report, put out by Good Harbor Consulting, assessing the risk of a proposed LNG terminal in Providence, Rhode Island, concluded that a successful terrorist attack on a tanker could result in as many as 8,000 deaths and upward of 20,000 injuries.

It is important to keep in mind that this is the worst-case scenario.

TWENTY-SIX

Admiral Edward Domville found the Swedish spy, Pia Valquist, dead. He had no time to mourn.

Over the ship's loudspeaker he said, "Attention. This is Admiral Domville, Royal Navy. This ship is sinking. Abandon ship. Abandon ship. There is no time to launch lifeboats, abandon ship immediately."

Finally, he keyed the radio and called out to the Hong Kong Police, who were calling frantically for the ship to stop all engines immediately, "This is the *Gemini*. The rudder is blown. I've ordered the scuttles opened but I fear the ship won't go down quickly enough. I'm ordering everyone over the port side. You must sink this ship. Repeat, this is Royal Navy Admiral Edward Domville in temporary command of this vessel. You must sink this ship if you are able."

The *Doll Ship* was turning in a long, steep arc into Victoria Harbor, the heart of Hong Kong.

Domville had an informed layman's understanding of the effects of an LNG leak and the likely results. The wind was dampened here, closer to land, which was unfortunate. Wind would be good.

The simple fact was that if the Chinese could not sink the ship, it would hit land, very densely populated land. The LNG might not escape. Then again it might, and if it did it would expand through the streets and alleyways of Hong Kong until it was ignited.

The better alternative would be to ignite the gas at the source of the leak. The result would be a blowtorch, but that was better than an explosion.

Domville sighed. He reached inside his jacket to the buttoned inner pocket. He drew out a six-inch-long, pale yellow tube bearing the red logo of Montecristo cigars. He twisted off the red plastic cap and tapped the cigar into his hand.

"Pia," he said, looking down at his friend, "if you're in heaven this is good-bye. If you're in hell, I'll be seeing you shortly."

He cut and lit the cigar, and strolled out onto the deck.

The president's limo was a tank in all but appearance. You could shoot bullets at it all day. You could hit it with a rocket-propelled grenade and it would roll right on.

The limo had secure communications, its own oxygen supply, and a stock of the president's own blood for an emergency transfusion.

The driver was a former navy SEAL with more medals than even he could keep track of. There were Secret Service in the front seat, in the backseat, in an SUV in front and a second SUV behind. Every one of them would take a bullet for the POTUS.

There was no person on Earth better protected.

And yet . . .

Ginny Gastrell was worried, very worried, about her boss.

Gastrell was fifty-six years old, six feet tall, a former forward on the women's basketball team at Duke University, and looked a bit like Camilla Parker Bowles. She had been married three times, divorced three times, and had no children or hobbies. She was loyal to the president, even more loyal to her party, and most loyal to herself.

Helen Falkenhym Morales had a paper script on her lap. In the end the White House speech writers had had to write something for her. All she had produced herself was ranting nonsense.

Ronald Reagan had shown the early signs of Alzheimer's while still in office.

Woodrow Wilson was completely incapacitated after suffering a stroke that was covered up by his wife.

Even Lincoln was known to suffer from depression.

But this was different. This was very different. Something was wrong with the president. And now Ginny Gastrell was playing the role once played by Mrs. Wilson and to a lesser extent by Mrs. Reagan. Gastrell was deliberately shielding the president from exposure.

That video, that goddamned video from those Anonymous creeps. That had been the straw that somehow broke Morales's back. Helen Falkenhym Morales—Mother Titanium, some pundit had tagged her. Tough. Fearless. Determined. Brilliant.

Look at her now. Look at her now.

The president was crunching the papers slowly in her fist. Crunch and release. Crunch and release.

It would be better once MoMo was good and buried. That was it, that was the thing that had derailed the president.

All she had to do was sit there in the front pew at the National Cathedral. Listen to the various speakers. Nod along. Then give one speech, the eulogy.

Then things would go back to normal.

No, they won't, a voice in Gastrell's head whispered. The boss is crazy. The boss has lost it. You should be briefing the vice president. Agnelli was a spineless idiot, but he was better than a crazy person.

One lousy church service.

One lousy speech.

"Come on, boss," Gastrell whispered under her breath. "One hour and we're home free."

As she glanced out of the window she saw the crowd lining the street to see the president drive by. And she saw the sign: WE KNOW YOU DID IT.

Vincent endured the assault by water. It was not the first time he'd been on the receiving end of a desperate attempt to dislodge him.

And he had never been beaten.

He grabbed onto the fine hairs on Bug Man's chin.

That name, Bug Man, how had it come to him? The gloomy creatures in his alternate universe? Had he heard it from them?

Bug Man. It meant something to him, but he couldn't quite place it. He just knew that this Bug Man was the game space, he was the terrain, and he was the opponent as well.

The razor was an opportunity, not a threat. As the horizon-wide blades descended he raced his biots to the end, to the plastic framing, and leapt aboard.

The razor swept down and down but then rose dizzyingly through the air before touching down again. This touchdown left Vincent able to jump free higher up Bug Man's face, up above the water storm.

From there he was equidistant between eye and ear. There would be enemy forces in the eye, but his opponent couldn't twitch as long as he was showering. This, too, Vincent knew. He had played this game before and he had won.

He had beaten a guy named . . . What was his name? The first one? He had beaten . . .

And then, up against Sailor099. No, wait, that was a different game. Not this game, that one had swords.

But he had won. And then . . . another.

He shook off the mental confusion. Play the game. Focus.

Vincent's instincts told him that if he could get past Bug Man's outer perimeter of nanobots he would have a free walk most of the way down the optic nerve. Unlike biots, nanobots were not always alert. They were machines, and when they were not being controlled or running on some program, they were as inert as toasters.

He could picture them clearly. Nanobots. No problem. Nanobots could not kill him; he was invincible.

Vincent found three nanobots waiting but off-line at the back of Bug Man's eye. He crippled them without any effort.

A faraway voice said, "I'm going down the shower drain!" but it meant nothing to Vincent.

Neither did a male voice yelling, "Sadie! Grab onto something, anything!"

Vincent knew these sounds meant something important and in some vague, distant way he even understood the words. But he did not care. That was another world. He was back in the game, down where he belonged, down where he was alive. He was a wolf, alert, nose sniffing, ears twitching, looking for prey, craving prey.

"The water stopped," the distant voice said. "I'm—one of mine is in the drain. Aaaaarrrrggh! Damn it! I don't know how far down I am. My other two are still okay, but one is way down south. Long walk back."

"Get out of the drain, just make it out of there," the male voice soothed. "This is over for you. Let Vincent handle it."

Vincent recognized that word, that name: Vincent. He nodded, yes, let Vincent do it.

"I can do it," Plath said.

In the macro Vincent frowned. But his attention was on the vital intersection ahead, the optic chiasm where the optic nerve connections crossed over to their opposite hemispheres. That's where an enemy would lie in wait, the crossroads. Yeah, how often had he battled here? Hah!

Left eye, right eye, it didn't matter, if you were headed for the deep brain you came this way. And whoever you were, whatever you were, however good you thought you were, Vincent was better.

Bring it.

And there they were, just where they should be, clinging upside down hoping to drop unexpected from above. Yes, of course, because a novice twitcher would be thinking in terms of up and down and imagining that the surface beneath his biot's legs was the "floor" and might not see them "up" there like bats on a cave ceiling.

Vincent heard a laugh and thought it might have come from him.

The nanobots were inert, off-line. Twelve of them, each with Bug Man's exploding head logo. Vincent felt disappointed: he wanted the game, not a cold-blooded job of destruction.

If he just kept moving he could pass by leaving no trace and be deep into wiring possibly without ever being seen. He hesitated. What was the object of the game? To destroy nanobots or to take over control of the brain?

The question confused him. That he didn't know the answer meant something was wrong with him. He remembered the game, he remembered the desire, he remembered tactics and even strategies, but things were missing, too.

There was a sound, fist pounding. Frustration. Why didn't he remember the object of the game? He had played the game many times and always won, so he must have known the object of the game.

It was as if he could reach toward something with his hands but when his hands were close enough to touch it disappeared. It was present only as an absence. It was like something that always moved out of sight no matter how you turned your head to see it.

His biots froze in place.

He blinked his eyes and focused on a tense, drawn face in front of him. It was not a biot face; it was in that other place, one of those slow, gloomy creatures.

"I think he's seeing me," the face said.

"What did you do to me?" Vincent asked Plath.

"Pay attention to Bug Man," Wilkes said, very agitated, "Damn it, don't let him get you."

Vincent held his breath. He had heard her and understood and all at once he was completely up in that shadow world, disoriented.

"Tell him," Keats said.

"He may —" Wilkes said, but stopped herself. "Nah. Blue eyes is right. Tell him."

"Vincent, we cauterized a part of your brain," Plath said.

"I feel it. I feel something missing."

"Daisy . . . Daisy . . ." Wilkes sang in a low voice and laughed her heh-heh-heh laugh.

"You were damaged," Plath said. "We . . . We did our best to fix you. We need you."

"You burned a hole in my brain."

"Yes," Anya Violet said. He recognized her, knew her, suddenly knew the taste of her lips and the smell of her hair. "Because they're the good guys and they needed to win."

Vincent did not hear the sarcasm. "To win the game?"

Plath nodded, and now there were tears spilling from her eyes. He knew her, too. "Yes, Vincent. To win the game. We had to try and save you. We needed you. We need you now. To win the game, to wire Bug Man."

Vincent's eyes narrowed. "Wiring is the win?"

Plath shot a desperate look at Keats, who looked for a moment as if he might be sick, but then clenched his jaw, nodded once, and said, "That's right, Vincent. The wire is the win. But we're going to need to send Wilkes and Plath in, too, for a complete wiring, and we can't do that unless Bug Man's forces are destroyed. So for you the 'win' is disarming him."

"Kill his nanobots, Vincent," Plath said. "Then lay some scrambling wire until we can get more biots in his brain."

"Thank you," Vincent whispered.

His three biots looked up at the clinging nanobots.

And just then, all dozen nanobots stirred.

Bug Man sat wet and naked and freshly shaved from wrist to face and shakily donned his gear.

He keyed the visuals for the nanobots guarding his nasal passage. They were fine and functional. Same with those in each ear.

Left eye, okay.

No contact with the other eye.

He switched visuals to the chiasm, an eye entry usually led here. Twelve screens opened in a snap. Hanging above/below his nanobots stood two identical biots and a third, similar but slightly longer.

Bug Man enlarged the visuals, not quite able to accept what he was seeing. It was hard telling one biot from the next, it was almost more instinct than recognition, but as the disturbing insect/human faces came into wavy focus he knew.

Vincent.

A thrill of fear went through Bug Man.

Back from madness? Vincent was back?

Twelve nanobots against three of Vincent's biots. Four-to-one odds. Against most twitchers that would be more than enough. Vincent was not most twitchers. The last time he'd faced Vincent the odds were heavily in Bug Man's favor and he'd barely come out on top.

He felt defeat coming. He was exhausted. He was frightened. He was eaten up inside with the loss of Jessica.

Bug Man had one small hope: he had to focus on killing one biot, ignore the rest, all it would take is that single kill and Vincent would be out of it again, this time, he fervently hoped, forever.

He platooned all twelve nanobots together. They would move as one.

One punch, that's all he would get.

The twelve nanobots released their hold and pushed off into the cerebrospinal fluid, descending on Vincent like a mailed fist.

Halfway there Bug Man saw the two original biots move aside. They each crouched down and folded their legs, a clear sign that they were out of this battle.

Vincent would fight using only a single biot.

Bug Man's mouth was dry. The water in his hair and on his body was making him shiver with cold. What would they do to him if he lost?

Twelve nanobots met the single biot in midair, except of course there was no air.

With unbelievable speed Vincent's biot snatched the first two nanobots by their retracted wheels, paddled back with its remaining four legs, and smashed the captives into the second row of advancing nanobots. In half a heartbeat four broken nanobots were sent drifting, and the odds had gone from twelve-to-one to eight-to-one.

Bug Man laughed in disbelief. This was some new kind of biot. It was stronger and faster and he was so going to get his ass kicked.

But hey: never say die.

Bug Man instantly split his eight remaining nanobots into two smaller platoons of four so that they could veer left and right, but Vincent had seen this coming, too, and used the split force against Bug Man.

Vincent's biot reached the chiasmic wall, grabbed a single handhold, and curled its body out so that the powerful hind legs were in position, claws stretched as the first two nanobots struck.

Vincent missed!

"Yeah! Yeah!"

Instantly Bug Man was back from the dead, hah!

Two of his nanobots hit the biot's midsection, stabbed, penetrated deep, hah-hah-hah!

But they couldn't stab again. Vincent's biot wrapped them in its legs, tangling them hopelessly, and began ripping the machines apart.

The detached four turned awkwardly, racing back to attack from behind, but the slow circulation of fluid was against them and they were just . . . a little . . . too slow.

It was like some ancient World War I aerial dogfight with Bug Man's four planes caught in a crosswind.

Anchored securely in place, Vincent had only to reach out and stab each one as it came helplessly within reach.

"Fuck!" Bug Man yelled.

What did he have left? A dozen other nanobots on board, but spread all around his head. He could bring them all against Vincent, but it would take minutes, and a second dozen wouldn't do any better than the first dozen.

With sick dread Bug Man realized that his brain, his own self and soul, was wide open, unprotected, vulnerable to the only twitcher on Earth who might actually be his equal.

"What's the move?" he asked himself. "What's the move?"

The only real forces he had left were not on board in his brain. They were a mile away in the White House.

The Twins would take him out if he screwed things up with the POTUS. On the other hand, hell, they'd probably already come after him. And if he didn't do something fast he'd be a wired-up little bitch, just like Jessica.

What a fool he'd been to trust her. What a fool he'd been to believe there was anything real there. He had made her, and then unmade her, and been shattered when she betrayed him. He was a fool.

"Okay, Vincent," he said. "You got me good, dude, you got me good. But the game isn't over yet."

"Those are bacteria," Nijinsky said to Billy.

"They're moving!"

"Of course they are, they're alive."

They sat close together, both just a few feet from Burnofsky, who tried to snort and sneeze and somehow dislodge their creatures from his nose. But a pretend sneeze is nothing like as powerful as the real thing, and they had moved from the nostrils, where air was compressed into the vast sinus cavity.

The sinus cavity was bigger in the m-sub than a domed football stadium. The sides of the sinus were covered by a fragile tissue stretched across a network of capillaries so dense that in places it seemed the membrane was little more than a sheet of waxed paper drawn tight over a nest of red worms, each pulsing with platelets and white blood cells that brought their heat to warm the passing air on its trip to the lungs.

In other places the surface was covered by cilia, little clumps made up of soft, slow-waving, overcooked noodles whose job it was to push along the smears and clumps and balls of gray mucus, like some bizarre volleyball game.

The walls of the sinuses were mountain ridges, three of them, with deep canyons between.

For a space filled with air it made Billy think, incongruously, of video he'd seen of the ocean floor, filled with waving anemones and distorted geography. Everywhere were strange, brightly colored shapes, some almost half the size of his nanobots, others no bigger than cupcakes.

Pollen, Nijinsky had explained. The sinus was full of pollen, some like starfish, others like blowfish, others like random bits of coral. And of course there were the smaller, more sinister bacteria, some scattered singly, some in slow-squirming clots.

"We're going up there," Nijinsky said and, with one biot's arm, pointed. It was dark, of course, they were far from external light and the tiny lights of the biots and nanobots did not reach all the way to the "roof."

They climbed, though of course with very little sense of gravity it soon ceased to seem as if they were climbing and became a horizontal—if hilly—walk.

They reached the "roof" and there was a long field of what looked at first like cilia. But on closer view they were more like yams, some of which were long enough to look a bit like handless arms.

"The olfactory cells," Nijinsky explained up in the world. "The sense of smell. They go up into the olfactory bulb, which is how we get into his brain."

"I don't like this," Billy said.

"It's scary at first," Nijinsky allowed. "Disturbing."

"Yeah, but . . . I thought we were going to fight some nanobots."

"Not on this trip," Nijinsky said.

"I don't like this," Billy said again.

"He doesn't want to mind-rape a helpless old man—imagine that," Burnofsky said. "What's the matter, boy? Don't you know you're saving the world?"

"It's tight getting through," Nijinsky said. "We'll have to cut some bone."

"Why not pick up some of those bacteria and bring them with you?" Burnofsky said. "Surely there's some strep and some staph and a few other lovelies close to hand. I doubt my immune system is very strong."

"We don't do that," Nijinsky said dully.

Burnofsky laughed. "See, Billy? He's the good guy. You can tell because he'll wire me, he'll use me, but he won't kill me."

"I . . ." Billy began.

Nijinsky didn't slow down and Billy's nanobots kept pace, following the monstrous biots into the dense forest of olfactory cells.

"You ever study World War II in school?" Nijinsky asked.

"Study?"

"Toward the end of the war we—the Americans, the British, our allies—we started bombing cities. Cities full of people, most of them not soldiers. We dropped firebombs and we even dropped atomic bombs. It was pretty terrible."

"Ah, here it comes," Burnofsky snarled.

"It was very bad, burning cities full of people. But we had to. And even though it was bad, it was necessary."

"Don't you have a flag to wave, Nijinsky?" Burnofsky said.

"You know why it was okay to do those terrible things?" Nijinsky asked.

Billy shook his head.

Nijinsky leaned close to Burnofsky, no longer really speaking to Billy. He put his face right up close to Burnofsky and looked into his eyes. "I'll tell you why it was okay. Because they started it. Because some madman decided he had to take over the world. And weak, pitiful, depraved people like Mr. Burnofsky here, helped those madmen. Evil men and the weak men who help them sometimes leave us no choice."

Burnofsky spit in his face.

Nijinsky didn't flinch.

"Just like the men who attacked the safe house you were in left you no choice, Billy. You didn't shoot them because you wanted to. You did it because you had to. That's one of the reasons we hate people like that, because they make us . . . Because they turn us into them."

Then Nijinsky leaned closer still, put his lips a millimeter from Burnofsky's ear. His next words were barely voiced, a whisper Billy did not hear. "Enjoy what's coming. You deserve it."

TWENTY-SEVEN

Minako could not stop shaking. She had never in her entire life been near violence of any sort. In the last hour she'd seen savagery and death.

A cultured British voice was speaking over the loudspeaker. It was saying to abandon ship. It was saying to simply jump off the side.

"Where is KimKim?" Minako asked, forcing herself to open her eyes and look outside the Plexiglas bubble. "Where is KimKim?"

Silver shook his head. "They got him. You don't want to see, honey."

Minako shrank back. She hadn't really known KimKim, of course. At first he'd terrified her. Then he had rescued her. But it still seemed impossible that he could actually be dead.

Silver slumped in the front seat. There came the flat crump of another grenade going off. The battle was still going on.

"Can you swim, kid?" Silver asked her.

The question made no sense to her. He might as well have asked whether she could dance. "Yes, I swim."

"Well, this time of year, here in the harbor the water shouldn't be too cold. We're not far from land, should be able to reach the wharf or at least one of these little islands if no boat picks us up right away."

"What do you mean?"

Silver turned to face her. "That loud bang and all of a sudden the boat starts turning? Well, it hasn't stopped turning. And the engines are still going full blast—you can feel it. That's why they're calling to abandon ship."

"You think we're going to crash?"

"I'd say there's probably no way to stop it," he said, looking very serious. "And this chopper, well, kid, I don't think we have time. The skids are still chained."

"Jump in the water?"

"Or I could throw you, but one way or the other, I didn't go through all this to let you die. So come on. Now!"

Minako said, "I'll do it. But we'll have to count to . . . to seven. That's my best number."

Silver looked nonplussed but said, "Seven it is."

They climbed from the helicopter. Minako felt something sticky under her shoes. Blood. There was no way not to look at KimKim, he lay like a rag doll, arms and legs twisted in impossible ways.

She followed Silver, moving at a fast trot now, to the railing. She could hear cries and gunshots from the split-open sphere that had been her prison. The battle still raged. The Sea Kings hovered helplessly, staying out of range of RPGs.

They went to the side, climbed over pipes and up a shallow steel ladder that brought them at last to where they could gaze down at swiftly rushing green water.

Suddenly Minako felt a terrible rage inside her. She was no longer afraid, she was no longer overwhelmed, she was feeling her fists clench. "I don't want to run away, I want to kill them."

Silver did not smile or laugh. He nodded and said, "Yeah. You and me both, kid. But for now, let's just get off this floating nightmare."

Minako counted. "One." The first prime. "Two." The second. "Three. Four," a bad number to be swiftly passed by, to reach, "five."

"Shove off as hard as you can and swim away from the ship."

"Six," a very bad number.

"I'll be right behind you."

"Seven," she said, and jumped.

As she fell she twisted in the air and saw a sharp-prowed gray ship, much smaller than the *Doll Ship.* A blossom of smoke erupted on the smaller ship's deck.

Minako hit the water before the sound of the cannon reached her.

She was still plunging down, down into chilly, nearly opaque water when she heard the loud explosion of the shell hitting the *Doll Ship* just at the waterline. The shock wave was strong but not deadly.

She kicked and crawled her way up toward light. It seemed to take forever for her to find the surface, and when she did at last the *Doll Ship* was nearly past.

Minako sucked in air and trod water as the Chinese vessel fired a second round followed by a second explosion.

Silver surfaced fifty feet away, looked frantically around, and when she yelled, "I'm here!," began to swim to her.

A third round, a third explosion, but now the Chinese ship was in danger of being crushed between the *Doll Ship* and the shore. It reduced speed, and the *Doll Ship*, damaged but still plowing ahead at full speed, crushed a vintage sailing yacht to splinters.

A wall of skyscrapers was directly ahead.

More people were jumping now, falling into the water.

From the too-near shoreline Minako heard alarms going off. There was a cruise ship docked almost dead ahead and looming up over it the row of forty-story buildings, built right to the water's edge.

"It's going to run right into those buildings!" Minako cried.

"Yes it is," Silver said. "That's Harbor City. A huge mall, office buildings, hotels . . . God save them."

The Chinese police vessels had now swung in behind the *Doll Ship*. The harbor was lit up by frantic machine-gun fire, by the sudden explosions of the cannon and the eruption of flaming steel from the LNG carrier's stern.

The *Doll Ship* was riding lower and slower, but it was less than a quarter of a mile from impact, still moving at ten knots, and nothing was going to stop it.

Helen Falkenhym Morales had been to National Cathedral only once before, for the funeral of a supreme court justice. That had been two years ago, and at that time she hadn't paid much attention to the location and the look of the place. It was north on Wisconsin Avenue, out past the Naval Observatory in a surprisingly green setting for so urban a location.

The cathedral itself might have been transplanted straight from medieval Europe. It was a pointy object seen from the outside, a bit like a hedgehog, if a hedgehog could be Gothic.

They were running late, so there was no sequestering in a secure side room, the Secret Service after some debate allowed her to walk in the front door like a regular person. Everyone in the cathedral—and it was jam-packed—had of course been checked out, and in any case these were congressmen, senators, White House staff, major donors, foreign prime ministers, first ladies and first gentlemen, and other well-behaved folks. It was a sea of black suits and black dresses and somber looks.

The president's pew was at the front. It felt like a very long walk between those massive columns, beneath that distant vault of a ceiling, past the eyes that followed her, that were always on the president. And of course the cameras, discreetly mounted on brackets, one aimed at the altar, one remotely controlled following her, and a third panning the room picking out this or that celebrity.

But there was no doubt that at this moment Morales was on just about every TV screen in America.

A rector preceded her, Gastrell and two Secret Service agents followed behind, but the president walked alone, arms at her sides, head high, eyes front. She walked at a steady pace, a reassuring pace, sending the message, that's right, world, the president of the United States was still strong and in charge.

She sat. A sort of sigh of relief rose from the audience, and shuffling as people got comfortable.

The Right Reverend Jenny Hayes did a reading, followed by MoMo's own parish priest, Father Miguel Richards. The choir sang. It was lovely. MoMo would have liked that, although he would have been bored by the readings.

Then the first lady of Canada, Hanna Ellstrom, gave the first eulogy. She'd been a friend to MoMo; they'd liked each other and had hung out at important functions while their more important spouses were doing their terribly important business. Ellstrom's voice broke when she described a joke MoMo had played on her.

Then at last it was time for the main event. No one was expecting great eloquence from Morales. She had never been an especially compelling speaker.

As she walked slowly up the steps to the special bulletproof podium, the president knew that all she had to do was read the speech. It was short, just twelve minutes long.

Twelve minutes.

Bug Man had a sketchy, grainy view out over the audience at National Cathedral. He had excellent positions for viewing through the president's eyes. After all, he'd had weeks to get it right. But there were still limits on the method, and none of the people were recognizable, they were just dancing gray pixels. The huge columns were just shapes and shadows.

The words on the autocue swam into view, ghostly and blurred. Only a few words could be made out. He might have brought in still more nanobots to refine the resolution, but he was going the opposite direction: his nanobots were retreating from the dark corners of the president's brain, rushing for the exits, and soon those nanobots still attached to the optic nerve would also be detached.

There was no winning this game, but there was a way to keep BZRK from winning: destroy the value of what they had. And what they had was him: Anthony Elder, Bug Man.

They were after him because he controlled the president. If you can't get the puppet, get the puppeteer. And if the puppeteer no longer pulls the strings?

It was bug-out time. Bug Man . . . out!

And then? And then what? The question made his stomach

clench in a knot. He would have to run very far, very fast. Get his nanobots out of the president and leave them somewhere they would never be found. If he did that BZRK would have no use for him. The Twins would still try to kill him, but they'd look for him a whole lot harder if he still had a grip on Morales.

Was Vincent seeing what Bug Man was doing? He had to hope so, he had to pray, and he did pray most fervently, that Vincent saw he was bailing on the president.

"I'm out!" he yelled, chattering. "I'm getting out!"

Fighter nanobots, spinners, all of them were assembling at the far end of the president's optic nerve, two dozen all together now, wheels down and racing for daylight.

Bug Man looked around for a piece of paper. Nothing. He pulled out his phone and thumbed text onto a note. Then as his tiny soldiers, all platooned together, ran full tilt, he held the message up in front of him. He pinched the text as large as it would go:

Bailing. No good to you now, Vincent. I quit.

If it is possible for a place to be both hellish and beautiful, the drainpipe was it. Looking through her biot's eyes, Plath looked up and saw hard fluorescent light from high above. It was a ring of light, brilliance around a dark center formed by the drain stopper.

A huge, rough pillar of steel rose up to the stopper and extended down, out of sight, to the levering mechanism. She would have liked to be there, climbing that steel post, because although it was tangled here and there, long stretches of it were clear.

But here, on the wall of the pipe, she was in a jungle. Hairs as big as anacondas, in every shape and type, formed a bewildering thicket. They soared free, or were squashed together; they were scaly and rough-barked; some were clean, others had joined to form nests of bacteria.

And such bacteria. Varieties she had never seen, some like soccer balls, some like tadpoles, some mere twitching sticks, still others busily dividing. They came in all the colors of a demented rainbow. These, here, were the great predators of the human race, the tiny bugs that twisted guts and dimmed eyes and burned humans alive from the inside.

If the bacteria were frightening, other things were startlingly beautiful—crystals of unknown provenance, bubbles of soap that turned the ring of light into a rainbow, fantastic sculptures of debris trapped in balls of hair.

Plath's biot climbed through the tangled wilderness toward the ring of light, claw over claw, a precarious handhold, a wild leap, like Tarzan swinging through the jungle, only here beasts were tiny and the "trees" seemed to ignore the laws of physics.

"Are you okay?" Keats asked her.

"As long as he doesn't turn the water back on, I think I can climb out."

"And what are you seeing through his eye?" Wilkes asked. "I haven't been able to tap in yet."

Plath focused on the visuals from another biot. "I see . . . Wait. Wait. I think he's sending us a message."

"A message?"

"Oh my God," Plath said. She read it aloud. "'Bailing. No good to you now, Vincent. I quit.'"

"What does that mean?" Wilkes asked.

Keats said, "He figured out his only move is to declare neutrality. He's making himself useless."

Plath focused her attention on the macro. Wilkes was frowning, not quite sure what Keats was saying. Keats looked troubled. He said, "I suppose that's a good thing?"

Plath heard the question mark. She said, "The Twins lose the president. But so do we. And we lose the chance to turn Bug Man. He'll leave, move out of range, and take our biots with him."

"We can't wire him in time to stop him," Keats said.

"No, we can't. However, he's just up two floors," Plath said.

Wilkes let go of her heh-heh-heh laugh. "Check with Lear?"

Plath hesitated. "No. Not Jin, either. When Vincent's back with us, he's in charge. Until then . . . It's me."

Domville watched his marines recede behind the *Doll Ship.* The Sea Kings were already starting to pick them up.

Benjaminia and Charlestown were still full of people. The fools were cheering, thinking they'd won something. They were singing some mad song about the Great Souls.

Well, the Great Souls were nowhere to be seen, and neither was the ship's crew. Hong Kong's Victoria Harbor was a place of great activity; most who had jumped would be rescued if they didn't panic.

His concern was with the people in the cruise ship and the hotel, dead ahead. He thumbed a text report. Not very official, but it was all he could manage at the moment.

Officers and men behaved very well. The fault lies solely with me.

He thought about adding a patriotic "God Save the King," but that didn't seem quite the thing, really. So he signed it:

Cheers. Domville.

The starboard bow of the *Doll Ship* struck the Holland America ship *Volendam* a glancing blow. A glancing blow that made a metal shriek like the sound of Godzilla in the movies.

Domville was knocked to his knees, and it was from that position that he saw cabins torn apart as the side of the *Volendam* was opened like a tin of sardines.

He saw men and women exposed, dressing, lounging, going to the bathroom, all suddenly revealed as the side of the *Volendam* was ripped off.

The hulls of both ships crumpled, railing buckling inward, bits of rigging suddenly everywhere, debris flying, and the all while that awful metal shriek that went on and on.

It was a lifeboat winch that tore the hole in the last LNG sphere.

The blast of depressurizing LNG actually jolted the *Doll Ship*. Domville jumped to his feet and began running to the powerful jet, made visible only by the heat-wave-like distortion of the lights of the cruise ship.

A spark would ignite it.

Domville wanted to be that spark, but not yet, not yet, not while natural gas was blasting into the last few dozen meters of open cabins. The jet of gas had to waft clear of the boat. It was at exactly that point, as it blasted over empty waters, that he wanted to light it—before it could spill into the streets and passageways of the Harbor Town complex and provide fuel for an explosion big enough to level the city.

A spark. A lighter. Anything and the gas would ignite.

He froze, listening to the cries of people on the cruise ship. The suddenly stopped scream as a man fell into the grinding metal. The now-distant noise of helicopter rotors. And the overpowering roar of the gas jetting out.

He felt the *Doll Ship* sag, slow. It was listing to starboard, which was good, good, bring that jet down to water level, let it blast harmlessly into the water until the ship rolled over and sank.

The *Doll Ship* moved past the docked cruise ship, sagged farther to starboard, and now was the time, now, now! Domville raced toward the gas jet and standing in the edge of the methane hurricane, puffed his cigar.

Nothing. The cigar had gone out!

Domville fumbled frantically for his lighter as the *Doll Ship*, slower but not stopped, barreled on toward the Harbor Town pier.

He found his lighter. Thought, *Too bloody late, most likely*, and flicked it.

Domville was hurled, a burning torch, into the dock at the waterline. He was dead before the impact.

A huge blast of flame burning at 1,600 degrees Celsius incinerated the dock, boiled the water, and sent up a vast cloud of steam that rolled across the face of the Gateway Hotel.

Then, the sheer force of the jet of flame began to shift the *Doll Ship*. Its starboard list became less pronounced and the blowtorch, that massive, terrifying blowtorch rose as the *Doll Ship* rolled toward its left side.

Three hundred and ninety rooms on thirty-six floors of the Gateway Hotel. The fiery blast burned its way from bottom to top. It blew out windows, incinerated everything and everyone inside instantly. In seconds the hotel was a shell.

The steel support beams were warping, collapsing inward like a tall man bent over from a blow to the stomach. A minute more and the building would be gone and the blowtorch would burn on and through and ignite the city.

But the roll that had begun was accelerating. The ship's ballast had shifted decisively. It rolled onto its side, sending the flame shooting hundreds of feet into the air.

Now at last the remaining residents of the *Doll House* panicked.

The inside of Benjaminia was a slaughterhouse—dead marines, many more dead villagers, hung from bloody catwalks. The sphere turned on its axis, and floors became walls. Bodies fell through the air.

Like the turning drum of a dryer, the sphere rolled on and now people clinging to desperate handholds fell screaming and crashed into the painted mural of the Great Souls.

Water rushed in through the opened segments.

The blowtorch submerged but burned on and turned the water to steam as the *Doll Ship* sank, and settled on the harbor floor.

There was a knock at the door. Bug Man knew who it was. His message had been delivered.

He set his platooned nanobots on their course, out of the president's eye, racing away down her cheek. Then he detached from the twitcher gear and went to the door.

Five people stood there: the strange girl with the creepy eye tattoo, a serious-looking boy with startling blue eyes, a pretty but angry girl with light freckles on her cheeks. And—supported by an auburn-haired woman—a young man with dark hair and an intense brow and eyes that stared straight past Bug Man.

"They're out of her," Bug Man said.

They all stepped inside.

"I guess, given who we are and what we do, we don't shake hands," Bug Man said. Then he looked at Vincent and laughed softly. "Poor bastard's still not right, is he? And he kicked my ass anyway. Well."

"We could kill you," the blue-eyed boy said.

Bug Man looked sharply at him. "That accent's not from around here."

"Not quite as posh as yours," Keats said.

"There are five of you. You could kill me, but what would be the point? I'm out of Morales. The Twins will kill me if they ever get a chance. The game is over for me."

"Proof?" Plath snapped.

Bug Man nodded toward his twitcher station. Wilkes went over and put on the glove.

"I burned it all down myself," Bug Man said. "I had everything. I beat Kerouac. I beat Vincent. Plenty of money. I had a girl . . ." He shrugged. "But I guess it didn't mean much, eh? Just a game, right?"

Keats swung his fist with every ounce of rage he could muster. Bug Man went down on his butt, blood pouring from his nose. Then Keats buried the toe of his shoe in Bug Man's rib cage. No one moved to stop him.

"Kerouac is my brother," Keats said. "That was for him. And now, you have something of ours."

Bug Man prudently said nothing as Keats stuck his finger in his eye and held it there as the biots left Bug Man.

Sitting at the twitcher station Wilkes suddenly jerked sharply. "His nanobots are out. But look at the news!"

A small TV monitor beside Bug Man's main screen was showing a CNN feed.

Wilkes tapped the keyboard and the news feed opened much larger on the main screen.

"What is it?" Plath asked.

"She's lost it," Wilkes said.

"I first met Monte when we were . . ." she began.

The autocue went on with the usual story, the story they had both told for a long time. It was an amusing and touching story. But it wasn't the truth.

They had met when Monte Morales, driving a bit drunk, ran her off the road. She'd been on a bike. When she fell off she rolled into a ditch. Monte had come running, yelling, "No, no, no!" and she had risen from that ditch covered in mud and spitting a stream of obscenities that turned the air blue.

The bike was ruined so he let her drive his car. She left him standing by the side of the road yelling, "Hey! I said you could drive it not steal it!"

The next day she had found him from the information on the

car's registration. He had apologized, she had not. She'd told him her only regret was not running him over. He'd said . . .

"I think your greater regret was in not kissing me."

The audience gasped.

She had spoken it out loud, all of it.

It had always seemed like an important secret, and now . . . Well . . . There were so many worse secrets now.

Gastrell got the news on her iPhone. Massive explosion Hong Kong. Likely terrorist. Threat condition Orange.

The president had begun her eulogy. And it wasn't going well.

The Secret Service had obviously been advised as well. The lead agent was already moving toward the president, protocol be damned, Condition Orange came with orders to immediately secure the POTUS.

"I loved him," the president said. "And now . . . How . . .?"

She stared at the Secret Service agent stepping briskly to her and said, "Are you arresting me?"

The agent froze. The audience stopped breathing.

Cameras zoomed in close on her face and what looked like a single tear rolled from her eye. It seemed dark, for a tear, almost as if she was weeping blood. Even with high definition cameras it was impossible to make out that the dark tear was a rush of platooned nanobots.

"Madam President, I'm—" the agent said.

The president stepped to him and suddenly shoved him back. He stumbled, tripped backward, and landed hard. Morales squatted beside him and reached inside his jacket.

Two other agents were rushing now, not knowing what was happening, just that something sure as hell wasn't right.

When the president stood up she was holding a pistol.

"Jesus Christ," Gastrell said.

The agents froze. In all their training, there was nothing about the POTUS wielding a gun.

Morales walked calmly back to the podium. The gun was in her hand. She looked out over the audience and at the world beyond and said, "I don't know why."

Then as a chorus of screams echoed, she raised the gun to her temple and squeezed the trigger.

Deng Shi had two jobs, one more profitable than the other. On the one hand, he was a shrimper. On the other hand he engaged in a little light smuggling—no drugs, just cigarettes, booze, a bit of tax avoidance really, no harm in it.

He had in his time seen a fair share of strange things in the waters of Victoria Harbor. But what he saw now beat anything.

He steered his boat a few degrees to starboard, veering toward the object—no, objects, there were two—in the water. He yelled down to one of his crew to get a grappling hook.

One man with a hook was not nearly enough. It took four strong men and a winch.

Ten minutes later Deng stood amazed and a little awestruck by what looked very much like two men melted together. There was also an elderly woman, but she was practically invisible standing beside the creature—he couldn't yet quite think of them as humans.

It seemed one single life jacket and the small woman had managed to keep them afloat. Deng spoke no English, and neither the Twins nor Ling spoke any Cantonese. But one of Deng's deckhands was Vietnamese.

It took an hour to work out the details, for Deng to lend his phone to Charles Armstrong, to wait while he contacted Jindal, and then to get confirmation that half a million U.S. dollars had appeared in Deng's bank account. The other half of the money would be delivered in cash when Deng put the Twins ashore in Vietnam. There was an Armstrong factory facility there that paid many bribes: the Twins would not need to undergo too many formalities, and there would be no questions.

AFTER

"Thrum has taken the bait," Stern said. "She is watching your accounts, and AFGC is following our search for Lear."

Plath and Stern were both enjoying a stroll through Central Park. It was a lovely day. Frisbees skimmed, kites bobbed and weaved against a pale blue sky, and skaters clogged the paved paths.

"Okay," Plath said. Then added, "Good," because her father had always taught her the value of praising the people who worked for you. "Is there more?"

Stern didn't answer at first, then he asked, "Do you want more?"

Now it was her turn to hesitate. She knew what he was asking. Did she want to know more? Did she want or need to know more? "Tell me, and I'll decide whether I want more."

Stern sighed. "I've been contacted by a person in Lebanon, a hacker who, as you might expect, says his name is Anonymous." Stern rolled his eyes slightly. "He's following AFGC following us. He had some very interesting information on the terrorist incident in Hong Kong."

"What does it have to do with us?"

"If this fellow is to be believed, the Armstrong Twins were aboard that LNG ship. In fact, they owned it, and used it as a sort of . . . as a . . . I don't even know what to call it. Some sort of cross between a zoo and an insane asylum, I suppose. A floating chamber of horrors. According to our Lebanese friend, Swedish intelligence and the Royal Navy are involved. The Chinese are trying to put a lid on everything, and they're damned good at cover-ups."

"Were the Twins killed?"

Stern shook his head. "No one knows. There are rumors both ways."

"And why would we believe this Lebanese guy?"

Stern smiled. "Because he gave us the keys to the kingdom. He showed us the way into the AFGC system."

The possibilities made Plath's head spin. Against all odds they had scored a victory. The FBI and Secret Service were frantically chasing down every rumor having to do with the president's bizarre and shattering suicide. And intelligence services the world over were investigating the Hong Kong incident.

Soon they would find out about BZRK, too.

But they had taken Bug Man out of the game. Burnofsky had been released—a changed man. Vincent was perhaps on his way back. . . . They walked on in silence for a while.

"There's an island," Stern said. "It's called Île Sainte-Marie and it's off the coast of Madagascar, quite inaccessible, easy to monitor the single small airport, and the local officials can be bought off for a song."

Plath smiled at him. "Beaches?"

"The most beautiful white sand beaches. Mile after mile of them. We could keep you safe there."

"I know you could. For a while, Mr. Stern. But the technology has been created, and if the Twins are still alive . . . No place would be safe if they take that last step."

"So."

She nodded. "I was trapped into this. I've seen some terrible things, and I've done some terrible things." She couldn't remember Burnofsky's exact words, but these were close. "Lear knew once I was in it would be impossible to get myself back out."

"But we can get you out, Sadie."

Plath looked past him, to Keats, who walked at a distance, watching, waiting until she was done, waiting to see whether, in the end, she would run or stand and fight.

And she looked on beyond Keats, to the man who stood under the trees, shadows muting the lilac and green of his clothing, silhouetting his tall hat.

"There is no out," she said.

She turned abruptly away, then stopped, looked back at him. "One more thing, Mr. Stern. You know the phony search for Lear? Make it real. Find him for me. Find Lear."

ACKNOWLEDGMENTS

There are so many people involved in the writing of a book, and I can't thank them all. But one name has to be mentioned: Leah Thaxton, my editor for the first *BZRK* and this one as well. Leah has left Egmont to take on even greater challenges than dealing with certain cranky writers. *BZRK* wouldn't exist without Leah. A lot of good books wouldn't exist without Leah, and because of her ongoing work, many more will be created.

The author thanks the Council on Foreign Relations for use of their backgrounder, *Liquefied Natural Gas: A Potential Terrorist Target?*

Turn the page for a sneak peek at
the concluding book in Michael Grant's
thrilling BZRK series.

Available in hardcover and e-book from
Egmont USA in October 2014.

ONE

Sandra Piper was having dinner with friends when it started.

She was eating chilled lobster on the teak deck of a producer friend's Malibu home, along with a former costar named Wade Talon (a ridiculous screen name in Sandra's opinion), her current director (Quentin—no last name necessary), a very rich and rather magnificently tattooed woman named Lystra Reid who had an odd vocal tic that added "Yeah" to random sentences, and an extraordinarily fit, tall, and broad-shouldered man whose name she kept forgetting but who might have been named Noble, or something very close to that.

The Noble creature was listening, rapt, while the more famous folk discussed work and mutual friends and more work. In fact, in one way or another it was all work.

Sandra had been nominated: Best Actress. Very tough competition. The oddsmakers called her a long shot at six to one. Long but not impossible. And despite the fact that Sandra Piper was a mother of two, a down-to-earth thirtyish woman with a masters in economics who had smoked pot exactly twice in her life and never drank more than two glasses of wine, she was thinking of seducing young Mr. Shoulders. Mr. Shy Grin. Mr. Large-But-Sensitive Hands.

Because he was definitely interested, and she had been divorced for two years and had dated no one in that time. And she was exhausted from long days on the current shoot, plus her son, Quarle (three years old), had just gotten over a two-week-long bout of the flu.

And really, what the hell was the point of being America's Sweetheart if you couldn't even get laid? Would a male actor in the same situation even hesitate? Well, some, sure. But lots wouldn't. So why should she? Wasn't that why Quentin had invited Noble . . . ? No, wait, now she remembered. His name was Nolan. Whatever. Wasn't he there for her, um . . . amusement?

Unless. Oh, had he come with the Lystra person? Was he here for *her*? She would be closer to his age, not a beauty but attractive enough, given that she was not Hollywood at all but some sort of health-care billionaire.

No. No, young Mr. Body of Steel was not eyeing Lystra. He was eyeing the next winner of the Academy Award for Best Actress. *Uh-huh.*

But the idea sighed inside her and deflated like a balloon with a slow leak. She shook her head, a tiny movement not intended for anyone else, and took a deep breath. She had to help Quinn (seven years old) with her stupid California Mission project, due tomorrow.

God, she was boring. Boring and responsible and definitely

America's Sweetheart, except that when it came right down to it, she was Mommy.

Suddenly her hand jerked and she tipped her wineglass over. The last ounce of white wine drained onto the wood surface, alarming no one.

"Sorry. I just—"

Sandra frowned. Shook her head.

"What's the matter, Sandy?" Wade asked.

"I'm just . . ." She shook her head again. Frowned, despite the fact that frowning would crease her ageless forehead. "Oh my God, is there something in the wine? I'm . . . I'm seeing something."

Nolan looked at her from beneath lashes that would probably have tickled her cheeks (and other places, too, if she'd just said the word) and asked, "Are you feeling ill?"

"It's . . ." She laughed. "This is going to sound crazy. It's like I can see something that isn't there. I'm . . ." She looked away from them, stared out toward the black Pacific Ocean, wondering if somehow what she was seeing was a reflection off the wineglasses.

But no. It was still there. It was as if she had a second set of eyes, and they opened onto a small TV screen in a corner of her *own* eyes.

"I'm seeing, like, like . . . just flat, but weird." Then, a sudden, sharp gasp. "Oh my God, a second one. Like another window in my head."

"Maybe you should lie down," Nolan suggested.

"Or have another glass of wine," Quentin said, and laughed. But now he, too, was staring at her sideways, with concern on his face.

"There's two . . . Oh! Oh! Oh! There's a giant insect. I'm going nuts. Maybe I'm having a stroke."

"I'm calling nine one one," Nolan said, and pulled out his phone.

"Jesus Christ! It's a huge bug. I can see it! It's turning, it's coming toward me. . . . Oh, oh God, I think I'm moving it! I think I'm making it move!"

She pushed back hard from the table. Glassware clattered and toppled. Wade leapt to his feet and caught her arm as she lurched away from the table.

"It has eyes! It has eyes! Oh, God. Oh, God. My face! My eyes! Those are *my* eyes!"

She pushed Wade aside violently, then, abashed, shocked by her own behavior, she tried on a fleeting smile, reached out a reassuring hand and said, "I think I need help. I think I'd better see a doctor."

"That would be best," Lystra Reid said coolly, then added, as if an afterthought, "Yeah." She had moved to place her back against the railing and was watching with detached interest. At least she wasn't taking a picture to tweet later.

"Ambulance is on the way," Nolan reported.

And Sandra thought, *Well, he certainly won't sleep with me now.* But that thought came and left in a heartbeat, because something else was happening on that eerie picture-in-picture view in her head. She was seeing a falling drop of liquid that must have been a million gallons. It was far bigger than the terrifying bugs with her face smeared across them, her eyes; those nightmare insects with *her own damned eyes*.

The drop landed. It swept around the two bugs, engulfing them. And instantly it began to eat away those insect legs. It chewed burning holes into those insect carapaces. It burned away those distorted reflections of her own face like an old-time filmstrip jammed in a projector that bubbles and caramelizes and is gone.

The picture frames in her head blinked out.

They were gone as fast as they had come.

Sandra stood now, seeing only through her own eyes, seeing only what was real.

She laughed. "Hah-hah-hah-hah. Hahahahahahahah!"

And then she screamed. "Ahhhh! Aaaaahhhh! You're devils! Devils!"

Nolan moved to grab her because she was climbing awkwardly onto the table. She slipped, skinned her knee against the edge, stared down at the blood, and shrieked, shrieked like a mad thing.

She snatched up a knife. Not a very big knife, just a dinner knife with a point and modest serrations. She stabbed it into Nolan's thick bicep.

The strong man screamed, a more feminine sound than one might have expected.

"Hah! Hah, devil!" Sandra yelled, happy at the sight of his blood, fascinated.

Wade and Quentin backpedaled, making sure to keep the table between themselves and the long shot for Best Actress.

In Sandra's eyes they were not backing away, they were coming for her, with their fangs out, and claws for fingers, and liquid fire dripping from their eyeballs—it was all about the eyeballs, it was there, in the eyes, the demons.

Sandra Piper turned the knife around and stabbed it into her belly. It didn't go far. It drew blood, but just a stain the size of a quarter.

"Hey, hey, hey!" Quentin yelled.

"No, no, stop that, stop that this instant," Wade said.

Nolan made another move—this time wary—to take the knife from her.

Sandra spit at him. "Hah!" she yelled, and stabbed the knife into her own eye. Her left eye. Pulled it out bloody and clotted with viscous goo.

Cries of horror, and now even she could see that they were backing away, the devils. It was working. *Hah! Run, devils, run!*

She then stabbed the knife into her other eye and pushed it through cracking bone, pushed it until the hilt was stopped. Then she twisted the knife around as if she was trying to churn her own brain.

Her knees gave way. The knife dropped from her hand.

"Stupid Mission project," she said. Then fell onto her back, laughing and howling, laughing and howling. "Devils! Dev—"

It was Lystra Reid who took the knife from her. And Lystra who placed a napkin over the bloody craters in her face.

Not that Sandra Piper could see that.

TWO

Her name was Sadie McLure. She had indifferently styled brown hair and smart, skeptical brown eyes that could take on golden highlights and even suggestions of green in certain lights. She had freckles on her cheeks and across the bridge of her nose. She'd never liked the freckles—they seemed to be accompanied by the word *cute* and she didn't like people thinking of her as cute. Cute was a belittling word.

The cute freckles had a second outpost on her chest, and a lesser presence on her shoulders. But all her freckles were now almost hidden by a rich, deep tan.

Her name was Sadie McLure, but in certain company she called herself Plath, after the great and tragically suicidal poet.

It was her nom de guerre. Her BZRK name. The name that defiantly acknowledged that there were only two possible fates in her future as a member of BZRK: death or madness.

She had a net worth expressed in billions of dollars. She had a small but effective private army in the form of McLure Labs security under a Mr. Stern. (She must have heard his first name at some point, but what had stuck was the Mr. and the Stern.)

She had seen terrible things, Sadie had. As Plath she had *done* terrible things, too, and had terrible things done to her.

She was sixteen years old.

A month had passed since that bizarre and fateful day when the *Doll Ship* had burned down much of the Hong Kong harbor waterfront. A month since the president of the United States had blown her own brains out on nationwide TV after being (correctly) suspected of murdering her husband.

A month since Sadie as Plath had sent her biots into Vincent's brain, one armed with acid to burn the biot-death madness from him. The great advantage of biots over their mechanical competitors, the nanobots, was the closeness of the connection between twitcher and biot. That was also the greatest disadvantage because that same connection meant that the loss of a biot sent its creator on a downward spiral into madness.

Vincent had spiraled following the loss of one biot and serious injury to a second.

From a desperate desire to save Vincent, Sadie had undertaken a grim mission to cauterize parts of his brain. But at this moment that terrible day was compartmentalized if not forgotten, and Sadie was doing something that was not at all terrible. She was on a white-sand beach beneath palm trees. A picnic was laid out on a woven mat of the kind the locals used. There was cold fried chicken, cold lobster, and a bowl of vanilla-spiked fruit in the local Madagascar style.

There was also a bottle of white wine, now empty, and a bottle of vodka, now partly empty.

And there was a boy.

He was naked as Sadie. His name was Noah, though like Sadie he sometimes used a nom de guerre: Keats.

Whether they were Plath and Keats or Sadie and Noah, she was on top and he was inside her. They were both smiling because the ash from the joint in Sadie's mouth had landed on the very tip of Noah's nose, and when she blew it away it made him sneeze. Which struck them both as funny, so they laughed, and that physical convulsion had interesting side effects.

"Laugh again," Noah said.

"Not yet," Sadie said.

"You're torturing me."

"I'm teaching you endurance," she said, voice slurring.

"I'm standing right at the very edge of a cliff," he said, and his eyes closed and his smile became dreamier. "If you laugh . . . or even move at all . . . or even breathe deeply, I'll go right . . . *mmmm* . . . over . . . the edge."

"You're going with a cliff metaphor?" she asked, and giggled.

Which was all it took.

She watched his face while his body arched and thrust and shuddered and finally subsided. His expression was more animal than human in the first seconds, and the sounds he made were definitely not witty banter. Or even half-drunk and quite stoned banter. But then that feral look softened into an expression like you'd see on the face of a saint in a Renaissance painting.

And then he laughed, too.

And opened his blue, blue eyes and said, "Don't go yet."

He remained inside her, in more ways than one. He was also inside her brain, and not metaphorically. A tiny creature smaller than the period at the end of a sentence—a creature that was built from an exotic stew of DNA that included Noah's own—was deep within Sadie's brain. This was a *biot*. One of *his*, Noah's biots, because biots were nothing if not unique to their creator. It was designated K2. Keats 2. His other biot, K1, was in a tiny vial stuck in the buttoned pocket of his shorts, which were . . . he looked around . . . over there, somewhere.

K2 had the job of maintaining the fragile latticework painstakingly built around a bulge in an artery in Sadie's brain. Left alone, the aneurysm might never pop. Then again it might pop at any moment, which would almost certainly kill Sadie, perhaps over the course of pain-filled hours.

Noah had worked with scarcely a break over this last month to strengthen the Teflon casing around the deadly bulge. It was tedious work. Fibers had to be carried through Sadie's eye, down the optic nerve, up and down the soggy hills and deep valleys of her brain—quite a long trip for a biot—then carefully threaded in place. Basket weaving.

All the while a sort of picture-in-picture was open in Noah's own mind, an artificially color-enhanced but grainy picture. Imagine a 3D special-effects movie but with the color flattened out and stripped of nuance, all shot through a dirty lens.

Noah knew Sadie with an intimacy that was impossible for people who did not travel *down in the meat*. When she became aroused, he could feel the artery beneath his biot's six legs pumping faster, harder. But it was not just the relatively monotonous, liquid-encased surface of the brain that he had seen up close. He had at various times, in the course of more than one desperate mission, crawled across her eyes, her lips, her tongue.

She kissed his mouth and then the place just beside his mouth and then his neck. Then she rolled off onto the blanket and looked toward the food.

"You didn't . . . ," he said.

"No." She struggled to find the right tone. Unconcerned but not indifferent. Nonchalant, not like it mattered. Then tried switching to a sexy purr. "But I loved every minute. That's not the only thing in the world, you know."

"It's not?" he asked, trying to be funny.

"Want some lobster?" she asked, deflecting him. She didn't like talking about sex. The effects of weed and wine were ebbing, leaving her tired and groggy. She could be cranky in a minute if she let herself.

There were things nagging at her, distractions. She wanted to keep pushing them away, but self-medication had its limits and all those niggling worries would resurface, frequency and intensity increasing. She had pushed it all away for a month and now "it" was pushing back.

"I do want some lobster, I absolutely do," Noah said.

"Then trot on over there and get me some, too."

He sighed. "It's always something with you. *Undress me. Make love to me. Feed me lobster.* You are so demanding." He stood up, and she saw that half his hard, lean behind was coated with sand. She lay back, head resting on one hand, enjoying that particular sight, and the view beyond. They were in a secluded lagoon on the western edge of the island, facing the much larger island of Madagascar, which was a blur of green ten miles off.

A quarter mile to both north and south, armed men—fashionably attired in white Tommy Bahama shirts and automatic rifles—watched for any threat to their privacy. Just out of sight behind a rocky point, a yacht crewed by ex-soldiers rolled in the gentle swell and kept a radar lookout over the area.

Noah brought her pieces of lobster on a small china plate.

"We're out of wine," he said.

"Good. Time to sober up, anyway."

"Is it?" he asked. "Why?"

She sat up and reached for her T-shirt. He interrupted her with a kiss and gently stroked her breasts as if saying good-bye to them. "I quite like these," he said.

"I guessed that. Can I put on my shirt now?"

"I suppose." He started to dress as well, shorts, a T-shirt, sandals. He reached down and pulled her to her feet.

"I'll call for our cab," Sadie said. She pressed the talk button on a handheld radio—there was no cell-phone reception this far up-island.

Five minutes later, as they packed up the picnic, a glittering white cabin cruiser appeared around the point.

The captain gave a little *toot-toot* on the horn, and the boat blew up.

It took a few seconds for the flat *crump!* of the explosion to reach them. It took a bit longer for the debris to splash into the water.

And just like that Sadie and Noah were Plath and Keats once again, running now, food and blanket forgotten. McLure security men were tearing along the beach from north and south, assault rifles in their hands, yelling, "Get under cover, get under cover!"

The boat burned for a while—there was no possibility of anyone having survived—and then it slipped beneath gentle waves that were a very similar color to Noah's eyes. The pillar of black smoke was smothered. A black smudge rose until it was caught by a breeze and blown away over the island.

Vacation was over. The war for the human race was back on.